A RAE GREYSON MYSTERY

THE SHRILL OF IT ALL

BW HOFF

Black Rose Writing | Texas

ISBN: 978-1-68513-045-9
PUBLISHED BY BLACK ROSE WRITING
www.blackrosewriting.com

Printed in the United States of America
Suggested Retail Price (SRP) $21.95

The Shrill of it All is printed in Baskerville

*As a planet-friendly publisher, Black Rose Writing does its best to eliminate unnecessary waste to reduce paper usage and energy costs, while never compromising the reading experience. As a result, the final word count vs. page count may not meet common expectations.

Thank you, Mom. On a scale between 1 and 10, you're a 400.
Thanks, Dad, and hey, you accidentally face-timed me again.
Much love, Brian. No, I don't know what's for dinner.
With fondness, Ella. Breakfast at The Hen House?
Danke, Hugh. And put on some pants!

THE SHRILL OF IT ALL

CHAPTER ONE

Rae Greyson was ten seconds from breaking her personal record. Facing her computer monitor, she secretly worked on a sudoku puzzle that rested on her lap. As Rae was close to solving it within her two-minute goal, a reminder about the three o'clock Monday meeting popped up on the computer screen, preventing her from beating her shortest time ever. Frustrated, she threw the incomplete puzzle into her desk drawer and joined the other three graphic designers on the march to the dreaded conference room B.

At the head of the table awaited Travis. He was the Art Director, the boss *and* the owner of Graphics Inc. In another life, he probably was expensive linen that was blinding white and stiffly ironed. He never had a hair out of place and made it a company rule to ban knick-knacks of any sort. Apparently, he suffered from OCD and didn't know it. Rae wasn't going to inform him either. Being six feet five inches tall and normally burning underneath his collar, Rae called him The Torch behind his back. And today, his face looked hotter than liquid fire.

As all five assembled, Tonya began the meeting by sugar-coating her mundane tasks. Kimmy, mild and meek, followed by quietly reporting on her projects and then Chuck proceeded. He nervously talked about his missed deadlines and then brilliantly switched topics to his newly purchased puppy. This softened Travis's expression a little, but not for long.

Just as Chuck described the difficulties in potty training a beagle puppy for the good outdoors, Travis interrupted, "Isn't that insensitive on your part to expect your beloved to use the bathroom outside? Where everyone can see?" He looked at the others. "Am I right in assuming that we all have neighbors?"

"I do." Tonya's fake smile flashed.

Travis ignored her. "I have neighbors. And you have neighbors too. Right, Chuck?"

Chuck looked sweaty.

A small spark ignited in Travis's eyes. "My neighbors don't live close to us. They're two acres away because we all have large homes on large lots. Know what I'm saying?" They all nodded and Travis continued, "I have a big yard full of big trees for privacy. And guess what, Chuck? I still wouldn't want to show my bare ass in my front yard to defecate. Got it, Chuck?"

Chuck gulped.

"I don't think you do, Chuck." Travis really emphasized the *ch* sound in that name this time. "If you did, Chuck, you would've already bought the Grassy Puppy Patch made for indoor potty use. They're not that expensive, Chuck, and can fit in any corner of the room." He glanced at everyone's faces. "That's what we do for our Tiny." He glared back at Chuck. "Because we love Tiny like a person and not like a four-legged, furry animal."

After this little tirade, Travis needed to rehydrate and drank a whole bottle of water. "Rae." He verbally punched her name like a boxer with a short left hook. "Still working on those logo designs?"

"Yep, I've designed one hundred twenty-eight so far."

"And your client disapproved all of them?"

"Yep. Even the ones you designed as me to try to trick her."

"Christ. What's wrong with her?"

Rae shrugged. "Other than being from New York?"

Travis stared her down. "I'm originally from New York."

Rae nodded to that. "I think she's dead set on Tom being the designer for the logo."

Travis scolded, "Did you explain to her that Tom doesn't work here anymore? You do. You're the new Tom."

Rae calmly replied, "No."

Travis shook his head. "Whatever. I'll handle it." He grabbed a new bottle. The crack of a broken seal cut through the anticipated silence. Travis took a quick gulp before announcing, "I'll be out of the office for two weeks starting tomorrow. My husband and I just received word from China that our adoption request has not only been approved but they also have a match. A little boy. About two years old."

Tonya squealed in delight. "You and Seth will be such wonderful dads!"

"Cut the crap, Tonya. We would've been wonderful dads fifteen years ago when this process first began. Now, opportunity knocked us up and here we are." He finished his second bottle. "God, I wish this was stronger." Travis gestured to the group. "I don't need false words of encouragement. What I need is someone to house-sit for us while we're gone." He leaned back in his chair and his eyes narrowed directly at Rae. "So, who's it going to be?"

Rae immediately pointed to Tonya. "That sounds like something right up her alley."

Tonya's eyes darted upward. "I can't. I'm fostering a family of twenty-five. They just lost everything in a fiery flood and need a place to stay for two weeks. Exactly. Starting tonight."

Rae knew a liar when she saw one. And heard one. "Well, isn't that convenient?" Rae said as Tonya merely shrugged. Moving on to Kimmy, Rae asked, "Are you available? Or are you going to be busy entertaining the Pope? For the next two weeks? Exactly?"

"No." Kimmy sighed and wilted in her chair like a limp tulip. "Just my in-laws. They're making my husband and me throw them an anniversary party for this coming weekend. They arrived last night and filled my bathtub with live lobsters that they bought with our credit card. The guest list of sixty keeps growing." Kimmy's eyes were misty. "That means more lobsters. Having the Pope over sounds nice. And a lot less stressful."

Chuck chirped up, "I'm able to house-sit."

Travis still focused on Rae. "If you make a grocery list, the fridge will be stocked full."

"I can't," Rae said.

"There's a tower guest room. What girl hasn't dreamed of being a princess in a tower?"

Rae pointed to herself. "This girl. I find towers to be too circular. I prefer to walk in straight lines."

"We have a wine cellar the size of this conference room with specialty wines from all over the world. You're welcome to any of them."

"I don't drink."

"I do." Chuck raised his hand.

Travis never took his eyes off Rae. He studied her closely and then dropped a bomb. "We have a heated pool."

Rae's eyes squinted. "So?"

"So, I know you like to swim. Don't deny it. You constantly reek of chlorine and your hair looks as soft as straw."

Rae said, "Stop the flattery." She then hooked a piece of her straw-like hair behind her ear and it stuck straight out. "I actually run more than I swim."

Travis smiled. "There's a nice path by our house that leads to a beautiful park. The path was specifically made for walkers and *runners*."

This made Rae inhale deeply. Living in the city of Monroe, she ran on uneven sidewalks and around strollers. One time, she tripped, flattening toddler twins. How nice would it be to not deal with that! She then exhaled. "Look, that sounds fantastic, but in all honesty, I don't want to house-sit because I don't like dogs. Or big houses. But mainly dogs."

Tonya gasped, Kimmy choked and Chuck said, "I don't mind big houses."

A vein pulsed in Travis's neck. He ordered everyone to leave, except for Rae. After the other three designers ran over each other through the door, Rae remained, looking at her bitten fingernails. A few tense minutes passed and then Travis surprised her by lighting up a cigarette.

Rae's eyes bulged. "You smoke?"

"No," her stern boss snapped. "I quit a long time ago." He took a long drag. "Seth and I asked everyone we know to help us and they all seem to have some planned emergency coming up these next two weeks." He pointed at her. "I know what you're thinking and I don't care that everyone is scared to death of me. I prefer that. However, Seth is bawling his eyes out. He's worried sick about leaving our house for two weeks unattended. We just sunk every penny into remodeling that six thousand square foot Victorian whore. If *anything* happens to it while we're gone, we'll be in financial ruin and I'll have to kill myself."

Rae mulled this over briefly, before asking, "Why me? We've only known each other for a month."

"Exactly. That's why you're my favorite. Right now. Besides, I figured out that you're a straight-talking, no-nonsense, sarcastic kindred spirit. You remind me of a female version of myself, if I stopped growing at the age of seven." He stomped out the cigarette on the carpeted floor. "So, like me, I know that you can be bribed and I'm just the guy who can bribe you. That's one of the benefits of owning this damn business. Bribing people. So, what is it going to take?"

Without missing a beat, Rae listed, "Your dog in a kennel, a reliable security system and the next two weeks off. Paid."

Travis lit up another cigarette and hazy fumes encircled his whole head. "Done. We have a regular dog-sitter who probably can watch Tiny. Our security system was one of the first things we put into this house. Two weeks off is fine, but you'll have to do some work from my home office." He eyed her coolly as smoke swirled out of his nostrils. "And stop calling me Torch behind my back. I don't like it. It's not accurate at all."

Rae corrected him. "It's actually *The* Torch and don't be offended. I give nicknames to everyone without their knowledge. Who told you? Was it Chuckles? Two-face Tonya? Klimpy?"

"It was Two-face Tonya." Smirking, he added, "I have a special nickname for you too. Wanna hear it?"

Rae returned his smile. "Nope." She then quickly left conference room B.

At five o'clock, Rae sent a batch of logo designs to that New York client. She received no reply, which actually meant none were any good. Rae, however, was not going to let that dampen her joyful spirit. She instead strode cheerily out the building with a whistle on her lips and Travis's spare house key in her pocket, anticipating a great two weeks at Travis's glorious manor.

The ghost stared at him with a yearning look. Stone indignantly ignored the spirit and remained behind the bar, vigorously rubbing the goosebumps that formed on his forearms. The bumps disappeared and he redirected his focus toward his drunk and amusing regular named Sally.

Sally was an older woman wearing a sleek bob wig the color of fire. Thin with draping skin, she spilled her upper body across the counter and slurred, "Your grandpa would've loved the changes you did to this place."

This place was called The Rail. Whereas some trendy cities boasted of cosmopolitan cocktails that glowed, the midwest city of Monroe bragged of their many corner bars that served local beer. There were also corn fields, but mainly bars, which actually began as tied houses during Prohibition. The Rail was an original tied house that rugged Stone Winters presently ran as his corner bar.

Massaging his eyebrows, Stone wore his stained Hank Aaron t-shirt and faded blue jeans with holes worn at the knees. He removed his battered baseball cap, running his fingers through his brown hair and awakening the unruly curls. Stone did nothing to change The Rail. He didn't like change. He liked things to stay the same, like his Hank Aaron t-shirt, which Sally was using to wipe her mouth.

As he resituated the cap squarely on his head, he said to her, "It's three o'clock. In the afternoon. On a Monday. I'm cutting you off."

Sally kicked up her foot onto the counter, declaring, "I stop drinking when I can no longer stand on one leg." Her front teeth were smeared with red lipstick, her one false eyelash was loose and her grip around the cocktail glass began to loosen. She could, however, balance surprisingly well on one leg for two seconds; then, she fell.

Stone watched as Sally used the bar stool to climb her way to a standing position. Once stable, she nodded to him. "Another gin and tonic please. Easy on the tonic."

Knowing that his gin bottles were becoming endangered, Stone rubbed his stinging eyes and gave her a stern look.

"Fine," she muttered. After surrendering her glass, Sally said, "You know, your grandpa fancied me once. It was at a time when he was into *younger* women." Her eyes narrowed. "We could have a go at it. You and me. If you're into *older* women, that is."

A smile spread across Stone's face. "That's the best pickup I've heard all month. You just earned yourself a free cup of coffee and a free ride home."

"From you?"

"From Uber."

Sally reached across the bar and patted Stone's cheek. "A rain check then."

Chuckling, Stone grabbed the coffee pot to pour stale coffee into a large mug. He then handed it to Sally and she drank half of the jet black liquid before wincing. After snatching four sugar packets from her purse, she tore open all four at once.

"I gotta tell ya," Sally said while dumping the crystals into her coffee, "he was glad that you agreed to run his bar instead of your father selling it. It was his dying wish."

Stone now glanced to his side. In the corner behind the bar was a simple stool. Grandpa Ed used to sit there, enjoying the crowd. His perturbed ghost was there now, staring at Stone before finally dissolving into nothing. Stone then filled his coffee cup and choked down three long swigs as uneasiness engulfed him. Holding his breath, he waited for the nausea to pass. However, it unexpectedly intensified.

Suddenly, a teen-aged girl materialized within a mist, wearing a yellow romper. Her blonde hair was pulled into a high ponytail and her brown eyes shone brightly. He didn't know her and as Stone studied the girl, her appearance began to change. Her clothes became tattered, her hair fell to her shoulders in tangled knots and her eyes filled with tears.

Paralyzed, Stone watched as severe cuts appeared on her face. With each laceration, he felt the heat of the strike on his own skin, stinging him. Bloodied, the girl reached for Stone with her blue fingers. She needed help, but what could he do? Closing his eyes, the vision overtook him and he found himself standing outside a large home with gabled roofs, columns, a wrap-around porch and a foreboding tower. Moisture hung in the air and his shirt felt cold and clingy. Then out of nowhere, a dog barked.

He turned his head when a familiar-looking woman formed next to him. Her playful smile was whimsically drawn across her lips and the red flecks in her brown hair flashed in the sunlight. She laughed at him. It was the same bubbly laugh that he remembered from years ago.

Looming behind her were thousands of birch trees and they began to sway, gracefully at first and then more violently. As the sky turned a stormy grayish blue, matching the color of her eyes, the slender white tree trunks bent over her as if trying to swallow her.

Extending his arm, his fingertips grazed her palm and she began to slowly shatter like glass. He watched helplessly as her body broke into millions of tiny pieces, leaving only her mouth. Her once amused smile now opened in surprise as a shrilling cry shattered the silence. He shivered and was instantly looking into Sally's eyes again.

"What the hell is wrong with you?" Sally asked.

"Nothing." Stone blinked. "I'm fine."

Stone was not fine. He clenched his fists to steady his trembling hands as he thought of that girl in the yellow romper and the woman, his crush from long ago. Staring into his coffee cup, he sighed and Sally unceremoniously slid off her stool. As she lay on the floor, giggling, Stone told himself that Rachel was somewhere safe. He was almost sure of it.

CHAPTER TWO

Rae awoke on Tuesday morning feeling a little anxious. Today marked the first day of house-sitting and she felt like she unintentionally gave herself a prison sentence. To calm herself, she ate a banana when Travis texted: *Left a small surprise for you.* Small surprise? Rae's mind raced around the possibilities. Chocolate? Loads of cash? Anti-anxiety meds?

An hour later, she stood at the bottom of the front porch steps, gaping at the small surprise and cursing Travis's wicked sense of humor. The so-called small surprise was his dog Tiny, except Tiny was enormously large and he dwarfed the wrap-around porch on which he stood, as well as the tower looming above it. The head was as large as a watermelon and the paws could easily palm Rae's whole face. His dark eyes reminded Rae of black olives, extra large and extra frightening.

Pure panic set in and Rae dropped her bag. She slowly removed her cellphone from her back pocket to dial Travis's number. After listening to his voice message, she waited for the tone before saying, "Your surprise sucks. You have some nerve. What am I supposed to do here? You promised." Suddenly, there was another tone and then she heard crackling. The call abruptly ended. Sighing, Rae studied the creature and after a while, she tentatively stepped closer with her outstretched hand palm-side up. She heard that this gesture meant she was a harmless person.

Her oversized greeter remained sitting at the top of the stairs. When she produced her hand, he cocked his head to the side. He then stood on his hind legs, readying himself to jump toward her. She screamed at the top of her lungs and he sat back down again.

The dog had balls the size of two hot-air balloons, which startled her. She gathered her wits and said, "You must be Tiny. Did you know that your owner is a jerk?"

Tiny cocked his head to the other side and softly woofed.

"Oh, so you do know." She looked past him, fearful of making eye-contact. "Why are you out here? Your owner described you as being a prince of some sort. Shouldn't you be inside, sitting on your throne?"

Tiny slowly rose on all four legs and descended the five steps in one large, gentle leap. Landing to the side of Rae, he carefully moved his body closer to her and the top of his head reached her collarbone. His ears could have tickled her cheeks, if she allowed herself to be that close. She didn't. Instead, she took a sidestep away from him.

Tiny cleared his throat and Rae quickly grabbed her bag, marching up the stairs. With the spare key and security code already in hand, she opened the door while informing Tiny, "I'm going inside. You're welcome to follow. At a distance." She waited for Tiny to enter, but he remained sitting at the bottom of the porch steps with his head cocked to the side again, looking puzzled or possibly frustrated. Rae couldn't tell what he was thinking. She wished that he would seek out a bush. Instead, he yawned, licked his chops and stayed at that spot. Not knowing what to do with the dog, she closed the door, remained in the foyer and immediately sensed someone standing behind her. Quickly turning around, she yelled a very loud and equally strong whoop.

It was an ugly, horrific mirror, fitted perfectly for Frankenstein. The wood frame looked as if a wild cat with sharp nails clawed at it before setting it on fire. The charred blackness gave the mirror an angry feel and Rae flipped it off.

Rae's attention drifted from that monstrosity to the rest of the home's decor. Travis and Seth apparently lived in a very expensive art gallery, starting with the floor in the foyer. Rae examined the hand-painted wood tiles made to look like three-dimensional marble blocks. She slipped off her dirty tennies and delicately placed her car keys on the ornate glass console table in the entry. Wearing socks and a look of astonishment, she moved from one breathtaking room to another. After twenty minutes, though, her head felt heavy. Between the lace floral wallpaper and the feminine mahogany furniture, Travis's home looked like a nineteenth century manor with a severe Victorian stomach virus. And it threw up all over itself.

The show-stopper was a very large portrait prominently displayed above a fireplace in one of the formal rooms. The portrait was of Travis and Seth, arm in arm, both holding onto a white, stuffed prop of a puppy. It had a cotton ball head and the tip of the little pink tongue stuck out between its lips. It almost looked real, but the fake black eyes were the give-away of it being a photography model. Rae wondered why they posed with a cute stuffed animal instead of their Tiny. Maybe this photograph was taken before Tiny was part of the family? Or maybe the photographer couldn't fit the drooling beast into the frame? Rae snorted. That sounded right.

Rae eventually found solace in the kitchen. The stiff white cupboards against the cool gray walls brought her back to contemporary decor. The white marble island matched the countertops, which acted as a fine backdrop to the gray tiled backsplash. Stainless steel appliances officially stamped the area as modern and sterile. One *might* say polished or streamlined. Possibly cold. Maybe unapproachable. Definitely snobby. Definitely Travis. Still, Rae preferred the surgical kitchen to the rest of the freaky human-sized dollhouse.

In typical Travis fashion, the space was void of any knick-knacks, allowing her to quickly notice the only item in the kitchen with any color. It was a tan straw basket wrapped in clear cellophane, sitting patiently on a thick base on the island. An arrangement of high-quality organic fruit and snacks awaited her. Just as she unwrapped her second small surprise of the day, Rae's mouth watered as the aroma of luscious pears, crisp apples and bright oranges filled her nostrils. After picking up a crunchy-looking apple, she saw a card sticking between two oranges and began reading:

Rae (Smartass),

Seth wants me to express his appreciation for you helping us. Now, just a couple reminders. Don't leave the lights on. Don't take more than a five minute shower. Don't eat on the furniture. Don't wear shoes inside the house. Don't touch the antique mirror standing in the foyer that you will never be able to afford after you break it. Don't forget to read the house-care information packet that I left for you underneath the fruit basket. Don't have any guests over. Enjoy.

Travis (The Torch)

Rae lifted the basket. Sure enough. That base was an instructional manual the width of a collegiate history textbook. There was even a Table of Contents with chapters titled anywhere from *Turning Off the Water* to *Where Is the Breaker Box?* Nothing about Tiny's upkeep, though.

Rae suddenly flinched as the doorbell sounded. As she approached the door, she expected to see the melon-sized head of Tiny, but an old woman stood on the porch. Her soft, white hair was pulled into a loose, messy bun with ringlets falling around her face. Her dark eyebrows and lashes were in extreme contrast to her pale, but clear complexion. Surprisingly, she wasn't very wrinkly. Wearing a black peasant skirt and a billowy green shirt, she looked elegantly disheveled with her best feature being her warm smile.

Rae opened the door and politely said, "Hello. May I help you?"

"Hello," returned the old woman. And then she said the craziest thing.

"Are you a channeler or an empath?"

"What?" Standing in the frozen food aisle of the supermarket, Stone held two bags of broccoli. He glared at the guy next to him who wore a goofy grin. Dressed in tan khakis, trendy shoes and a polo shirt, the stranger was tall with thin arms and legs, but he still had a couple of spare tires around the middle. Store lights from above reflected off his dark bald head, giving the stranger an angelic halo effect. One eye seemed surprised while the other drooped slightly, yet both were deep brown in color, showing care and concern. More perplexing than the man's appearance was the strong butterscotch aroma, wafting from this man's pores.

"Oh," the guy said, "you don't know yet. Or is it that you don't want to know?" He pointed to the broccoli. "You should try brussel sprouts. They're really scrumptious."

Stone replaced both bags of broccoli into the freezer and slammed the door. Then he fled, looking like a frantic escapee from prison. He hunched over his cart, walked forward while looking backward and crouched by the end of the aisles, peering around the corners. Stone exhaled after seeing no sign of the man nor smelling anything butter. Or scotch. Ten minutes passed without incident and while waiting at the deli counter, he felt a shoulder tap.

Stone turned around and the same man said, "You seem agitated. Have a butterscotch. Bibi always told me that butterscotch calms the nerves." The candy, wrapped in gold foil, shone brightly in the man's palm. "Bibi is the Swahili word for grandma. My Bibi's from Kenya."

Stone snatched his pound of honey ham. "How do you say *I hate all candy* in Swahili?"

This made the man smile wider. It was a full, ear-to-ear, genuine smile. Tucked underneath his arm was an economy size package of toilet paper. Forty-eight rolls. He patted it. "All of this for only six bucks."

Without a word, Stone left the deli counter and maneuvered around the produce. Paying no attention to his unwanted companion, he quickened his pace. This time, however, the man kept up with him rather well, even past the bananas.

"You sure walk fast," said the man. He was breathing heavy at this point. "I'll tell you what. Just tell me what my name is and I'll leave you alone."

Stone replied impatiently, "I don't know you."

"I know that. And I don't know you either, Stone. Never met you before, Stone. I know nothing about you, Stone. But I know your name."

Stone stalled by the checkout lanes and asked, "How? Who are you?"

The man shrugged. "I know your name because I'm just like you. As far as who I am, well, let's play a little game and you tell me."

The little game sounded stupid. Stone's upper lip rose in disgust. Feeling trapped, he only wanted to find the self checkout lane and run the hell out of there. Unfortunately, all four self checkout computers had paper taped to the screens with the words *out of order* written on them. Stone instead nodded to the man, released his shopping cart and shrugged in an I-totally-give-up sort of way. Then turning on his heel, he tried to simply stroll out of there. He took three steps and, to Stone's amazement, a name popped into his head. It was a unique name that he had never heard, but he knew it was right. Turning around again, Stone said, "Zalen. Your name is Zalen."

CHAPTER THREE

Rae scrunched up her face and asked, "What did you just say?"

"I said," the old woman spoke sweetly, "you have a great figure for nude bike riding."

Taken aback, Rae still managed to comment, "Sounds painful."

"Not necessarily. I've learned you need a real wide and padded seat." The old woman then winked. "And one for the bike too." Rae chuckled as the woman continued, "Please let me introduce myself. I'm Maeve." Maeve presented her hand and they shook. "I've lived in this neighborhood for the past year. Travis and Seth are my next-door neighbors." Maeve smiled while spreading out her arms in a bird-like fashion. "Welcome to Birch Grove."

"Thank you, Maeve."

"You're welcome, dear. Now, here." Maeve dug into her purse to retrieve a piece of paper. "Take this." It was folded three times lengthwise. Poorly. On the front in black letters were the words: Save the Trees from Corporate Expansion. "It's my version of a pamphlet," Maeve explained. "You see, we are trying to get the word out. The woods bordering our secluded neighborhood are in danger of being cleared for another strip mall. We are peacefully protesting this possible wrongdoing with a nude bike ride. Here's our thinking." Maeve had a twinkle in her eye. "If the Big Corporate Man is going to strip this area of our beautiful birch trees for a strip mall, then we are going to strip to make them see how ludicrous this whole situation really is."

"And bike ride."

"Of course." Maeve beamed. "That will help us spread our message faster. The nude bike ride is next Saturday, eleven days from now. You should still be here for it. Keep your fingers crossed for a warm, sunny day. All you're expected to wear is a helmet."

Rae shook her head. "Oh, no, no. I mean, I support your cause and everything, but I can not ride around naked. In daylight. Plus, I don't have a helmet."

"Oh." Maeve frowned. "I was under the impression that you would help."

"Well," Rae raised her eyebrows and said, "if Travis told you that, he lies. Constantly." Rae glanced at the pamphlet. "But I can help in another way. I'm a graphic designer and would be more than happy to redesign your pamphlet. Even add some color. It won't take long. I could easily have this ready by tomorrow. How many do you need? Twenty-five? Fifty?"

"Only five hundred." Maeve then gushed, "How wonderful! Are you sure about this?"

Rae almost swallowed her tongue and coughed. "Sure," she finally said, "no problem."

It was a problem. Five hundred pamphlets? For tomorrow? How? As she waved farewell to Maeve, one horrible solution came to mind. It involved a printer she knew from her recent past. He was her one contact and the thought of him instantly twisted her stomach. His name was Chad and he had a face and body comparable to Adonis, the handsome Greek god, which was why she called him ChAdonis. His mind, however, was comparable to soggy oatmeal that sat out for days and was often driven by sordid thoughts. She knew that he would be willing to print them for a small price. Would it be worth it? Rae reluctantly dialed the phone.

The phone conversation with ChAdonis lasted three minutes. For the small fee of treating him for dinner, he agreed to have her pamphlets printed and ready tonight. It sounded innocent, except for the way he emphasized the word *tonight*. Did she just make a deal with a Greek god devil? Rae gulped.

Hopefully, unpacking would brighten her mood, so Rae followed the map inside the house-care manual to her tower guestroom. As she opened the door, a thrill in the pit of her stomach actually developed. It wasn't bad. Very dainty and circular, but okay. The appeal was welcoming in an English aristocrat sort of way.

There were three tall windows highlighted with sheer curtains, allowing in an abundance of sunlight. Divine sunlight. The fabric cascading across the top of the full-sized bed looked like it was made from fancy paper. From China, perhaps. The covering on the decorative pillows was white, delicate and lacy. From Belgium, most likely. The dresser was beautifully carved out of mahogany with five drawers, a shaped skirt and a large rectangular mirror sitting on top while extending its two wings. Forget-Me-Nots and daisies filled three white stone vases. From the Taj Mahal, no doubt. Dark wood floors contrasted with the light blue, cream and lilac decor, giving this room a romantic feel. All in all, the bedroom was too beautiful for words.

Carefully setting her bag onto the canopy bed, she tried not to wrinkle the pale blue silk comforter. She then removed her folded clothes and filled the dresser with her yoga pants, yoga shorts and tank tops before grabbing her pouch full of toiletries and placing it in the adjoining bathroom. The walk-in shower was the star of this spectacular room. Completely tiled from floor to ceiling, it was circular and large enough for a party. Each tile was a different shade of earthy tones as well as vibrant greens and blues with splashes of pink and purple across the walls. As Rae stepped inside, she felt like she transported herself into one of Monet's paintings. She looked at the square rain showerhead overhead and the many side showerheads and gasped. This piece of heaven was made for long showers. To prove it, Rae took one immediately, lasting twenty minutes and quickly breaking one of Travis's rules.

After dressing, she left her regal tower and followed Travis's map to his home office. On the way, she passed a closed bedroom door with a pink plaque hanging on it. Bedazzled in pink glitter, Tiny's name was written across it in a cursive flair. Wondering how the bedroom of the dog prince would look, she put her hand on the doorknob when her phone rang. It was Two-face Tonya, acting as the boss substitute, and she had Travis down pat by demanding Rae to send ten new logo designs to the New York client before noon. Rae forgot about the dog and his bedroom.

For the next ninety minutes, Rae worked feverishly. At one point, the doorbell rang again and this time no one stood on the porch. No Maeve. No Tiny. Strange, she thought and returned to her work. Ten new logo designs later, she sent the batch electronically to the New York client. Again, there was no reply and again, she knew they were no good. Needing a change, she completed a sudoku before redesigning Maeve's pamphlet. She sent the improved brochure electronically to ChAdonis by early afternoon and he responded: *Yummy. See you at 6.*

"I need to learn how to say *no*." Rae sighed while calling her sister-in-law.

Clare eventually answered, "Hey, Rae, what's up?"

"Nothing much. I just wanted to say hey and thought that I should tell someone in my family where I am. I'd tell my parents, but they're on that Alaskan cruise and told me that I couldn't call them. So, I'm telling you and my dear brother, Danny, instead."

"Yay," said Clare dryly. "Aren't you at work though?"

"Kinda." Rae then quickly summed up her temporary living housing arrangement, prompting Clare to softly snicker. Rae asked her sister-in-law, "What's so funny?"

"Well, don't get upset, but while being married to your brother for the past fifteen years, I've noticed a few *things* about you."

"Like what?"

"You're a magnet for *weird* situations. And to some extent, *death* follows you."

Rae shrugged. "I try to live a normal life."

"I'll never forget that time in France when you somehow locked yourself in that Picasso museum and then were almost eaten by guard dogs."

"Nobody died though," Rae reasoned.

"And weren't you attacked by gypsies in Amsterdam?"

"No." Rae explained, "That happened in France too. You're making my stomach hurt."

"And now you managed to get yourself into another *weird* situation."

Rae defended herself. "I'm just house-sitting a mini mansion for my boss while he and his husband travel to China in order to adopt a little boy. It's an old cliche."

"Did anyone die yet?"

"Not yet."

"Well, the sun hasn't set." Clare teased. "Is the big mini mansion scaring you?"

"No, but there is this mirror."

"Oh, brother." Clare tsked and then said, "You're worse than my four kids put together."

Rae had two nieces and two nephews, all belonging to Clare and Danny. The ages ranged from two to fourteen. Rae adored all of them and would never think of favoring one over the other. Lately, though, her oldest nephew had a couple squeaky wheels, causing her to eye him a little more closely. His name was Sebastian Connor Greyson. Known as Bash to everyone.

Bash was twelve, had blue-gray eyes similar to Rae's and was more than proud to finally be an inch taller than her. His interests included Sasquatch, detective shows and irritating his older sister. Not interested in sports, he was involved with his school's student government, played trumpet in band and excelled in all classes. Despite all these accolades, he was still a twelve-year old boy who, Clare now informed Rae, was grounded.

"Why?" Rae asked, "What did he do?"

"Well," Clare began, "last night, he got arrested."

. . .

Bash slumped over his desk. He did not see what the big deal was. So, he broke the law. Well, two laws: curfew and trespassing. As he pointed out to his parents and Officer Howie, of all the laws to break, those were the two *mildest*.

Blowing out a long sigh, he knew that he got off easy, all thanks to Officer Howie. However, it was still torture. His sentence was to write an apology to ol' Mrs. Hodge and his sixth attempt was sitting in front of him, taunting him. He picked up his pencil and began again.

Bash wrote to dear Mrs. Hodge, explaining that he did not mean to scare the bejeezus out of her in the wee hours of the morning. His intention was not to trespass onto her property out of mischief; it was to trespass out of his intense interest for science. Science of the paranormal, to be more specific.

His letter carried on about how his actions should not be punished, but revered. He continued to persuade old Mrs. Hodge that instead of being ticked off, she should be tickled pink by his interest in her farmhouse, which dated back to the late 1800s. That was according to his research at The Village of Polk Historical Society. She should also feel absolutely lucky to have a young investigator, such as himself, eager to explore her homestead, particularly the abandoned barn. At three in the morning. This was the hour when supernatural activity reached its peak, as stated on Wikipedia.

He ended his letter by suggesting that next time, she should not be so hasty in calling the police and should, perhaps, first find out if the disturbance was him. Now, all he needed to end this time-wasting ordeal was his mother's approval.

"There's no apology in this one either, Sebastian." His mom pointed out once again. "And do you honestly think that there will be a next time?"

"Mom," Bash said, "I'm doing this in the name of Science of the Paranormal."

"Yes, you keep writing that. Just out of curiosity, whatever happened to your interest in Bigfoot? That seemed to be a better obsession with you just sitting on the couch and remaining inside the house."

"That was the whole problem. All I could do was watch shows about Bigfoot. You wouldn't let me investigate the state of Washington to really find him. So, I lost interest."

"Well, I still stand behind that decision. Washington is halfway across the country."

Bash shrugged off her comment. "When can I have my paranormal equipment back? It took me two whole years to save up for all of it."

"You can have it all back after you write a sincere *apology*."

Bash snatched a new piece of paper and quickly began writing his seventh attempt. He felt his mother's breath on the back of his neck as he wrote. She then said into his ear, "In your neatest handwriting."

Bash sighed. "Now you're asking for the impossible."

"And," his mom continued, "you need to call Officer Howie and thank him."

"Do I have to?"

"Definitely. He *is* the one who got you off the hook again."

"I know, but he only does it because Dad bribes him with a beer every time."

"Your dad isn't bribing Officer Howie with beer. He just knows that Officer Howie likes beer. They've been friends since college. They were both going to be EMTs, but Officer Howie hated the pressure."

"Then why is he a cop?"

"Technically, he's a part-time cop. His full-time job has something to do with security for a bank."

Bash was perplexed. "Isn't there pressure in that job?"

His mom shrugged. "I guess he likes that kind of pressure."

Bash nodded as he asked, "Will I be ungrounded after all of that?"

"Yes, but with a warning. I'm tempted to put you in a summer camp again."

"Even after what happened last summer?"

His mom nodded. "That's how desperate I am."

Bash thought briefly before the idea struck him. Looking at his mother with big round eyes and a sweet smile, he asked, "Speaking of desperate, what's Aunt Rae up to these days?"

CHAPTER FOUR

Rae hustled across the busy street, running late and cursing out alarm systems and large dogs. Tiny never returned home, which worried her the *tiniest* bit. She actually wasn't worried about the dog vanishing, but was more worried about her job vanishing because she lost the dog already. After searching the bushes in an attempt to find Tiny, she whistled, but the dog never returned. Even more unsettling was the incomprehensible house alarm system. She precisely followed the instructions, so why wouldn't it work?

Sighing, she hurried to meet ChAdonis, the Greek god printer, just as her phone rang. It wasn't the normal ring tone. Being a music lover, especially of jazz, she set her ringtone to play the song, "When the Saints Go Marching In". The trumpets caused a smile to spread across her face, even though the familiar number instantly gave her gas. Why was her brother calling her?

Rae cautiously answered the phone. "Danny? Everything okay?"

Danny gave his usual one-worded reply. "Mostly."

Rae asked, "Well, then, what's up?"

"Bash. Slide show presentation. Mini mansion."

Rae understood her brother's meaning immediately. "So, Bash presented a slide show presentation to you and Clare about the benefits of him staying with me at my boss's mini mansion." Chuckling, she asked, "What are the benefits?"

Danny replied flatly, "Quieter evenings. No morning arrests."

Rae smiled. "Did he present a slide regarding *my* benefits?"

"Yep." In a rare Danny moment, he strung a sentence together. "You need a companion to keep your over-active imagination from leading you to hysteria and hullabaloo."

"What?" Rae yelped. "For the record, it's *his* companionship that leads me to hysteria and hullabaloo. Usually."

Danny continued unphased. "So. Bash. Yes or no?"

According to Travis, Rae wasn't allowed visitors. Then again, according to Travis, she wasn't supposed to be watching his dog. He broke the rules first. So, of course, she broke a third rule and finally answered, "Sure, sounds great." They quickly finalized plans as she entered the restaurant, ending their conversation.

Slipping her phone into her back pocket, Rae spotted ChAdonis easily. With hair as yellow as the sun and skin permanently bronze, he literally glowed. When he saw her, he bobbed his eyebrows before standing to give her a tight bear hug. Then he licked her cheek before planting a sloppy kiss on her mouth.

"That's enough, Chad," Rae managed to say while wriggling out of his hold.

"Dating anyone?"

"Yes. Tons. So, don't ask me out."

"Wanna go out?"

The waitress arrived, fortunately, and Rae ordered the big, greasy cheeseburger with extra cheese and lots of onions. ChAdonis ordered a salad.

Rae asked disgustedly, "A salad? Really?"

"Doctor's orders. My blood pressure's high. I have to cut down on fats."

Rae asked, "Don't you mean salt? Salt affects your blood pressure. If you have to lower your fat intake, then you have high cholesterol."

ChAdonis shrugged. "Whatever. It's one of those two things." He smiled at her hungrily. "I knew you would call me. I was just counting down the hours."

"Hours? I haven't seen you in five *weeks*."

"And now you're crawling back to me."

"You know that we never dated."

"Still playing hard to get." He winked. "I like it." Then he handed her a rectangular box. "Here you go. All five hundred pamphlets ready for action. Nice design. I actually read one. Well, most of the words. And to show what kind of great guy I am, I'll be happy to strip right along with you for protesting the building of this mall."

"Well," she began, "I don't have a helmet and would be breaking the one requirement. So, I'm not participating in the nude bike ride."

ChAdonis only winked. "I'll look forward to it." He drank some water and continued, "I grew up around there. My parents still live there. They definitely don't want a strip mall next door to them."

Rae's eyes popped open. "You grew up in a mini mansion?"

"Christ, no. I'm normal. I lived on the other side of the haunted woods past the park."

"Haunted woods?"

He looked at her very seriously and whispered, "Yes."

Rae laughed. "What? Are you five years old?"

"No, and don't laugh about it. The banshee will hear you and come looking for you."

Rae laughed harder. "Ha! Now there's a banshee?"

ChAdonis usually wore a smirk, but his mouth was a straight line. "Yeah, and she lives in the haunted woods. I'm telling you, she's real. And legendary. Look it up. She's called The Birch Grove Banshee."

"That doesn't sound scary," Rae scoffed. "That sounds approachable. Like someone who sells essential oils."

"This banshee doesn't sell oils. She's roaming those woods, looking for her head that was somehow chopped off."

"I think you're confusing stories."

"Whatever." He drank some more water. "There's a path around the haunted woods. You're safe as long as you stay on the path."

"So, the banshee has an aversion to paths?"

ChAdonis nodded. "Apparently. Just don't stray off the path. Or go near those mini mansions, as you call them. They're more like asylums for the wealthy. A lot of weird shit goes on behind those front doors. Murders. Killings. Homicides."

"You just named three of the same things," Rae stated.

ChAdonis continued, ignoring her, "You couldn't pay me enough to step foot in one of *those* places." He cast his emerald green eyes onto Rae. "So, where are you living these days?"

Rae smiled. "In one of *those* places." She then explained how her boss did pay her enough to house-sit his manor and that all was well. "Except," she said, "there is this mirror that looks like a gateway to Hell."

"Which mansion is it?"

"The one with the tower."

"There are a lot with towers."

"Well," Rae added, "this one also has a large dog."

"Is it near the haunted woods?"

Rae eye-rolled. "There is a forest of trees near my boss's house, but none of them have said *boo* to me."

"Joke all you want, but I'm warning you." ChAdonis's face was serious. "Don't enter those woods. Especially at night. One girl a couple years ago walked into those woods around midnight and was *never seen again*."

Rae was half-listening at this point. "She should've stayed in bed."

"The second year of her disappearance is coming up this Saturday. It's been on the news." ChAdonis continued, "The girl was young. About thirteen. I think she was meeting her boyfriend or something."

Rae asked incredulously, "She had a boyfriend at thirteen? And was sneaking out of the house to meet him in some woods? Isn't that kind of asking for trouble?"

ChAdonis gave her a quizzical look. "Didn't you ever do anything reckless with your friends when you were young?"

"I watched my friends toilet paper a neighbor's house once." Rae nodded. "And then I reported them."

"So, you had no friends." ChAdonis looked at her disappointedly. "Moving on, no one knows exactly what happened to the girl, but I do." He paused for effect. "The banshee got her."

Rae shook her head at him. "How old are you?"

"Thirty." He bobbed his eyebrows. "How old are you?"

"Twenty-five." Rae shook her head. "We're both too old to believe in ghost stories."

"This isn't a ghost story. It's a banshee story."

Rae sighed. "What about the boyfriend then? Why didn't the banshee get him too?"

ChAdonis shrugged. "I dunno. Maybe she let him live for the price of the girl? I personally think the police should hire a psychic or ghost hunter to find out what happened."

"Right." Rae was finished with this joke of a story. She inhaled her food, paid the bill and thanked ChAdonis for his speedy work. He retried the bear hug move, but Rae used her tiny physique as an advantage and squirmed out of his hold like a hamster. They parted ways.

While strolling to her car, the thought of that missing girl invaded her mind and, just like a missing piece to a puzzle, it frustrated Rae. Nothing caused her more anxiety than an unsolvable riddle. But what could she really do about it? She was just a graphic designer who knew other graphic designers and one printer guy. It wasn't like she was a coffee-drinking cop who kept company with detectives, paranormal investigators or even psychics, nor did she know of any. And, she hated to admit it, but more pressing than the missing girl was her boss's missing dog.

Rae grumbled at her tiny problem that was quickly becoming a huge pain.

· · ·

It was fifteen minutes past six. Sharp. A few hours ago, Stone not only met a strangely friendly man in the grocery store, but also agreed to have dinner with him at a quarter past six sharp. That was how Zalen stated it, which should have been another red flag. But Stone accepted. Why? He could not answer himself, but instead tried to reassure himself that the bar was in Sally's good hands during the next hour. That reminded him. He forgot to tell her to keep her hands to herself and not on any of the young men's bottoms. Or the gin bottles.

As he entered the meeting place, Stone immediately spotted Zalen sitting at a round table with a big grin on his face, showing off his dazzling white teeth against his dark skin. Stone took the chair opposite his new acquaintance and immediately felt Zalen's wide eye on him.

The quick-service coffee/sandwich shop called The Espresso Lane buzzed with energy. It was a typical chain cafe with the same trendy artwork, the same mismatched tables and chairs, and the same authentic drinks in each location found all over the midwest. The workers all had the same monotone voice inflection too. As well as the bored, comatose eyes.

Just as Stone's awkwardness was building, Zalen broke the silence. "I don't really like coffee," he admitted.

"Same here," said Stone.

"But I love their tasty sandwiches."

"They are the best."

"The lemonade is pretty good here too." Zalen smiled. "Lemonade is my favorite drink."

"I like beer," Stone offered.

"Never touch the stuff." Zalen smiled. "Have you tried Kvass?"

"Never touch the stuff."

"Oh, so you've heard of it?"

"No."

"Well." Zalen's voice slightly rose in excitement. "It's made from fermented stale dark, sourdough rye bread. It's rich in vitamins, helps digestion, and promotes healthy flora in your digestive tract."

"All good reasons to stick with beer."

Zalen's smile grew. "You're funny."

Stone shifted uncomfortably in his seat. "I'm not sure why I'm meeting with you. I left my bar in very incapable hands. I need to go."

"You're meeting with me because you're relieved. You're relieved to know that you're not going crazy and that you're not alone. What you have is a gift. You just need some time to accept it. Then you can learn about it. Then you can do good things with it."

Stone asked, "Are you speaking from experience?"

"Yes. I am what one might call an intuitive empath. I have the ability to just know things about people, places, or things."

Just then, a young girl in her teens and wearing tons of eyeliner approached their table, carrying a tray with two glasses and two plates overflowing with sandwiches and chips. First, she unloaded the drinks by giving the lemonade to Zalen and the dark soda to Stone. Then she carefully set the spinach artichoke and mushroom sandwich in front of Zalen and the ham and cheese on rye in front of Stone. With a dull voice and blank eyes, she said, "Enjoy."

Stone looked confused until Zalen said, "I ordered for you. I hope you don't mind. You looked like a ham and cheese on rye guy. I'm pretty sure I read that right. If not, I'd be happy to buy you something else."

Managing to shake his head, Stone said, "No. This is what I always eat here."

Zalen smiled bigger. "I know."

"But," Stone said, "I don't drink soda."

Zalen's smile vanished. "What? At all?" After Stone shook his head, Zalen ate a chip and explained, "I don't get it right every time." He drank some of his lemonade and unknowingly dribbled down his shirt. "I'm better at knowing names. Sometimes, names hit me like a kidney punch. Yours did. When names hit me with such great force, I've learned it's a sign that I'm supposed to get to know that person."

"Why on earth are you supposed to get to know me?" Stone crossed his arms.

Zalen shrugged. "Not sure." He took another huge bite of his sandwich and said, "But I think I'm supposed to help you find a girl. She's in danger, but you already know that."

CHAPTER FIVE

Rae weaved somewhat absentmindedly around other cars until she parked inside Travis's garage, which was not attached to the home. Walking to the front porch, a chill on this hot evening caused her to shiver. She glanced into the forest of birch trees lined on the one side of Travis's property. They seemed to be watching her. Or, at least, it felt like someone in there watched her. Pausing, she peered back. There were hundreds of trees, in Rae's estimation. Their white trunks illuminated the first few rows and then there was nothing, but black. Why any thirteen-year old would enter that unsettling darkness, day or night, was beyond her. She took a step toward the woods. Eerily still, the trees generated a lively buzz about them. Rae was drawn. One step after another brought her toward them. And then she abruptly stopped. Turning her attention toward the house, Rae clenched her fists at a sound of a woman loudly hollering something about a large dog.

Approaching the front porch, she reluctantly rounded the bend for fear of her suspicions being correct, which they were. On the sidewalk, right in front of the house, Tiny stared quizzically at an attractive blonde in a tailored beige suit with purple stilettos. She clutched a thick canvas bag like a shield to block Tiny's non-encroaching behavior, screaming at the top of her lungs, "Help!"

Put-off, Rae sauntered over. "It's okay. I don't think he bites."

Tiny recognized Rae's voice and immediately hung his tongue out his mouth to pant. Sitting down on his hind legs, he tilted his ear in Rae's direction. The gold charm on his collar jiggled when he shook his head, causing the engraved capital T to sparkle. She had a sneaky suspicion that he wanted his ear scratched.

Rae did not touch his ear. Instead, she raised her eyebrows at the blonde who looked great from a distance, but not so good at close range. Frown lines were carved deeply into her forehead and her dark red lipstick melted into the creases on her lips. Bulging bags hung underneath her eyes, resembling filled potato sacks. The sunken cheeks did her no favors either and gave her a very mean and skeletal appearance.

Unlike her fragile appearance, however, her voice was strong as she yelled, "Get your damn dog away from me!" The heavy-looking canvas bag probably weighed three times more than the woman, but she clutched it for protection.

Rae said in her most apologetic voice, "Sure." Then she looked at the dog. "Tiny, go."

Tiny tilted his head to the left as if to say, "Really?"

"Yes, really," answered Rae and she pointed to Travis's house. "Go home right now."

Tiny stared at her for a quick second and sighed. Then suddenly, he stood on all fours and exploded down the street past Travis's house toward the park.

Perplexed, Rae could only watch. Was she supposed to catch that? How? Her bewilderment was interrupted by the woman's threats.

"I'm calling the police!" Still shrieking, she asked, "What's your name?"

Rae quickly replied, "Travis."

"Well, Travis, it's a law to keep dogs on a leash, especially untrained, malicious dogs." She walked shakily in her heels to her silver Honda, which was parked on the side of the road. "Your dog almost attacked me! You're going to have a lawsuit on your hands one day soon if you don't figure out how to control your damn dog!"

By now, the woman struggled to steady her hands as she opened the car door and dropped her bag. Rae bent to pick it up for her, noticing the design of two hexagons on the front of it. "Neat bag," Rae said, but the woman snatched it from her and quickly settled herself inside the vehicle, starting the engine and driving away.

Hands on hips, Rae stayed on the sidewalk. She stared in the direction of the park, wondering about Tiny. How could she catch a dog that made the speed of light look slow? Cupping her hands around her mouth, she inhaled deeply and yelled, "Tiny!" The dog never appeared and Rae shrugged in hopelessness. Her thoughts switched to the blonde woman with the purple high heels. Rae gave her the nickname of Purple Stiletto. If Purple Stiletto called the police, maybe they could use their squad car and help Rae retrieve Tiny?

"Don't *worry*."

A voice suddenly sounded next to Rae, causing her jump. She jerked her head to see a tall woman with wavy cherry red hair pulled back into a ponytail, standing less than an arm's distance from her.

The redhead realized that she startled Rae and raised her hands with her palms facing outward. "Sorry! I didn't mean to *scare* you." Wearing the latest runner's outfit, complete with expensive new shoes, she didn't look like a runner. She looked like someone who would run only to a late hair appointment. Her legs were painstakingly thin while her stomach protruded slightly over her waistband.

Rae's first thought was, who was she trying to kid? Regardless, her hazel eyes sparkled as she smiled genuinely at Rae.

"My name's Jessica Baraton," she said. "I saw the *whole* thing and don't *worry*. You and your dog did nothing wrong. Your dog didn't even *touch* her." Jessica gestured to a tall boy in his teens standing behind her. He had light yellow hair with natural gold highlights. "This is my *wonderful* son, Bryson. He *loves* dogs." Jessica looked at Bryson. "Don't you, sunshine?"

Bryson didn't answer. He just picked up a stick on the ground.

Jessica continued, "We live down the *road*. Are you *new* around here?"

Rae shook her head. "No, I'm just house-sitting for someone. My name's Rae and just to be clear, that's not my dog."

Confused, Jessica asked, "Whose is it then?"

Rae was just about to explain when Jessica's phone beeped. Jessica quickly glanced at the number. Gritting her teeth, she stifled a small scream. "I *swear*," she said to Rae, "working from home isn't all that it's cracked up to be." Then she beamed. "It was *so* nice meeting you. You're *so* pretty. We should hang out sometime." With that last remark, she looked at Bryson. "Come on, *sunshine*." She turned and loped off, bringing the phone to her ear and remarking into it, "I told you that we're done."

In her wake followed her son. Bryson playfully kept a stone rolling down the sidewalk with a stick. He glanced at Rae and opened his mouth to speak, but Jessica stopped him. "Bryson, I said we have to *go*." He nodded toward his mother and struck a stone forcefully. It rolled off the sidewalk and into the middle of the street. He trailed after his mom in silence.

Rae debated about following the path to the park *just* for a dog. Although, it was her boss's dog. Her boss who promised her that she would NOT have to watch his dog. Travis also failed to mention that Tiny was high-maintenance. So, was it really her responsibility? She pulled out her phone and texted Travis to call her immediately. She had no idea what time it was in China or even if his plane landed, but she hoped he would call her immediately. He didn't and she glanced at the path again, praying to spot the dog. She spotted a man on the path instead, partly hidden behind a tree trunk. He sat in a wheelchair, wearing a tan cowboy hat and facing her. She waved at him, but his hands remained on his lap. His face looked contorted and she squinted at him a little harder. Was he scowling at her? Did he just shake his head?

That was when Rae heard it. Startling her out of the squint, it was a long, ear-splitting shrill from the woods. It started to dip, slowly and mournfully. The eerie call fell into the deepest, lowest timbre that Rae ever heard. She scanned the wooded area, waiting for ChAdonis's banshee to spring out of the trees. Nothing happened, of course, and when she turned toward the cowboy again, he was gone.

And that was when Rae felt it under the heat of a fiery sun. It was an icy breath all around her. So cold. So hopeless.

It pricked her skin.

Stone was unnerved, so unnerved that he instantly left The Espresso Lane. No good-bye. No thanks for the meal. He just stood wordlessly and departed.

Zalen had been in mid-bite. Maybe his one wide eye popped out of his head from Stone's abrupt departure? Or maybe he knew that Stone was going to leave like that even before Stone knew himself? No matter. Stone was now driving away from that lunacy toward a milder lunacy of Sally running his bar. Albeit, he was driving with very white knuckles.

In fact, Stone maintained that white knuckle grip after arriving at work. He stood motionless in front of the counter with a straight face. He felt like his normal aloof self, except his hands gripped the railing tightly. The twisted wood railing ran along the whole long length of the entire bar, branding the establishment as The Rail. However, at that moment, it was more than a prominent feature. It was also his backbone. His twisted backbone that kept his legs from collapsing underneath him.

Zalen wasn't supposed to have known about that girl. No one was. She was Stone's secret. That way, he didn't have to deal with it. He didn't have to accept it. He could just ignore it. Could he still? And what did Zalen mean she *is* in danger? Stone pictured the girl's whipped face and her blue fingers. No, the girl *is* not in danger. She *was* already dead.

Stone's hands ached from intensely holding onto the railing while Zalen's words turned inside Stone's head. His psychic ability wasn't a gift. It was a curse. And he had it since he was a kid. His teenage years were the worst. That was when his arms began to tingle whenever he felt a pair of invisible eyes on him, or when he saw a dark shape around corners that nobody else saw.

Suddenly, goosebumps instantly formed on his forearms again. He furrowed his eyebrows. Looking at his grandfather's stool, it rested peacefully in the corner. Stone turned his head, searching for the young girl's apparition. She was nowhere to be seen. So, why were pins and needles prickling every inch of his body?

CHAPTER SIX

That animal howl from the woods disturbed Rae. It had to have been a bear. Or a cougar. Could Tiny howl like *that?* Rae gasped. What if Tiny was in danger? Confused by her new-found feelings of concern, she stood on the sidewalk with her hands on her hips. Why was she feeling this way? She wasn't aware that she could feel this way toward a dog. Wait a minute, she said to herself. What was happening? Travis somehow tricked her into caring for his dog. Well, she refused to fall into his sticky web of manipulation. Shaking her head, Rae headed into his manor as that troubling scream echoed through her mind.

Rae patrolled the Victorian home under the protection of Travis's golf club, the big one, while checking the locked doors and unsuccessfully activating the alarm system. Then after a few minutes, she rechecked the doors and still had no luck at activating the alarm system. She jumped and screamed three times at the sight of another person in the foyer, carrying a golf club. And all three times, it was just her own reflection in that large, heinous mirror.

To calm her beating heart, Rae produced ten more logo designs. After sending the new batch to the finicky New Yorker, she timed herself on how fast she could finish an online crossword. Nine minutes and twelve seconds later, she looked at her completed puzzle, shaking her head in dismay. It was not a quick finish, but her anxiety had the best of her that night. Knowing what she had to do, she searched the kitchen for her favorite evening snack. After spreading generous amounts of peanut butter and jam onto warm toast, she relaxed and hunted for the nearest television.

She eventually found a flat screen TV hanging over the mantel in one of the more casual-looking rooms. With toast in hand, she broke another one of Travis's rules and settled herself on an oversized sectional, spilling crumbs all over the couch. She then placed every throw pillow on either side of her and rested the golf club across her lap.

Around ten o'clock, those same feelings of mixed concerns surfaced regarding Tiny. She never agreed to dog-sitting; she only agreed to house-sitting. Regardless, Travis stuck her with this responsibility, even after *promising* that she would *not* have to watch his dog. Still, Tiny was a just a dog caught in the middle. Poor dog. Rae gasped. *Poor* dog? This dog lived better than Rae. She was poor, not this dog. And how dare Travis force her into staying in this creepy manor by these creepy woods and then dump his creepy beast of a dog on her? And Tiny had the nerve to run off. Twice. Well, she wasn't going to look for him. Or should she try and look for the beastly dog at least once? Glancing out the picture window into the blackness of the night, images of herself being stuffed into a trunk or hunted by a cougar made her decide to remain on the sofa and eat more food on it. Another image of the spa shower suddenly flashed in her mind though, and a new decision was made. After turning off the television, she headed upstairs, passing the front door just as the doorbell rang.

Rae's pulse quickened. Every scene from every horror movie came rushing at her. She waited for a few minutes and finally worked up the nerve to drag a wingback chair to the door and peek out the transom window, but no person was there. There was a car, however, parked at the end of the street right by the woods. It was a black Ford Taurus and someone sat behind the wheel. An overwhelmingly wide figure with a bulbous head filled the space.

She could see the outline as well as the red glow of a burning cigarette, periodically piercing the darkness.

Fifteen minutes later, Rae still stood on the chair, spying on the driver. The veil of the dark night covered any hopes of her acquiring a clear physical description of this person, but she remained at her post as questions swirled inside her head. Did the driver of the Ford ring the doorbell? Was this some kind of neighborhood watch? How long was this person going to sit there? She finally raised her phone to her ear and called her brother, Danny.

Danny answered on the fourth ring. "Yo."

"Hey, somebody rang the doorbell and took off."

"Ding-dong ditch."

"Yeah. Now there's a car parked across the street and someone's in it. What should I do?"

"Nothing."

"Really?"

"Yep. Work emergency. Gotta go." With that, Danny disconnected.

Peering at the car again, the car's engine roared to life and the driver circled the Ford around slowly, passing the manor. Rae listened as the rumbling sound of the engine gradually diminished into silence.

While trying to set the alarm system, it squealed in protest. Frazzled, she turned the system off, relocked the front door and cemented the chair in front of the door. Feeling a little safer, she trudged up the stairs to her tower guestroom, telling herself that everything was fine. Sleep was the necessary medicine, not a shower. She didn't want to star in any version of an Alfred Hitchcock movie. As for Tiny, if he didn't return by morning, she would then google how to hunt down a supersized pet dog with an enormous head. But for now, she was not unlocking any doors and going outside in the dark all by herself. The better choice was to pull the covers over her nicely-proportioned head and sleep. However, her anxiety might make it hard.

Soothing sounds should help. Once in bed, she reached for her phone and found a recording of relaxing typing sounds on YouTube. She closed her eyes and inhaled deeply for three counts. Then she exhaled for three counts. This deep-breathing continued until she felt the tension in her eyelids and mouth lessen. Maybe rest was in her near future after all?

She really should've known better.

• • •

Time crawled by. At two in the morning, exactly, Stone kicked out the last patrons and locked the door. Sally was the only exception and remained leaning against the bar, wearing an electric blue bouffant wig this time. She wanted to talk, but Stone wasn't in the mood to listen to her slurring. Instead, he called Uber for her again, helped her into the backseat and then left the scene himself. Neglecting all of his bar ownership duties, he just wanted to fall into bed. No more talking. No more thinking. No more counting the gin bottles. Just a whole lot of forgetting.

Stone tried to turn off his mind. As he lay on his back in his bed, fully clothed, he thought of football. The feel of the leather. The sound of the cheering crowd. The brilliant stadium lights. They were blinding at first, and then suddenly dark. Stone was out cold.

He slipped into a deep slumber until something startled himself out of it. The red numbers on his alarm clock glowed angrily in the darkness. He tried to shield his eyes from their glare, but couldn't move his arms. Eventually, he focused on those bright numbers. It was five o'clock in the morning. With his breathing even and his pulse regular, Stone felt unusually calm. Nothing seemed out of the norm, except for two things. First, he apparently was paralyzed. Second, his bed had been replaced with leaves. Still flat on his back, fully clothed, he was now outside on the ground. Somehow. Although, it didn't feel like outside.

There was a forest of trees around him. They all were tall with smooth white trunks leading straight up to the starry morning sky. The foliage crowning the top of the trees danced and swayed high above him. It was a beautiful morning, except for the fact that Stone was incapacitated. He could only turn his head, which he did, and that was when he saw her.

Rachel was beside him on his left. She was not on her back in a peaceful, straight position though. Her body was broken and contorted. It looked like the trees tore her limb from limb. Only her beautiful face remained intact with those blue-gray eyes glimmering in the early sunlight. However, a glistening brown liquid dripped down her face, leaving streaks. It wasn't blood and it was runnier than syrup. Whatever it was, Rachel's hair dripped with it.

Stone felt utterly helpless. He yearned to wipe her face clean and dry her hair. He wanted to take her into his arms and put her body back together. That would make her smile the way he remembered. But he still couldn't move a muscle.

Suddenly, a whitish gray mist formed next to Rachel. That same young girl who Stone saw at the bar materialized. The cuts on her face still bled and her brown eyes were pleading. Using her hand, she beckoned Stone to follow her deeper into the woods. He couldn't budge and she eventually gave up on him. She turned from him and he involuntarily sucked in air at the sight of the gash on the back of her head. Walking away, the girl was soon swallowed up by the trees' shadows.

The cool morning breeze caressed his skin, causing a shiver to run down his spine. He closed his eyes and listened. Hearing nothing but dead silence, he inhaled deeply. Familiar scents lingered in the air, like the fresh smell of damp dirt, the sweet fragrance of wildflowers, and butterscotch. Wait. What?

Then someone tapped his other shoulder.

When Stone turned his head to look, his confusion mixed with frustration. He groaned.

"Hey, Stone."

It was Zalen.

"How ya doin'?" Zalen smiled. He, too, was laying flat on his back next to Stone on the other side.

Stone opened his mouth with a few choice words in mind, but he could only grunt.

Zalen chuckled. "You should really call me, man. This is pretty crazy. Now, you're going to tell yourself that this is a dream. It's not. And then you're going to tell yourself that you don't know my number. You do. You must give yourself a chance. Just relax, clear your mind and try."

A loud snap of a bird flapping its wings caused Stone to jump. He sat up, sweaty and breathless. Looking around frantically, he no longer saw trees nor stars. Rachel was gone. And so was Zalen. He now recognized the silhouette of his dresser and felt the damp sheets tangled around his legs. He was back. He returned from the forest to his bedroom. Alone.

And with Zalen's damn phone number stuck in his head.

CHAPTER SEVEN

Tossing and turning, Rae had continuous nightmares. The last one really jolted her. She was with Travis on a plane, naked except for the helmet on her head. She was sharing her seat with Tiny, the largest dog that she ever saw. A cougar suddenly appeared in the overhead compartment, trying to swipe at her. She pressed the assistance button for help and it sounded like Travis's doorbell.

Gasping, Rae opened her eyes and sat up in bed. It wasn't a dream. The doorbell really had sounded. She was sure of it. Puzzled, she wondered if it would sound again.

It did.

Who kept ringing the doorbell? With a thumping chest, she glanced at the time on her phone. It was five in the morning. She muttered profanities and threw off the covers. Peeking out her bedroom window, she looked down onto the driveway. At the bottom of the front porch steps sat Tiny. He looked up at her and cocked his head to the left. Any feelings about her doing the right thing regarding this dog flew out the window, as well as her loyalty to her job. The mumbling began, "I didn't sign up for any of this. This is ridiculous. I don't even like dogs, especially ones who ring doorbells at five in the morning." She rummaged around her tower bedroom for a sweatshirt and flip-flops before slumping down the stairs.

Rae opened the door. "Tiny, you're a naughty dog. What gives?"

Sitting even straighter, he cocked his head to the other side. He woofed quietly.

Exasperated, Rae said, "Don't talk back to me. The sun is barely over the horizon. It's too early for arguing. Are you coming in or do you want a parade in your honor?"

He gave her a side look. Shifting his paws, he moved like he wanted to enter, but something stopped him. His watery eyes seemed unsure.

Rae yawned. "Look, dude, I don't know anything about dogs, except I thought dogs usually wake people up to go *outside*. I haven't heard of a dog ringing the doorbell to come *inside*. That is what you want, right? To come inside?"

He lifted one paw and froze.

"What does that mean? Do you want to shake? Is that it?" Rae reached for his paw, but he set it down on purpose.

"Hey," Rae snapped. "That wasn't nice."

Tiny shook his entire body, flashing the letter T on his dog tag again.

"I think that *T* really stands for *Terrible*." Anger reached a new level for Rae. "You're either in or out!"

Tiny shrugged and sniffed. His red eyes looked tired. After nodding once, he bounded through the door and up the stairs. Rae closed the front door and followed Tiny's trail, stopping him when he tried to stroll past his bedroom.

"Your stop is right here." Rae opened the door and gasped. Her body swayed backward as if she were about to be blown over by all the pink. There was a small pink fuzzy dog mattress underneath a pink wooden structure shaped like a large doghouse. A string of rosette globes were strung along the roof beam. They were a dark pink. The wallpaper had various tones of pink dots all over it. The circular light pink rug in the middle of the room had various-shades-of-pink stuffed animals sitting on it, waiting for playtime. A hand-sewn flannel blanket, pink, covered the small mattress perfectly. Everywhere Rae looked was pink and fuzzy. She now knew how it would feel to be forced to live inside high end cotton candy. Her teeth hurt.

Rae asked Tiny, "Do you like pink because it compliments your fur?"

Unamused, Tiny ignored the question by turning his head away from Rae.

She smiled and walked around him, saying, "*Sweet* dreams."

Leaving him in the hallway, she found solace in her tower bedroom where there was absolutely no pink. First, she slipped off her sweatshirt. Then she kicked off her flip-flops. Climbing into bed, Rae pulled up the silky sheet to her chin and settled in for more sleep. Four more hours. At least.

As she sighed in delight, someone else arfed. Rae then felt hot breath on her neck and cringed at the sound of a wet tongue licking lips. Before she even opened her eyes, she knew who her new bed companion was.

"Tiny." Rae was agitated. "You have your own bedroom."

Tiny whined.

"I don't care if you don't like it. You can't stay in here. I don't sleep with dogs."

Tiny yipped.

Rae yipped louder, "This isn't up for debate. Now, go to your room." In a dramatic flair, she extended her arm and pointed toward the door.

Tiny merely yawned and licked his chops again. Then he rolled onto his other side, taking the whole silky sheet with him.

Rae grabbed what little edge of the sheet she could and pulled. It was like a little Volkswagen towing a semi truck. "C'mon, Tiny." Rae's voice was strained. "You need to go." Placing both of her feet on his back, she pushed, but the force almost moved her off the bed instead. She moaned. "Please go."

Tiny only softly woofed again. Then he flicked his ear and settled two of his paws on top of her feet.

Rae surrendered. Grabbing a pillow, she left her tower bedroom and returned to that oversized sectional. She used the throw pillows like a blanket to cover herself and snuggled into the cushions. Content to be rid of the dog and his sharp toenails, her body relaxed. Soon, she entered the dream world.

. . .

Bash was pumped. His plan not only worked, but he also was on his way to a thrilling destination. He read about this particular area in a library book titled *Ghosts and Ghouls in Your Own Backyard!* He smiled at the thought of the ghost that he was interested in pursuing, except it wasn't a ghost. It was a banshee. Now, he just needed to pack appropriately.

On his bedroom floor was a suitcase and piles of clean clothes that his mother ordered him to place inside of it. Bash sighed at the socks, underwear, pajamas, swimsuit and matching outfits. Opening the suitcase, he reached past all the lavender-scented clothes and grabbed a hard black case, setting it on his lap. He unlocked the lid for the third time and triple-checked the items: one EMF and temperature meter, a spirit box, an instant camera, a new guide called *A Ghosting We Will Go: Becoming the Hunter,* one mechanical pencil, a highlighter and a red spiral notebook. Satisfied, he closed the lid and placed the case in his suitcase. Next to it, he stuffed his dad's utility flashlight and some extra batteries. It was a snug fit. With the remaining space, he managed to squeeze in one pair of shorts, a swimsuit and binoculars.

Ready to go, he said farewell to his oldest sister, Emma, through her bedroom door. She did not respond. He then said good-bye to his younger brother, Henry, who was more absorbed with his science kit than Bash's departure. Meg, his youngest sister, was at daycare, but had already given Bash a sloppy kiss on the cheek. That was more than enough. Carrying his suitcase and pillow to the car, he waited for his mother.

A few short minutes skipped past the eight o'clock hour and his mom emerged from her house, carrying a purse, satchel and a briefcase. Out of breath, she threw everything in the backseat, except for the satchel. She plopped the bag on his lap, saying to him, "I packed this with everything you forgot to pack." She gave him the stink eye.

"Thanks," Bash said absentmindedly. He stared out the window in deep thought.

"Hey," his mom said, "you'll only be staying there for a few days. So, be on your best behavior and remember to help out."

"Right," Bash said slowly again.

His mom asked, "What are you thinking about?"

Bash turned his head in surprise. "Me? I'm not thinking about anything." It was a lie. He was thinking about catching that banshee.

His mom scoffed at Bash's statement. "That's a lie," she said. "What are you up to?"

Blinking quickly, Bash answered, "Nothing. I'm just excited to see Aunt Rae. It's going to be fun. Helping out and stuff. Looking forward to all of it."

"Hmmm," she hummed, "it might be a little boring at times. She still has to work."

"I'll be fine, Mom."

"Well, promise to call me or Dad every night. And if you want to come home earlier than Sunday, that's fine. We will come anytime."

"Can I stay later?"

His mom squinted in thought. "We'll see," she finally said.

"Thanks, Mom." Bash smiled. "And thank Dad for me again. And don't worry about us, okay? You have a tendency to overreact."

"I'll be good." Nodding at him, she said, "I'm actually glad you and your aunt are so close. I think it's nice that you two will be spending this time together. Just be smart."

They both remained quiet for the rest of the hour. It wasn't until they drove down the impressive street with grandiose manors and beautiful birch trees when they both gasped. As his mom parked at the apron of the driveway, Bash noticed that she started perspiring a lot.

Turning toward him, she squeaked, "This place looks very unaffordable. Please remember to lift the seat and don't touch anything."

Bash smiled. "How am I supposed to lift the seat then?" He quickly left the car with his satchel, snatched his suitcase from the backseat and hustled across the front lawn to the porch. Climbing the steps, he banged his suitcase along the way.

Standing next to her car, his mom hollered, "Bash! Careful of the stone steps!"

"Don't worry, Mom." He raised his fist to knock on the door.

She hollered again, "Don't touch the door with your dirty knuckles!"

"Mom," Bash snapped, "it's a door. Made for knocking. What am I supposed to do?"

His mom held her face. "Everywhere I look, I see marble and lawsuits."

Bash sighed. "Mom, you're overreacting. Remember your mantra?"

His mom nodded. "It's all about finding the calm in the chaos."

"Exactly. Keep repeating that. Between Aunt Rae and me, we'll keep this house and all of its valuables safe and unharmed. Trust us."

Her voice tilted toward the hysterical side. "You're right, everything will be fine."

Footsteps then sounded from behind the front door. The doorknob turned and the whole door yanked open. There, with untamed hair and crazy eyes, Aunt Rae stood in the doorway. Frantic. Sweaty. She first looked at Bash. Then at his mom. Then back at Bash. Finally, she asked both of them breathlessly, "Have either of you seen a very large dog?"

CHAPTER EIGHT

Rae saw Clare's look of concern mixed with amusement and fear as she joined Bash. "You know," Clare stiffly joked, "history has proven over the years that a mother repeatedly faces tough decisions regarding her children's well-being."

"Mom." Bash moaned. "Don't pick on Aunt Rae."

Clare continued to speak. "Take Alexander the Great, for instance. His mother, Olympias, probably struggled fiercely with herself when deciding if she should or should not murder people for her son's career advancement. I can kind of understand that now."

Bash looked at his mom. "I'm just visiting Aunt Rae, not climbing the corporate ladder."

Speaking to Rae, Clare said, "Just promise me you won't lose Bash too."

Rae jogged down the steps, protesting. "I didn't lose the dog. He seems to come and go as he pleases. I'm just surprised he left so soon, since he didn't come home until five o'clock this morning." She looked around the front yard. "I don't get it."

"This is lit." Bash's face shone with excitement. "I love big dogs. The bigger, the better."

Rae said, "You're in for a treat then. This dog is huge, like a walking mountain." She scratched her head. "I don't see him anywhere."

"You can't *see* a walking mountain?" Clare laughed. "And to think I was going to set you up on a *blind* date."

Rae scoffed. "That's a terrible joke."

"At least I'm trying to see the humor," Clare reasoned before turning to Bash. "Call me tonight and, if you and your Aunt Rae find yourselves in any kind of *weird* situation, just save yourself and get out of there. Okay? What's *your* mantra?"

Bash mumbled quietly to his mom, "It's every Bash for himself."

"Remember that and here." Rae watched as Clare slipped her son a fifty dollar bill. "Just in case." She then gave Bash a squeezing hug. "Call Howie in a *real* emergency, okay? Not me. Not your dad. You call Howie."

Rae asked, "Who's Howie?"

Bash answered, "My parole officer."

Clare tsked. "No, he's not. If you keep saying that, people will start to believe you." She explained to Rae, "Howie is a policeman and a good friend of your brother." After digging in her purse, she produced a slip of paper and handed it to Rae. "Here's his phone number, in case you need him."

Rae read his name and said, "Can Officer Howard Scott catch large dogs? If not, I probably won't need him."

Clare didn't laugh. "I'm being serious. Take precious care of my son."

Rae asked Clare, "Have I ever let you down before?"

"No, never." Clare smiled. "That's one of the reasons why Bash is here." Clare slid behind the steering wheel, started the car and slowly backed onto the street. Rae and Bash remained on the lawn, waving for the three long minutes it took for Clare to finally drive away.

With bright eyes, Bash asked his aunt, "Where should we look first?"

Rae shoved Howie's phone number into the front pocket of her yoga shorts, nodding toward the trees. "There's a path around the woods that leads to a park. We should probably start there. Dogs naturally like parks, right?" Bash nodded and Rae continued, "C'mon. Let's put your bags inside the house first. Then I guess we're going on a dog hunt."

After Bash threw his belongings into the foyer, he closed the front door behind him and asked, "Do you have a leash?"

"Yep. Right here." She pulled out a short, thin pink leash that was tucked in the other front pocket. "Although, honestly, I don't think this will help much. Just like it wouldn't help lead around a pygmy elephant." She stuffed it back into her pocket and they began their hunt on the path. The *safe* path, as ChAdonis told her. The one from which no one should stray.

By two minutes into the walk, Bash strayed from the safe path many times. In fact, it was impossible for him to stay on the path. Rae wondered about him as he weaved in and out of the trees. Looking up. Looking down. Looking in every direction, except forward. He walked into a tree. Four times.

Rubbing his forehead, he said, "These birch trees are breathtaking."

Rae replied dully, "Yep. Now, be on the lookout for a dog the size of a naval vessel."

Bash raised his eyebrows. "Okay. What kind of dog is it?"

"Possibly a Great Dane or German Shepherd and part Russian transport helicopter."

"Could he be both? The dogs, I mean."

"Only if such dogs really exist."

"They do," Bash answered while staring at his cellphone nestled in the palm of his hand. He searched for something. When he found it, he held up his phone displaying the image of such a dog. "This is a Great Shepherd, which is a Great Dane and German Shepherd mix. They are known to be patient and friendly." After a short pause, Bash added, "They're big dogs. They stand at twenty-eight to thirty inches tall."

"My boss's dog seems bigger." Rae glanced at the picture. It showed a proud-looking canine turning his head to the side with his chin held up high in the air. The specimen was mostly a short-haired tan dog with darker ears and big brown eyes. The upturned smoky snout gave this creature a conceited look. Rae sniffed. "Yeah, that looks like him. He's not very patient though. Or friendly. Or even polite. And he has a much more smug look on his face."

Bash grinned. "Well, I can't wait to meet him. What's his name?"

"Tiny."

Bash snickered. "That's funny. Your boss has a wicked sense of humor."

Rae turned to face her nephew. "My boss Travis is definitely wicked. I call him The Torch because he's a tall demon. I really do believe he came from Hell."

"How did Tiny get out of the house without you knowing it?"

Rae shrugged. "He left when I was asleep. To make a long story short, Tiny can apparently open doors. Don't ask me how." Sighing, she added, "This dog is very annoying."

Bash's hand patted Rae's shoulder as he said, "Don't worry. We'll find him."

When Rae turned toward Bash, something in the corner of her eye caught her attention. It was something, or someone, crouched behind one of the trees. Rae normally had crisp eyesight, but today, her tired eyes blurred everything in the distance. Squinting at the form, she tried to figure out what was behind that distant tree.

She looked at Bash and said, "I think someone's in the woods, watching us."

Bash asked, "Could it be Tiny?"

Rae turned from her nephew and scrutinized the wooded area again. She watched as the hunched-over shape swiftly scampered on two legs deeper into the woods. Rae said, "It's a person and he's on the move." She stepped off the path.

Bash grabbed her hand. "Why do you care?"

Thinking about the doorbell ditcher, Rae answered, "I just want to check it out."

"Or, we could keep walking. Dogs naturally like parks, remember? We should just go there and forget about the possible entity lurking in the woods."

"Entity?" Rae shook her head as the feeling of curiosity rose. She said, "Stay here."

Bash sighed. "Haven't you ever heard of the proverb, 'curiosity killed the cat'?"

Rae retorted, "Haven't you ever heard that the original form of the proverb was actually '*care* killed the cat'?"

Bash shrugged. "Either way, the cat dies."

* * *

Every time Stone dozed back to sleep, he dreamt of Zalen's round face, which he thought was highly irritating. He had enough. By quarter to nine, Stone stood behind his bar, still closed for business, and rubbed his temples. His forehead felt slick from oil. His scalp itched from lack of a good shampoo scrubbing. More unsettling than the way he felt was the desperate atmosphere he sensed around him.

Scattered on the bar's counter were many napkins with illegible words scribbled all over them. His hand moved fast as his hand raced to keep up with his mind. Anger rose in Stone with each strong stroke of the pen. At first, all of his focus was on the written words. Then he smelled it. A combined scent of mossy grass and a heavy musk lingered in the air. It wasn't from him. That was the cologne his Grandpa Ed wore. Stone actually appreciated lighter aromas and took out a bottle of cologne that he kept under the bar. He sprayed it in front of his face. Then he spritzed it three times toward the corner stool, his grandpa's stool, inhaling the simple fragrance of a beach bum. After taking out his phone, he finally dialed those damn numbers.

Zalen answered half-way during the first ring, "Hi, Stone!"

Stone wasn't as zealous and spoke thickly, "I'm done with you and all of this bullshit."

"Oh, come on now." Zalen's tone was irresistibly engaging. "You just had a rough night."

"Exactly my point." Stone adjusted his cap the same way a batter adjusted his right before hitting the ball out of the park. He was more than ready to unload. "I've been reading up on all of this nonsense for nearly the past two hours and I found out the *real* reasons why people think they see ghosts. Or have out-of-body experiences. Or even have nightmares, for that matter. It has nothing to do with psychic abilities. It all has to do with stress, anxiety, or insomnia. And after meeting you, I now have all three." As Stone spoke, his pointer finger angrily struck the air, and he heard his grandfather's empty corner stool slightly wobble.

Zalen's soothing voice remained even. "Calm down, buddy."

"No," Stone shouted, "you calm down! I don't know how you do your parlor tricks, but they're not going to work on me. Anymore!"

Zalen interrupted calmly, "Parlor tricks?"

"Yes. Parlor tricks." Stone's voice cracked. "Stop following me or stalking me or whatever you're doing to find out my information. And if you ever come near me again, I'm calling the police!" With that last bit of anger, Stone disconnected at the exact time the stool flipped over itself, landing with a reverberating bang inches away from him.

He jumped. Ears ringing. Heart thumping. His cap was no longer fixed squarely on his head, but was pushed up and a little sideways. "What the hell?" he said softly to himself while staring at the stool. The musk scent was overpowering and angry.

Stone closed his eyes and concentrated on something else to steady his breathing. It was her smile. Rachel's easy smile. He focused on it. And after a few deep breaths, the smile faded, making room for his blood to boil. His fingers curled into tight fists and he pounded them on the bar. A spark in the pit of his stomach ignited, growing into a huge ball of fire. It climbed up and into his throat. Arching his back, he released a thunderous roar. It lasted a few seconds, but the echo made it last a few seconds more.

Then peace. No movement. No sounds. No smells. Until there was a knock on the door.

Stone peered at the person standing on the outside of the bar and the person peered right back at him. It was Zalen. He had his face pressed to the glass door with one hand cupped around his eyes while his other hand waved eagerly at Stone. Then with the same wide grin, he hollered through the glass, "What do you mean by *near*?"

CHAPTER NINE

"Just stay on the path," Rae ordered her nephew as she softly stepped off the path. With bent knees, she moved soundlessly from tree to tree. This reminded her of a game she played with her neighborhood friends when she was eleven years old. They called the game Chase. She remembered the loud laughter as all eight of them ran through the suburban yards late at night. Rae smiled at her memory of the never ending game of tag under the summer night sky. One would be the tagger while the others ran like they were on fire. No one knew when the tagger changed; everyone just kept running. No one was ever really safe. And no one could ever catch Rae, which drove *him* nuts. Her then best friend. He lived next door and always started the game at ten o'clock. She could still see his face shine in the moonlight. He was so cocky in the beginning of the game, betting her that he could catch her. Rae, however, not only ran fast, but also *silently*. He never knew where she was. He never had a chance. By the end, he would be sprawled on his back, trying to catch his breath instead.

She smiled at another memory. The one where she let him catch her. And, to her surprise, he kissed her. Under the moonlight. At age eleven. And, to his surprise, she gut-punched him.

Rae shook that recollection out of her head as she approached the spot where she saw the dark shape. It was now vacant. Standing with her hands on her hips, her eyes scanned the area. She wasn't nuts. Something had been there. She knew it.

Looking over her shoulder toward the path, she saw Bash still standing there. His hand held his cell phone. Was he videotaping her? Rae shrugged at him and he returned the shrug. Then shaking her head, she turned away from him and ventured a little deeper into the woods.

So, these were the woods that ChAdonis warned her about. Gazing at the tall alluring birch trees, they were breathtaking, not scary. The forest didn't look like the home of an evil banshee who kidnapped children. Rae actually felt very comfortable and headed deeper into the woods. Soon, the path and Bash were completely out of sight.

At one point, though, she heard a rustle. Were those leaves blowing across the ground? Or someone crawling toward her? Don't be silly, she told herself. Rae then remembered the cougar scream. Would a cougar really be living in these woods? Turning around, she saw nothing. Standing motionless, she flinched when she heard a breath. It was heavy and to her left. She quietly picked up a broken branch and hid behind a tree, waiting. There was another breath. This time, it wasn't to her left.

It was behind her.

Rae spun around with the branch at her waist, ready to jab. No one was there, but then she felt it. It was the skin on her right arm. It started to prickle, and the sensation spread to her whole torso. It could have been from the sudden cool breeze. Or maybe it was from the sound? It was a strained, gaspy sound of someone crying.

Rae crouched behind the tree, listening to the weeping. Did banshees weep like that? She smacked herself for thinking that silly thought and then peered through the shrubbery and criss-crossing branches, trying to find the source. Squatting low, Rae suddenly felt stupid and like a snoop. A stupid snoop. Someone was definitely having a very bad and very personal moment in the woods, clearly hoping to be by themselves. Maybe she should leave the person alone? Her mother always told her that nosy people didn't live long.

She began to move stealthily away from the crier. Rae understood bad days. Maybe the crier also had a nasty boss who was forcing him or her to dog-sit his nasty dog? That made perfect sense to Rae as she crept quietly away, trying not to make any sound. It was all going to be good, she told herself. Except, at that moment, her phone rang. And it rang that very loud, very peppy Mardi Gras party song.

Brass instruments overwhelmed the whole forest while playing "When the Saints Go Marching In" and it caused little forest friends to scurry away in pure terror. It also scared Rae and she hopped backward, yelping as she jumped. Then she quickly reached for her phone from her back pocket, only to bobble it in her hands a few times before accidentally throwing it into a nearby bush.

It was still ringing. Rae had no choice, but to dive on top of the bush and wrestle with it until she retrieved her phone. By then the call ended. The music stopped and so did the crying.

The woods were silent once again, but something was off. Everything was still. Too still. Where were the fleeing footsteps? Wouldn't a self-respecting crier run away after all of that?

Rae stood, holding her phone and staring in the direction of the mournful wail that now completely ceased. She knew the crier was still near. She felt someone's eyes on her, but Rae couldn't see the watcher. Whoever it was. Whatever it was.

Rae took a small step to the side and then saw a partial face between a heavy cluster of leaves on a branch. Two dark eyes stared at her. The rest of the face and body were hidden by thick foliage. Was all of this her imagination? She took another small step toward it and leaned in ever so slightly. The shaded face was about fifteen feet from her. Nonmoving. Was this really a face? Or was her eyesight failing?

Then the black eyes blinked.

The face wasn't her imagination after all. Perplexed, Rae at first just stared back, feeling frozen from indecisiveness. With each passing second, she grew more uncomfortable. For some reason, she wanted to laugh, but concentrated on keeping her own straight face. Lengthy seconds stretched into minutes and strange thoughts of her spending eternity in these woods invaded her mind. Rae wanted to end this. She opened her mouth to say something, when suddenly, a loud flapping sound broke the tense placidity. Rae gasped and looked up, expecting to see a large prehistoric bird hovering above her. But nothing was there, except for the canopies of taller trees framing a blue sky. The sound left as quickly as it came. Returning her attention to the forest stranger, she searched for the face, which was now gone, but finally heard the fleeing footsteps.

Her phone rang loudly in her hand again. It was Bash. She answered a little breathlessly, "Did you just try to call me?"

"Yes." Bash sounded unusually anxious. "I need you to get out of the woods."

Rae panicked. "Why? Are you okay?"

"*I'm* fine." Bash sighed, now sounding annoyed. "But *you* just disturbed the banshee."

▪ ▪ ▪

"He's worse than a bad penny," Stone said aloud. "At least a bad penny is still worth one cent." He stared at Zalen through the glass door for a minute or two. Zalen only stared back with a very content look on his face as if he was used to being excluded, which pulled on one of Stone's heartstrings. It wasn't a hard pull, but more like a light tug.

Walking slowly over to the door, he hesitantly unlocked it and opened it. Straining a lopsided smile, he said, "Please. Come in."

"Only if it's not too much trouble," Zalen said and was already sitting at the bar by the end of that sentence. With hands folded on the counter, he added, "Nice place."

Stone maneuvered around the fallen barstool, completely ignoring it, and grabbed a tall glass. "What can I get you?"

"Some water would be refreshing. It's already near ninety out there."

Perplexed, Stone said, "You're at a bar and you want water?"

"Water hydrates. Cools the body down naturally." Zalen smiled. "Tap water is fine."

"Sure." Stone shook his head. Instead, he opened a bottle of mineral water and filled a tall glass with ice before pouring the fizzy water into it. He handed the glass to a gleeful Zalen.

"Thank you very much. I like bubbles. They tickle my nose." Zalen picked up the glass, nodded it toward Stone and took five long swigs. He emptied it. And sneezed. Leaning to remove his wallet from his back pocket, he asked, "How much do I owe you?"

"It's on the house."

That made Zalen's smile spread even wider. "Alrighty. I must then thank you again."

Stone was studying Zalen. "How did you know I was here?" He leaned against the back counter with his ankles casually crossed. His arms, however, were defensively crossed over his chest. "And don't tell me that you sensed I worked at this bar."

"Oh, I didn't sense it. I felt it."

"That's the same thing." Stone sighed and rubbed his temples. "Now, be honest. Have you been in my bar before? Have we actually met?"

Zalen chuckled at that. "Oh, no, I don't go to bars. Crowds aren't my thing. Besides, I always say that I like to remember my good times. You know? I hear about other people's drinking escapades and have learned from their stories that alcohol erases memories. So, why would I want to do that?" He smiled again.

Stone was gently pulling on his bottom lip while deep in thought. Then he asked, "Do you have a job? Or family? Or a guardian?"

Zalen chuckled at that too. "Yes, I have a family. Two parents who are now living in Arizona. And three married sisters. Two on the west coast and one on the east. Kinda makes the holidays hard." He shrugged and then continued, "No, I don't have a guardian, but thank you for asking. And yes, I have a job. I'm a special education teacher. I work primarily with kindergarteners through the second grade. It's a great job."

"Is that a joke?"

"Nope. I'd tell you some stories about the little rascals, but I would be breaking the confidentiality agreement that I had to sign." He was still smiling. "I could lose my job."

A pain was forming at the base of Stone's skull. "What's your last name?"

"Richards." Zalen beamed. "It used to be Richardson, but my great-great-great-great grandfather shortened it to Richards. I don't know why. I think it had to do with slavery ending."

This triggered a Richards' family history timeline to unfold as well as a migraine for Stone. He grabbed the nearest bottle of beer and said, "I normally don't drink before noon." He then twisted off the cap and drank half of it.

Zalen nodded. "I'll have to tell you about my family tree some other time. You're right in thinking that we should really be talking about your psychic ability."

The cold beer bottle rested across Stone's forehead. "I wasn't thinking that at all."

Zalen chuckled again. "Your sense of humor is one of a kind. Now, what I find interesting is that I can only feel things and sense stuff here and there, but you can see things and experience surroundings. Your abilities are stronger than mine, Stone. You were able to pull me into your forest vision this morning. I've never had an experience like that before."

Stone asked incredulously, "Are you kidding me?"

"No. Like I said, I usually just feel things. And I *feel* that our paths were supposed to cross. I *feel* that we are supposed to be a team."

What Stone felt was sick. "Look," he said, "the only team I've ever played on was my high school football team. I know that you think you can help me, but I honestly don't want to be helped. I don't want to accept or understand any of this. So, if you can accept and understand that, then feel free to stay and have another refreshing drink on me. Otherwise, please leave."

Stone stared into Zalen's one wide eye. He mentally prepared himself for more of Zalen's crazy comments, but was surprised when Zalen only said, "I'd love another mineral water."

"Okay." Stone grabbed a new bottle. "And just to be clear, no more weird talk about dreams or having psychic abilities."

"Got it." Zalen smiled again. "I accept and understand your feelings." Zalen picked up the sparkling refill and nodded it toward Stone. "No more weird talk." He even put a finger to his lips. And winked.

Stone grinned for the first time that morning and drank more of his beer, feeling the pain in his head subside. With his temples no longer throbbing, he began breathing normally again.

Until Zalen asked, "Who is Rachel? And is she *already* dead? Or is she *going to* die?"

CHAPTER TEN

Rae disconnected her phone. Shaking her head in disbelief, she muttered, "The banshee?" How did Bash know about the banshee? Then again, how would he not know? She began trudging back toward the path, asking herself, "Is it even possible to disturb a banshee?"

As she stepped out of the woods, Bash said to her, "Thank God you're not dead. I'd have a hard time explaining to my parents and the proper authorities about your death resulting from meeting The Birch Grove Banshee."

"Not you too." Rae said before her attention shifted to the tall boy standing next to Bash. It was Bryson Baraton, the sunshiny boy. The teenager stood heads above Bash with very broad shoulders and lanky, but strong limbs. In his hand was a string about the length of a ruler with a paperclip attached to one end. He swung it around in circles. Rae looked up into Bryson's face and said, "Oh, hello."

Bryson stopped twirling the string and said amiably, "Hello, we meet again." Flashing a brilliant smile, he flipped his long golden bangs from his clear, bright eyes. They were a palette of layered paint with flecks of gold, green and blue in them, reminding Rae of abstract art that was both beautiful and complex. The combination of his hair and eyes definitely marked him as a walking sunbeam.

Rae smiled politely while thinking he looked way too happy to be the crier from the woods. "Out for a stroll?"

Bryson nodded, explaining, "My mom was going to come with me, but she needed to take a call. She's a marriage therapist and works from home."

Rae said to Bryson, "Cool. So, you don't believe in this banshee stuff too, do you?"

Bryson fanned out his lips into the widest smile. "Not really, but who knows?" Then looking at Bash, he said, "Well, I gotta go. It was nice meeting you. Maybe we can hang out sometime?" With a small nod toward Rae, he turned and trotted down the path.

After Bryson rounded the bend, Bash said with a lowered his voice, "He's strange."

Rae looked at Bash. "Really? He seems like a regular kid to me."

"He told me he's fifteen."

"So?"

"I'm twelve."

"And?"

"I don't know any fifteen-year olds who want to hang out with me."

"Well," Rae began, "Bryson apparently does." As Bash scrunched up his face, she changed the subject. "How is it that you know about the witch?"

"Banshee." Bash corrected. "And I like to put my reading skills to use as well as my library card. I know," he continued, "I'm strange too."

She needled her nephew. "And irritating at times." Being strange and irritating were what made him so interesting to her though and she loved hearing about his new fascinations, even if she didn't believe in them herself. Smiling, she asked her highly irritating and strangely fascinating nephew, "What's the scoop on this birch banshee?"

"Well." The excitement rose in Bash's voice as he gestured with his hands. "It's been hard finding a notable resource, but from my research, which is ongoing, The Birch Grove Banshee lives in these woods. Her age is anywhere between eighty to one thousand years. She's possibly a sculptor who sold her soul to the devil. She also most likely killed her husband and buried him in one of her sculptures. Plus, there have been reports about how she eats trespassers or sucks out their souls to give to the devil for her immortality. Something like that."

Rae only said, "Of course. Anything else?"

"Well," Bash began again, "there's another theory out there that this banshee might not have been a sculptor at all. She might just be a retired teacher who feasts on bad children."

Rae said with a hint of sarcasm, "I'm glad your research is ongoing."

Unphased, Bash explained, "The original legend of the banshee is quite interesting. Banshees are usually regarded as an evil old lady with a high-pitched shrill that is heard anytime, usually at night. If *you* hear it, *you'll* die. But that's not really accurate. For starters, banshees have taken many forms. People claim to have seen an older woman with long gray hair, wearing rags. Others claim to have seen a beautiful young woman with long red hair, wearing a green dress. Some say she's carrying a bowl of blood. Some say she's headless. It goes on and on."

"What do you think?"

"I think it all depends on the person who the banshee reveals herself to."

Rae was impressed. "That's very good."

"And the famous banshee scream is more of a mournful wail that's supposed to warn the person of danger. Not necessarily death. And only that person in danger can hear it. But there is another sound that she can make to let a person know that they're entering a situation where they may not come out alive. It's a flapping sound. Like a bird flapping its wings."

Rae thought of the flapping sound that she just heard. Then she caught herself from falling victim to Bash's bewitching tale. "Why is a banshee living in these birch woods? I thought they preferred Ireland."

"Or Scotland. Or even Wales. But I don't know why she would be here." He glanced at the forest. "Maybe she's attached in some way to these birch trees? Did you know that birch trees are indigenous to Ireland?" Bash shrugged. "That's not out of the realm of possibilities."

By now, they reached the park, which was devoid of any dogs or activities. However, a black Ford Taurus sat across the park in a parking lot that led to another subdivision. The driver's seat was empty. Rae was certain it was the same Ford from the prior night. Then scanning the park again, she noticed a man slouched in his wheelchair in some shade under a tree, wearing a tan cowboy hat. Rae recognized him from yesterday. He was a good thirty feet from them and presumably asleep with his chin lowered onto his chest.

Returning her attention back to Bash, Rae continued their conversation. "Or," she said, "maybe there is no such thing as a banshee? People love to tell scary stories just to create hype. No doubt, banshees are a great ghost story, but honestly, they are as real as Bigfoot."

Bash gasped, clearly personally injured. "Can you prove that Bigfoot *doesn't* exist?"

Rae smiled. "I'm not attacking you or your core belief system. I'm just saying you can't believe everything you read or hear. Or even see."

Bash looked confused. "What do you mean?"

Rae opened her mouth to explain, but stopped. Glancing over her shoulder, she noticed that the man in the wheelchair was no longer across the park, but instead directly behind them.

As Rae and Bash turned to face him, he said to Rae with a gravelly voice, "I've been watching you."

Rae stepped in front of Bash and asked the cowboy, "You've been *watching* me?"

The cowboy glanced to his right and then his left. "You shouldn't be staying in that house. Someone disappeared from that house and was *never heard of again.*"

Rae heard Bash speak behind her, "Disappeared? Who disappeared?"

The cowboy spoke to Bash, "A girl. About your age."

Just then, a slim young teenager, wearing a black t-shirt and baggy jeans, appeared from the woods. Looking at his face, evidence of dried tears remained on his cheeks, leaving a trail of streaks. Rae immediately wondered if he was the crier in the woods. He noticed her staring at him and he glared at her.

The teenager strode briskly past her, clipping his shoulder against hers. Then he nodded toward the old man, saying quickly, "Hola, Bronco." Bronco only nodded in return and the teen broke into a fast run down the path, past the woods and into the other neighborhood.

Rae looked at the cowboy and asked, "Do you live around here, *Bronco*?"

Using one foot, he rolled even closer toward them. "You should forget my name." He then added with a warning tone. "It would be best if you mind your own business."

■   ■   ■

The pain instantly returned to Stone's head. He gritted his teeth. "It took you two lousy seconds to break our agreement. I want my water back. Including the water you swallowed."

Zalon waved off Stone's remarks. "C'mon, Stone. I didn't say anything weird about the dream or mention a word about our shared psychic ability. Can I have a lemon wedge?"

"No."

"Alrighty. I only wanted to know more about Rachel. I can feel how important she is to you." He smiled wider. "And I get the feeling that she might not be dead. Yet."

Stone heaved a heavy sigh. "She's *not* dead."

"Yet."

"Stop saying that." Stone's voice shook. He never thought of Rachel as actually dead.

Zalon took notice and reversed a bit. "Okay. So, who is Rachel? Where is she?"

Massaging his eyebrows, Stone answered, "Just a girl, and I don't know."

"Hmmm...can you at least tell me her last name?"

"Nope," he replied. "Why do you care so much?"

"I already told you that. I feel that I'm supposed to help you find her."

"Rachel?" Confused, Stone asked, "Not the other girl?"

"What other girl?"

Stone drummed his fingers on the counter, thinking about the apparition of the girl with the facial cuts and head wound. He was surprised and relieved that Zalen didn't know about her. Zalen seemed to only know about Rachel. Somehow. Deciding to keep it that way, Stone merely shrugged. "No one important."

"Oh, okay." Zalen nodded. "So, was Rachel a past girlfriend? The one who got away?"

"No, nothing like that. We never dated."

"Oh." Zalen nodded again. "She was the one way out of your league then. I could *feel* that she was a cheerleader." He winked. "I get it."

"Actually," Stone said, "Rachel would never have been caught dead wearing a cheerleading skirt."

Zalen looked surprised. "Oh. Then I *feel* she was the academic scholar."

"Nope." Stone shook his head. "She hated studying."

"Musically talented?" Zalen's eyebrows scrunched together.

Stone said, "Wrong again." He smiled as he watched Zalen squirm uncomfortably on the stool. "But she was talented in something."

"Public speaking?"

"Not with her anxiety." Stone studied Zalen briefly before commenting, "You're not very good at this psychic thing, are you?"

Zalen cleared his throat. "I already admitted that I'm not right all the time."

"Obviously." Stone winked. "I'll help you out this one time. Rachel was a talented artist."

"I was just about to say that." With pursed lips, Zalen asked, "How did you two meet?"

Stone drained the rest of his beer and opened a new bottle, explaining, "We were best friends. Grew up next door to each other. When we were eleven, I kissed her. She didn't talk to me for a whole month after that and I learned my lesson. Then as we grew older, we drifted apart. After graduation, I never saw her again."

Zalen sat on the edge of his stool, keenly interested. "So, you pulled yourself away from her because of your ability. You didn't want her or anyone to know about it and you gave up. Too bad. You should try to reconnect with her. You obviously still like her. I can *feel* it."

Stone swallowed hard. Zalen nailed it. While keeping his eye on this nosy annoyance, Stone sliced a lemon and dropped a wedge into Zalen's glass. He said lightly, "Has anyone ever told you that you're an odd duck?"

Zalen nodded. "It takes one to know one." They raised their drinks and clinked them together. As Stone began guzzling, Zalen said, "Rachel prefers to be called Rae, though." Smiling very broadly, he added, "Rae Greyson has a nice ring to it, doesn't it?"

Stone managed to set his bottle of beer down on the counter before spraying the liquid from his mouth all over Zalen's face.

CHAPTER ELEVEN

Rae headed toward the manor with Bash following. She heard him say behind her, "I wouldn't worry about what Bronco said. Obviously, he's just an old guy who likes to tell stories and spook people. None of that was probably true." Bash jogged to catch up with his aunt. "We should go back and look for Tiny though, don't you think?"

Rae kept stride and absentmindedly asked, "Tiny who?" In her mind, she mentally calculated the chances of Bronco's missing girl story being the same one that ChAdonis told her yesterday. One side of her felt the chances were pretty high. The other side thought she needed more facts. Regardless, one unsettling detail was possibly factual. A girl who used to live in Travis's manor, the same manor that Rae was house-sitting, disappeared and was *never heard of again*. Rae shivered under the heat of the sun.

Bash nudged her with his elbow. "You okay?"

Rae sighed. "Look, Bash," she began, "are you sure you want to stay with me?"

"Definitely."

"I mean, there's some strange stuff going on. Maybe your mom's right? Maybe I am a magnet for weird situations?"

"And I'm loving it."

"It's disturbing that the Bronco guy's been watching me."

"He's just bored."

"And why did he warn me about staying at the house as if I'll be the next one to go missing? I think you should go home."

"No way. First of all, he didn't *warn* you about staying in the house. He said that you *shouldn't* stay in the house and that's his own opinion. Second, he *warned* you to mind your own business." He looked at Rae. "I get warned that a lot. It doesn't mean anything." Swinging his arm around his aunt's shoulders, he said, "We're going to be fine, staying here. Together. All three of us."

"All three?"

"Yeah. You, me and Tiny." Bash smiled brightly. "Once we find him."

Rae found her nephew's words to be reassuring. "You're right," she said as she slowed down, "everything is going to be fine. Bronco is just a pot-stirrer."

Bash nodded. "A trouble-maker."

"A rabble-rouser." Rae grinned. "I'm not going to let anything he says bother me."

"Exactly," Bash agreed. "He probably made that missing girl up."

Rae smiled, hoping her nephew was right. Maybe this story was something that locals like Bronco and ChAdonis told people for teasing purposes? Yeah, that was it. She nudged Bash. "We'll have fun. Travis has a heated pool and hot tub. We can stay up late, watch movies and eat popcorn on the furniture. It'll be great." She carefully studied Bash. "But you have to promise me that if, at any time, you want to go home, just tell me. You won't hurt my feelings."

"I promise. But I have to tell you that if I do go home, there's a good chance my mom will sign me up for summer camp again."

Rae gasped. "Even after what happened last summer?"

Bash nodded and they both exploded with laughter.

■　　•　　■

Zalen asked for a napkin. After Stone tossed a clean bar towel to him, he did a complete wipe-down. Face. Chin. Back of the neck. Even the upper chest. Zalen handed the towel back to Stone, but the speechless bar owner just told Zalen to keep it as a remembrance.

"Thanks," Zalen said cheerfully. "This is my first bar towel. I may frame it." Zalen smiled wider. "Now, I think we should first find Rae. And then save her. Any ideas?"

Still dumbfounded, Stone said, "Not at the moment."

"She should be easy to find. Especially these days. With all those little gadgets."

"Gadgets?"

"Whatever those young people use to find information."

"Cellphones?"

"Can a cellphone find a person?"

"Yes. You don't have a cellphone?"

"Just a landline. How can your phone help us find Rae?"

Shaking his head, Stone leaned over his phone and was about to show Zalen the search engine when he realized what he was doing. "Wait a minute, I'm not doing this. My bar opens at two. That's in five hours. I don't have time for this."

"Really? That sounds like a lot of time." Zalen asked, "Are you nervous to call her?"

Stone tried to reason with him. "She'll think I'm nuts."

"Scared?"

"Of course," Stone stated. "What reason would I give her for hunting her down? For old time's sake? She'll see right through that." Stone asked sarcastically, "Should I tell her that I've been having horrible dreams about her and her broken body?"

Zalen shook his head. "I personally wouldn't start the conversation that way. Maybe you can tell her a funny joke first?"

Exhaustion suddenly hit Stone. This conversation needed to end. Not bothering to stifle his yawn, he asked, "Can you do me a favor?" He looked solemnly at Zalen. "Leave."

"Of course. I understand. You want privacy when you call her. Start off with a knock-knock joke. They always make me laugh. Do you know the one about the banana?" He then tapped his temple before asking, "Or is it an orange?"

After Stone escorted Zalen out of his bar, he locked the door. To his astonishment, Zalen did not press his face to the glass, but ambled down the sidewalk.

Now standing by the counter, he absentmindedly spun his phone. He felt relieved that Zalen didn't know about that young girl. He could continue to keep her as his little secret. For all he knew, that girl found her peace by now and no longer needed him. As for Rachel, why was she suddenly haunting him after all these years?

A few minutes passed and the phone was now still. He inhaled deeply and held his breath as he searched for any information on Rachel Greyson. His heart raced. He swayed slightly. In the end, he found nothing on her.

Surprisingly, his spirits fell. Placing his phone in his back pocket, he yawned and ambled to his office, commonly referred to as the back storage area. Sitting on the folding chair at the card table, a thought struck him. Zalen's phone number just came to him the other day. He didn't need to look it up. The numbers just appeared. All he had to do was relax. Right?

Stone closed his eyes, slowed his breath and unclenched his fists. He concentrated on the rhythm of his deep inhales and slow exhales. Seven digits eventually flashed through his mind. He smiled. His eyes sprung open and he grabbed his phone. Without waiting another second, he dialed the number. Maybe Rachel would love to hear from him? So, what could really go wrong?

CHAPTER TWELVE

"Hello?" Rae answered. Her cellphone was pressed against her ear as shock spread across her face. Slowly. Alarmingly. "Why in hell are *you* calling *me*?"

"Well, since you asked so nicely, I wondered if you would like to have dinner with me."

"No."

"Then how about breakfast?"

"You're not turning this into some kind of fatal attraction again, are you?"

"Not yet. Now, let's stop this game. I know you're into me. That's why you really asked me out last night."

"It wasn't a *date*. It was *payment* for printing the pamphlets." Rae sighed. "I explained that to you very clearly, Chad."

"We both know that the pamphlets were a cover up. Speaking of, the nude bike ride is ten days from now. You want to see me naked and you know it."

Rae hung up. She looked at Bash and said, "Let's go swimming. I need strong chlorine to clean my pores after that phone call."

Bash wiped the sweat from his eyebrows. "What about Tiny?"

Rae didn't have a chance to answer. Ahead of them erupted the annoying racket of incessant barking.

"Is that Tiny?" Bash asked.

Worried that Tiny met Purple Stiletto again, Rae jogged around the bend toward the guttural howl. As she rounded the last curve on the wooded path, she saw Tiny standing on the porch, guarding it as a couple walked by the house. A good-looking man with movie star qualities held the elbow of a sporty-looking woman as they quickly passed the porch toward the expensive homes and away from the woods. The movie-star man caught Rae watching them. He had a devilishly handsome face, complete with dark eyebrows and a square jaw. The woman then spotted Rae. Wearing a white headband to keep her thick brown hair out of her face, she rested her hand on her cheek, seeming to be upset. They both quickly strode out of sight.

Rae shifted her eyes toward Tiny as he turned his whole balloon head in her direction. She glared at him angrily for scaring the neighbors again. With his ears straight up, he nodded at her in a dignified manner. After slowly circling his body toward the front door, he lifted his two front paws, turned the knob and muzzled his way into the home.

Bash now stood behind her. "Was that Tiny? He really can open doors? I thought you were joking."

Rae's tone was flat. "No joke."

"I want to meet him." Bash dashed the last fifty yards to the porch with Rae on his heels. It turned into an innocent foot race as they bounded up the porch steps and pushed each other through the front door. Doubled over from hysterics, neither could breathe nor talk until Rae straightened up to her full height and let out a horrific, ear-piercing scream for two good reasons. The first one was that the horrid, charred-looking mirror startled her again. The second reason involved the older man standing in the foyer, reading one of her pamphlets. He was squatty, broad-shouldered and had wispy strands of orange hair stuck to the sides of his head. Wearing a long maroon leather coat, he looked like an orangutan as a pungent odor of smoke mixed with bacon swirled around him.

Her scream startled the orangutan man and he knocked all the pamphlets off the console table, scattering them onto the floor. He also dropped a small bag of bacon treats for dogs. Looking at her, he scolded, "What's the matter with you? You could give a guy a heart attack with a scream like that."

Rae roared, "What's the matter with *me*? How did *you* get into this house?"

The orangutan man struggled with his belly to bend over. He was trying to pick up some of the pamphlets that landed around his feet. He grabbed two and gave up. Upon standing, he explained, "I rang the doorbell and the dog answered. Then the dog let me in." He motioned to Bash. "Can you pick up that bag for me?" Bash obliged and gave the bag to the orangutan man who tucked it into his coat pocket.

Rae said incredulously, "You bribed the dog with treats. Who are you?"

Fortunately for him, the orangutan man wore a watch which suddenly beeped. Lumbering toward her, he gave Rae the two pamphlets. They had greasy fingerprints smeared across the front. He said, "Sorry to have bothered you, miss. I'll see myself out." However, just as he was about to step through the threshold of the front door, he turned to her and said, "You should really keep your door locked."

The door closed and Rae listened to the heavy footsteps descending the porch steps. She gaped at Bash. "What is going on in this neighborhood?"

Bash shrugged and, at that moment, both he and Rae heard music and voices, coming from the other room. Rae pulled Bash behind her and said, "Who else is in here?"

Bash answered, "I think you're hearing the TV."

As they crept down the hallway, Rae heard someone changing the television channels rapidly. Then a show was finally selected. It was a grilling show about steaks. They followed the sound of the grill master's voice into the room with that oversized sectional.

"Oh my Lord," Rae said as she and Bash approached the cushy sofa. Glaring down on its drooling occupant whose breath reeked of bacon, Rae asked Tiny, "Where have you been?"

Tiny raised his head and looked at her. He licked his lips as one ear flicked. Then he lowered his head before stretching out the entire length of the designer couch, sighing loudly.

Bash looked elated. "This dog is huge." Smiling, he said to Rae, "Too bad he can't talk. I bet he has some good stories."

Tiny looked at Bash and nodded once. Then he fell instantly asleep.

"Useless." Rae removed the remote from Tiny's paw and steered her nephew to the foyer again.

As they surveyed the spilled papers, Bash asked, "Why do you have hundreds of pamphlets about riding a bike naked?"

Rae replied, "I designed those as a favor for Maeve."

"Who's Maeve?"

"A neighbor."

Bash studied the information. "People want to get rid of those trees?"

Rae nodded.

"What will happen to the banshee?"

"Well, I guess she'll have to flap and shrill her way back to Ireland."

Bash reminded her, "Or Scotland or Wales."

Rae barely listened. Her mind was in puzzle-solving mode, except she wasn't trying to solve crosswords or cryptics. This puzzle involved a few pieces that didn't fit together, like a handicapped cowboy, a man who resembled an orangutan and a legend of a banshee taking a girl.

Bash read one of the pamphlets. "We should hand these out for Maeve."

While nibbling her thumbnail, Rae asked, "Why?"

"Because we're *nice* people."

"Are we? I mean, it's near one hundred degrees out there. I don't like to burn."

"We'll use a lot of sunscreen." Bash smiled innocently. "It'll be a great way for us to meet the neighbors."

Perplexed, Rae asked, "Why do we want to do that?"

Bash shrugged. "I'm not exactly sure. It just seems to me that we're at a disadvantage here. I mean, many of the *neighbors* already noticed *you*. We need to level the playing field."

Her nephew was right. Many neighbors noticed her and were flat out watching her. "Alright," Rae said as she grabbed a decorative basket sitting on the floor full of yarn and needles. It was artfully put together. Obviously, Travis or Seth sacrificed a lot of their time in arranging this ornamental, yarn show-stopper. She dumped everything into a heap on the floor. Turning to Bash, she said, "You put the pamphlets in here and I'll find us some suntan lotion."

* * *

As soon as Stone heard the thick accent on the other end of the phone line, he knew that he made a mistake. "Lo siento," Stone apologized and quickly hung up. That definitely wasn't Rachel's number.

He remained in his office for the rest of the morning, trying to work on finances while fighting off the urge to sleep. Another nightmare of twisting trees tearing Rachel apart would break him. Instead, he focused on inventory until the yawning started, causing tears to flood his eyes. A voice inside his head told him to stay awake and the next thing he knew, his whole body slid down in his chair. Then his head leaned against the back. Then his baseball cap somehow moved from the top of his head to his face, covering it. With his arms crossed against his chest, he fell into a deep sleep.

When he awoke, he was very confused. Still behind his desk, everything was exactly the same. He smelled must and not the great outdoors, and strangely enough, he was alone. He cautiously said out loud, "Zalen?" No one answered. It was just him. Nobody was around him. No contorted body of Rachel Greyson. No apparition of a young dead girl.

Stone exhaled very slowly. Then he suddenly barked with laughter. He slept without dreaming and he felt more than fantastic. As his mind emptied, a content smile formed on his lips. He felt like a healed patient who just received dismissal papers, even if he knew deep down that this good feeling was only temporary.

He had moments like this all of his life. Moments of feeling normal, but knowing he wasn't. Eventually, the same thoughts would invade his mind, bringing him right back to his miserable state. Thoughts like, why was he like this? Was it hereditary?

He didn't know. The earliest memory of him experiencing this was at the age of seven in the second grade. His teacher was an elderly woman with gray wiry hair and flabby arms. Her name was Mrs. Anderson and she always wore tent-like, colorful shirts made from sheer material. At first, her appearance frightened him, but her melodic voice and genuine kindness erased those wary feelings.

A gentleman always stood beside Mrs. Anderson. He had a receding hairline, thick hands and wore the same black suit to school every day. He knew the man as Mr. Anderson and thought nothing more of it until his parents came home from parent-teacher conferences.

They were livid. They honestly believed that he, their son, tricked them into thinking that Mr. Anderson helped his wife in the classroom when he had been deceased for ten years. Stone felt his cheeks warm as old feelings of embarrassment grew. The look on Mrs. Anderson's face during his apology to her was still humiliating.

And then he remembered his Grandpa Ed's words after he told him all about Mr. Anderson. His grandpa was cleaning glasses behind the bar, listening to him explain that he didn't trick anyone. He really saw Mr. Anderson. Without ever looking at Stone, Grandpa Ed said, "It's better if you just keep stories like that to yourself."

Stone followed that advice ever since. Glancing at the time on his phone, it was just after noon, which meant the three cooks would be arriving soon. Stone rose, leaving his office as well as leaving the thought of Rachel behind him.

CHAPTER THIRTEEN

As Rae and Bash stood on the front porch, the scent of coconut overwhelmed the air. Rae inhaled deeply, enjoying the beachy fumes, and then surveyed the area. Travis's red brick Victorian manor situated itself near the road with a long driveway off the side, leading to a separate garage behind the house. It was the last of the expensive homes on the street before the forest of birch trees, marking the dead end. Across the street sprung evergreen trees and beyond that was the distant sound of traffic. Looking to her right, she regarded the curvy road leading to the other residences. Travis was right when he said the private large yards had a lot of trees. There were tall oaks, evergreens and a sprinkling of maples, not to mention a sea of bushes that all worked together to create beautiful, exclusive lots between each resident. Above the trees, Rae glimpsed the gabled rooftop of the next-door neighbor. She counted three chimneys and two points of what she assumed were the tips of towers.

Bash held the basket full of pamphlets with his arms and looked at Rae, "Who should we see first?"

Rae bit her fingernail in thought and then replied, "Maeve. I'd love for her to approve the pamphlets and she might have some information regarding the people around here. Plus, she lives next to my boss." On her left were the woods full of bears, cougars and mysterious criers. Obviously, Maeve lived down the street in the other direction toward Wealthyville, which made Rae wonder. All of those stately homes were huge and Maeve didn't look like she would live in a small castle. She looked like somebody who would be happy in an apartment or village hut. Maeve did say, however, that she was a neighbor to Travis and Seth. Sighing, Rae said, "I guess we'll go this way. We'll start with the house right next door."

"Alright." Bash bounded down the steps. "Let's get to know the neighbors."

Right next door turned out to be a six-minute, two-acre hike in the intense heat. The Tudor style mansion sat proudly on the land and Rae felt as though she were shrinking with every step on the long and winding walkway to the front door. Fortunately, there was no moat or chewed-up signs warning them of biting territorial pitbulls, so Rae kept putting one foot in front of the other until she reached the brass knocker, striking three times.

Her eyes widened when the owners appeared. It was that movie-star man and, standing next to him, was a blonde, not a sporty brunette with a white headband. He flinched when recognizing Rae, but made a smooth recovery by flashing a handsome smile. He introduced himself, "Hello, I'm Bob Harrison and this is my wife, Candice." At the mention of her name, Candice raised a brandy glass at them, winking and clicking her tongue at the same time.

"Hello, I'm Rae and this is my nephew, Bash. We're house-sitting for Travis and Seth. We just wanted to introduce ourselves since we'll be here for the next ten days."

Bob said, "Oh yeah, Travis and Seth. The brothers."

Candice spoke into her glass. "They're not brothers." She then drank the rest of the gold liquid, belched and turned away. Rae watched as Candice lost her balance and needed the aid of the wall to steady her. She carefully walked into the other room and out of view.

Bash cleared his throat. "You have a beautiful home, Mr. Harrison. I hope to live in a beautiful home like this someday. May I ask what you do for a living?"

Rae gave Bash the side-eye at his obvious attempt of getting to know this neighbor.

Bob, however, seemed delighted at the question and replied affably, "I graduated from Berkeley in finance and founded my own mortgage company. The key to making money is working with money. Do you like math?"

Bash said politely, "Nope. Just the sciences. Is your wife in finances too?"

"Well, she used to work for me as a loan officer until we tried to start a family." Bob looked uncomfortably over his shoulder. "Unfortunately, we never could have children of our own and she now busies herself with charities, church and golf." Looking at the pamphlets, he cleared his throat and asked, "What do you have there?"

Rae explained about the removal of the birch trees for the mall expansion and Bob shook his head. As it turned out, Bob's grandfather helped plant those trees nearly one hundred years ago. Uncoerced, Bob began telling the story of how his heritage was intimately connected to the area. When he finished, he asked if he could help in some way.

With the heat of the sun sizzling Rae's scalp, she selfishly dismissed wanting Maeve's approval of the pamphlet design and gave Bob ten pamphlets to pass on his own. Bash gave Bob ten more and now there were only 480 more to go.

Just as Rae and Bash were leaving, Rae asked Bob, "Do you know where Maeve lives?"

Bob looked confused. "I don't know anyone around here by that name."

Rae asked, "Really? I met her yesterday. She said she lived next to Travis and Seth."

"Nobody by that name lives *here*." Bob nodded politely and closed the door.

As Rae and Bash strolled down the driveway, Bash said, "So, Movie Star Bob is married to Boozy Candice. Who's the brunette with the white headband then?"

Rae grinned. "Nice nicknames and I am also wondering about Ms. Headband."

"I guess Movie Star Bob is living the movie star life," Bash said.

Chuckling, Rae said, "You know, your manner of questioning is a little transparent."

Bash shrugged. "Movie Star Bob didn't seem to mind."

This routine of meeting and questioning neighbors continued as Rae and Bash searched for Maeve. They instead found doctors, lawyers and other CEO's living in their French Provincials, Greek Revivals and up-scale Ranches. all the friendly neighbors had some kind of connection to the woods and everyone was eager to help. Since Rae and Bash were losing hydration, they were equally eager to unload piles of pamphlets.

It bothered Rae, however, that no one knew Maeve and this casual hunt for her turned into a burning quest. While trudging up to the sixth majestic home, she wouldn't allow her optimistic spirit to wilt. She rang the doorbell and waited. Resting felt good. She closed her eyes, listening to the light brushing sound move across the leaves. She loved sounds and this one seemed very relaxing. Very hypnotic. Almost lulling her to sleep until a friendly voice said, "Hello again."

Rae and Bash were greeted by Sunshiny Bryson, standing on the lawn and holding a rake. He flashed a bright smile. "What's up?" Suddenly, the front door opened and Jessica quickly joined them, carrying a guinea pig. Bryson resumed raking, straight-faced.

"It's *so* nice to see you again." Jessica gave Rae a quick, one-arm hug and then noticed Bash. "And who might you be?"

"I'm Bash." He pointed to Rae. "I'm her nephew."

Jessica gushed. "You're *adorable*. Would you like to hold my Fluffy?" She laughed. "Actually, it's Bryson's Fluffy, but he lets me *snuggle* with her whenever I want." She handed the guinea pig to Bash before he could answer. Smiling at Rae, Jessica asked, "So, what's up?"

Rae explained to Jessica about the clearing of the woods, but Jessica was more interested in Bash. She asked him, "Would you like to stay for lunch?" Bash politely declined, handing Fluffy back to Jessica. Looking pained, she asked, "Why not?"

Bash loudly gulped and then explained, "I wanted to help my aunt pass out the pamphlets. We were going to swim afterward." He smiled nervously.

Jessica's face brightened. "You have a pool? Bryson *loves* to swim. My son's been on a swim team ever since he was seven. He was on the path to the *Olympics* until he hurt his back from competing too much. But that's okay. Whenever a door *closes*, another one *opens*. Now, he's *very* involved in student government. I see him being a *senator* one day, don't you?" She beamed at Rae before continuing, "It's a *perfect* day for swimming. I'm *so* envious."

Reading the expectant facial expression on Jessica's face, Rae said, "Well, we're house-sitting the manor at the end of the road. Would you like to join us? Say, in an hour?"

Giving Rae another one-arm hug, Jessica said, "That sounds *great*. Bryson is *thrilled*." Bryson barely raised his head. He instead raised the rake like a sword, poking the end of it at his mom's arm. She tried to laugh. "Typical teenager."

Rae and Bash quickly left the Baratons dueling it out on the front lawn. Once on the sidewalk, Bash groaned. "Why did you invite them over to swim with us? They're *weird*."

"Oh, stop it. They're not weird, just a little desperate. Besides, I'm trying to be *nice* because, according to you, we are *nice* people." She smiled. "So, how many pamphlets are left?"

"Two hundred." Bash's hair dripped with sweat. "And I'm thirsty." Three horse flies dive bombed his head over and over. He rolled one of the pamphlets into a tube and swiped at them. "Can we go back now?"

Rae bit a fingernail and spit it out. "But we didn't find Maeve."

"And drink some water?"

"Or her house."

"All I taste is salt."

Rae bit another fingernail on their walk back to Travis's manor. "I don't get it. I could've sworn she said that she was the next-door neighbor. But Movie Star Bob and Boozy Candice live next to Travis. No one lives across from him and everyone else lives houses away."

"Why does it even matter?" Bash tried to lick his lips with his dry tongue.

"Because I should've already solved this puzzle, but it's getting harder."

"Well, it's easy to me. On one side of Travis's home lives the Harrisons and on the other side lives the banshee in the woods. And the banshee's first name is apparently Maeve."

Rae opened her mouth to argue when her phone rang suddenly. It was her brother, Danny, and she quickly answered. "You called me *yesterday* and *today*? When did you turn clingy?"

"Dog?"

Rae mentally cursed Clare's name. "I didn't lose the dog. He's actually on the couch, watching a grilling show."

"Bash?"

"No, I didn't lose Bash. He's right next to me. Do you want to talk to him?"

"Later." Danny disconnected and Rae looked at Bash who was supposed to be right next to her. Surprisingly, he wasn't. He was, however, among a group of boys behind her, all with bronze skin and dark hair. Did they materialize from thin air? As they encircled Bash, his voice rose above them, saying something about his phone and pamphlets and the number fifty.

Pure panic set in and using her deepest, manliest voice, she hollered, "Hey!"

All five boys looked at her simultaneously and then bolted in different directions, except for one. Rae recognized him as being the same teenager who shoulder-bumped her. He nodded to Bash before sprinting toward the woods, making sure to glare at her as he passed.

Rae asked Bash, "What was that all about?"

"Nothing."

"Who were they? What did they want? Your phone? Did they want your phone?"

"Wow. You're asking a lot of questions all at once." Bash sighed. "First, they didn't want my phone. Second, Gio recognized me from the park. He asked for my name and wanted to know if I just moved in. Third, they're all very friendly and interested in the pamphlets."

"They look guilty. Only the guilty run away like that."

"You scared them. And me." Bash gave her a not-so-cool look.

"So, is Gangsta Gio the leader? He glares way too much."

Bash blew out another sigh. "Only at you. If you gave them a chance, you'd see that they're all pretty nice. I mean, they offered to pass out the rest of the pamphlets. That's cool."

"They *want* to pass out two *hundred* pamphlets? That's not cool. That's *suspicious*."

"They like the woods. Gio says the woods protect them from the banshee."

Rae whined. "I've heard enough. Just stay away from Gio and his horrible gang."

Bash said with a smile, "I will as soon as we're all done swimming."

Rae groaned. "Why did you invite them over to swim with us? They're *weird*."

Bash nudged her. "I was just trying to be *nice*."

Rae replied, "Well, nice or not, they all give me the creeps."

■ ■ ■

By the time they entered the manor, Bash noticed that his aunt had bitten three fingernails. Now, he stood next to her in the foyer, studying her face. She looked concerned.

He asked her, "What's wrong now?"

"When we left, the television was on." Aunt Rae crossed her arms. "I bet he left again."

Bash lifted his eyebrows and followed his aunt to the oversized *and empty* sectional.

Aunt Rae nibbled another fingernail. "See? He's gone. This is what he does to me."

Bash nodded. "At least, he turned off the TV. That was considerate of him." Puzzling over the dog's whereabouts, he asked his aunt, "Where do you think he went?"

"Beats me." Aunt Rae sighed heavily. "This has been a trying day and it's only noon. Are you hungry?"

Shaking his head, Bash replied, "More dehydrated than hungry. All I need is a bottle of water and a swimming pool."

"You're on. Let's take a water break first and then grab your stuff. Travis has some cold bottles of expensive specialty water in the fridge. We should drink all of them. Then we'll head upstairs and find you a nice guest room. After that, we can swim."

Bash asked his aunt, "Should we be worried about Tiny?" He saw Aunt Rae's stormy gray eyes turn a shade darker and said, "Never mind. I'm sure he's good."

Four cold bottles of expensive specialty water later, Bash and Aunt Rae trudged upstairs with all of his gear and perused the other two available guest rooms. He chose the smaller guest room right across from his aunt's tower bedroom and now gazed out the large window overlooking the backyard. He had an enticing view of the woods.

Aunt Rae offered to help him unpack. As she placed his clothes from the satchel into the dresser, he covertly shoved his suitcase underneath the bed with his foot. When he turned, she was watching him and asked, "What don't you want me to see?"

Bash desperately wanted to keep his paranormal investigative equipment a secret, especially since he was supposed to have left it all at home. He had no choice and answered, "Underwear."

"Liar." She smiled at him. "Is it alive?"

Bash shook his head. "Of course not."

"Okay," she said, "I guess I'll have to trust you." Aunt Rae walked toward him. "Give me fifteen minutes and I'll meet you by the pool. Alright?"

After they slapped a high five, he watched his aunt stroll out of his guest room and cross the hall. She closed her door and he shut his. Raising the cellphone to his face, his fingers quickly tapped at the screen. It took a few searches, but he soon found the information of a missing girl from The Birch Grove area. Her name was Honey Ward and she disappeared from this house two years ago. Next, he found his red notebook and opened it to the first page where he wrote the headline *Suspects* and added two names: Movie Star Bob and Maeve, the banshee.

CHAPTER FOURTEEN

Rae sat on the edge of the bed in a red racer swimsuit with her cellphone in the palm of her hand. She just finished leaving another terse message to Travis in China, asking him again to call her back. How dare he leave her with the responsibility of dog-sitting a vanishing dog! Then another curiosity overtook her and, presently, she read an article on the internet, involving a missing thirteen-year old girl. Her name was Honey Ward and she disappeared from The Birch Grove area two years ago. The anniversary of her disappearance was approaching this Saturday, three days away. This had to be the same girl who Bronco mentioned. Upon further reading, Rae learned that Honey's parents divorced and her father died a month ago. How awful, Rae thought.

Rae stared at the image of Honey Ward. She had big brown eyes and long blonde hair that was pulled into a high ponytail on top of her head. In her arms, she held a puppy with floppy ears and a dark brown face. Bringing the image closer, she studied the puppy when a knock at the bedroom door sounded.

It was Bash. He wore lime green swim trunks, bare feet and goggles already fastened to his face. All he needed was a towel. After Rae grabbed two from the bathroom, she tagged him with one and they raced each other through the house to the pool. Rae and her competitive demeanor won, but Bash quickly retaliated by creating an entertaining game of repeatedly cannonballing over

Rae on a raft. She didn't mind though and actually enjoyed the rocking. As the afternoon was on the cusp of merrily floating away, they all arrived. Sunshiny Bryson. Gangsta Gio. And his non-gang.

Bryson entered the pool area first from the backdoor of the manor. Surprised, Rae asked him, "Did you just walk through the house?"

He nonchalantly explained, "I rang the doorbell, but you didn't come. So, I let myself in. Don't worry. It's cool." He wore trunks with a matching swim shirt. He slipped out of his cloudfoam slides and said to Rae, "You should really keep your door locked."

Rae nodded. "Yes, that is a good idea." With a half-grin, she asked Bryson, "Where's your mom?"

"She got a call and won't be able to make it." His strong, broad shoulders and flipper-like feet instantly branded him as a swimmer.

Rae asked, "So, you're on a swim team?"

"I've been on a swim team ever since I was five."

"I thought your mom said since you were seven?"

"Five. Seven. Same thing. I won at state many times." He smiled triumphantly and his eyes scanned over Rae's body. "You look like a swimmer too."

Rae fought the urge to use her hands as a cover. "I was on a swim team in high school."

Bryson asked, "What was your specialty stroke?"

Rae squirmed. "The backstroke, but I loved swimming the butterfly."

"I bet you were amazing." Bryson smiled.

Rae cleared her throat. "I won some stuff."

The sound of stampeding feet interrupted them. Rae's eyes opened in horror as Gio and his non-gang bounded into the backyard and scaled over the pool fence with practiced ease. Trampling over each other, they shrilled like wild coyotes. They wore nothing, but cut-off jeans. No shoes. No towels. Only one wore a tank top.

She hollered above the raucous whoops and cheers, "You can all swim, right?"

This made the pack laugh harder as they bombed the pool with their balled-up bodies. They caused so many rolling waves that Rae couldn't hold onto the raft and she bounced off within two seconds of their invasion.

When she surfaced, two of the boys had Bash high above their heads. Ready for launch. Before she could open her mouth to stop them, she heard Bryson yell, "Hey! Stop!"

The two boys paused, saw that it was Bryson who spoke to them and then launched Bash high in the air. He sailed from one end of the pool to the other. When his body made contact with the water, Rae gasped. His head missed hitting the concrete edge by a millimeter.

Bash seemed unphased. In fact, his face broke into the biggest, widest smile Rae ever saw on him. It was pure elation. He excitedly shrieked, "Do that again!"

"No!" Rae yelled, but the two boys already lifted Bash over their heads.

Then another voice boomed, "No!"

The boys froze. They knew instantly who spoke that time and looked straight at Gio. He was standing on the edge with clenched fists. A very angry glare ignited in his deep brown eyes. He said something else to them in Spanish. Rae couldn't understand the words, but she understood the tone very well. The boys lowered Bash, looked at Rae and said, "Sorry."

The rest of the afternoon went swimmingly. There were no more near death experiences. Rae didn't participate in any of the pool games though. She became the unpaid lifeguard instead, patrolling the pool and carrying a rescue tube that she suspected was supposed to be a decoration. All she needed was a whistle around her neck, but her two fingers worked just fine.

Neither Bryson nor Gio swam either. Instead, Rae noticed that they sat on opposite ends of the pool. Gio sat upright on a patio chair, staring or glaring at Bryson. Brooding, dark Gio. Directly across from him was Bryson. Gold and glittery. He was reclined in a chaise lounge, drawing in the air with a stick.

And then there was Bash, who still horsed around in the pool with boundless energy, unknowingly in the middle of it all. He seemed so free. So happy.

Three boys. They were just like the three primary colors. Or like rock, paper, and scissors. Maybe even like a BLT? Rae was suddenly reminded of a wise old saying about the number three. Her grandmother would always mumble it under her breath whenever she had to watch Rae and her two older brothers. How did it go again? Something like...three things cannot be long hidden: the sun, the moon, and the truth. Rae understood it to mean that the truth will always come out. People might be fooled, but only for a while. Regarding the three boys, she wondered which one was going to fool her the most? Sunshiny Bryson, the golden sun? Or Gangsta Gio, the dark moon? And how exactly did Bash fit into all of this?

The pool guests left one by one. By five o'clock, all were gone and Rae's stomach felt hollow. Adorned in swimsuits and towels, she and her nephew rummaged through the freezer. Bash pulled out a frozen cheese pizza and Rae preheated the oven. Grabbing paper plates, he asked, "After we eat, shouldn't we *try* to find Tiny?"

Just then the doorbell rang and Rae said, "I bet that's him now." To her surprise, poised on the other side of the front door was Maeve, standing amid the fumes of vanilla, chocolate and mint. She held a plate loaded with squares of fudgy sinfulness.

"Hello, dear," said Maeve. "I heard that you and your nephew passed out all the pamphlets."

Rae nodded. "I wanted to show you the new design first, but I couldn't find your house. Unfortunately, I don't have anymore to show you."

"Oh, that doesn't matter. I'm glad you got the word out so quickly." Maeve lifted the plate to Rae. "I made my famous Mint Witch Brownies to thank you both."

Bash stood at Rae's elbow now, leaning in to smell the fresh goodies and listening very carefully to the conversation. "*Interesting* name for a recipe."

Maeve laughed. "Yes, it is. This recipe has been in my family for many generations." She looked at Bash and introduced herself, "I'm Maeve."

"I'm Bash." He smiled before asking their visitor, "How many generations exactly? Ten? Fifteen? Four hundred? And from where? Ireland, perhaps?"

"Ignore him," Rae quickly said to Maeve. "He thinks there's a banshee living in the neighborhood and I guess that your Mint *Witch* Brownies checked all the right boxes for him to suspect that you're The Birch Grove Banshee."

Maeve had a gleam in her eye. "Me? A banshee? Oh my, I'm delighted! But why would I bring brownies if I were a banshee? A pail of blood would seem more appropriate, don't you think, cutie pie?" She winked at Bash and then eyed Rae. "Have you changed your mind about riding in the nude bike ride next Saturday? I have an extra helmet."

"Nope."

Maeve smiled slyly. "Well, we'll see. Now, I should really go."

Rae quickly asked her, "Maeve, can you tell me about some of the neighbors around here? Do you know the man in the wheelchair who wears a cowboy hat? His name is Bronco."

Maeve shook her head slowly and a loose strand of hair fell from the bun twisted at the nape of her neck. "No, I never heard of him."

"How about a man who looks like an orangutan? He has wispy red hair, broad shoulders and long arms. And he wears a maroon trench coat."

Maeve chuckled. "No, but what an unfortunate description." Turning away, she stated, "I'm sorry, but I must leave." She glided quickly to the steps and descended them as Rae and Bash remained on the porch. Her long green chiffon hair scarf flowed behind her, resembling a billowy cloud of smoke behind a steam engine.

Rae called to her, "Did you know the family who used to live here?" Bash looked surprised at her question. "I'm just wondering," she said to him.

Keeping her face forward, Maeve replied, "The Wards? Not at all. Now, you should stay in the house. A wicked storm is about to brew."

Rae and Bash both peered at the sky in unison. It was blue and cloudless with the friendly sun brightly shining down on them.

"It was nice meeting you, Bash!" Maeve called over her shoulder, "Good luck catching that banshee!"

Bash returned the call, "Good luck evading me!"

Rae heard her nephew chuckle as her eyes followed Maeve down the sidewalk toward the woods. Her eyes then widened as she spotted the black Ford Taurus parked across the street again and the orangutan man sat in the driver's seat, watching her.

Rae took three steps down the front porch, when very suddenly, the sky darkened and the wind picked up. Soon after, the heavens opened to unleash wildly barking thunder followed by large drops of rain. Straining her ears, she heard a sound over the slaps of raindrops hitting the pavement. It was a laugh, possibly a cackle, coming from the woods.

· · ·

While passing through the bar, Stone saw Sally, mingling with all the younger men. There was a group around her, enjoying her stories. She was like everyone's grandma, especially if everyone's grandma loved to drink gin and wear trippy wigs. She was famous at The Rail and, without Sally even realizing it, she became the bar's icon over the many years. If for some reason she would realize it, she would buy everyone a gin and tonic. Easy on the tonic.

Sally had been the bar mistress to Stone's grandpa. She was the exact opposite of Stone's grandmother. Fun and loose. Throughout the years, though, she became his grandpa's unofficial assistant. Grandpa Ed showed her how to run this bar. He wanted to show her and she wanted to help. At first, it bothered Stone to always have her around. But Stone quickly realized that she had more of a natural business sense than he did, even with his business degree. And, at that particular moment, he was extremely grateful.

"Sally," Stone called through the chests and biceps, "I have to go."

She sat on a stool with long blonde curly hair sprinkled with glitter tonight. The ends were highlighted in lime green, which contrasted with her purple lipstick. "I'll say you have to go. Get some dinner. Or a drink. You look like hell." Stone thought to himself that if anyone knew what Hell looked like, it would be Sally. At least, she wasn't slurring.

Relieved at her sobriety, he asked, "Can you handle the bar for me tonight? I'll pay you."

She smiled. "Of course, handsome. Anything for my doll."

As he turned to leave, Stone heard her yell after him, "How much?"

He didn't answer. Instead, he sped home and showered for the first time that day. Not bothering to use a towel, he threw on some shorts, remained shirtless, and fell onto his lumpy comfy couch. Dialing the pizza delivery number by heart, he ordered his usual: meat lover's deep dish with extra breadsticks. Next, he opened a cold can of beer that somehow found its way into his palm and then grabbed the television remote. His team was up to bat and he let his body relax into the couch. The only thing left to do was jot down Rachel's phone number that just popped into his mind. He looked at it while waiting for his dinner, deciding to call or not to call.

CHAPTER FIFTEEN

The rain soaked Rae within three seconds. Still in a swimsuit with a towel wrapped around her waist, water dripped off her chin as she remained on the steps, peering into the distance. The cackle was gone, but the orangutan man wasn't. She could feel the hotness of his stare through the windshield even though she couldn't clearly see his face. Rae could only decipher the round shape of his head and hunched shoulders.

Rae lifted the towel skirt above her knees and took the last two steps down the front porch. She hollered at him, "Hey! What're you doing?" As the engine of the Ford Taurus erupted heatedly, the orangutan man drove out of the neighborhood. Rae smiled, catching and mentally noting the license plate number.

Bash stood at her side now. "Isn't that the same car at the park? And wasn't that the guy who bribed Tiny with bacon treats earlier today?"

Rae paused, wondering how to answer his question without causing alarm. She finally answered, "Maybe or maybe not? I couldn't tell if it was Orangutan Man for sure."

Bash asked, "Why did you yell at him then?"

Trying to sound casual, Rae replied, "I always yell at Fords." The rain struck her skin hard and goosebumps formed instantly. "I'm cold. Let's go in." Gently grabbing Bash's hand, they both trotted up the steps and through the front door. Rae locked it behind them, saying over her shoulder, "Let's change into dry clothes and watch a movie."

Bash pulled on his bottom lip. "What does Orangutan Man want?"

Rae shrugged, wringing her hands. "Does this make you nervous? Do you want to go home? I'll understand if you do."

Bash's eyes almost popped out of his head. "No," he declared and then beamed. "I'm staying. This is way too exciting."

"Really?"

"Yeah! I mean, we get to stay in this ghoulish manor next to some terrifying, yet beautiful, woods and then we're stalked by not one, but by two ominous old guys. Not to mention that there's a banshee who bakes good brownies. What could be more thrilling?"

"A hammock at a beach resort."

Bash pulled on his bottom lip again. "There is one thing that bothers me though."

"Only one?"

"What about Tiny? It's storming out there. We should look for him, don't you think?"

Rae's eyelids felt like sandpaper, scraping along her eyeballs. She sighed and placed both of her hands on his shoulders. "Don't worry about it. I know he's fine. He'll be back later. Probably at five o'clock in the morning." Bash opened his mouth to debate the issue, but Rae was ready. "Please," she said, "just get changed. I *want* to watch a movie. I *don't want* to call Clare or Danny and have you sent to camp."

Bash's mouth fell open. "You're playing hardball already? That's not nice, Aunt Rae." Turning his back to her, he bounded up the stairs.

The rest of the stormy evening was spent with Bash and Rae settled near each other on the oversized sofa. Bash found his favorite movie series on TV and laughed continuously at the four men trying to capture ghosts. With Travis's home manual sprawled on her lap, Rae read the section *How to Handle a Power Outage*. She already followed his map to locate two flashlights.

Bash asked her if they really needed them. Rae shrugged. "According to the weather app, it's supposed to storm all night. Better to be safe than sorry."

It was ten o'clock when the sequel ended and Rae smiled. There had been no banshee shrills, bird flappings or mysterious doorbell ringings. Not that she believed in anything unexplainable like that. She believed in real stuff like toast, diet soda and fuzzy socks.

Bash flinched at a loud boom of thunder. Looking at Rae, he anxiously asked, "You're still not worried about Tiny?"

Curling up in the corner of the sectional, Rae yawned. "Tiny's fine." Rae yawned again. "I have everything under control."

"My mom claims that whenever you say that, hell's about to break loose."

Suddenly, her phone rang. "Speak of the devil," Rae muttered aloud while answering the call. "What do you want?"

Clare sniffed. "Where's Bash? I called him eleven times and he never picked up."

"How curious," Rae replied dryly, tossing her phone to Bash. She listened as her nephew painted a beautiful, and not exactly accurate, picture of his first day staying with Rae and she heard Clare sigh in relief on the other end. They said their goodbyes and then Bash tossed the phone back to her, stating that his mom still needed to talk to her.

Clare informed Rae, "I have arranged a meeting between you and a very nice gentleman."

"This better not be a blind date."

"It's not a blind date. It's a meeting between you and someone you have never met. It's for Thursday afternoon."

"Oh, my nauseating Lord. That's tomorrow."

"At the art museum down by the waterfront."

"What? Why there?"

"Because you like art and he works there as a Coordinator of Vehicular Locations."

Rae didn't miss a beat. "He parks cars?"

"And is a very nice gentleman."

Rae moaned loudly. "I can't. I am coming down with lockjaw. Call another victim."

Clare sighed. "I already told him that you agreed. You'll be meeting him at three in the Impressionists wing. His name is Michael."

"And what about Bash? I can't leave your son here alone to go and meet some guy whose ambition in life is to align cars in an orderly fashion."

"You're right. That's why you are taking Bash with you. He loves any type of museum. End of story." It also was the end of the conversation because Clare hung up before Rae could.

Rae was stunned at Clare's forcefulness and relieved that Bash was also ordered to go on the date. He would be the perfect buffer. With Bash's eyes on her, she said to him, "Your mom set us both up on a blind date. Tomorrow." She then turned off the television. "I now have a throbbing headache and may throw up. Time for bed."

To Rae's surprise, Bash didn't protest or even ask questions. Instead, the evening ended with each in their own guest room. Rae kept her flashlight on the nightstand, wide-eyed and listening to the sound of rain. Normally, the light tapping of the drops against the window glass relaxed Rae; however her mind reeled uncontrollably about stalkers, an overbearing sister-in-law and a snobby Great Shepherd. To make matters worse, Bash suddenly hollered, causing her to sit straight up in bed.

"Aunt Rae!" Bash yelled, "Come quick!"

Rae leapt out of bed and stumbled over her own feet. After grabbing the flashlight for a weapon, she bounded across the hallway to find Bash in his room. She flicked on the light and saw his body plastered against the window, holding binoculars.

She breathed heavily. "You scared me." Noticing that Bash had the binoculars pressed to his face and frantically searched for something outside, she asked him, "What are you doing?"

"I heard noises." He spoke quietly and carefully.

Rae wasn't so quiet. "Well, yeah," she said. "It's raining. You're probably just hearing water hitting things."

"No, not *things*. I hear *voices*."

"Outside? Right now?"

"Yes." Bash whispered, "Someone's out there."

Rae intently peered. At Bash. "Are you nuts? No one in his right mind would be outside in this weather. Not in an electrical storm."

Still whispering, Bash said, "I didn't say he was in his right mind."

Rae studied Bash as he surveyed the backyard. His hair stuck up in places and his tongue hung out. She was pretty sure that his eyes were crossed. Glancing at his bed, she saw a book resting on his pillow.

Shaking her head, she said, "Your choice for bedtime reading is a book called *A Ghosting We Will Go: Becoming the Hunter*? Well, congratulations. You passed over the hunter stage and moved right on to lunacy." She ordered him, "Give me those binoculars."

Bash handed them over with instructions. "Just take a look." He pointed to the woods.

"I'm only doing this to prove to you that you're nuts. And then I'm taking these and that book and you're going back to bed. Got it?"

"Yep. Now look in that corner section. By that cluster of trees. I swear someone's moving in there."

Frustrated at her nephew's demented behavior, she thrusted her flashlight at him before bringing the binoculars up to her eyes. After a few seconds of focusing, she zeroed in on the trees. They were about a football field away. At first, she saw black space. Nonmoving. Nondescript. Then the lightning flashed. Her first reaction was to lower the binoculars and clean the lens, which she did.

"You saw it too. Didn't you?"

Rae refused to answer him. She scanned the trees again with the clean binoculars, waiting for the lightning to strike.

It did and she saw the shape again. This time, it moved a few feet and was shorter. Darkness fell. She waited. Lightening then flashed and the shape moved again. Rae briefly saw the head and shoulders before the shape was completely swallowed by the blackness of the night.

"Who do you think it is?" Bash asked earnestly.

"Well." Rae waited. There were a couple of bolts illuminating a larger area of the woods, which helped her vision. Rae gasped softly as her suspicions were right.

"What? Do you see him?"

"Not *him*," Rae said calmly. "But I do see *them*. I think it's Gio and his troop."

"Why would they be outside now?"

"Who cares?" Rae gave the binoculars to Bash. "All that matters is you're safe inside."

"Do you care about Tiny not being safe inside?"

She gave him a sideways glance. "Not really. Did you know that dogs eat their own poop? And they drink toilet water."

Bash tried to hide a smile. "Regardless, we should at least call for him."

"No way. Besides, I think he's staying with someone else."

"What? You're crazy." Bash shook his head.

"I may be crazy, or I may be a genius. I can't prove it, but I have a feeling that Tiny leads a double life." Rae opened her eyes to show suspense.

Bash rolled his eyes to show annoyance. Then the doorbell rang and he gasped, looking at Rae. "Who could that be?"

Rae groaned as Tiny's face flashed in her mind. A couple of heartbeats later, they both stood at the open front door, staring into the darkness. She said to Bash, "That's strange. I thought it would be Tiny. He can ring doorbells, you know."

"I didn't know that. I thought he could only open doors."

"Nope, he can do both. I think." Rae stepped onto the front porch and searched the scene in front of her. She saw only raindrops hitting puddles and felt the cool breeze of a summer storm. The street was otherwise empty. "I don't know who it is, but someone around here keeps ringing the doorbell and then leaving. It's happened four times now. I found Tiny on the porch after it rang one time and honestly thought he was the doorbell ditcher."

Bash stood next to her. "Maybe it's a ghost?"

Rae slugged him, causing him to laugh. He then cupped his hands around his mouth and hollered Tiny's name over the pounding rain. Tiny never appeared, but the rain suddenly lightened to a drizzle, allowing the quieter sounds to once again be heard. Bash yelled for Tiny three more times and as Rae strained her ears, she heard wild music in the distance.

"Do you hear that?" She looked at Bash who stepped closer to her.

"That doesn't sound like any music I listen to. I hear a base and a fiddle. Lots of fiddles." Rae added, "It sounds like something a gypsy band would play."

He looked at her. "It also sounds like it's coming from the woods."

They both looked at the forest just as lightning struck and flickered over the tall trees moving side to side in the stormy wind. Rae heard Bash gulp at the sight.

With wide eyes, Bash begged. "Please, Aunt Rae, Tiny's out in this storm. He's a living being and could be in a dangerous situation. We should drive around and look for him."

"Or," Rae began, "he needs to learn a lesson and we should go to bed."

Rae lost the argument. The next thing she knew, she and Bash drove slowly through the subdivision. With his forehead pressed against the window, Bash searched the area fervently. After thirty minutes without a Tiny sighting, Rae drove into the garage, ending the hunt.

Dodging raindrops, they sprinted to the front porch and entered the home. Standing in the foyer, Rae heard Bash's melancholy exhale as she locked the door and fuddled with the alarm system. She thought that she had it set until it gurgled. After turning it off, she moved the chair against the front door again.

Bash looked at the chair. "Offering the burglar a place to sit?"

"We'll be fine. I locked the door."

"What about Tiny?"

Rae groaned. "If Tiny isn't back by morning, I'll drive all over *again*. Okay?"

Bash nodded and asked sheepishly, "Can I stay with you in your room tonight? I mean, you never know what crazy frolicking banshees will do, especially ones who play fiddles during electrical storms."

Rae chuckled. "It's just a group of teenagers led by Gangsta Gio."

"Still," Bash reasoned, "there's safety in numbers. I promise not to hog the covers."

As they now both lay in the queen-size bed, Rae and Bash continued the debate about Gio. "No, Aunt Rae, you got it all wrong. Gio's not a gangsta and he told me that he doesn't go into the woods. He's afraid of the banshee. I mean banshees." He yawned and then asked, "Why aren't you scared about those people out there?"

She shrugged. "I guess when you live in a big city where you hear people shouting, sirens blaring and music blasting from all of your neighbors throughout the night, things like this just seem tame. I mean, I hear strange noises all night long, every single night."

Bash's snoring interrupted her. He was asleep with one of his heavy legs draped over both of hers, feeling like a column of swampy concrete. Reaching for her phone, Rae knew that the only way for her to find dreamland tonight was to listen to the soothing sounds of a brush being pulled across a mic.

• • • •

Stone slept through the thunderous storm. In fact, he never slept better. No night terrors rattled him. No dead people appeared to him. No woods. No Zalen. No nothing. He awoke with actual energy and a bright disposition for the first time since forever. Whistling while frying eggs, he felt like a new man and after breakfast, he was ready to climb.

Grabbing his bag packed with rock climbing gear, he soon drove through city traffic toward an indoor climbing facility called On The Rocks. Stone actually preferred free soloing, where he, alone, relied on his own strength and skill rather than on ropes or harnesses. However, since he took over The Rail six months ago, the opportunity to free solo became rare and he resorted to joining the indoor climbing gym. It wasn't ideal, but it worked. Rock climbing, indoor or outdoor, helped him to focus his mind on something other than his weirdness and today, it would help him to forget about Rachel. After giving it much thought, he realized that her danger may only be connected to him. Just like in rock climbing, he needed to cut their linked line before it snapped on its own, securing them only of falling to their deaths.

It was just after eight in the morning when he arrived. Hustling through the parking lot, he jogged through the drizzle. He entered the main doors, wearing a misty smile and a damp white compression shirt, which showed off his abs. This melted the young receptionist's hard facial expression like butter in a skillet.

"Hellooooo," she sang a little too long and breathlessly. "So good to see you, Stone."

Stone merely answered, "Hi, how are you?" He handed his membership card to her.

"Still single," she replied. "Your guest is waiting for you by the vending machine."

Stone's heart stuttered. Guest? What guest?

CHAPTER SIXTEEN

At five o'clock in the morning, the rain pounded on the manor's roof as the doorbell punctually sounded. Rae stormed down the steps, kicked the chair over and unlocked the door. Swinging it open, she was ready to unload her wrath onto the rude Tiny, but he wasn't there. No one was. The doorbell ditcher struck early this Thursday morn. She closed the door, leaning against it in bewilderment. Just as she turned the lock, the doorbell sounded again. Rae waited for a minute before cautiously unlocking the door and peering through the crack. A smoky snout greeted her. Swinging the door fully open, she glared at Tiny. "You think this is funny? Your nasty antics have Bash worried. Me, not so much."

Four rain puddles formed underneath each paw as his doleful brown eyes fell upon her. His gold charm around his collar dripped water like a leaky faucet and even his ears drooped.

Rae said in an exasperated tone, "I don't think the *T* on that charm stands for *Tiny*. I think it stands for *Taxing*." Taking the charm, she turned it over with her fingers. The back of the charm was blank. They stared at each other for a moment before Rae said, "I'm on to you. You have a girlfriend, don't you? Why don't you stay with her?" Then her heart surprisingly softened as he wiped the water from his eyes with his paw.

With one hand, she tentatively reached for him. Her palm hovered above his head before eventually landing on the top of it.

At first, it was awkward petting the large melon head, but then she found the spot behind his ears. As he leaned into her for more ear-scratching, she smiled at him and some of the weight on her shoulders lifted.

As she stepped aside to let him enter, Tiny strode into the foyer and shook his entire body, spraying the excess water all over the walls, the floor and on Rae. She jumped back and yelped. He cocked his head to the left, giving her a quizzical look, and then galloped up the stairs to the tower bedroom with her close behind him. He trotted past the pink bedroom and stepped easily into her bed, sniffing Bash's head. Glancing at Rae, he yawned while snuggling closer to the sleeping boy.

The tension in her shoulders began to mount again. Muttering expletives to herself, she left the bedroom and spent the next few morning hours working on logo designs in Travis's office. During which time, he texted her. His question was to the point. "House still standing?"

She texted back. "Of course."

He replied, "It better be."

Rae responded, "We need to talk about a Tiny situation."

Travis answered, "You can handle Two-face Tonya."

Rae wrote back. "I'm not talking about Tonya. I'm talking about Tiny."

"Tonya isn't tiny. Her ass is as big as Texas. Gotta go. Don't touch the mirror."

Rae sighed at Travis's superpower of evasion. Or maybe, she thought, Travis really was not aware that there was a Tiny situation? Whatever. For the rest of the morning, she absorbed herself in logo designs.

Around ten o'clock, she heard Bash and Tiny rummage in the kitchen for breakfast. Bash then appeared at the office door, balancing a small pink dog dish in the palm of his hand. "Why does Tiny have such a small food dish?"

He raised it and Rae narrowed her eyes, studying it.

"He doesn't seem interested in the kibble either." Bash added, "I think Travis bought the wrong kind of dog food. The bag says it's for small breeds. Maybe that's why Tiny won't eat it?"

Rae shrugged while continuing to work. "Maybe?"

"I'm going to make Tiny and me some eggs. Want some?"

She shook her head and leaned in closer toward the screen.

Hours passed and at one o'clock, Bash strolled into Travis's office, carrying buttery, crunchy, toasted bread oozing with gooey cheese on a plate. With ketchup. Rae gazed at him with heartfelt appreciation and he jumped back from fright.

"My god," he said. "What have you done to your eyes? They look bloody and wet. Like all of your capillaries burst at once. How long have you been staring at the computer screen?"

"Only eight hours. Straight. Logo design. So close."

Bash shook his head at his red-eyed aunt. "And now you can only talk in fragments. May I suggest that you find the nearest emergency eye wash station and douse your entire face with some potassium chloride and tetrahydrozoline hydrochloride? Immediately."

"Why can't you say eyedrops like everyone else?"

"Where's the fun in that? Seriously," Bash continued, "you're disgusting to look at. Fix yourself. We have a blind date today at three, remember? Let's try to look good."

"I'm fine," Rae said to Bash, but he was already out of the room. That was when she noticed all the blur. Nothing had defined lines anymore. It was all just a lot of fuzziness. She saved her work and shut down the computer. Sighing, she cringed at the idea of her upcoming blind date. What could be worse than a car parker? Just then, she received a text from ChAdonis. He wrote, "Nine more days til we ride in our birthday suits." Her question was answered.

. . .

That could mean only one thing. But how? At first, Stone refused to look. He instead focused on the floor, but then he heard his guest call to him, "Hey, Stone! Want some organic vegetable chips? Processed foods really aren't my thing, but the sea salt helps. A lot."

"No thanks." Stone reluctantly looked up and faced his fear. It was Zalen, wearing red baggy basketball shorts and a plain yellow t-shirt that was tight around his middle. Simple brown sandals were strapped to his feet and a black harness stretched itself around his torso and thighs.

Raising his hand, Zalen shook the bag of organic vegetable chips. "Are you sure? They're really good." He shook the bag a little harder.

Stone begrudgingly moved his legs toward Zalen. "How did you get in here? I don't think this place even has guest passes."

"A smile goes a long way." Zalen smiled wider.

Stone was still confused. "How did you know that I was even coming here?"

Zalen actually looked hurt by that question. "Aw, man. You know my answer to that."

"Because you're a serial stalker and you're trying to make my life a living hell?" Stone gestured toward Zalen's feet. "You can't climb in sandals."

Zalen chuckled. "It's funny when you joke around like that."

"Why do you always think I'm joking?" Stone rubbed his forehead. "Why are you here?"

Zalen ate an orange chip. "I'm proud that you've reached the base of the Rae climb. In climbing terms, I believe it's called the approach. To keep you moving upwards, I'll act as your personal ascender, a device to aid you in reaching the top of Rae. Once you're there, I'll leave."

"Well," Stone began, "then we have four problems. First, I'm not climbing Rachel. Second, I need you to leave. Third, you're not my personal ascender. You're more like drag, which is friction caused by the rope not being able to be pulled. In climbing terms, it can be disastrous. This leads me to our fourth problem. Stop defining climbing terms. It's annoying."

Zalen was now eating a vibrant green chip. "But Rae's in danger and you could be her top rope, which, in climbing terms, is a rope that will protect her from falling very far."

"I know what a top rope is." Stone then explained, "Look, I really started thinking about all the dreams and visions, and I strongly think that Rachel will only be in danger if I'm in her life. See? The dreams and visions were all warnings for me to stay away from her. If I'm near her, then she'll be in danger. If I stay away, she'll be safe."

Zalen's face was straight. His eyes looked concerned, almost pained. "Well," he finally said, "do you really *feel* that way?"

"Yes," Stone replied, "I *think* that all I will do is bring destruction to her life."

"Okay," Zalen spoke slowly, "so you *feel* that she'll be safe without you around her?"

Stone nodded. "I *think* she'll be better off without me."

"All right." Zalen's face was void of any glee. "If that's how you *feel*, then I should be going."

Stone paused briefly before saying, "I *think* that would be best."

They spent the next twenty seconds staring at each other silently until Zalen suddenly brightened and said, "I have to meet someone special this afternoon anyway."

Stone asked, "At the insane asylum?"

Zalen had a big twinkle in his eye as he answered, "No. At the art museum."

CHAPTER SEVENTEEN

Bash looked sharp. He wore a black crew neck t-shirt with white block lettering written off-centered and vertically down the front. His matching silky shorts had a white logo that pierced the black canvas of the flowing material. He even gelled his bangs to stand up. Bash smelled good too. His minty breath shamed any plant from the mentha genus and Rae detected a musk, woodsy fragrance emanating from his body.

"Are you wearing cologne?" Her faded blue tank top had a chocolate stain on her belly and the brown yoga shorts lost its string around the waist. Fortunately, she managed to shower and her damp hair was now pulled into a ponytail with a few strands falling around the sides of her face. She hooked them around her ears and then wiped her nose with the back of her hand.

"At least I'm trying to make a good impression for us," Bash replied as he scratched Tiny's rear end. "We better go, or we'll be late for our date. What's his name again?"

"Mitchell. Or maybe it's Mark? Something like that."

"It's *Michael*. Even *I* remember that and *I* wasn't part of the conversation." Bash gave Tiny a quick pat on the head before Rae shoved her nephew out the back door.

Sternly looking at the dog, she asked him, "Are you going to stick around this time?" He only cocked his head to the left in that judgmental way of his and blinked. Rae tried to sound authoritative. "When I get back, we need to have a little chat."

Tiny yawned. Then his ears sprang to attention. He looked next to her and his tail wagged excitedly. Next thing Rae knew, he bowed, but not at her. He bowed at the space next to her. She gave him a curious look. "What's wrong with you?" When he rolled over and started kicking his hind leg, she blew out a sigh and left, slamming the door behind her.

. . .

The Great Shepherd stopped kicking his leg when the back door slammed. Now on all fours, he watched the angry lady and the nice boy walk toward the garage. He glanced behind him and knew that the sad girl would be gone. She never stayed long and he missed her. But the nice boy gave really good belly rubs, even better than the sad girl. As for the angry lady, she had a good heart. He could tell. And she smelled like sugary bacon.

As the car's engine came to life, he waited until he no longer heard it. The angry lady and nice boy were gone and he whined for them. He missed them too, but knew he had things to do. He also knew that the angry lady didn't set the alarm or even lock the back door again. He was going to have to teach her how to do that. For right now, however, he stood on his hind legs while reaching for the knob with his front paws. He turned it and the door cracked open. Nuzzling his nose further into the crevice, he widened the opening and strolled out of the house. He paused on the patio, making sure the door closed behind him. After leaping over the pool fence, he galloped toward the park and onward to the meat lady. She always made him bacon that tasted real good.

CHAPTER EIGHTEEN

The blind date was a bust. It turned out that Michael liked long legs. He himself stretched way past the six foot mark and Rae was about ten inches too short for his standards. Before Rae really knew what hit her, Michael ended the date, explaining that he'd rather work another hour and bank more bucks. The sting of rejection hurt, even for a disinterested Rae.

Now standing in the ticket line, Rae heard Bash clear his throat. "Hey, Aunt Rae, you dodged a bigger bullet than he did."

Rae appreciated Bash's attempt of cheering her up and tenderly squeezed his shoulder. "Yeah, I know. Do you still want to stay?"

"Of course," Bash answered. "It's just us now. You can teach me all about art. It's like I have my own private guide."

Looking at her enthusiastic nephew, she said, "I can draw better than I can talk about art."

"Well, I'm sure that you can figure out something interesting to tell me."

By now, they strolled into a rectangular room that had white walls, white track lighting and a white ceiling. Rae thought they entered what static noise would physically look like if static noise could be a room. The seven large paintings hanging on the walls thankfully broke the white silence. There was also a welcoming black bench in the center. It faced the largest painting of the group, spanning almost the entire wall. Rae and Bash sat to admire the landscape.

"Well?" Bash asked after a few minutes ticked by. "What can you tell me about this?"

Respecting her nephew's attempt at salvaging this afternoon, she played along. "This particular artist used strong brushstrokes to create dramatic movement to this piece. At first glance, you might think he used a simple palette mainly of muted yellows. However, if you look closely, you can see he actually used all the warm colors of reds and oranges with some cool greens and blues." A small group of interested listeners gathered behind her as she continued. "Do you see that dark shape in the middle?"

"How can I miss it? It looks like an upside-down burnt chicken."

"It is outlined in black and then filled in with thick colors, mostly dark violets. I strongly believe that this artist was influenced by Van Gogh or Japanese prints or both." Rae read the small metal plate squeezed in next to it on the wall. "It's titled Dandelion Field."

"Dandelion Field? What's that large shape then?"

"That's what is so interesting about art. Art is what the viewer makes of it. For me, it's always changing. Paintings have mood changes, just like people. And just when I think I figured something out in a painting like this, I look at it in a new light and see something completely different. So, for today, that black shape represents hope to me."

"Hope? Are you being sarcastic?"

Rae laughed. "Nope. I look at it this way. The shape is black and overwhelming the space, but the warm colors around it make me feel hopeful of the unknown."

"Well," Bash said, "it looks like death to me." He then looked at Rae and licked his lips. "I suddenly have a craving for butterscotch."

The small group surrounding Rae dispersed, leaving one man to remain. His loud lip smacking compelled Rae and Bash to turn around and face him. He wore red baggy basketball shorts and a yellow t-shirt that was too tight around his middle. More alarming than his appearance was his stretched smile. It seemed comically exaggerated.

"I agree," he said to Rae. "I see hope too."

The stranger had a genuine kindness about him, but Rae remained cautious. He held out his hand and nestled comfortably in the cup of his palm were two butterscotch candies, wrapped in shiny gold foil. The happy man asked, "Would you like one? I find they calm the nerves."

"No thanks," Rae answered and thwarted Bash's hand from accepting the treat, friendly man or not.

"I understand, Rae. Stranger danger should always be taken very seriously." He smiled.

"Do I know you?" Rae asked this happy man while knowing full well that she didn't. When he shook his head, she asked, "How do you know my name then?"

"Well, Rae, it's like this. I am what you would call an intuitive empath."

Bash sprung up from excitement. "Really?" His voice rose. "You have a psychic ability? I read about this in a book called *Wake up and Smell the Psychic Roses*. This is so cool. You can sense things, right?"

"I can *feel* things about people. Sometimes I can sense when things *might* happen."

Bash pointed to his aunt. "And you felt my aunt's name? Why?" He gasped. "Is something going to happen to her?" His eyes sparkled with excitement. "Good or bad?"

Contradictory, Rae felt frustrated, snapping crossly at the man, "Who are you?"

Still smiling, the man replied, "I'm Zalen Richards."

Bash asked, "What's my name?"

Zalen paused. He shifted his weight uncomfortably. "Kyle?"

Bash shook his head, quickly saying, "Try again."

Zalen stared at Bash and eventually guessed. "Charlie?"

"Wow." Bash sighed. "You're way off. Let me help you. My name starts with a B."

"Barnaby?"

Now Bash was offended. "Do I really look like a Barnaby?"

"I'm not right all the time," Zalen said defensively.

"Obviously." Rae wore a wide smile now. Hooking her arm through her nephew's, she turned to Zalen and said, "See you around."

"Wait. Please." Zalen's eyes filled with concern. "I do really feel that something with you is off. You might be in trouble, Rae, and I know someone who can help. He's a really good friend of mine. I guess you could even say he is the yin to my yang. Go to him."

Rae mentally scoffed at the preposterous words escaping from Zalen's mouth. However, Bronco flashed through her mind, as well as Orangutan Man loitering around Travis's house. Then Bash flashed through her mind along with Clare's words about weird experiences and death. She reluctantly asked Zalen, "What's your friend's name?"

"I can't tell you. That would mess things up. I will tell you that he's a *mutual* friend and owns a bar downtown called The Rail. I recommend the sparkling water. It's very refreshing. You'll have to ask for a lemon wedge though. He doesn't like to hand them out freely."

Rae wrinkled her eyebrows together. "Are you a scam artist?"

Zalen said with a bright expression, "No, but my ex-wife was. I found out ten thousand dollars too late." He dug into the pocket of his red shorts and held out his fist. "Trust me." Pouring a handful of gold treats into her hands, he added, "They really do calm anxiety. Now, please excuse me, I must go home and start packing." Before completely parting, Zalen turned toward Bash. Placing his hands on Bash's shoulders, his one wide eye became rounder and larger. "As FDR once said, when you come to the end of your rope, tie a knot and hang on. Got it, Bash?" Then he popped an unwrapped butterscotch candy into his own mouth and strolled casually out of sight.

. . .

Standing in front of the bar, Stone puzzled over many things. Like why was he being hunted by one of the happiest guys he ever met? And why couldn't he kick Rachel out his head? Was he doing the right thing by not contacting her? The corner bar stool jiggled quickly and without looking, Stone said aloud, "Not now, grandpa."

He redirected his attention to the many different liquors resting on the shelves. Stone's eyes eventually traveled upwards toward the five large whiskey bottles lining the very top. A buried memory flickered through his mind like an old home movie. Closing his eyes, he watched the scene unfold. Grandpa Ed and he worked quietly together at the bar. Toothpicks and wires were strewn all over the counter. Somehow, these dull objects transformed into an impressive boom and mast. Stone could still feel the smoothness of the basswood, smell the tea-soaked paper used for sails, and hear the quiet grunts of Grandpa Ed as he squeezed the surgical forceps. It took many afternoons before they finished, and Stone remembered when Grandpa Ed handed off the final baton to him for their project's completion. It was the cork, and as Stone plugged the bottle's opening, thereby winning a marathon, he never felt more proud.

He still felt proud. Their ship in the bottle was the largest of the five, bringing a smile to Stone's face. The entrance doors suddenly burst open, however, and wild whoops of laughter overtook the quiet atmosphere, changing the content smile to a grim line of a businessman.

CHAPTER NINETEEN

"Well?" Bash said with a mouthful of butterscotch, "should we go to The Rail?" In his hand was his phone, displaying a map of downtown Monroe. He showed the screen to Rae. "The bar is just around the corner and I could use a lemonade."

Rae was also sucking on a butterscotch. Her fourth one. While shifting gears, she said, "No. I can't take you to a bar. Your parents would kill me."

"They don't have to know. Besides, the website says that The Rail is also a restaurant. We can tell them we stopped for cheese curds. They're the big seller and rated two stars out of five."

"I'd rather go to Half Pounders. They have great greasy cheeseburgers and onion rings that are rated ten out of five."

"You're making that up."

"Listen, if the cheese curds are rated that poorly and those are the big seller, then the food at The Rail isn't safe to eat."

"Fine. Let's just have drinks then and find out who the mutual friend is." He looked at her. "I know that you're just as curious as I am because you parked the car right in front of the bar and are now staring at it."

Bash was right. Rae was slightly curious and presently peering at the bar's entrance doors. She asked her nephew, "What if that Zolift character is a coo-coo nut job?"

"It's Zalen, not Zolift."

"How many people accost others in art museums, quote dead presidents and talk about yin-yang? He sounds like a certified ying-a-ling."

"Well, that ying-a-ling got my name right."

"Eventually."

"Come on, Aunt Rae. We'll only stay for a few minutes. And we're drinking lemonade and soda, for Pete's sake. Do I have to literally twist your arm?"

Rae surrendered. "Don't tell your parents we're here. And turn off that tracking app on your phone."

"I already did."

As Rae and Bash entered The Rail, they were blown over by the roaring crowd of young men. There were fifteen of them and they all wore old shirts and shorts, splattered with paint. Their skin was speckled with round, red welts; their eyes shimmered with inebriated elation at the flat screen television. A baseball game was somewhere in the eighth inning with the losing home team up at bat. They only scored one run so far, which paled considerably to the other team's seven run lead. The men gathered around three small pub tables, filled with beer mugs, and they were jovially yelling obscenities at the players and each other.

Rae steered Bash away from the wild, fraternity-looking crew. She spotted a quieter corner and was full steam ahead for that safe haven. After they climbed on top of the tall bar stools, Rae heard the umpire call the third strike and a chain of events began inside of The Rail.

First, one of the men hollered, "Bullshit!" This word triggered the others to grab one of their buddies, hoist him above their heads and then pass him over the crowd. Reclined on his back, the buddy seemed happy, laughing the entire time, even when he was unceremoniously dumped on the ground after reaching the end of his ride. The loud thud caused everyone to cheer heartily, including Bash.

Bash shook Rae's shoulder and shouted, "That looks like fun!"

Rae rolled her eyes. "Absolutely not!"

Her nephew transfixed his googly eyes on the group of men and watched them with wild envy. Rae, on the other hand, ignored all of them and looked around the surroundings, soaking in the ambience. It was an old tavern. The color scheme was dark wood on darker wood. Pub tables and chairs were scattered all around the room and the air was thick with the smell of yeast, frying oil and Old Spice. Every inch of every wall was adorned with signed jerseys, signed balls and signed bobble heads. The style reeked of tackiness and masculinity with a general midwest comfort. She liked the place, especially the railing. It was long, knobby, twisted and followed the whole length of the large bar, which took center stage.

An older woman stood behind the counter, laughing at the young men. Her chortle was almost as loud as her spiky, rainbow-colored wig. She was drinking, flirting and occasionally wiping down her area with a ratty old rag. Her interest was on the young men, not on Rae.

Ten minutes crawled by and Rae's serious doubts turned to grave convictions. Being there was so wrong. What was she doing? She should be working or running. She should not be there, following the directions of some unbalanced stranger named Zooloo. The only real danger she currently faced was being overcharged for a soda.

"Bullshit!" The chain reaction soon began again and another man was picked up, passed and tossed to the ground in the same manner as before.

Bash squealed in delight. "This is so cool!"

Rae shook her head. "Nah, this is a waste of time. We should go."

Bash's eyes popped open. "But what about the mutual friend? What if you're in trouble?"

"I'm not." Noticing the worry filling Bash's expression, Rae consoled him. "If it makes you feel better, I could call that cop you know." She hopped off the stool.

Bash nodded. "Maybe we should call Officer Howie?"

"You can't have me arrested for bad service," joked the voice of that older woman from behind the bar. Only she wasn't behind the bar anymore and was now standing in between Rae and Bash, wearing rainbow leggings that matched her hair. Grinning, she said, "I'm Sally. I normally don't work here. Just helping out today because I believe in giving back to the community. Now, what can I get you two?"

Bash quickly answered first, "Do you have lemonade?"

"Anything for you, doll. I'll hand-squeeze the lemons myself." Sally winked at him and spoke to Rae next. "And what about you, honey?"

She sighed at Bash as he smiled at her and she climbed onto the stool again. "Diet soda."

Sally nodded. "Anything else?"

Bash blurted out, "Is the owner here? It's imperative for us to see him."

Sally gave him and Rae the side-eye. With a protective tone, she asked, "Imperative?"

"Yes. You see, a guy by the name of Zalen told us to come here and see the owner. I'm Bash and this is my aunt. If you could please tell the owner that we're here, we'd really appreciate it." He then gave her his best smile, showing off his dimples.

Sally's guarded disposition dissolved instantly when she saw the deep depressions on both of Bash's cheeks. She pinched them affectionately. "I'll see if he's feeling social today." As she walked away, she said to Bash over her shoulder, "Call me in ten years."

Rae groaned and her eyes searched for the restroom sign. Her anxiety was on the rise and the thought of crawling out of a bathroom window appealed to her. But she couldn't leave Bash.

She could, however, splash cold water on her face. Rae said to her nephew, "I'll be right back."

She crossed the room at the same time the umpire on the television yelled, "Strike three! You're out!"

Again, a man from the crowd hollered, "Bullshit!"

Before Rae knew it, someone grabbed her by the waist, lifted her over his head and passed her to the next guy. He then passed her to the next guy who passed her to the last guy. Above all the cheers rose Bash's voice as he hooted and hollered enviously for her. She felt her body lighten as she was tossed high into the air. Upon falling, her stomach dropped and she braced herself for the impact of a wood floor. Pain never came though. Instead, she suddenly found herself in the arms of the one and only Stone Winters. His electric blue eyes locked with hers and they both stared speechlessly at one another for a full minute.

Finally, Stone spoke first, "Oh, shit."

Rae said flatly, "It's nice to see you again too."

Another full minute ticked along awkwardly and Rae looked deeply into Stone's eyes. It was easy to do because they were as wide as caverns and seemingly as bottomless. Rae felt his body tremble against hers. She cleared her throat, "A very happy man named Ziploc or Zany told me to find the owner of this bar. He said we're all mutual friends. I take it he means you?"

Stone unexpectedly dropped her to the floor. "Zalen," he muttered aloud. Then he quickly helped Rae to her feet while saying, "Sorry."

"So, that's a yes." Rae brushed off her backside. "Can you just tell me what's going on? He said something's off about me and you could help. Is this a joke?"

With her feet firmly planted and hands on her hips, she faced him, or rather, faced his chest, noticing his chiseled, smooth pecs. Well, she guessed they were smooth underneath his tight t-shirt. Smooth and easy to lick. Rae forced her chin to tilt way up to see his face. He looked down on her with furrowed eyebrows.

Every memory of Stone in high school made her want to wince. From the time between sixth and seventh grade, something caused him to change drastically. He was no longer the easy-going best friend. His expression became hard. Stone-cold hard. His mouth straightened to a severe line and his icy blue eyes literally had the ability to freeze people in their tracks. By their senior year, his personality matched his name perfectly. Stone Winters was the coldest name she ever heard and the unfriendliest man she ever knew. And they were no longer friends.

Except now, his features softened a little. They weren't so judgmental and the frost in his eyes melted with each passing second. She noticed his full lips were not the usual hard line as she remembered and were curving upwards at her. A cascade of tingles erupted all over her body while standing underneath his gaze.

And then there was his chest again. Rae licked her lips.

Stone spoke warmly, "It's nice to see you, Rachel."

"Bullshit!" After another strike out, the men searched for someone to pass.

A small familiar voice yelled from the corner, "Pick me! Pick me! *Please* pick me!"

Rae groaned at her nephew and said to Stone, "I need to grab my chest. I mean, my nephew, Bash, before someone else does. But can we talk sometime when you have time?"

Rae searched his eyes for an answer, but he just stared into hers. At one point, he glanced backwards and shook his head at the corner bar stool behind the counter. Sighing, he turned back to Rae and coughed once before asking, "How about now? Are you hungry?"

Rae pictured a burger dripping with cheese. "I'm a little hungry."

Stone said with a knowing smile, "How about Half Pounders?"

Giving him a skeptical look, she replied, "It's like you're reading my mind."

Stone heard Rachel's question and gulped. She wanted to *talk*? An image of her broken body invaded his mind, as well as that brown liquid trickling down her shocked face. His answer stalled. He needed time to think, but his grandpa's stool was antsy and wobbled slightly.

Feeling conflicted, he wanted to take Rachel anywhere she would let him. After all, it was beautiful Rachel Greyson with the auburn hair, stormy gray eyes and spunky wit. On the other hand, what if *he* was the reason why she would be in danger?

The stool gently rocked and Stone could hear the legs softly tapping the ground. His grandfather's voice whispered inside of Stone's head, "Be with her."

His feelings of confliction switched to feelings of protection. As she stood there, his new impulse was to wrap his arms around her and be her shield, made of 100% stone. Looking at his grandpa's bar stool, he shook his head and the stool returned to its lifeless state. Stone blew out a sigh of relief, knowing that he gave his grandfather no reason to flip it over this time.

Rachel was watching him with one arched eyebrow. He coughed once and then asked, "How about now? Are you hungry?" Suddenly, he envisioned Rachel sitting at a round table with a tray of food in front of her. She was biting into a half pound cheeseburger.

"I'm a little hungry," Rachel said to Stone.

He asked, "How about Half Pounders?"

Her eyes narrowed slightly. "It's like you're reading my mind."

Stone didn't say a word. He just shrugged, trying to look casual, but really looking stiff and awkward. Rachel only chuckled and turned from him. She quickly crossed the floor to her nephew. He was still waving his arm at the group of men, pleading with them to be passed over their heads. Rachel grabbed him just before he was picked and led him to the door, calling to Stone, "Let's meet at the one on Eighth and Lincoln."

Stone nodded, inhaling deeply. Once Rachel and Bash left his bar, he exhaled and began planning out what he was going to tell her and what he was going to keep a secret. His strange ability? That was a secret. His horrid visions of her? Those were also secrets. His inkling of her being in danger? It would be better to keep that a secret too. What should he tell her?

Sally walked up to him, carrying a tray with one soda and one lemonade on it. "Damn," she said flatly. "I worked hard at squeezing the lemons."

Stone smirked. "Our lemonade is premade. All you had to do was unscrew the cap."

Sally chuckled. "I know. Where did your attractive friend go? More importantly, why aren't you with her?"

Stone rubbed his temples. "I actually do need to leave for an hour or so. Would you mind handling things while I'm gone?"

She asked, "Really? Only an hour? Your grandpa had more stamina than that."

"Sally, it's not like that."

"Right." Sally grinned. "What's her name?"

"None of your business."

"That's a long name." Sally put the tray on the counter, taking the lemonade for herself. "So, if I dressed in tank tops with stains and yoga shorts and pulled my hair back into a messy ponytail, you'd leave your bar with me for an hour too?"

Stone ignored the question. "I have to go," he finally said. "Behave yourself."

CHAPTER TWENTY

Half Pounders was hopping and packed, both inside and out. Stone entered and caught Rachel elbowing her way into line right after she ordered her nephew to scout the restaurant for a table. Stone quickly joined the same line as Rachel, but stood behind her and another couple. He then watched Bash circle the dining area like an opportunistic Great White Shark with a poor sense of attack. Three times, he walked by a table and three times, the people left without him noticing. Other patrons then descended on the available table just as Bash turned his back. Stone heard Rachel sigh each time this happened. Then he chuckled as she snapped her fingers and clapped her hands, trying to catch her nephew's attention. Another table became available and she wanted to direct Bash to it.

Cupping her hands around her mouth, Rachel hollered, "Bash, on your left!"

He turned to his right and missed the sighting.

Rachel's hands dropped as she muttered out loud, "You've got to be kidding me."

Although Stone enjoyed watching this show, he began to worry about where the three of them were going to eat when, suddenly, Bash dove toward a newly vacated table. It was smack-dab in the center of the whole restaurant, surrounded by a sea of other tables. Rachel groaned loudly when her nephew used his forearm to wipe off crumbs from the previous eaters. Then he looked at her gleefully and gave her a thumbs up.

Ten minutes later, Stone trailed Rachel as they both carried their trays piled with wrapped food and drinks. As all three settled at the round table, Stone felt Bash's eyes on him.

Stone held out his hand. "Hi, Bash. I'm Stone." They shook hands, quietly regarding each other before the ping-pong conversation between Stone and Rachel began.

"So, Stone, you own a bar?"

"Yes." He unwrapped his burger and tucked in some loose onion strings back underneath the top bun. "I inherited it after Grandpa Ed passed away."

Rachel's expression became pained. "Oh, I remember Grandpa Ed. He always laughed at me for some reason. I'm sorry to hear he passed."

Stone smiled and changed the subject. "What do you do?"

Rachel munched on a waffle fry. "I'm a graphic designer. I work downtown for a studio called Graphics Inc." Bash snatched a fry from her basket as she took one of his onion rings. Looking at Stone, she asked, "Are your parents still living in our old neighborhood?"

"Yep. I heard that your parents moved away."

Rachel nodded, slurping her soda. "They live in Florida."

"Nice. Where are you living these days?"

"I live in a duplex downtown. Although, right now, I'm house-sitting my boss's Victorian manor in the Birch Grove area. It has a wrap-around porch and a tower with a creepy fairy tale vibe. Staying there has just been a dream come true." Rachel slabbed on the sarcasm thickly.

Bash reminded her, "Don't forget about Tiny."

She gave Stone a playful sneer. "Tiny is this very large dog hanging around my boss's home. Picture a manatee with four legs and big saucer ears and you got Tiny."

Bash shook his head. "He's a Great Shepherd and a great dog. We're dog-sitting him."

Stone smiled at Rachel, even though the description of her boss's manor was the exact one in his vision, making him nervous. And she spoke of a dog too. However, she didn't mention scary trees or a shrilling cry. Plus, she didn't shatter yet. Regardless, Stone felt his stomach lurch, but he maintained his composure as Rachel asked him, "So, where are you living?"

"Downtown. I live on the lower level of a duplex and rent the upper."

"You're a landlord, too?"

"Well, I just have one property to landlord. Does that really qualify?"

Rachel shoved an onion ring into her mouth. "Of course."

As she continued conversing, Stone didn't want to think about anything except for her face. Staring at her button nose, long eyelashes and tongue dabbing at her salty lips, he decided to ignore that crazy psychic *business*. Creepy Victorian manor? What creepy Victorian manor? Psychic ability? What psychic ability? In fact, he decided to squelch the idea of *business* entirely. He hated that word. *Business* was no longer accepted in Stone's vocabulary.

Bash interrupted Stone's thoughts. "Let's get down to *business*. Your very good friend, Zalen, said my aunt needs help and you're the guy to help her. So, what can you tell us?"

Sighing, Stone picked up a pickle and clarified, "He's not my very good friend."

Rachel took her third bite of the cheeseburger. Still with her mouth full, she asked, "You're not the yin to Zalen's yang?"

Now choking on a pickle, Stone pounded his chest twice before answering, "Good God, no, and I've only known Zalen for two very long days. I met him at the grocery store. He kept following me around with toilet paper." He adjusted his baseball cap. "What did he say to you?"

Rachel took two gulps of her soda to wash down her burger bite. "He told me that something's off about me and I should see you about it. That's it."

"So, what do you think?" Bash gulped his root beer malt, looking earnestly at Stone for an answer.

"Where did you guys even see Zalen?"

Bash answered, "At the art museum this afternoon."

Stone sighed at the recollection. "Zalen mentioned to me this morning that he was going to the art museum to meet someone." Looking at Rachel, he added, "I didn't know he meant you. I'm sorry that he alarmed you. I'll talk to him about that."

"Is he deranged?" Rachel asked.

Bash interjected, "More importantly, is there any truth to what Zalen said? Is he an empath? Is my aunt in trouble? Do you know something?"

Truth? Trouble? Stone sheepishly glanced at his food as his mind was at a crossroads. Was Rachel in trouble because he was in her life? Or was she in trouble because he was not in her life? The truth was he didn't know if Rachel was even in *real* trouble.

Rachel secretly dipped her waffle fry in Bash's malt without him knowing. "I'm not in trouble. Zippy or whatever his name is just likes to talk a good game."

Bash disagreed. "*Zalen* knew my name though."

"Eventually," Rachel corrected.

"Well, riddle me this then. How did he know that we were at the art museum?" When neither Stone nor Rachel answered, Bash looked at Stone. "Does my aunt need your help?"

Before Stone could answer, Rachel argued with Bash, "I don't need his help or anyone's help. I am a strong woman who needs no help from any man, boy or large dog."

Bash stood. "I'm going to the bathroom, not because I have to use it, but because I've heard this speech before." As he strolled away, Bash stepped aside to let an older man pass whose hands trembled as he carried a tray with one super large drink on it.

Stone's arms tingled as the old man approached their table. He stopped in front of it, his eyes darted around the room while his wrists shook. The bucket-sized soda cup teetered. Leaning toward Rachel, Stone began, "Listen, Rachel-"

Rachel interrupted him, "I don't need you acting as some kind of protector. I'm not a weak little person. I can take care of myself."

Stone said nothing, rubbing his stinging forearms. The vision of Rachel's face dripping in brown liquid popped into his mind again and again. Why?

Rachel carried on, "I'm very smart and always keep my head on a swivel. In fact, while studying abroad in France during college, I aided the French police in capturing two drug dealers in Nice. Granted, I mistakenly thought they were giving me money just and the French police were actually trying to get me out of the way, but you get the idea."

The old man nodded toward someone and moved around the table, squeezing behind Rachel's chair. After successfully lowering the tray onto the table, he sat down next to his wife. Stone's forearms still tingled though. Something was about to happen. He could feel it. Suddenly, a tall girl on the other side of Rachel jumped to her feet with a large cup of soda in her hand. The momentum caused the girl to lose her grip. With her hand above Rachel's head, Rachel was unknowingly the direct recipient of the dark soda drenching. Fortunately for her, Stone stood and reached up to catch the cup, saving Rachel from a carbonated shampoo. After handing the soda back to the apologetic girl, he sat down again and Rachel continued talking without ever noticing this event. His vision of her face dripping with a dark liquid now made sense to him and he smiled, knowing that he stopped a part of his vision from actually happening. The tingles stopped too. His heart soared as he realized that his visions were things that *might* happen. They weren't necessarily things that would *definitely* happen.

Rachel wiped off the small drop of liquid that landed on her forehead and studied it. "Great, I'm sweating soda again. Anyway, don't worry about me. I'll be just fine on my own."

By now, Bash returned and sat on the chair. Looking at Stone and Rachel, he asked, "Did I miss anything?"

Rachel replied, "Nothing at all."

Stone disagreed. Suddenly, he realized that he, himself, missed everything. The visions weren't realities, only suggestions. More importantly, he could control the outcome. She was in trouble and he could help her. The Rachel road ahead of him was going to be tough, though, and riddled with potholes. Her independence was one of those pockmarks as well as her stubbornness. He knew that her statement of needing no help from him was as serious as a thirty car collision. He would have to act like an orange barrel, guiding Rachel without her knowing it. After all, he was the guy who could help her, even if she might lead him to a dead end.

•   •   •

In the car after dinner, Bash fretted. Aunt Rae declined Stone's offer of protection and he couldn't understand why. "You might really be in trouble, Aunt Rae."

"From what?"

"From disasters, like Orangutan Man or Bronco. I personally think Maeve, the banshee, has it out for you."

Aunt Rae reasoned, "I took a self-defense course in college. I know how to get myself out of disastrous situations involving attackers."

"How about other disastrous situations like extreme loneliness or isolation? Maybe Stone can help you with those?" She playfully slugged him in the shoulder as he continued. "Please tell me that you didn't already delete his phone number that he just gave to you. You may need it."

"I still have it, so don't worry your cute little self about it."

During the rest of the drive, they sang along with the radio, wrong lyrics and all, and arrived at the manor in good spirits. However, his cheery mood sobered upon entering through the back door. As they stood in the kitchen, Bash immediately felt Tiny's absence.

Worried, he said, "Tiny's gone again."

Aunt Rae smiled with a twinkle in her eye. "I had a feeling he would be." Turning from him, she headed out the kitchen. "I've got some more work to do."

Bash quickly asked, "You're really okay with him being gone? If something happens to him, won't Travis fire you or something?"

Hollering from Travis's office, Aunt Rae said, "There's always a silver lining."

Raising his voice even higher, Bash asked, "Don't you care about Tiny at all?"

There was silence. Bash then heard his aunt's footsteps walk from the office, through the foyer and into the kitchen. She looked Bash squarely in the face. "Of course I care. In fact, I care so much that I've been closely watching him and developed a theory about him."

"Is it the double life theory again?"

She stuck up her nose. "All I'll say is that I'm a master puzzle solver and there are clues to this dog's puzzle everywhere. You're smart. Figure this one out on your own." She then poked the tip of her tongue out through her lips and made a thwapping sound at him.

Bash sighed. "What clues?"

Aunt Rae studied him, drumming her fingers on the counter. "Here's one clue. I told Travis to have Tiny stay at the dog-sitters and Travis promised me that he'd do that."

Bash shrugged. "So? Travis broke his promise and now you're mad. That's a clue?"

She shook her head. "Upon further inspection, I don't think Travis broke his promise."

"I don't understand what you're saying. Is your theory that Tiny stays with the dog-sitter, but still comes home every once in a while to see *us*?"

Aunt Rae gave him a quizzical look. "Does that make sense to you?"

"None of this makes sense to me."

"Then keep thinking. Especially think about Tiny's leash, Tiny's food dish and Tiny's food." As Aunt Rae backed out of the kitchen, she casually added, "He'll be back in the morn." She turned and breezed through the kitchen into the foyer where Bash heard her scream at the top of her lungs before cursing angrily.

Bash called to her, "Did the mirror scare you again?"

"Yep," she replied before heading into Travis's office and closing the door.

He smiled at that when the doorbell unexpectedly rang. "I'll get it!" Bash hurried to the front door and opened it. No one was there. Curious, he stepped onto the porch and looked at the vacant surroundings. Staring down the street, he saw nothing. Then, out of the corner of his eye, he spotted Gio on the path. Gio held up three fingers and Bash raised a thumb in agreement. The plan was set. They would meet in the morning at three to hunt for a banshee. Gio quickly turned and left as Bash entered the house.

He spent the rest of the evening sprawled on the oversized sofa, watching reruns of his favorite paranormal investigative show. At one point, he checked in with his mom and kept their conversation brief. He learned that the less she knew, the happier she was. Then, as each hour passed, he salivated at his own planned adventure that was fast-approaching. Speaking of salivating, where was Tiny? Glancing at the time, it was ten o'clock. Turning off the TV, he approached the doorway to Travis's office and said, "I'm going to bed. Tiny's still not back."

Aunt Rae never took her eyes off the screen. "Trust me," she said, "he's fine and will return at five this morning."

Bash left, muttering to himself about how frustrating his aunt was. Now, sitting on the bed in criss-cross fashion, he wrote in his red notebook. His observations included more theories about Movie Star Bob and his wife, Boozy Candice, as well as Sunshiny Bryson, Gio, Bronco and Orangutan Man. He also added two new people and one dog to his notes: Zalen, Stone and Tiny. Flipping to the front of his notebook, he reviewed important information that he gathered from the internet regarding Honey Ward. His first reference was from an informative website created by a brilliant young researcher named Jimbo. Filled with facts and some misspellings, Jimbo confirmed Bash's suspicions of Honey not only being taken by the banshee, but also now haunting this house.

The second reference was from an article giving more facts about Honey's disappearance. Her mother, Laura, stated that Honey went to bed at ten and never came out of her bedroom. Bob Harrison, the neighbor, a.k.a. Movie Star Bob, was quoted in the same article as seeing a white form run through the Wards' backyard and enter the forest around midnight. He took his dog out at that time and, fortunately, was able to help the police with the timeline. Bash thought that was very convenient for Movie Star Bob and marked Bob as his number two suspect.

His number one suspect to Honey Ward's disappearance remained the banshee. The plan was set to prove it. Kinda. Kneeling on the floor, he pulled out his case full of paranormal equipment and glanced at the bedroom door, making sure that his aunt didn't appear out of thin air. She didn't, so he opened the case and began checking over his devices. Everything was in perfect working order, especially considering that he just placed new batteries in the EMF meter and spirit box. He even made sure that his mechanical pencil had new lead in it.

The only things left to do were charge his phone and wait. So, after connecting his cellphone to the charger, he reached under his pillow and removed his book called *A Ghosting We Will Go: Becoming the Hunter.* With only about four hours left, he reread the sections that he highlighted to pass the time. Once, he heard the doorbell ring and he listened to his aunt open the front door, curse loudly and slam the front door shut. His ears then followed the sound of her footsteps as she ascended the stairs and walked toward his bedroom door. He quickly turned out his light, pretending to be asleep. Aunt Rae opened the door a crack, waited for a few seconds and then closed the door. Bash exhaled.

Now, hours later, Bash laid on his back with his ankles crossed and arms behind his head. He was completely dressed and even wore his tennis shoes. He could feel the fifty dollar bill rolled up and stuffed in his sock. He never trusted pockets and his wallet was too bulky. He hoped Gio wouldn't mind a sweaty rolled-up bill. Money was money, after all. He also hoped Gio would show up like he promised. Only time would tell. Speaking of, Bash glanced at the clock sitting on the nightstand. He could barely contain his excitement. One more hour to go before supernatural activity reached its peak.

CHAPTER TWENTY ONE

Rae finished her two hundredth logo design and sent off the new batch of twenty to the New York client. After waiting a few minutes, her mailbox remained empty and she shut down the computer in anguish. She knew the New Yorker didn't like any of the logos and it was back to square one. Shuffling to the front door, she peered through the window. A small part of her hoped to see Tiny. He and his puzzling ways were beginning to grow on her. The whole street, however, was vacant. No Tiny. And no Orangutan Man sitting in a Ford. She locked the door, futzed with the alarm system until it fizzled, moved the chair in front of the door and turned.

The doorbell rang.

Rae spun around and her hands moved quickly, pushing the chair and turning the lock. Swinging the door open, she was too late; the doorbell ditcher was gone. She hollered a profanity into the night, slammed the door and relocked it. Staring at the alarm system, she again tried to set it, but was zapped. Tired, she shoved the chair against the door and trudged upstairs, checking on Bash briefly before collapsing on her bed. She felt guilty about abandoning him this whole evening for work and flopped onto her stomach. She would have to make it up to him somehow. Pulling her phone from her back pocket, she deliberated her next move and then began searching for information on Honey Ward.

According to the first article on the internet, Honey Ward was the only child of Ryan and Laura Ward. Ryan ran his own laser tag business with the help of his wife, Laura, and they were very successful at it. The article described Honey as a social and popular thirteen-year old. She played the piano and had recently been elected as her class president. Her favorite movie was *The Wizard of Oz*, prompting her to name her puppy after Dorothy's dog, Toto.

Rae then searched for another article and found a more recent one written about a month ago. In this article, the reporter interviewed the homicide detective assigned to this case from the beginning. His name was Detective Nelson and he didn't say much. It was a short article.

The third article dated back to one year ago and was more interesting. It talked about how the family of Honey Ward seemed to be cursed. After Honey disappeared, the laser tag business fell into financial ruin, leading Ryan into depression. Laura divorced him and moved to the west. Ryan ended up fleeing to the east as the bank foreclosed on their historic Victorian manor.

Rolling onto her back, Rae began a new search about The Birch Grove Banshee. Bash was right. The story was legendary, according to one of the goofiest websites Rae ever saw. While scanning the information, Rae chuckled at all the misspelled words and incorrect use of punctuation. It was written by a young author named Jimbo. Just as she decided to leave this mockery of a website, the last paragraph caught her attention. Jimbo mentioned other legendary hauntings in the area and listed the top five. As luck would have it, Travis's manor was listed as number four and being haunted by none other than Honey Ward who, according to Jimbo, was taken by The Birch Grove Banshee.

Chuckling, Rae ended her search and then studied her guest bedroom. Spooky thoughts suddenly invaded her mind. Thoughts like, *was this Honey's room? What if Honey was still here? Like in the closet? Or under the bed?* Still wearing her street clothes, she slipped underneath the covers, pulling them up to her nose.

Grasping her phone, she wondered about calling someone. Danny? Hell no. Clare? *Hell* no. Stone? Her cheeks flushed.

A decision was made. Instead of calling someone, Rae used her phone to search YouTube for soothing sounds of keyboarding. She dimmed the lamp on the nightstand, telling herself that ghosts didn't exist. Suddenly, she widened her eyes at the thought of Bash. She had to make sure that he didn't find out about this house possibly being haunted by Honey Ward. That would be disastrous. Fortunately, he didn't seem the least bit interested in Honey Ward and seemed to only be fixated on the banshee.

Breathing deeply, she listened to the relaxing computer keys as they lightly tapped along and Rae smiled as a new thought struck her. Even though some things were out of her control, right now, both she and Bash were safe in their beds and all would be well. And it really would be, at least for her.

• • •

Bash stood in Travis's backyard, facing the birch trees and staring into the blackness. His left hand grasped his ghost hunting case tightly by the handle while his right hand held a flashlight. Around his neck hung his instant camera and his cell phone was stuffed in his back pocket. He was at the meeting spot, just like Gio instructed, but where was Gio? The plan was to meet here at three. That was why Gio held up three fingers. Bash made sure to arrive on time, which was ten minutes ago. Then he heard a footstep on his right and Gio emerged from the night's darkness.

"You got the money?" Gio asked while eyeing Bash. "Why are you carrying a briefcase?"

Bash handed over the emergency fifty dollar bill that his mother gave to him and explained, "This is my case for all of my paranormal equipment. I'm interested in the science of the paranormal and this stuff will help me obtain proof of the supernatural."

"So, you want to catch a ghost?"

Bash shook his head. "No. I want to catch a banshee."

"Ghost. Banshee. Whatever. You never told me why."

Bash lowered his voice. "I think the banshee is responsible for the disappearance of Honey Ward. Did you know her?"

Gio stood motionless. Finally, he replied, "No, man, not at all." He turned on a flashlight the size of a pen. "Okay, let's do this."

"Awesome." Bash flicked on his flashlight. It was the size of a small utility box. "And you know the way for sure?"

"I've seen the banshee's house a few times. It's down this trail." Gio answered.

Bash couldn't see a trail. Gio moved in front of him and stood on the edge of Travis's yard and the woods. He pushed some branches to the side, revealing a narrow footpath.

Aiming his flashlight at Bash, Gio said, "Stay close."

Bash nodded and stepped into the trees' shadows. With the branches closing in behind him, the beam of his flashlight struggled to light the way. He strained to hear ominous sounds, but only heard the crunching of dead leaves and the breaking of twigs underneath his feet. Otherwise, it was silent. The trees didn't even dare rustle their foliage. It was like they were holding their breath.

Worse than the quiet was the darkness. Bash couldn't see his own body and had to aim his light directly on Gio at all times in order to see where he was going. Gio, however, moved with ease, scampering quickly along the trail.

"How long have you lived around here?" Bash asked Gio in a whisper.

"All my life," Gio whispered back. "I used to play in these woods with my friends."

Bash asked, "Really? Were you here last night? Dancing? And playing a fiddle?"

Gio answered, "What? Are you high, man? I never come into these woods. Not after that time I saw the banshee. She stood by the cliff. Her back to me."

"There's a cliff?" Bash became uneasy. He didn't like unexpected drops. Ever since his aunt pressured him into riding The Scorpion's Tail with the two hundred foot hill descending below ground at a very high speed, he avoided drops. And cliffs. "Is it a big cliff?"

"Maybe about twenty feet? There are big rocks on the bottom that would kill you." Gio lowered his voice even more. "Sometimes, I feel like the banshee was trying to keep me away from the cliff. Like she was protecting me. But that's nuts, right? Aren't banshees evil?"

"What gave you the impression that it really was the banshee?"

Bash felt Gio next to him. They stopped walking and stood together in the darkness. Gio said, "Her long white hair was blowing. Plus, she wailed. What else do banshees do? Right?"

Curious, Bash asked, "When was this?"

"Two years ago when I was thirteen."

"Really? That's when Honey Ward went missing."

Gio started walking again. "I don't know anything about that. All I know is these woods give me the creeps. Come on, let's go."

"Wait, Gio." Bash stopped him. "Then why are you helping me tonight?"

"Simple," Gio said. "I need the money. "

Bash would have nodded in understanding, however, his attention suddenly switched from Gio to his own forearms where all of his hair stood up. And then his attention switched again from his forearms to the hot breath, which was warming the back of his neck. Bash saw the whites of Gio's eyes grow in alarm as they popped open in pure terror.

CHAPTER TWENTY TWO

With his flashlight still in hand, Bash swiftly turned and felt the slimy soft texture of a tongue touch his chin. It slowly moved up his face to the top of his head and right back down again. The stench of dog chow overwhelmed him. Corn gluten meal mixed with some poultry-by-product and then added to animal slime. Tiny's tongue lathered Bash's entire face with that concoction, causing a smile to spread from one wet ear to the other.

Bash returned his large furry friend's greeting by wrapping his arms around Tiny's thick neck. He squeezed it gently. "Thank God it's you."

Tiny nodded and yipped. Then he cocked his head to the left and nodded it toward the other boy.

"This is Gio," Bash said to Tiny. "He's helping me find the banshee's house." Tiny shook his head and nodded it toward the direction of Travis's manor. Sensing Tiny's apprehension, Bash explained, "I have to do this. In the name of Science of the Paranormal."

Tiny only arfed.

Gio chuckled. "It's like your dog can understand you. What's his name?"

"Tiny and he's not my dog. He belongs to my aunt's boss. We're just watching his house and dog for the guy."

A low growl from Tiny's throat interrupted this quick explanation. Suddenly, he broke out in multiple loud barks.

Bash asked worriedly, "What is it?" He searched the darkness for an intruder. Possibly a banshee. He had the feeling of being surrounded by a whole clan of them.

Remaining on the trail, the large dog transfixed his eyes on something behind Gio. Or were they on Gio? Tiny opened his mouth to unload another round of frenzied barks, but abruptly closed it. A chipmunk scurried past them. After two quick head shakes, a satisfied-looking Tiny licked his lips and began panting happily.

Gio said to Bash, "We should keep moving."

As the three of them carefully meandered down the footpath, the empty night sky acted as a veil. No stars. No clouds. Even the moon left. The visibility was so low that Bash had to rely more on his sense of touch than his flashlight while trying desperately to follow Gio. Tiny stayed at his side, but Gio walked farther ahead.

Bash heard a distant rushing sound of waves. Were they near the cliff? He whispered to his fast-footed guide, "Gio?"

No answer.

Bash froze. He strained to hear Gio's footsteps ahead of him, but only heard Tiny's breathing. With his flashlight, he scanned the area for Gio. After a few panoramic swipes, he found his friend's dark shape, standing to his right and a few steps in front of him.

"Gio?" Bash whispered a little louder.

Still, no answer. Gio only remained on that spot. His torso was stiff, however, and his head awkwardly tilted to the left, looking unnatural.

Bash took one step closer to Gio and Tiny whimpered. "It's okay," he said to his furry sidekick and slowly approached his guide who was obviously waiting.

However, as he drew near, the brand new batteries in his flashlight died. Bash shook it vigorously and the beam of light stuttered once before completely ceasing. Tiny whined and Bash reached into the darkness for Tiny, but flinched when a light breeze brushed his cheek. The trees then swayed slowly and the sound of the rustling leaves softened as a raucous buzz of laughter grew. And music? It reminded Bash of the same gypsy music from the other night.

Swallowing hard, Bash inched closer to where he last saw Gio, extending his own arm and feeling the darkness with his fingertips for Gio's shoulder. He had to be close to him, but felt nothing. He stretched a little more and Tiny gave a low grumble. Bash leaned into his stretch, telling himself that something didn't seem right. It didn't feel right.

Tiny growled, but Bash couldn't react. A hand abruptly grabbed his shoulder as another hand forcefully covered his mouth. He didn't have a chance to scream.

▪ ▪ ▪

It was a quarter past three and the paintballers left The Rail an hour ago. That party was almost completely out of control. They even outdrank Sally. Now, all the chairs rested on top of the tables and all the glasses were clean. The Rail was officially closed.

After making sure that Sally settled herself safely in the backseat of another Uber driver's car, Stone walked to his own red Dodge. He now sat behind the steering wheel, contemplating the quickest route to Rachel. Instinctively knowing where her boss's manor existed, he debated about taking the scenic lakeshore road or heading through the seedy, but speedy, part of downtown. His plan was to guard Rachel from his car overnight. She would never know that he was there and he would feel better knowing that he was. He made up his mind to take the lakeshore route and turned the key. Instead of pulling onto the road though, he inhaled quickly and couldn't release. He felt his eyes bulge as he gripped the wheel. Wanting to scream, it felt like someone covered his mouth with a hand and he couldn't utter a single sound.

What was happening to him? A stroke? A heart attack?

Slowly, the whole paralyzing sensation began to fade, leaving him with such weakness that his head dropped onto the steering wheel. Sitting in bewilderment, his heart stuttered. Apparently, it was just as confused as his brain. He closed his eyes and tried to go to his happy place, but he didn't really have a happy place. So, he concentrated on the only happy face he knew. Not Zalen's. It was Rachel's face.

He pictured her lips, her nose, her hair. Just when her full portrait formed in his mind, Bash's image edged out Rachel's face and monopolized the area. Stone mentally pushed Bash's face out of the way and focused on Rachel's eyes, except her eyes suddenly became Bash's eyes. What was going on?

Stone tried one more time with Rachel. He focused on the warmth he felt when he held her in his arms. He thought about the way she looked at him and the way she dipped a fry into Bash's malt without his knowledge. It was working. A smile formed in the corner of Stone's mouth. He remembered how she used to cup his face with her hands when they were kids. It always consoled him during those psychic attacks or what she always thought were panic attacks. He never corrected her. And now, he could feel the weight of her hands on his face. Her thumbs caressed his skin, calming him. He opened his eyes, expecting to see that warm smile.

He saw Bash instead, standing in front of the car. His arm reached out for Stone as his mouth gaped open in horror. Fright filled the boy's eyes and Stone's veins, but only for a split second. Then in a blink, he was gone. Poof. Like magic.

Forgetting all about the lakeshore, he punched the accelerator and raced downtown. He knew exactly how to find her boss's house. As soon as Rachel said Victorian manor earlier at dinner, it was all too familiar. The wrap-around porch. The tower. He somehow knew exactly what the address was and fifteen minutes later, he now stood, facing the foreboding structure.

The dark manor stared back at him. Stone closed his eyes and cleared his mind. His urge was to turn away from the home and walk toward the woods. Following his instincts, he stepped onto the path and walked until he felt the urge to stop. Peering into the blackness, the trees suddenly came to life, violently bending and rocking insanely in the wind. And, just like in his vision, he heard that far away, familiar sound of a dog barking. Snapping his head to his right, he waited expectantly for the ghost girl to appear. The white mist formed among the angry trees and she eventually materialized, beckoning him to enter. His feet cemented themselves on the pavement where he felt safe.

As they stared at each other while the world twisted around them, he did not feel fear, but sadness. With her brown eyes imploring him to step closer, she slowly raised her arm, pointing into the woods. He couldn't do it though. Stone wasn't there to help her. He was there to help Bash. Shaking his head at the apparition, he refused to budge. She sadly turned away, exposing her large head wound. Walking into the woods, her image dissolved a little more with every step.

Once the girl vanished, Stone breathed in deeply and roared as loudly as a state quarterback could, "Bash! It's Stone! Get out of there!"

The wind immediately settled, allowing the birch trees to become still and other sounds to echo, like a dog wildly barking, a large bird flapping its wings and, finally, the sound of fast footsteps, advancing.

CHAPTER TWENTY THREE

Bash pushed Gio's hand off his mouth and wiggled his shoulder from Gio's firm grasp. He shrieked, "Don't grab me like that!" He heard Tiny woof angrily in agreement.

Gio quickly shushed him. "We're here," he said, "but we have to be very quiet." He took Bash by the wrist and led him down a stone pathway. The music and raucous voices heightened.

Bash stuck close to Gio who moved stealthily around the tall slender bushes in what Bash suspected was the banshee's front yard. Gio's flashlight pen still worked, giving small glimpses of the strangely pruned shrubbery. They were all sculpted to look like people and they all stood side by side, leading to the banshee's front door.

Tiny whined and Gio flashed his light in Bash's face. "Keep him quiet."

On the outside, the house was small, from the little Bash could actually see. Low and broad, the single-story building had a pitched gabled roof and a large chimney plunked on top.

On the inside, the house seemed hollow. Dead. No lights anywhere. But there was a heart beating behind the house. Bash could see strobing lights in a clearing of the trees. His feet even vibrated from a strong pulsing bass. Floating above the low notes was the high strumming of fiddles and a ukulele and he heard a female's voice crooning along like someone in a trance.

Tiny looked over his shoulder. His two front paws anxiously scratched at the ground. Bash turned his head in the same direction as Tiny and saw the kind of blackness that swallowed up people whole before eating their souls. He gulped.

Gio tugged on Bash's wrist. Crouching to the ground, they scrambled on their hands and knees to the back of the house. Tiny trailed behind and lay down on his stomach by some bushes just like the two boys. All three peered at the scene in front of them, trying to figure out what was happening.

Bash counted seven people. They all wore dark robes and tribal-looking masks. The singer wore an orange one with black markings around the mouth and eyes. Yellow strips of paper stuck to the top, giving her the appearance of having blonde spiked-up hair. She stood on a boulder, singing and strumming the ukulele. Four others wore similar masks, just other color variations and danced together in a circle around a blazing fire. Two of them played fiddles while the other two twirled each other and sometimes fell over each other. All were laughing hysterically in a broken shrilling kind of cackle.

Another larger fellow wore a blue mask with orange paper ringlets. He remained in a patio chair, plucking a bass guitar. Every now and then, he'd stop to reach into his shirt pocket. After partially lifting his mask to expose his chin, he'd pop something small and round into his mouth. Then he'd lower the mask over his chin again. Although his feet never moved to the groove of the music, he dripped with sweat.

The seventh participant was a hooded figure and the most mysterious-looking one of the bunch. Round and graceful, Bash felt this person was a woman by the way she flitted around the perimeter, observing and encouraging others to indulge in frivolity. She wore a green robe that looked velvety and heavy, yet flowed freely. Bash watched her closely. She was definitely the host of this shindig, making sure everyone was well taken care of by refilling their glasses with a red liquid. Her movements were calm and engaging, which was in complete contrast to her mask. It was light gray with frenzied lines scribbled all over it and red colored paper hair was bent in a zigzag way, making her look crazed.

All three spies were speechless. The wet ground began to soak through Bash's shirt and he involuntarily shivered. Tiny's nose nudged the side of Bash's head as if to say that enough was enough. Bash nodded. Something in the back of his mind nagged at him to go. At the same time, however, he wanted proof.

Bash elbowed Gio. "Which one's the banshee?"

"They all are." Gio shook his head. "This was a mistake. We shouldn't be here. The banshees are doing some kind of ritual dance. We need to get out of here before they see us." He looked at Bash very seriously and said, "I think I just got us in a bad situation."

He belly-crawled away from the clearing, motioning Bash to follow.

Bash didn't. He stayed right there, mesmerized by the seven banshees as they danced and laughed the night away. Slowly, he raised his instant camera that looped around his neck.

Tiny softly woofed.

"Just a second," he said to Tiny who was already on all four paws, prancing nervously.

Bash brought the camera to his face, carefully aimed it at the group and gently pressed the button. An unexpected bright light flashed, illuminating the dark space around Bash and revealing his hiding place. He gulped at his mistake and then everything stopped in a finger snap. The music ended. There were no more singing voices and no more amusing shrieks. Most unsettling, there was no more movement. Everyone froze, including the graceful host. They all turned to stone like a spell. Then without any warning, each of the seven masked people snapped their heads toward Bash right before the strobe lights cut and the fire died, leaving Bash and Tiny in what felt like a black hole.

The heart of the woods stopped beating in an instant. The same instant it took for Bash to snap that picture. The same instant it took for Bash's heart to stop beating as well. Bash sprang to his feet, grabbed his case and took off.

With arms full, Bash ran without the control of his legs, or his mind, for that matter. Not able to find the trail, he just ran. Probably in circles. In blind, hysterical circles. He knew the banshees saw him. After all, they looked straight at him. Did they know that he was there all along? Who was watching who exactly?

His burning chest forced Bash to slow to a walk. He was in the middle of the woods. Looking behind him with wide eyes, he saw only the silhouettes of the trees swaying wildly. A strong wind encircled him, rustling the leaves all around him. He was overtaken by fear and fell limply to the ground. Where was Gio? Where was Tiny? The banshees obviously took them and now they searched the forest for him.

The jig was up. No one would ever see him again. He was only to live a life of twelve years. The real kicker came when he realized that his hands only held the case and the camera. The instant photograph, the proof, was gone. Thumping his head with the case, he closed his eyes and readied himself for surrendering. He was to become another victim of The Birch Grove Banshee.

As the strong wind persisted, an unexpected paw the size of a ping-pong paddle patted the top of his head. Bash raised his face, exclaiming, "Tiny!" He exhaled a long breath that he didn't even know he held. "You're safe!"

Tiny nodded and howled something that sounded like, "Let's go!" To speed things along, Tiny nuzzled his huge dome underneath Bash's arm and began pushing him upward with his nose. Upon standing, Bash picked up his flashlight, prayed for some good luck and turned it on. The shining beam of light brought tears to Bash's eyes. For the next few minutes, they hiked through the forest with the wind blowing at their backs. Bash followed Tiny, putting his faith into Tiny's dog nose intuition, but he felt uneasy.

If only he recognized a familiar tree or heard a familiar sound to signal that they were headed in the right direction. Suddenly, Tiny stopped with the tips of his ears pointing straight up to the night sky. Bash gasped when he heard it too.

"Bash! It's Stone! Get out of there!"

The trees instantly stopped swaying, but Tiny barked threateningly. Bash jumped when a stick cracked loudly on his left. Something moved behind a tree. It was a wide shape of someone. Bash then heard strenuous huffing. The smell of nicotine wafted underneath Bash's nostrils. Who would be smoking in the middle of these woods this early in the morning?

"Let me go!" Gio's cry interrupted Bash's thoughts. Tiny looked at Bash and they both bolted toward Gio in hopes of saving him from the knobby grips of the banshee.

■ ■ ■

The fast-approaching footsteps belonged to a teenager who frantically slingshotted out of the woods, but Stone managed to grab the boy's wrist as he passed by him.

"Let me go!" the boy yelled while trying to twist out of Stone's vice grip.

Stone held on and asked the young teenager, "Where's Bash?"

Before the boy could answer, a large dog exploded from two birch trees like an iron ball out of a cannon. He startled Stone so much that he lost his grip, releasing his hostage into the night. Bash then stepped out of the woods, holding a briefcase, and jogged tiredly up to Stone. Bending over, Bash touched the ground with his fingertips as the large dog sat down next to him. Stone noticed that Bash trembled. He asked him, "Are you okay? Did that kid hurt you?"

Bash straightened slowly. "Gio? Oh no. He's a friend." Bash cleared his throat. "I'm fine. Nothing's going on here. We're just out for a stroll. No big deal. Don't tell my aunt."

Stone narrowed his eyes at Bash and pointed at the briefcase. "What do you have there?"

Bash glanced down at his hand and explained, "This is my paranormal investigative equipment and nothing worth talking about. My aunt doesn't need to know about this. Don't tell her." The dog shook his head and Bash cleared his throat again. Looking at Stone, he asked, "So, what're you doing here?"

Stone also cleared his throat. "I just came over to see how you and Rachel were doing."

"At this hour?" Bash and Tiny cocked their heads to the left. "That makes no sense."

Stone tilted his head too. "Neither does your story about being out for a stroll." He smirked. "I think you should tell me what you're up to, or we could wake your aunt."

Bash sighed and looked behind him before explaining. "Have you ever heard of The Birch Grove Banshee?"

Stone nodded. "Yes, it's an urban legend that people like to tell. It's not true."

Bash shook his head at Stone. "You're wrong. I saw her and her banshee family." The dog whined as Bash continued, "There are seven of them and they almost ate me, Tiny and Gio."

Stone smiled while looking at the dog. "So, you're the manatee with four legs and big saucer ears?" Tiny raised his paw for a shake. Stone gently accepted the paw that enveloped his own hand. "You're the biggest dog I ever saw."

"He's awesome," Bash said. "Anyway, I had a photo of the banshees, but lost it, which sucks. You have no idea what I went through to get that proof. I almost *died*." Tiny nodded.

Stone said, "You still might die. Your aunt will kill you for sneaking out."

Bash shook his head. "How will she know? If you tell her, she's going to wonder why you showed up in the first place. And then she'll start thinking. She'll think that either you believe Zalen about her being in trouble or that you're an empath too. Do you want that?"

Shit, Stone thought. Who was this kid? Stuffing his hands in his jeans pockets, he tried to sound casual. "I'm not an empath or a psychic or anything."

Bash and Tiny looked at each other. Then they both looked at Stone. "You're a psychic?"

Stone felt warm. "No, I'm just a bar owner. Look, I only wanted to check on your aunt. That's all. No big deal."

Tiny whined as Bash chuckled softly. "Okay, psychic, if my aunt finds out that you are *checking* on her, she'll kill you."

Stone groaned. "First, I'm not a psychic. Second, how will she know?"

The three of them quietly studied each other. Finally, Bash stuck out his hand and said to Stone, "I got your back, if you got mine." Smiling, Stone shook Bash's hand and then they both shook Tiny's paw.

"Let's get you two home," Stone said.

Before departing, Bash glanced behind him, peering into the woods. Leaning toward Stone, he asked, "Did you see anyone walk into the forest for a smoke?"

Stone raised his eyebrows. "No. Is someone seriously smoking in there *now*?" He squinted into the forest and saw nothing.

Bash shrugged. "Can fear make you see things that aren't really there?"

Stone nodded. "It's possible."

Bash looked at Stone. "Maybe you should stay until morning? There's a great couch you can sleep on." Tiny woofed in agreement as Bash quickly added, "Just sneak out before my aunt wakes up or you know what'll happen."

Stone grinned. "Yep. She'll kill me."

CHAPTER TWENTY FOUR

Rae startled herself awake. She thought she heard the front door close and footsteps on the front porch. Did Honey Ward finally leave? Or was it that dog? She grabbed her phone off the nightstand and her eyebrows raised at the realization of the time. It was a little past eight in the morning, which meant that the dog never rang the doorbell at five. Rolling out of bed, she peeked out the middle window and saw nothing out of the ordinary. As she rubbed the sleep out of her eyes, she realized that she probably imagined those sounds. What she needed now was a jog. After finding her arm strap and in-ear headphones, she quickly changed into her running gear before crossing the hallway to check on Bash. To her surprise, the dog was sleeping soundly next to him. Baffled, she quietly closed the bedroom door.

She trotted downstairs while fastening the arm strap on her upper arm. As she approached the front door, she paused after noticing that the chair had been pushed to the side and the front door was unlocked. However, the alarm system was set. But how? Did Bash do this? Maybe he let Tiny in this morning and figured out the alarm system? Yeah, she told herself, that could make sense.

Her stomach growled. Wanting a small bite to eat before her run, she headed to the kitchen while salivating over a banana and yogurt when the doorbell suddenly rang. She ran and slid across the floor, hoping to catch the doorbell ditcher. After fumbling with the alarm system, she opened the door and found Maeve standing on the porch. Rae invited her into the foyer.

Maeve was short in stature and round. Rae towered over her, which actually made Rae quite uncomfortable. She was used to looking up and it felt very unnatural to tilt her chin down. Despite Maeve's tiny appearance, her presence demanded attention and she looked very striking in her black floor-length cotton dress and long green robe.

Gazing past Rae, Maeve's black eyes twinkled merrily as she admired her own reflection. "What a beautiful mirror." Returning her attention to Rae, she said, "I can't stay. I must get ready for tonight. My only intention was to quickly give this to you." She handed Rae an envelope, just as Bash and Tiny trotted down the stairs.

Maeve had a classy way of talking. There was a lilt to it, almost southern and almost English. Really, it was neither. It was just how Maeve talked. She gave Bash a good once-over while saying, "You look like you had quite a night."

Bash raised his eyebrows. "You would know."

"What?" Rae asked him.

Bash quickly replied, "Nothing." He pointed to the envelope. "What's that?"

As Rae opened the invitation, Maeve explained. "I'm inviting you to a meeting held tonight by The Crafters at my house. That's what we call ourselves. We're really just some friends who get together to do arts and crafts and since you have a background in art, I thought you'd like to come."

Bash nodded disbelievingly. "And you call yourselves The Crafters. Because of art. Not because of witchcraft. That's a nice cover-up."

Maeve eyed Bash and said to Rae, "There's a trail along the cliffside through the woods that you can walk from this backyard all the way to my place. I drew a map to show you."

Rae felt her mouth drop open. "Whoa. *You* live in the *woods*?"

"Of course. It's very peaceful. Now, like I said, I must get ready. There are a lot of preparations to do. Any questions before I leave?"

Bash crossed his arms. "I have one. Are you The Birch Grove Banshee? Be honest."

Rae moaned, but Maeve laughed. "I'm worse than a banshee. I'm a retired elementary art teacher."

Bash mumbled, "That is worse."

With a gleam in her eye, Maeve said, "Everyone in The Crafters loves art. We meet. Have snacks and drinks. Then we make art. Last night, we made traditional African masks out of construction paper."

"*That's* what you were doing? At three in the morning?" Bash rolled his eyes.

Rae gave her nephew a sideways glance. "What are you talking about?"

Maeve said to Bash, "Yes, that's what we were doing. We were all having a splendid time too, until your peeping face scared the life out of us." She dug into the front pocket of her cotton dress, pulled out an instant photograph and handed it to Bash. "I believe that you dropped this. In a hurry too, I might add."

Rae snatched the picture from Bash, which showed seven fuzzy white shapes against a black background. She gasped at him. "You peeped on them? At three o'clock in the morning? And took a terrible picture of them?"

Bash's mouth was now agape. He said to Maeve, "*I* scared the life out of *you?* How can one kid scare seven banshees who can put out a blazing fire in an instant?"

Maeve chuckled while speaking to Rae, "He certainly has a wonderful imagination." She then reached for Bash and tenderly squeezed his forearm. "You be careful now. After all, sneaking around people's homes in the middle of the night can be dangerous. You never know what terrible harm is out there, waiting to get you." She looked at Rae. "So, what do you say?"

"Well, I think I should ground him, but he is just a kid."

Maeve shook her head. "No, dear. I'm talking about the party."

"Oh." Rae smiled. "I'd love to come."

"Great." Maeve clasped her hands together. "I'll be expecting you around eight. Just follow the map, and the trail will end at my home." Suddenly, her arms engulfed Rae. "Welcome to The Crafters. I can't wait to tell the others. They're all going to love you."

Rae forced a smile. "Who are they?"

Maeve glowed with excitement. "Other retired educators."

"Can I come?" Bash asked.

Maeve's eyes danced when she looked at Bash. "Children aren't allowed." Turning back to Rae, she said, "Now, we all bring a snack and remember to B.Y.O.B."

Rae asked, "Bring my own *beer*?"

Maeve clarified to Rae while smiling slyly at Bash. "No, dear, bring your own *brew*." She winked at him before turning to waltz through the front door and descend the porch steps. As she glided down the sidewalk, the wind blew at Maeve's back, causing her long white hair to come to life. The strands of silky curls tapped playfully at her shoulders and the long green robe flapped behind her, making her seem as though she were floating.

■ ■ ■

The oversized sofa with the thick, comfy cushions should have lulled Stone to a blissful slumber, but the image of Bash screaming unsettled him. Instead, he watched the sun rise and read Travis's house manual, learning the code for the security system. Around eight, he decided to leave before Rachel caught him in her boss's home, making certain to set the house alarm since he could not lock the door.

Now hunched over the bar, Stone leaned on his elbows while desperately yearning for a cup of coffee after foolishly swearing off the caffeine. He thought it was shifting his brain into overdrive and causing these bizarre nightmares, visions, whatevers to strengthen. So, he decided to cut back. It couldn't be too hard, right?

Now, an hour later, he sweated from withdrawal. Maybe just one small cup of coffee? No, he told himself. Lately, the more caffeine he ingested, the more his hands shook. He instead imagined that the tall glass of chocolate milk staring at him from his grasp was the same as a coffee milkshake. It didn't work, but he held strong, just like the way he preferred his coffee.

Sighing, he placed his empty chocolate milk glass in the sink, cradled his head with his folded arms and closed his eyes for a quick second. In that quick second, he allowed his mind to wander to Rachel again. He instantly smiled as he remembered Rachel's laugh. It was so bubbly and infectious, but not in a bad way where an antibiotic was needed. It was infectious in a very good way, warming his heart. Inhaling, he could almost smell her naturally fresh aroma. She always reminded him of clean linen or a recent rainfall of lavender leaves or coconut shavings or butterscotch drops.

Butterscotch? Stone's eyes snapped open and bright white teeth flashed before him. Startled, he stood straight up and stammered, "What the hell, Zalen?"

"Hi, Stone," Zalen greeted cheerfully. "How are you?"

"How did you get in? I locked the door."

"Actually, it's your lucky day. You forgot to lock it." Zalen stood before Stone. One hand held onto a handle attached to an upright suitcase with wheels while the other hand grasped a piece of paper.

Stone fixated on Zalen's clothes. His patterned Dashiki shirt was a brilliant blue with yellow and brown embroidery at the neckline and cuffs. It was just a little too tight and a little too short, unfortunately revealing his too small shorts. Unknowingly, Zalen was on the cusp of looking obscene.

With a big smile, Zalen asked, "Would you do a favor for me?"

Stone raised his eyebrows. "Are you wearing spandex?"

"I have no time for chit-chat, my friend. We'll have to catch up when I return."

Stone's tone lightened. "You're leaving?"

"Yes. Since I fulfilled my obligation to help you find Rae, and I know that you will now help her because you finally *feel* it's the right thing to do, I decided to go to South Africa." His smile brightened. "Did you know that the world's first heart transplant was in South Africa?"

"How long will you be gone?"

"I'm not going for a heart transplant, so don't worry. I'll actually be teaching and assisting in a primary school for children with special needs."

"In those shorts? For how long?"

"Since I'm a special education teacher and of African descent, this is a great way for me to give back to the special education community in South Africa." He dazzled joyfully.

"That's very kind of you," Stone spoke sincerely. "For how long?"

"Six weeks. Approximately. My plane leaves in three hours." He waved the paper, showing Stone his printed ticket.

Stone also dazzled joyfully now. "Do you need me to drive you to the airport?"

"Oh, no, I have an airport taxi picking me up here in a few minutes. My favor involves you checking on my apartment from time to time. You know, doing the mail thing."

Thinking it over, Stone said, "Where do you live again?"

"Nearby. It won't be out of your way at all."

Stone studied his beaming friend and eventually shrugged. "Sure, why not?"

Zalen was beyond beaming now. His face looked like it could blast off his skull from pure joy and excitement. "Thanks, Stone, I'll bring something special back for you from my African travels."

Fearful of what special thing Zalen could bring back from a country known for contagious diseases, Stone shrieked, "No, don't!"

Zalen didn't hear Stone's protests. The arrival of a honking taxi distracted him to the point where he immediately took off. Stone dashed after him and watched as Zalen gave his luggage to the driver who was giving the black spandex shorts a good once-over. Zalen raised his one leg to step inside the car and kept the other foot on the ground, unconsciously presenting his goods like a showpiece. There was such detail that Stone instantly knew Zalen only wore the spandex and no underwear. The driver also noticed, shielded his eyes and then dove for cover behind the steering wheel.

Zalen said, "Oh, man, I'm going to miss our talks. Now, here." He handed Stone an envelope. "This is a key to my apartment, my address and the name of *my* lawyer, if you should ever need a good one."

Stone tucked the envelope in his back pocket as Zalen seated himself comfortably in the backseat. The taxi varoomed down the road, carrying Zalen to the airport where he would soon be flying to a whole different continent separate from The United States. For six weeks approximately. And Stone dazzled again.

CHAPTER TWENTY FIVE

Rae, Bash and Tiny retreated to the kitchen. Bash patted Tiny's large dome as he fell onto a chair and Tiny collapsed on the floor by his feet. "Are you really going to the party, Aunt Rae? What I saw last night was not my wonderful imagination. It was strange and real."

While studying the invitation, she said, "You have to admit that this sounds intriguing."

Bash shrugged. "Swimming sounds more intriguing."

Rae frowned. "I'm surprised. You love investigating the unknown. What gives?"

Bash shrugged again. "Nothing gives."

Sensing a strange phenomenon, Rae asked, "Are you seriously *scared* about this?"

Glaring, Bash protested. "Absolutely not." He and Tiny looked at each other briefly before Bash said, "Just be careful of the cliff. And if you could do me a favor and find out if Maeve smokes, that would be great too."

Rae said, "What are you talking about?"

Glancing at the ground, he said, "There was someone smoking in the woods this morning. I think it was Maeve."

Rae smiled. "A smoking banshee? How entertaining."

Tiny groaned and Bash slumped over the table, saying, "Fine. Whatever. But just so you know, my mom and dad won't like to hear that you're leaving me alone to go to a party."

Shifting her stance, Rae said, "I won't be gone for long."

"Still." Bash sat up and smirked. "I'll be alone. All alone."

Rae pointed to the large panting dog. "You have him. What more do you need?"

"Stone," Bash said matter-of-factly.

Confused, Rae asked, "Why him?"

"He's cool. Plus, he'll be good back-up, just in case I have to save you."

Rae roared with laughter. "Fine. Whatever. I'll give you his number and *you* can call him later." She then reached for a box of pancake mix and presented it to Bash and Tiny like a game show model. "How about some pancakes?" Both Bash and Tiny nodded right before the doorbell rang. Rae squealed, dropped the box and raced to the front door in record time. Swinging the door open, she hollered, "Gotcha, doorbell ditcher!"

A chubby man, wearing a white collared shirt with a conservative tie, gray trousers and black Oxford shoes, stood on the porch. "Just call me Howie." He yawned. "You must be Rae, Danny's little sister. It's nice to finally meet you. I've heard stories about you for the past fifteen years. Danny told me about how you escaped from a band of French gypsies, beat off ferocious guard dogs in a Picasso museum, and then almost fell off the Eiffel Tower. All on the same day."

Rae sighed. "The wind was very strong in Paris."

Bash joined them. "Hey, Officer Howie, what're you doing here?"

"Your mom asked me to do a welfare check on the both of you." He gave Rae an apologetic look. "You both look good. If you'll excuse me, I must go to my bank job."

Rae stopped him. "I thought you were a cop?"

Howie explained, "I'm a part-time cop on the weekends. During the week, I work as an IT Security Manager at a bank." Glancing at his watch, he said, "It was nice meeting you."

Rae stopped him again. "Actually, if you have a few minutes, I was wondering if I could pick your brain about something."

Howie chortled. "I don't have much brain left for picking."

Rae spoke quickly, "It shouldn't take long. Do you like coffee? I can make you a cup."

"Cups."

"Of course. How about pancakes? Would you like some?"

Howie said seriously, "It's a little past nine now and I need to be to work by ten. How fast can you make a stack?"

"Really fast."

"Faster than you can open doors?"

Rae smiled and nodded.

Flying around the kitchen, Rae shamed any tire changer on a pit crew with her speedy pancake-making ability. Soon, everyone enjoyed their own stack of five, dripping with butter and syrup. Tiny sat next to the table, watching the others eat while licking his chops. Rae smiled and gave the dog one of her own. After pouring more coffee into Howie's large cup, she said, "There are some strange things happening around here. For starters, I think a man who strongly resembles an orangutan and drives a black Ford is following me."

Howie dwarfed the kitchen chair on which he sat. His bear arms were crossed and resting on his big belly. With short grayish hair and a bristly goatee, he peered at Rae with exhausted eyes. "You're picking my brain about a Ford-driving orangutan?"

Bash interjected, "Wait til you hear about the banshee, Officer Howie."

Howie perched his elbow on the table and leaned his head against his fist. "Besides the orangutan and the banshee, is there anything else?"

Rae flipped another pancake at Tiny who caught it in mid-air. "Since you asked, it all really started after being forced to house-sit this manor for my boss, Travis. First, I met a man named Bronco who threatened me and told me to leave the area. *Then* Orangutan Man entered my house without my invitation, by way of bribing my boss's apparent dog with dog treats. *Then* I was approached by an empath who said I might be in trouble. *Then* I find out that Honey Ward used to live here. Does that name ring a bell?"

Howie nodded. "She went missing two years ago."

Bash reasoned, "*Obviously,* she was taken by the banshee who lives in the woods. Her name is Maeve, by the way." Tiny yelped softly in agreement. "My aunt is invited to Maeve's party tonight. *Obviously,* my aunt is the banshee's next target."

Howie sighed. "Where's my aspirin?" Patting himself down, he eventually found two pills in his shirt pocket and swallowed them with the remaining coffee. After belching, he asked Rae, "Don't you have any friends that you can talk to about this stuff over salads?"

Rae scrunched up her face. "I hate salads."

Howie smiled. "Me too. Well, then let's tackle one thing at a time. First, I can't help you with the empath. I think it's all nonsense." Bash gasped, but Howie continued, "I also don't believe in banshees." Bash gasped louder and Howie still continued, "So, my advice is to go and enjoy the party. As for Honey Ward, I remember that story well and it's an unlucky coincidence that you are house-sitting the same house where she lived. But that's all it is. A coincidence." He jiggled his cup for more coffee and Rae quickly delivered. After taking a gulp, he said, "Let's move on to the Ford. Did you get a good look at the driver?"

Rae sighed. "Yes. He looks like an orangutan."

"Not helpful." The bags underneath Howie's eyes were bulging. "What *exactly* do you want me to do?"

"I was hoping that you could run the license plates. I wrote them down for you." She handed a post-it note to him.

Leaning back in his chair, he didn't look at the note. "I should've been a plumber, just like my dad." He then stood up and headed for the door with Rae, Bash and Tiny following him. "Look, Rae, I'm thirty-seven, but look and feel closer to fifty. I'm way too out of shape to be dealing with crime and violence. That's why I mainly handle traffic violations in my police car. My back hurts. I take blood thinners for a blood clot in my leg. Not to mention that I have six kids all under the age of ten. To put it simply, I don't have the time or motivation to run after ape men and witches."

Bash corrected, "Banshee."

Pausing in the foyer, Officer Howie sighed. "I might know someone who can help you. Or he might think you're nuts."

"Who is he?"

"He's a retired cop who turned private investigator. His name is Cook and he's always looking for things to do." Howie shrugged. "That's the best I can do. I'll have him call you, just give me your information." Rae recited her phone number as he added it to his contacts. He then turned and left through the door, yelling over his shoulder, "You two be safe and don't go looking for trouble. Okay?"

Bash rocked back on his heels as Tiny whined. He asked the dog, "Feel like a nap?" Tiny woofed and they both hurried upstairs.

Rae remained at the front door, watching Howie struggle into his car. She bit a fingernail and then spit it out, muttering to herself, "The problem is trouble always looks for me."

.   .   .

Sitting cross-legged on the bed, Bash studied the instant photograph that Maeve gave to him. The blurred shapes against the black canvas were weak proof. No scientist in the paranormal field would take this seriously. He then noticed a handwritten message written along the bottom: *Nice try. ∞ Maeve.*

"What do you think about this?" Bash asked Tiny, stretched out on the bed. The dog glanced at the picture, yawned and dropped his head onto his front paws. "I think she's sneaky too." He then pulled out Stone's phone number that Aunt Rae wrote down for him. "I also think Stone is hiding some psychic ability from us." He glanced at Tiny who blinked. "I'm glad we're on the same page."

Bash placed the photograph in his red notebook and then surveyed all of his paranormal equipment that was sprawled in front of him, particularly his spirit box. It was his favorite piece. Unlike the EMF meter which showed spikes in the electromagnet fields, suggesting that a ghost was nearby, the spirit box actually gave the hunter a chance to experience live listening. In other words, Bash could hear and respond to a ghost's voice instantly, instead of pushing the pause button, rewinding and then playing back the EVP. Or Electronic Voice Phenomenon. Or ghost voice, as Bash like to say.

Unfortunately, he never had a good opportunity to use it. His last two attempts ended in police chaos at Mrs. Hodge's home and banshee mayhem at Maeve's. However, his third attempt might be notably victorious. After learning about the missing Honey Ward and how she once lived here in this very home, Bash missed an obvious possibility. Why creep around the woods at night to catch a banshee when all he needed to do was communicate with Honey here? Her ghost would surely tell him that his suspicions about Maeve being a dangerous banshee were correct.

He grabbed the spirit box, turned it on and listened to the static, interrupted by the steady pulses, as the spirit box scanned channels. Using a strong voice, Bash said, "Honey Ward. Are you here?" There was no response. Tiny raised his head as Bash continued, "Is Maeve a banshee? Did she hurt you?" Again, no response. Tiny, however, smiled and began panting excitedly. Bash patted the dog's head and spoke into the recorder, "Will she hurt my aunt?" There was only static. Suddenly, however, Tiny rolled onto his back and his hind leg began kicking. Bash watched the dog. "Are you okay?" Tiny stopped kicking and flipped to his stomach again. "Hey, Tiny, I kinda need you to calm down." Tiny answered by sticking his rump into the air and howling gleefully. Bash took a deep breath and exhaled. "New plan." Reaching for his cell phone, he dialed Stone's number.

CHAPTER TWENTY SIX

Rae sat on the bottom step of the front porch, pondering her conversation with Howie. Did he really know a private investigator? Was he just placating her? Staring at the evergreen trees across the street, she began deep breathing exercises. Within a few minutes, her head became clearer and she decided to follow her own advice, which was to mind her own business. If trouble had the balls to find her, she would look in the opposite direction and never turn back. This was her life, after all. And she was in control of it. Sort of.

With newfound resilience, she jumped down the porch steps, shoved her earphones into her ears, turned her music on and raced toward the path for a morning jog. Each time her foot hit the pavement, she stomped out the stresses pertaining to ghosts and banshees. She pictured herself smashing logos, ugly mirrors and headlights on the black Ford Taurus with a sledgehammer. Running freely, nothing was going to depress her mood anymore. Not even Bronco, she said to herself as she spotted him in the park.

She stopped running and leaned against a tree while grabbing her foot for a hamstring stretch. Bronco hadn't seen her and she took some interest in watching him for a change. He seemed agitated while sitting in his wheelchair, bouncing both knees. After glancing at his watch a few times, he shook his head and suddenly stood. Rae gasped as he picked up his wheelchair and walked with it toward a white convertible parked in the lot.

What? He can walk? For real?

Rae inconspicuously hid behind the tree to spy, turning her music off and removing her earphones. Her eyes narrowed as he lifted the wheelchair into the back seat of the car. Then he leap-hopped to the driver's seat and slid right in with the ease of a man with two healthy legs. Reaching for her phone strapped to her upper arm, she unfastened it and took a picture of Bronco sitting in his car. Just when she thought this couldn't be more interesting, a familiar silver Honda pulled up next to Bronco. Rae immediately took another picture as Purple Stiletto emerged from the Honda with that same canvas bag hooked over her shoulder, which instantly fell to the ground. Rae heard the thump and watched as the frail-looking woman struggled to lift the bag over her shoulder again. She then hustled to Bronco's car and slid into the passenger's side. Without any greetings, Bronco and Purple Stiletto drove off together. Checking the time on her phone, it was twelve minutes past ten.

Rae bit a fingernail. Trouble found her again. What was she going to do? Mind her own business? Yeah, yeah, that was right. She was to mind her own business. Quickly refastening her phone to her arm strap, she smiled, turned around and faced Gio, almost bumping into him. Their noses were an inch from touching.

Rae stepped back and roared, "Why are you always sneaking around?"

"Hey, I'm not the one taking pictures of people with my phone." With dead black eyes, Gio's hand swiftly moved to the inside of his jacket and he suddenly produced a fifty-dollar bill. "Will you please give this to Bash?"

Puzzled, Rae asked, "What for?"

At first, Gio only stared at her. Then he said, "It was his."

Rae snatched the bill from him. "You stole my nephew's money?"

Gio's eyes bulged and he took two steps from her. "No way, lady. He gave it to me. And now I'm giving it back." With a shaky voice, he added, "I'm not a thief, okay?"

"I tend to not believe liars," Rae replied.

Gio's mouth dropped open. "What have I lied about?"

"The woods," Rae answered in an exasperated tone. "You told Bash that these woods scare you and yet you're always in them."

He seemed genuinely offended. "I only go into the woods when I absolutely have to."

"Well, I guess that's all the time then?" Rae gave him a disbelieving look. "See ya." She ran around him, leaving him in her wake.

Rae sprinted all the way back without music and earphones. The thoughts in her head provided the motivation needed to run. Her mind reeled with expensive purple stilettos, old tank shirts and forest dwelling teens who didn't understand how personal space worked.

As Rae entered the manor, Bash and Tiny met her in the foyer. They just ended an apparent kitchen raid. Giving them a look of disgust, she said, "The stacks of pancakes weren't enough for you two?"

Bash smiled. "We needed the salt after the sweet."

"You both have a healthy dusting of cheese across your faces." She pointed to Bash's hands. "There's an inch of that cheesy stuff on your fingertips too."

"It's called cheetle," Bash replied and began licking one hand while Tiny licked the other.

"I call it gross. You know junk food is very unhealthy for you and so is dog slobber." She suddenly changed the subject. "Hey, guess who can walk and doesn't need a wheelchair at all?"

Bash raised his eyebrows. "Bronco? Really?"

Rae nodded. "Yep. I just saw him walk to his car and drive away with Purple Stiletto."

Both Bash and Tiny tilted their heads to the right. "Who's Purple Stiletto?"

"She's this lady who wears purple high heels and hates dogs. It doesn't matter. What matters is that you stay away from Bronco. He's probably a wanted criminal." She then handed the fifty dollar bill to Bash. "Speaking of criminals, Gio wanted me to return this to you." She arched an eyebrow, waiting for an explanation.

Bash shrugged. "I paid him fifty dollars to show me where the banshee lives."

"Oh, good lord."

He looked at the bill. "Did he say why he's giving my money back?"

Rae put her hands on her hips. "No, but he probably knows that he shouldn't have taken it in the first place."

"Oh." Bash nodded at Tiny who nodded in return. "See, Aunt Rae? He's a nice guy." He brushed by her, saying, "I'll put this away and then we can swim."

Rae listened to Bash's climbing footsteps and sighed. Then she heard the dog sigh next to her and she looked at him. They were almost eye to eye. Instead of feeling frightened though, she felt very comfortable and even stepped closer to give him a whole head scratch with both of her hands. The gold charm on his collar jingled, causing Rae to examine the engraved capital T. After releasing the charm, she stared deeply into his dark brown eyes. "What are you up to?"

The dog shifted his two front paws and looked at the door.

"Don't avoid the question." Rae continued, "I know that you don't really live here and that you're not my boss's dog. So, fess up."

The dog whined and huffed once.

"Fine. Be that way." Rae crossed her arms. "Just to let you know, I'm very good at puzzles. Now, I haven't figured you out completely, but I will."

The dog sniffed her feet and knees. Then he licked her ankle.

After giving him one more head rub, Rae walked away, saying to the dog, "Please excuse me while I change." She turned to face him. "Will you be joining us or must you leave again?"

The dog glanced at the door again and she smiled knowingly before bounding upstairs.

.   .   .

The Great Shepherd sniffed the angry lady's feet and knees. He did like her general aroma. Too bad she said that she didn't taste good. He licked her anyway, savering her salty ankles. What was not to like? As she stood at the bottom of the stairs, he cocked his head to the left, wondering about his next meal. After she left him, he loped to the front door, turned the knob with his two front paws and nosed the door open, scuttling through as it closed behind him.

He rushed along the path, passing the woods and stopping briefly when he saw the sad girl. She stood just inside the woods, waiting for him. The leaves on the trees around her blew in the wind, but her blonde ponytail remained still. His head urged him to go to her, but his stomach told him that he was late. He glanced toward home and then right back at her, but she was gone.

He arrived at the small bungalow in no time and entered the home the same way he left it: using his snout and front paws to turn the doorknob before pushing the door open. It was a great trick he taught himself and he proudly wagged his tail. It was a dog's way of patting himself on the back.

Gingerly stepping into the room with the television, he saw the old man asleep on the couch. Next to him was a machine that beeped and hummed constantly. The dog crept softly past the old man and followed the scent of meaty deliciousness coming from the kitchen. The old woman stood in front of the stove, glancing back at him. Nodding toward the corner, the old woman smiled at him and he retreated to where a large bowl, overflowing with food for a large dog and topped with bacon, patiently waited to be devoured. Tiny felt that the old couple liked him and he liked them. The angry lady, however, smelled a lot better than either of them and he noticed that she began to smile at him a little more each day.

CHAPTER TWENTY SEVEN

The morning dragged. Stone yawned as the hour approached noon. With caffeine withdrawal symptoms mounting, he now experienced fatigue and poor concentration, along with sweating and tremors. Sitting at the folding table in the storage room, he thought of a way to keep himself awake and away from coffee. Pulling out his phone from his back pocket, he researched information on empaths and found that there were fifteen shared traits such as isolation, trouble fitting in, boundary issues and the need for *caffeine*. Stone rubbed his eyes and reread that last one. Whoops, he thought. It was actually the need for *rest*.

Stone yawned again and ran his fingers through his hair, accidentally knocking his cap off his head. He forgot that he wore it. Bending to retrieve it, he draped himself over his knees and stayed in that position while thinking. He had lots to think about, but couldn't remember what. What were the traits again? Trouble isolation? Caffeine issues? No, no, he said. He remembered now. They were isolating coffee cups and fitting in boundary caffeine. His mouth involuntarily stretched open as he inhaled air. On the exhale, he drooled on his shoes.

Forgetting about the traits, he tried to create a plan of watching over Rachel that night after work without her knowing it. I'm the orange barrel, he said aloud and immediately pictured himself squatting in the middle of the road while cars passed by him. Then he pictured himself as a large orange cup of coffee and he drank himself.

His eyes were about to roll back in slumber when two hands shook his shoulders. Lifting his head, he saw Sally standing over him.

"Go home," she said.

"I can't."

"Then go wherever your attractive friend is. You know, the one with the yoga pants. I'll handle the bar. You need a break." Sally handed him a can of caffeinated water and smiled. "It's not coffee."

"I just can't show up without some kind of reason."

"You'll think of one." Sally turned and left the storage room.

He smiled when his forearms tingled. Straightening in the chair, he knew what this meant. This psychic ability had some advantages after all. He looked at his phone, knowing that Bash was about to invite him over. He found a way to Rachel through Bash. Cracking open the can, he took a long and much-needed swig, just as his phone rang.

"Hey, what's up?" Stone greeted.

Bash replied, "Hey, psychic, you know what's up."

Stone smiled, trying to play along. "I'm not a psychic."

Bash spoke quickly and quietly. "Anyway, psychic, I need you to come over tonight. The Birch Grove Banshee has a ringleader, Maeve. She invited my aunt over for a party tonight. She *claims* she's a retired art teacher and hosts these parties with other retired teachers. They call themselves The Crafters because they *apparently* do arts and crafts, but I don't buy it. They obviously do witchcraft. And listen to this, Maeve lives in the woods. Who does that? A banshee. That's who. So, I may need your muscle to help my aunt. Are you in or out?"

Even with the sketchy details, Stone replied, "I'm all in."

· · ·

Rae spent a memorable afternoon with Bash, swimming in the pool. After many competitions involving cannonballs, penny dives and underwater races, they both reclined on chaise lounges, surrounded by bags of cheesy snacks and pretzels. Covered in cheese dust, Rae said to Bash, "I need to work on some logo designs."

Bash looked at her. "Can you tell me where Tiny is first? I know that you know."

Rae chuckled. "All I know is that he's not Tiny. I have no idea where he is."

"How do you know he's not Tiny?"

She looked at her nephew. "Travis said he would have the dog-sitter watch Tiny."

"He could have lied."

Rae shook her head. "Travis is many terrible things, but I don't think he's a liar. And he's such a particular guy. He left a thick manual for me to read about maintaining his six *thousand* square foot home and a list of rules. For instance, I'm not supposed to take showers longer than five minutes."

Bash looked horrified. "Really?"

"Yeah. And I'm not supposed to have guests over or touch that horrifying mirror in the foyer or eat on the furniture or wear shoes in the house."

"We've done all of those things."

Grinning broadly, Rae said, "I know! I haven't touched that mirror though. Only because I think it's a portal to Hell. Anyway, I realized that a particular guy like Travis would have a section in the manual about how to care for his precious dog, but he didn't." Bash wore a look of skepticism, so Rae continued, "If the large dog you know as Tiny is really Travis's dog, then why would Travis have such a small leash for him? A small *pink* leash for a *male* dog? And why would this dog who is the size of an elephant seal have such a small bed? Or eat kibble that's intended for small dogs in such a small *and pink* dog dish?"

"Males can wear pink, Aunt Rae."

Snickering, Rae said, "It's fine if you don't believe me, but I'm right."

Bash turned onto his side, facing her, "If Tiny really isn't Tiny, then shouldn't we try to find out who he is or where he's from? Maybe we should follow him?"

Rae patted Bash's leg and said, "Sure. You figure out how we can do that." Rising to her feet, she brushed off the cheese dust. "In the meantime, I have some logo designs to massacre." With that, she left her nephew on the patio.

After reworking logo designs well into the early evening, Rae ended with only twenty decent ones to send to the New York client. Knowing that she wouldn't hear any response, she rose and followed the smell of frying cheese and butter. It was nearly seven o'clock and all the junk food in her stomach dissolved, leaving her famished. Feeling weak, she slouched next to Bash who stood at the stove, holding a spatula.

Rae smiled with imploring eyes. "Smells delicious."

"Yeah, yeah, yeah. I'll make you one." With a half smile, Bash flipped over his sandwich in the pan and began preparations for hers. Soon, the two of them sat at the kitchen table, devouring their grilled cheese sandwiches with ketchup and a side of potato chips. Since Rae wanted Bash to eat a vegetable with their meal, she searched the refrigerator for a jar of pickles and they each ate two.

After dinner, they helped one another with the clean up. It didn't take long to make the kitchen sparkle and Rae turned to her nephew with a grateful smile, raising her hand for a high-five. They smacked palms when Bash suddenly grasped her wrist and slapped a watch on it.

She gave him a quizzical look and he quickly explained, "It's seven-thirty. You have just enough time for a quick tutorial on my spy watch before heading to the banshee party. It's a video recorder and you'll have ninety minutes to record any banshee happenings."

Rae sputtered, "What?"

"Please be extra careful with this." He raised her wrist to her face so that she could take a good look at it. "It cost me eighty-five bucks."

"Are you crazy?" She removed the watch from her wrist. "I'm not doing that. I thought you didn't even want me to go to this party."

"I don't."

"Then why are you trying to enlist me as one of your paranormal investigators?"

"Well, since you're not listening and are still going to the banshee party, you might as well do something inspiring for the scientists of the paranormal."

Rae chuckled. "Do you know both of them personally?"

Bash narrowed his eyes. "There are more than just two scientists of the paranormal. From my own research, which is on-going, I happen to know of six that are certified."

Rae rolled her eyes. "I have to get ready. Did you call Stone? Is he babysitting you?"

Bash faked a laugh. "Bahaha. He's coming at eight."

Raising her eyebrows, Rae asked, "But doesn't he have to be at the bar?"

Bash shrugged. "He said he'll be here." He then looked her up and down. "Time's a wastin. You better get yourself together."

She raced upstairs. After breaking a new world's record for showering, which involved shaving two legs practically at the same time, Rae returned to the kitchen and found that Stone already arrived. Slouched on a chair at the kitchen table, he smiled tiredly at her.

She said to him, "Thanks for keeping my nephew company while I'm gone. I hope your bar won't suffer without you."

"It won't." Stone shifted in his seat. "I have someone who can take over for me."

Rae asked, "Like a manager or something?"

Stone's head bobbed. "Or something."

Bash walked over to the stove and asked Stone, "Would you like a grilled cheese sandwich? It's my specialty. I make it with four different cheeses."

"Sure." Stone sounded appreciative. "That sounds great."

Bash began spreading butter on each slice. He then placed thick sheets of provolone, white cheddar, colby and jack cheese on top of one slice of bread and topped it with the other. Soon, the heated pan sizzled and the aroma of melted butter filled the kitchen.

Rae caught Stone watching her and he asked her, "Where are you going again?"

Evading his stare, Rae replied, "To Maeve's house." She searched the cupboards for crackers to bring. "I won't be gone long. Or, I should say, I don't want to be gone long. Unless, things get real interesting. If there's a chocolate fondue bar, I may stay all night." She looked at Stone and snickered, causing Bash to look at her. She pointed to Stone. His arms cradled his head, his eyes were shut and his breathing was regular and deep. With her crackers, she crossed the floor to the back door. "Have a rip-roaring time."

CHAPTER TWENTY EIGHT

Rae held the invitation and followed the footpath to Maeve's house. Fortunately, it was the longest day of the year, so it wasn't too dark among the birch trees. Meandering down the trail, the walk lasted over five minutes before she found the edge of Maeve's property. She stood there, motionless and awestruck. The front yard was riddled with topiaries. The shrubs were all very human-like and in action poses. Rae felt small and uncomfortable, yet impressed. Furry and green, these plant artforms showed graceful movement and exploding action. One was leaping like a ballerina while another was in the middle of a roundhouse kick. All of them sprung to life as a light breeze caressed the leaves. A thought suddenly struck. Thinking of the electrical storm from the other night, Rae realized that she and Bash confused these topiaries for Gio and his non-gang. Rad nodded. Yep, she said to herself, a puzzle completely solved.

Between the sculptures was an uneven cobblestone path, leading to the front door. Rae followed the stones and smiled as she reached the modest Cape Cod. Maeve's home immediately exuded a tranquil and calm feeling. Short in stature, it was a proud structure with smoky gray cedar clapboard and dark green shutters. A central brick chimney sprouted from the middle of the roof. A little worse for wear, the tired stack slumped to the left, clinging to its waning self-worth. It was definitely an old home, but mostly in good shape. It should've seemed out of place as it sat in the middle of a forest. However, it actually seemed to be right where it was supposed to be.

Rae stuffed the invitation into the pocket of her yoga shorts and read a note taped to the front door: *Just come in, dear. We're all downstairs.* Entering the house, she instantly spotted seven pairs of shoes. They were all lined up against the wall of the entry. There were lumpy tennis shoes, hot pink clogs, cheap tan flats, pristine penny loafers, tattered flip-flops, dusty black ankle boots and strappy glitter sandals. Rae added her running shoes to the line-up and followed the voices to the basement. The farther she descended, the cooler the air became as it brushed her arms like a soft whisper.

It was a typical old basement with stone walls and exposed beams along the ceiling. The large room was set up for entertaining. Two faux leather sofas, both dark brown with floral throw pillows, sat opposite each other with a distressed teal coffee table placed in the middle. A couple of wingback chairs finished the conversational square. In the corner of the room was a wooden stage and next to it was a long dining table filled with snacks, desserts and lit candles. Rae's boxes of assorted crackers fit right in with the rest as she placed them on the table. Glancing around, there were no arts and crafts anywhere. There were no paints or glue or even pencils. Suddenly, she felt warmth on the back of her neck. Slowly turning around, she soon realized the warmth was coming from the seven people behind her, staring at her. They all had very white faces. She smiled meekly as The Magnificent Seven raised their drinks in a toast-like gesture.

"To Rae," said a lady, wearing a yellow silk top with black high-waisted shorts lined with four gold buttons on each side. Slim with snow-white hair in a pixie style, she seemed like one of those ageless models. Rae thought she must be the one who wore the glitter sandals.

The others repeated, "To Rae!" Then they all drained their glasses.

Maeve was the first to approach. Grabbing her hand, she brought Rae into the circle and squeezed her onto the sofa between the model and a heavier-set man.

He looked at her as he administered a shot in his own thigh. "I'm a diabetic," he explained before digging into his shirt pocket and pulling out a handful of M&Ms. "Would you like one?" She shook her head and he shoved them into his mouth. "Medicine," he said and winked at her.

Maeve introduced him. "This is Dave. He is our retired gym teacher." Rae instantly connected him to the lumpy tennis shoes. Maeve then gestured to the model-looking lady. "And this is Helen. She was our guidance counselor." Rae thought that made sense. She seemed unnecessarily ostentatious, just like most of the guidance counselors she remembered. Helen definitely owned the glitter sandals.

Maeve pointed to a woman with long strawy gray hair, a plaid shirt and a fringed jean skirt that was twenty years too old. "That's Dotty, our very talented music teacher who now just gives private voice lessons." Rae nodded as she said flip-flops to herself.

As Maeve continued with the introductions, Rae placed a pair of shoes with each of the old, white-faced retirees. The boots belonged to the tough-looking special education teacher, Mo, who seemed content, bouncing on one of those large exercise balls. The pristine loafers obviously belonged to the librarian, Phil, in the collared shirt and tie. The tan flats made for comfort and not for style paired with the classroom teacher named Jane. This meant one thing.

"I'm surprised that you're the owner of hot pink clogs," Rae said to Maeve.

"Well, dear." Maeve's eyes twinkled. "Even banshees like other colors than just green."

Maeve's comment caused an eruption of cackling from the other guests. Rae, however, sat silently until Maeve explained, "I told them about your nephew's suspicions of us being banshees. That's why we moved our meeting indoors. We don't want any more peeping toms."

Shrugging, Rae said, "Yeah, he reads too much."

"There's nothing wrong with that," said Phil. "In fact, kids these days should be reading more." He nodded at the group.

Dave huffed. "Kids should be outside exercising. They sit around too much, playing video games and *reading*." He dug into his pants pocket and shoved more candy into his mouth.

"Reading is exercise for the mind." Phil's lips trembled from anger.

"Here, Phil, you look like you need this." Mo held up a fidget spinner, a hand-held metal device that twirled between the fingers. "It's supposed to relieve psychological stress." She tossed it to him.

Phil dropped the fidget spinner instead of catching it and Dave laughed. This sent Phil into a small fit of rage. He picked up the stress-relieving object and whipped it at Dave, hitting him squarely in his chest.

"And that's what the kids always did with them too," Mo grumbled and bounced higher on her exercise ball.

"What we need is music to bring us together." Dotty took out her ukulele that must have been hiding in her long jean skirt and began strumming it. And humming. And swaying.

"Another drink, please?" Dave raised his glass for someone, anyone, to refill it.

Helen leaned over Rae and took Dave's glass. Standing up, she said, "Come on, everyone, stop acting like children." Then she smiled. "Speaking of children, my grandson did the most exquisite thing on our trip to France last month. Would you like to hear about it?"

Everyone, except Rae, answered in unison, "No."

Helen's shoulders dropped and she brought her hand to her tearful eyes. Jane promptly stood and patted Helen on the back. She said to her, "Helen, this is a small problem. Remember your coping strategies."

Straightening herself, Helen sniffed, gave the glass back to Dave and said to him, "Get your own damn drink." She claimed her seat once again.

"I have to leave in an hour," Rae said to Maeve when she waltzed over with a wine bottle to refill Dave's glass. Upon hearing this, Dave shifted his weight to his right butt cheek and passed gas. Rae corrected herself, "I have to leave in fifteen minutes."

Maeve chuckled. "Ignore him. Now, I see you didn't bring anything to drink for yourself." Maeve held an empty wine glass with the bottle in one hand. "Don't worry. Nobody ever does. Would you like to try my wine? I made it myself."

"No, thank you," answered Rae, when suddenly a full glass of wine somehow materialized in her hand. The scarlet liquid carried a scent, reminding Rae of a basket full of grapes and apples. However, the surface looked fuzzy. Was that pulp? Without tasting it, she set the glass on the coffee table. Glancing at Dave, she noticed his glass was empty and he was licking his lips while staring at hers. She asked him, "Can diabetics drink wine?"

Dave nodded. "Red wine or any alcoholic beverage can lower blood sugar for up to twenty-four hours. And I'd drink it even if it didn't." He nudged her playfully.

Rae liked Dave and pushed her glass over to him. "Go ahead. Take it."

When he reached for it, Maeve's booming voice rose over the others. "Dave, you can't drink that." She shook her finger at him. Then turning to the whole group, she gestured warmly with wide arms. "Let's start our meeting, shall we? As you all know, my fellow crafters, tonight is a very special evening. We have gathered together for one important reason. I trust you all brought what I asked you to bring?"

The other members nodded. Feeling out of place, Rae sunk deeper into the couch cushions. Her anxiety was building. Maybe she should drink that fuzzy wine after all?

Rae's wine-drinking thoughts were interrupted as Maeve began handing out robes. Everyone received one, except for Rae. However, she remained quiet and watched as the seven crafters put on their robes, extracting a sandwich bag from their pockets or purses. To Rae's surprise, each bag was filled with grass and she panicked. She never ever smoked weed. Her older brothers did, though, when they were young. What did they call it? The devil's lettuce?

Dave patted her knee. "Don't worry. We're just making an herb jar. It's all harmless fun." Then Phil and Mo placed a large black pot in the center of the coffee table. It wasn't necessarily a cauldron, just a ceramic mixing bowl.

Looking at Dave, Maeve said, "Let's start with you."

Dave laboriously wiggled himself to the edge of the couch to pour the contents of his bag into the pot. "Allspice," he stated. "For energy." He huffed his way back to the reclined position.

Helen was next. "Chamomile. For reducing irritability." She then poured her ground herb into the pot and the rest followed this strange pattern around the whole circle. Mo added holy basil for stress reduction. Phil threw in lemongrass for inner peace. Dotty gave rosemary for wisdom, while Jane contributed brahmi for mind clarity and reflection.

Last was Maeve. She held her bag for a lingering moment. Her dark eyes stared into Rae's. Finally, Maeve spoke, "Ground ferns. For the protection against evil." Once all the herbs were in the black ceramic bowl, Maeve used a wooden spoon to mix them. Then she produced a necklace from the pocket of her green robe. There was no gold chain, just a black leather cord. Clinging to this cord was a small glass pendant in the form of a teardrop with a cork topper.

Rae squinted at the pendant and soon realized it was actually a very small bottle, which Maeve filled with the herb mixture. After securing the cork top, she floated toward Rae and looped the necklace around her neck. "There," Maeve said with satisfaction. "This is for you." Handing the untouched wine glass to Rae, she said, "Drink up."

On cue, everyone raised their glasses to Rae and cheered, "To The Crafters!"

Rae felt obligated to return the toast, but paused. Dave nudged her playfully again and said, "It's okay, Rae. One glass of wine won't hurt you." He turned to the group and chanted, "Rae! Rae! Rae!" Soon, all seven were cheering her name in unison.

Rae's wall of uneasiness crumbled. Maybe from feeling safe among the group? Maybe from peer pressure? Either way, she lifted her glass and shouted, "To The Crafters!" Then like the rest, she sipped the wine and applause erupted. Smiling, Rae studied the wine. It tasted like fruit punch mixed with a white soda or some very sugary cereal mixed with syrup. At any rate, she loved it. She didn't even mind the fuzziness. So, she drank the rest of it, winked at Dave and immediately passed out.

* * *

Once it was past midnight, Bash wondered if his aunt was securing strong paranormal evidence. At one o'clock, he looked out the window and ate some potato chips. At two o'clock, he checked Stone's pulse. At half past two, he began to worry about his aunt. On impulse, he approached Stone who hadn't changed his sleeping position at the table. Then with as much gentleness as a stormy sea, he shook Stone awake.

Sitting upright with wide eyes, Stone clawed the air while muttering, "Don't touch me." He blinked at Bash a few times and said, "Oh, hey, Bash. What's up?"

Bash spoke matter-of-factly. "Aunt Rae is still at Maeve's party with the other banshees. We need to get her."

For a moment, Stone was silent. Then rising to his feet, he said, "Lead the way."

They darted to the trail. Bash held two beacons of light: the utility flashlight and his cell phone. Stone only had the light on his phone to brighten the dark path as they stepped onto it. Moving quietly through the woods, neither spoke. Bash stopped only once to warn Stone about the cliff and, even the darkness, Bash noticed that Stone's face paled.

Bash whispered, "You don't like heights?"

"I don't like this cliff. A body could shatter into a million pieces, falling off this cliff."

Bash's beams of light moved from the cliff, to Stone, and then back to the cliff. "That's a morbid thought. Come on, let's go."

"How much farther?"

Just then their lights went out. Both phones were dead, as well as the utility flashlight. Bash heard Stone curse, but he remained calm and replied, "We're almost there."

As Bash turned to continue to Maeve's home, he heard rustling ahead of him and saw two small dots of flames against the blackness. They were moving back and forth in short bursts. Stone moved in front of Bash and shouted, "Who's there?"

The rustling turned into mad scrambling. A low grumbly voice ordered another to run. The two flames took off in the opposite direction of Bash and Stone until one flame fell to the ground and a woman screamed. A gravelly voice ordered her to get up and follow him, telling her to just leave everything. Bash watched as the one flame bobbed away from him.

Bash trailed Stone in the darkness as they felt their way to the flame laying on the ground. Surprised to find a glass lantern, along with a tan cowboy hat and one purple stiletto, Bash said to Stone, "The hat belongs to a guy named Bronco and my aunt knows a woman who wears purple high heels. She saw them together. I wonder what they're doing out here."

Stone picked up the gas lantern and smiled. "I think we interrupted their midnight rendezvous." He raised the lantern. "At least things are looking brighter for us."

Bash pointed to the hat. "What about those things?"

Stone shrugged. "Leave them."

Armed now with a gas lantern, they continued their walk for another ten minutes, but the end of the trail never came. Confused, Bash told Stone that they should be near Maeve's house and they walked a little farther. They never found her home. Stone suggested that they turn around and retrace their footsteps. Maybe they passed the house? Maybe there was another trail?

Bash shook his head. "Impossible," he said. "I know this trail is the one my aunt took to Maeve's house. I don't know why we can't find her house. It's almost like the house is moving or Maeve is using her banshee powers to keep her house hidden from us."

"Isn't there another trail leading to the path? That's where we met yesterday."

"No. I made my own trail out of here from fear. What should we do?"

Stone suggested that they continue walking toward Maeve's house. After ten more minutes, however, they arrived at the end of the trail, which was actually the beginning.

They both looked at Travis's house and then at each other. Perplexed, Bash turned toward the opening of the path, wondering how they made a full circle. He debated whether or not to try again when Stone nudged him and motioned with the lantern toward the house.

He said to Bash, "Maybe your aunt is back? Let's go in and double check. If she's not, we'll come up with plan B."

Bash looked at his phone, hoping to call her, but he knew Maeve and her banshee powers drained his battery. As he stared at the empty battery icon, he said, "Fine, let's hurry."

They sprinted to the house and burst inside the kitchen through the back door. Both repeatedly called her name as they split up to search the home. Stone remained on the lower level while Bash scoured the bedrooms. They convened in the foyer and stared at each other.

"Well," Bash said, "what's plan B?"

Just then the doorbell rang. Stone furrowed his eyebrows and he hesitantly opened the front door. Bash gasped at the sight. There was a wheelbarrow at the bottom of the steps with his aunt lounging in it, giggling in her sleep while muttering, "Stop the screaming already."

CHAPTER TWENTY NINE

The spine-chilling scream interrupted Rae's swirly, drunken dream. Fluttering her eyelids open, it was very bright. A large white light hovered over her. It burned her eyes and hindered her vision, warping the two forms standing over her into dark and globby shapes. Raising her head an inch caused her face to wince in pain. Her whole body felt stiff and sore and crumpled. She closed her stinging eyes. "Who screamed like a girl?"

"No one screamed, Aunt Rae."

Rae recognized Bash's voice. "Really?" She opened her eyes, focusing on him. "Then what's happening?"

Bash replied, "The banshees did something to you."

"Banshees?" She shielded her eyes from the bright light. "What banshees?" She blinked rapidly. "And why am I blind?"

The light lowered and Bash's face began to materialize out of the darkness. He looked concerned. "I'm talking about Maeve and her banshee party. Don't you remember?"

Rae searched her memory and could only picture various shoes. Checking her feet, she wore her running shoes, which she remembered taking off, but didn't remember putting on again. Confused, she pushed herself up and sat in the wheelbarrow. Rae shrugged. "Where did I go?"

Bash crossed his arms. "Seriously? You went to The Crafters meeting at Maeve's house. You got an invitation and followed the trail through the woods. You even brought crackers."

Rae shook her head and Stone interjected. "What's the last thing you remember?"

Rae narrowed her eyes at Stone. He held a gas lantern, the blinding light. Puzzled, she asked him, "When did you get here?"

"This is worse than I thought." Bash's arms dropped to his side and he looked at her neck. Bending over her, he reached for the pendant dangling from the leather cord. "What's this?" He stepped closer to examine the small object.

Rae squinted at the tiny glass container full of grass grindings and a word popped out of her mouth. "Herbs." Finally, a memory formed as she continued, "I remember herbs and a pot. Maeve put the herbs in this thing and gave the necklace to me. But I don't know why."

"I do," Bash said gravely as he held the teardrop charm. "This is a witch bottle. Maeve made a potion and put it in this witch bottle. She then turned it into a potion bottle necklace just for you and only you."

Stone sounded agitated. "What are you talking about?"

"I read about this in a book called *Dragons and Fairies and Potions, Oh My!* When making a potion for someone, a witch chooses her ingredients with that specific person in mind. So, the potion will only help that intended person."

"Really?" Rae was perplexed. "Its purpose is to *help* me?"

Bash contemplated, nodded and then replied, "Or possibly *harm* you." He scratched his ear. "I'll have to reread that chapter. I'm more concerned about the scream that *only you* heard. Was it a wail? Or a shrill? When did you hear it?"

Rae giggled. "Just a few minutes ago."

"Mhmm." Bash pulled on his bottom lip. "I bet my spirit box that you heard the banshee's wail. I think you're in danger."

Rae snorted at the comment and Stone helped her out of the wheelbarrow. It took both Stone and Bash to carry her into the house and up the stairs, only because she was so wriggly. She kept insisting that she could walk, but whenever they lowered her to the ground, she would collapse like a three-legged wooden chair. In the end, Bash gripped her ankles while Stone held underneath her arms and they swung her on top of the bed. She instantly fell asleep upon impact.

When Rae awoke at eight on Saturday morning, she had the sunniest of dispositions, even after reading ChAdonis's text. He thought of her last night while at a strip club and couldn't wait for the nude bike ride, which was one week away. She wrote back, Shut up.

Without a hint of a hangover, a morning run appealed to her and she changed into her running attire, noticing the charm around her neck. Herbs, she said to herself. Squinting, she tried to remember exactly what happened at Maeve's, but she could only remember shoes and herbs. The rest of her memory was fine though. Only the night's details were amiss and fuzzy. Fuzzy? That word reminded her of something, but she couldn't recall. Shrugging, she fastened her arm strap, grabbed her earphones and checked on Bash before leaving the house. He was still asleep in his bed without his smelly companion. The large dog never visited that morning after all, which was strange. Roaming around the house in search of him, Rae couldn't find the dog or Stone. She tapped her bottom lip. Was Stone even here or was that a dream? After disarming the alarm, which curiously armed itself again, she opened the unlocked door and stood on the front porch. No sign of a car. No sign of Stone. Trotting down the steps, Rae left the manor.

While running on the path, the large dog's disappearance bothered her. Maybe she should buy him some appropriate dog food and a large food dish? Although, why would she do that? On the one hand, he seemed to be a nice dog. On the other hand, he wasn't her responsibility. On the other hand, the dog really liked

Bash. On the other hand, he wasn't her dog. On the other hand, it was kinda nice to have him around. He seemed to fit with her.

Smiling at the thought of this large dog invading her life, she increased her speed and raced through the park when she abruptly stopped. The black Ford was parked in the lot this time. Taking her phone out of the arm strap, she snapped a picture of the whole car. Then an idea struck. Walking closer, she approached the driver's side with her phone raised and thumb ready to punch the white button for a second photograph. Unfortunately, the driver's seat was unoccupied. Rae lowered her phone and looked around. Nobody was outside that morning; it was eerily silent. With her anxiety on the rise, she continued her run on the path. Soon, she felt more relaxed since the exercise always calmed her mind. As she rounded a curve, with a spring in her step, she felt like she could run forever. Nothing could stop her stride, except for the pile of dead leaves that spilled onto the path. She tripped over it and her body skidded across the narrow pavement before rolling to a complete stop.

Dazed, she glanced at the pile of leaves. It looked as though it crawled out of the edge of the woods to settle on that spot. She slowly stood, limped over to the pile and kicked it in anger. Her foot struck something solid. Surprised, her toes tapped at the leaves again. There was definitely something under there. Rae used her foot to brush away some leaves and froze when she uncovered blonde hair stained with red. A timely strong wind blew more leaves off the pile, exposing a pale hand with stiff, curled fingers. However, it was the one purple stiletto poking out on the other end that really alarmed her.

Within minutes after her emergency phone call, the quiet path turned into a fast-paced crime scene with paramedics, a medical examiner and other tense people. Rae bit three fingernails while police encircled the body with caution tape. She didn't want to see Purple Stiletto, yet her eyes kept drifting toward the face where jagged slashes ripped her flesh apart.

Rae looked up as an officer lumbered toward her, shaking his head and saying, "I should've known I'd find you here."

Her eyes widened. "Officer Howie. I'm so glad it's you."

"Please," he said, "just call me Howie." Gently touching her elbow, he steered her toward a shaded tree and took out a small notepad from his shirt pocket. "I'm so glad it's me too." His expression, however, reminded Rae of someone who drew the short stick. "I have to ask you some questions, starting with how did you find the victim?"

"I was out for a run." She waited for him to finish writing. "Then I tripped over it." She cleared her throat. "How did she die? She looked like she was attacked by a tiger."

"There aren't any tigers in this area. What time did you find the victim?"

"I left the house past eight. I must've tripped over her around eight fifteen. Did she die from the facial cuts or from something else? Why is there so much blood at the back of her head? Was she hit first? With what?"

The officer scratched his beard. "Look, Rae, I'm the one who has to ask the questions." He lowered his eyes. "Did you know the victim?"

"No. Well, yes. Actually, not at all. However, I met her once. What's her name?"

Howie no longer wrote. "How could you not know her and know her at the same time?"

"I met her one day when my boss's dog scared her. She threatened to call the police and then she left. We never exchanged names. So, I don't know her. Except we kinda talked that one moment. When she threatened me. I also saw her getting into Bronco's car yesterday."

"Bronco?" Howie narrowed his eyes.

"He's the guy in the wheelchair, remember? He's faking a disability and can actually walk. They drove off together. I took a picture of them. Do you want to see it?"

Howie gave her a quizzical look. "Why did you take a picture of them?"

"I thought their movements were odd. By the way, her bag's gone. The two times I saw her, she had this big heavy bag." Rae looked around. "It's not here. That's a clue." Snapping her fingers, she said, "Bronco has it. He did this. He's the killer. Case solved. You're welcome."

Howie sighed. "I'll look into him. Is the Ford still showing up around here?"

"Yes," Rae answered excitedly. "It was just parked down there. I took a picture of that too. Do you want to see that picture?"

"No and stop taking pictures." Howie returned the pad to his pocket. "Where's Bash?"

"He's at the manor, sleeping."

"Good. Now, I hope that I'm wrong, but I can see you two monkeys getting caught up in this. Please, don't. Just stay out of it. Understand?"

Rae smiled. "Of course. Although, it's kind of an interesting puzzle."

Howie groaned. "If I see you or Bash around here, I'll tell Danny. *And* Clare." He motioned with his head for her to leave. "Get outta here already."

Rae was unceremoniously dismissed. Deflated, she turned from the crime scene and noticed a group of onlookers. Among them was Gio, scowling at her once again. Turning from him, she spotted Movie Star Bob, steadying his swaying wife, Boozy Candice. However, she was lifting her elbow out of her husband's grasp. Behind Candice was Sunshiny Bryson. Like a skyscraper, he hovered a head above the others. Rae searched for Bryson's mom and found Jessica across the street, waving for Bryson to join her. He rolled his eyes and begrudgingly left the area. Rae then turned back to the group and surprisingly saw Bash with fallen shoulders next to Tiny whose ears drooped. Talking amiably with them was a gray-haired lady.

As Rae approached Bash, she overheard the woman say to him, "I'm sorry that Toto has been bothering you and your aunt. I'm having a hard time keeping him home."

Bash shook his head at his aunt. "Why did you have to be right about this?" He shook his head again. "Aunt Rae, this is Judy. She lives in the older subdivision on the other side of the park. She says this is her dog, Toto. Toto has been their dog for the past two years."

Why *did* she have to be right about this? "Hello, Judy, I'm Rae. Your dog hasn't been bothering us." She glanced at Toto. "In fact, I was just starting to really like having him around."

Judy replied, "That's good to hear. He always gets out of the house somehow."

Rae chuckled. "He opens the door with his paws and noses his way in or out."

"I'll have to tell Frank." Judy explained, "Frank's my husband. He's bedridden. It's getting harder for me to watch Toto. I'm afraid we're just too boring for this adventurous dog." She jiggled the long rope-like leash attached to his collar. "Toto *really* isn't our dog. He belonged to past friends of ours, Ryan and Laura Ward. They bought him for their daughter, Honey. She named him Toto after the dog in *The Wizard of Oz*."

The image of Honey Ward holding a puppy flashed in Rae's mind. After realizing that that puppy grew into this Great Shepherd, she mentally smacked herself.

Judy asked, "Have you heard that story?" When neither Rae nor Bash answered, Judy continued, "Two years ago, Honey disappeared. Her parents couldn't cope and divorced. Ryan never forgave himself for being gone that night and Laura never forgave herself for being home. We agreed to take Toto temporarily, but Ryan passed away last month." Judy covered the dog's big ears and whispered, "We may have to figure out other living arrangements now."

Rae looked at Toto and cupped his face in her hands. "All this time, you came to Travis's house, looking for Honey?" He nodded and she touched the charm on his collar. "And your name is Toto, not Terrible or Taxing or even Tiny." Caressing his head, she said. "I'm so sorry."

Judy then gently tugged at Toto to follow her. He woofed at Rae, his big brown eyes pleading, and against her own wishes, she told him to go. As they watched Judy and Toto slowly saunter home, Rae sighed heavily. Then she looked at Bash and he shook his head again.

Feeling distraught, Rae shifted her attention back to the crowd. After blinking away foreign tears, she suddenly felt a strange absence. Looking around, she noticed that Bronco was missing. Where was the nosy cowboy? After all, wasn't his partner just killed?

• • •

Stone didn't want to leave Rachel that morning, but Sally called him an hour ago about a grease fire that happened last night. Now, while cleaning the stovetop, his mind swayed back to Rachel. What did the banshees do to her? It wasn't like Stone to believe in such nonsense; however, last night's events changed him a little.

The difference between banshees and witches was a mystery to him, except that he knew banshees shrill and witches fly on broomsticks. Putting that aside, in his first vision, he heard a shrill and Rachel's name. In another vision, he found Rachel in the woods, broken and twisted. In both visions, he saw the ghost girl with her face cut up. What was the connection?

A light tapping on the kitchen window caused Stone to look. In disbelief, he gawked at the happy face, pressed against the glass.

Groaning loudly, Stone dragged himself over to the locked back door. He hollered through it, "Why aren't you in South Africa?"

Zalen yelled, "I guess all good things don't always go according to plan."

Stone unlocked the door and gestured for Zalen to enter. Relieved at seeing Zalen wearing sweatpants, Stone led him to the bar and offered him a glass of sparkling water.

"Can I have a lemon wedge?" Zalen asked.

"What happened?" Stone handed Zalen a glass of fizzy water with a lemon.

"After my shorts ripped, security pulled me aside. Asked me some questions. Went through my stuff. Ticketed me for indecent exposure. Detained me for a day. Gave my luggage back eventually. I sat in this nice room with no windows. Lost in my thoughts. And now I'm here." He drank all of his water. "This was worth the wait."

"So, no South Africa?"

Shaking his head, Zalen said, "They took my passport."

"Security?"

"Or the police. I couldn't tell. By then the sunlight was blinding me because I hadn't seen it in thirty-two hours." Zalen raised his glass for more water. "They also took my spandex shorts and gave me some sweatpants. Then they told me to leave, so I came here." He smiled.

"Damn." Stone didn't smile.

"So, how is Bash?"

Stone felt pain forming across his forehead. "Fine. Why?"

Zalen nodded. "For some reason, he's on my mind."

As if on cue, Stone received three texts from Bash in quick succession. The first one informed Stone of Rae finding a woman's dead body, missing her purple shoe. The second text mentioned how the victim's face was cut up and her head was bashed in. Stone gulped and immediately thought of the ghost girl again. She also had a head wound. Then the third text came. Should Bash tell the police about what they saw in the woods while looking for the banshee party? Stone sent a text to Bash, directing him to keep a tight lip and that he would come over later to talk. Setting his phone down, his palms instantly began to sweat.

CHAPTER THIRTY

Rae and Bash sat silently at the kitchen counter, trying to eat a late breakfast of pancakes drowned in maple syrup. However, the memory of Purple Stiletto's beaten face turned Rae's stomach into a clump of acidic glue and her throat lurched.

Bash also stared at his food without touching it and muttered, "Tiny liked pancakes."

"You mean Toto."

Bash sighed.

Rae thought back to the beginning of her stay, realizing that Travis intended the small surprise to be the fruit basket. Toto just showed up coincidentally on the same day that Rae arrived, confusing Rae into thinking that he was the real Tiny. The charm on his collar with the capital T confirmed her misconceptions. She chuckled. What a dope, she told herself.

Bash asked, "Why doesn't your boss have any pictures of the real Tiny in this house?"

"There is a portrait of Travis and Seth holding a little dog. At first, I thought the dog was a prop, but I'm now thinking it's real and its name is Tiny."

"One portrait? That's it?"

"Look around. There's no clutter anywhere. You've heard the term hot mess? Well, Travis The Torch is a hot orderly system. He absolutely hates knick-knacks of any kind. He handles his OCD affliction with sterile gloves and lots of disinfectant spray."

Bash asked, "Where's this portrait?"

Rae led Bash to a mantel with the large portrait of Travis, Seth and Tiny above it.

Bash told her, "That's a Bichon Frise."

"It looks so fake. Especially the eyes."

"I like our Tiny better."

"You mean Toto."

Bash sighed again, walking out of the room. He called to her from the kitchen. "I talked to my mom this morning and asked if I can stay another week. She said yes." He paused and then hollered, "You're welcome. Do we have anymore chips?"

Rae heard her nephew, searching the kitchen cupboards. Salty chips sounded delicious to her too. On her way to join him, there was a knock on the front door. To her surprise, Sunshiny Bryson stood on the porch, holding a book and an apple pie that looked too small for the dish.

"Hello, Bryson," Rae greeted. "How are you?"

"Fine." He offered her the baked good. "My mom made this for you. I guess she wanted to cheer you up after this morning."

"Wow," Rae said, "she's a fast baker."

"She actually didn't make it. She just wants you to think she did. She bought the pie, took it out of its box and put it in this pie plate." Bryson then raised the book. "Can I give this to Bash? I'm never going to read it and thought he would like it."

Rae read the title. "*Baiting a Banshee and What Not To Do*." She looked at Bryson. "This was your book?"

Bryson nodded. "There was a time when I believed too."

Bash suddenly appeared at her elbow. He gawked at the book in the same way most pharaohs gawked at their gold. "Thanks," he said while leafing through the information. "This tells you which traps will fail, so I won't be wasting my time." Bash showed Rae a picture.

She was confused. "I thought you weren't interested in the banshee anymore."

"That was yesterday. Today's a new day."

Rae grinned at Bryson and her mind instantly entered puzzle-solving mode. Ignoring her promise to Howie, she innocently asked him, "Would you like to come in?"

"Sure," Bryson replied and followed her into the kitchen with Bash trailing.

"How about some water?" Her guest nodded and she placed the pie on the counter before filling three glasses with ice and water. "Speaking of this morning, it grew quite a crowd. Fast."

"The police sirens drew us out. It was exciting."

She asked, "Did you recognize the victim?"

Bryson shook his head, picking up the glass of water. "She didn't live around here."

Rae continued, "But did you know her?"

He drank a few gulps. "How would I know her if she didn't live around here?"

Rae shrugged. "How do you know she didn't live around here if you didn't know her?"

Giving her a dull look, he said, "I grew up around here. I know everybody pretty well."

"Everybody?" A thought struck Rae. "How well did you know Honey Ward?"

Bryson sat casually on a stool, contemplating his answer. "We were in the same grade. She was very popular, but I didn't care about that kind of stuff. I was in higher courses, so we rarely had any interactions. We did have student government together though."

Bash looked up from his book, holding a highlighter. "Hey, I was a representative in student government. What were you?"

"The president. And still am." He sipped his water. "Did you like being a rep?"

"I liked having lunch in the student government conference room every Wednesday, instead of the lunchroom where Logan tried to dump his tray over my head."

Rae gasped at Bash. "Did your mom know about that?"

"No, and don't tell her. She'll stir things back up."

"I understand how mothers can be," Bryson said and set his glass down.

Bash continued, "My dad, on the other hand, is pretty cool. Mainly because he's never home." He highlighted a line of text. "I don't think he even knows my name."

Rae scoffed. "Yes, he does."

"He called me Bart the other day."

Bryson said matter-of-factly, "My dad died five years ago."

"Goodness," Rae said as Bash raised his eyebrows. "I'm sorry to hear that."

"Don't be." Bryson picked up his glass. "I was ten at the time."

Bash asked, "How did he die?"

"He fell down the stairs in the middle of the night. His head split open." An awkward silence filled the kitchen until Bryson said, "It's okay. Don't worry about it. I mean, my mom and I are good." He then flashed another one of his brilliant smiles.

Rae nodded and continued her quest. "Do you know Gio?"

Bryson nodded. "We're in the same grade too. So, I know *of* him, but I don't hang around him. He hates me. I think he's a sociopath and needs a psychiatrist."

Bash turned a page in his book and asked, "Why does he hate you?"

"Apparently, Honey liked me while they dated."

Bash asked, "Who dated? Honey and Gio?" When Bryson nodded, Bash argued, "Gio told me that he didn't know anything about Honey."

Bryson shrugged. "Sociopaths lie." He then looked at Rae. "What's with the questions?"

Rae tapped the edge of her glass, wanting to keep her sleuthing ambitions private. Finally, she replied, "Just curious, that's all. Were Gio and Honey dating when she went missing?" Bryson nodded and Rae asked, "Was she supposed to meet Gio in the woods on the night that she disappeared?"

At first, Bryson remained silent, staring at his empty glass. Then he replied, "Yes."

Rae sipped her water. She was onto something. "Do the police know that?" Bash stopped highlighting and looked at her.

Bryson nodded. "I think everyone knows that. They did it a lot." He abruptly stood. "I promised my mom that I'd be home soon. I have to mow the lawn. Thanks for the water."

"Oh, okay." Rae followed Bryson as he approached the front door. "Have a good day," she said, but he left without a word.

Bash stood behind her as they watched Bryson stroll out of view. "He acted kind of strangely, like he was spooked. Are you thinking what I'm thinking?"

"That Gio killed Honey?"

Bash objected, "Gio had nothing to do with Honey Ward. My gut says he's a good guy."

"Even though he lied to you?" Rae smirked. "Gio definitely knows something."

Bash asked, "Like what?"

"Like where he put Honey's body after he killed her."

Bash crossed his arms. "And what about that lady you found this morning? Do you think Gio had something to do with her too?"

"Purple Stiletto? Now that you mention it, yes. And I bet he took her shoe too."

"That was Purple Stiletto?" Bash suddenly choked. After a few good coughs, he said, "Maybe she lost her shoe in the woods really early this morning?"

She glanced at her nephew. "How early?"

"Sometime after two-thirty." Bash then told her about how he and Stone found a purple high heel and Bronco's hat while walking to Maeve's house to rescue Rae.

Rae's mind turned. "Why were they in the woods at that time?"

"Stone thought they were making out."

Rae shook her head. "He wouldn't have thought that if he saw Purple Stiletto's face."

"Well, Bronco is no looker either," Bash added. "Stone said I shouldn't tell the police."

Rae raised her eyebrows. "Really?"

Bash shrugged. "Do you think that I should?"

If only Bash's story didn't involve banshees, Rae thought. Maybe that was why Stone told Bash to stay quiet? Feeling conflicted, she answered, "I don't know. We *could* call Howie."

Bash nodded slowly. "We *could,* but *can* we *trust* him to not tell my mother?"

The sound of her phone ringing stopped their conversation. Recognizing the number, she said to Bash, "Too late. Howie's calling us." She answered, "Any news about the victim?" Bash plastered himself against Rae, leaning his ear toward her phone.

The officer finished yawning. "No and I couldn't tell you even if there was. I'm calling about the private investigator, Cook. He's tied up in a case, but he might be close to finishing it. When he does, he'll give you a call. It still might take a couple of weeks."

"That's fine. I'm actually onto more important things, like Bronco and Gio." Rae and Bash nodded to each other as she continued, "I have it on good authority that Bronco--"

"I'm going to stop you right there, Rae. I checked out Bronco and he's not a murderer."

Rae looked at Bash who furrowed his eyebrows. "Are you sure?"

Officer Howie sounded peeved. "Drop it now and move on."

"Fine." Rae straightened her back. "Did you know that Gio met Honey Ward in the woods on the night she disappeared?" Rae felt Bash nudge her, but she ignored him.

Sighing, Howie said, "Yes and did you know that trouble starts with a T that rhymes with D that stands for donut? Have one. There's nothing wrong with stress-eating." He then hung up.

Tension in her shoulders tightened and her right temple throbbed as a migraine formed immediately. Rummaging through her purse on the console table, Rae found four painkillers and popped the pills into her mouth, wrenching her neck. She shrieked.

"Are you okay?" Bash asked.

"No." She clasped the back of her neck. "I need to lay down."

Bash nodded. "You should go upstairs and lay down for a very, very long time."

Still holding her neck, she narrowed her eyes at him. "Are you up to something?"

•　•　•

Bash pushed Aunt Rae up two steps. "I'm not up to anything, just gonna watch TV." When she finally reached the top, he watched her shuffle down the hallway and listened to the faint sound of a bedroom door closing. Hurrying to the television, he turned it on and then tiptoed through the kitchen, grabbing his new book before creeping out the back door.

Bash ran to the garage full speed. Once inside, he opened his book to the first chapter and searched for the materials needed to trap Maeve: one stinky sock, barbed wire, wooden planks, some screws and nails, a hammer, blowtorch, a long rope, safety goggles and something called melatonin. Using his phone, he quickly learned of its sleep-inducing purpose. He was at a loss. Not owning that supplement, he wondered if painkillers could be used instead.

The afternoon passed and he had everything except for melatonin, wooden planks and the blowtorch. He had four steel stakes, however. Working with those supplies, building the trap began and when he finished, the structure looked more like refuse from a house fire than a banshee trap. Then again, who was to say what a banshee trap really looked like?

Unfortunately, the book did. The picture in the book looked like something that could trap a banshee whereas Bash's structure looked like something that could trap tetanus. His was a flat square with four stakes being held together by barbed wire and it should have looked more like a large squirrel trap. Knowing what he had to do, he scrapped his creation entirely and found a small squirrel trap on a shelf. After placing his sock inside of it, he admired his effort and headed in for dinner.

CHAPTER THIRTY ONE

A sunlit haze settled in the room as time stole most of the day. Surprised she slept so long, Rae sat up in bed, grateful that the pain was gone. Feeling better, she left her guestroom and heard voices in the foyer.

Rae found Bash at the front door, holding two pizza boxes and salivating. He turned to her. "Hey, zombie, I used your credit card to pay for dinner. I hope that's okay." Without waiting for her response, he strolled into the kitchen.

She joined him at the counter, noticing his one bare foot. "Where's your other sock?"

He looked down at his feet. "I didn't even know I was missing it."

Rae stared at him, debating if she should believe him or not.

He beamed, showing his dimples. "Let's keep breaking rules and eat on the couch."

One hour later, Rae and Bash sprawled themselves on the oversized sofa. After devouring the thick cheesy slices of pizza and garlic sticks, their stomachs bulged.

Bash could barely raise his head. "How about some pie?"

Rae rolled off the couch and stumbled into the kitchen. When she returned, she carried two plates, each with an enormous slice of apple pie topped with vanilla ice cream and caramel. Sitting next to Bash, she gave him his treat. "We should stay up all night and watch TV."

"Done," Bash said as he grabbed the remote and selected an action movie.

The hero in the film had a square jaw, piercing blue eyes and a chiseled chest. Rae thought of Stone and, raising her phone to her face, she searched for The Rail's business hours. His bar was open from two in the afternoon until two in the morning every day of the week. How horrible, Rae said to herself. His work schedule was not good boyfriend material.

After the movie ended, she and her droopy-eyed nephew found an old detective series. Wide awake, Rae watched episode after episode while Bash eventually fell into Snoozeville. She regarded his sleeping face, feeling calm only because of him, when suddenly, the charm began to burn her skin. It left no marks, but she removed the necklace and placed it on the coffee table. The burning sensation only intensified. Worried, she looked at the time, wondering if she should wake Bash. It was just past two in the morning.

Then she heard the scream again. This time, it was louder and more desperate. Cutting through her like an electric sword, it made her heart stop and instantly turned her blood to ice. She leapt to her feet, clutching her ears in horror, but nothing silenced the long screeching wail.

• • •

Stone never talked to Bash that day, like he promised. It was all too much. After Rae found a dead body with a head wound and facial lacerations, just like the ghost girl, he panicked and ran from that madness toward his sane bar duties. That was the real reason why he agreed with Sally's request to keep the bar open past closing time. It was to have a reason not to talk to Bash. "I'm a coward," he said aloud.

His arms tingled as he searched the crowd for Sally, spotting her hair first. Her wig of choice for tonight was long and wavy with a silver crown cascading into purple locks. Dressed in skinny jeans and a black crop cami, she looked very comfortable in the midst of the attractive male herd. As Stone watched her flirt, he involuntarily shivered. He wasn't feeling well. The tingling sensation escalated to burning. It felt like biting fire ants crawled all over his forearms.

He waded through the crowd toward Sally, hoping that she would agree to watch his bar so that he could leave. As she turned to face him, he noticed that her eyes were crossed.

She said to him, "Hey, hanshum."

The gin fumes on her breath singed the hair inside his nostrils. He asked, "You good?"

She nodded. "Fantasm."

He looked at her skeptically. "Do you mean fantastic?"

She nodded again. "Terrifish."

Stone's heart sank. Her insobriety ruined his plan. Helping Sally to a chair, he quickly filled a cup full of stale coffee and poured it down her throat. Maybe he could sober her up? She licked off the coffee mustache, lost the strength in her neck muscles and dropped her forehead onto the table, making a thud noise.

Then the ticking began.

It came from the old grandfather wall clock. Each passing second was loud and crisp. Tick, tick, tick, tick. No one in the bar noticed the noisy sound though, except for Stone. He hummed to silence the rhythmic clicking. It didn't work. He started singing, but that didn't help either. Desperate to end the ticking madness, he turned on the stereo system and cranked the volume to the point of bottles vibrating. The bass pounded his chest, but it didn't help. Soon, his armpits were soaked and sweat trickled down his back. The music needed to be louder and he raised the decibel, letting his mind dissolve into the electric guitar's solo. Some patrons yelled in protest, but Stone did not lower the volume.

He almost found solace until he heard the hopeless shrill, just past the two o'clock hour, causing his blood to freeze and his heart to shatter. Clutching his ears, he hoped to end the scream. It didn't end and he, instead, felt Rachel's fear in the pit of his own stomach. Covering his face, he relented to the hollowness and despairing mood fallen unto him.

Arching his back, a guttural roar escaped from his throat, instantly stopping the ticking, the music and the scream. With heaving breaths, Stone wildly looked around and the patrons stared back at Stone in silence. Then Stone heard the sound of a chair, scraping its legs across the floor. Stone's roar awakened Sally and she stood with one hand covering her heart.

She said to him, "You can turn into a werewolf? That's hot."

Stone didn't acknowledge Sally's comment. He was remembering the scream that he heard after seeing the girl's ghost for the first time. It was the same shrilling cry as tonight. A warning. Stone instantly knew what he had to do. Walking quickly to the front door, he opened it and hollered to everyone in a loud, deep voice, "Bar's closed!"

CHAPTER THIRTY TWO

Thirty minutes passed and the scream stopped long ago, as well as the burning sensation around her neck, but her heart still thumped. Biting a fingernail, Rae studied Bash and felt grateful that he never woke to hear the cougar. Or bear. If he had, he'd insist that the scream was from Maeve the banshee and now Rae's life was in danger. How silly! Reaching for the coffee table, her fingers snatched the herb necklace. Was it to help or harm? Quickly slipping it over her head, she felt that it was right to wear it. Suddenly, her phone vibrated in her pocket and she reached for it, surprised to see Stone's text. He was here, standing on the front porch.

After unlocking the door, she opened it, smiling at the sight of Stone and then frowning at the purple-haired lady who hung precariously on his arm. At first, she wondered who this woman was, but quickly recognized her face from The Rail.

In a joking tone, Rae said, "Well, it's about time. I ordered a waitress five hours ago."

Stone grinned before asking, "Are you okay?"

Rae eyed him suspiciously. "Yes. Are you *checking* on me?"

The woman looked at Rae and burped. "I'll have a gin and tonic, easy on the tonic."

Stone turned toward Sally. "This is Rachel. She doesn't have gin or tonic." He then explained to Rae, "This is Sally. She's not a waitress, just a friend who helps at the bar sometimes. Sally actually knew my grandpa. I met her through him."

Sally blinked hard a few times. "What kind of bar doesn't have gin or tonic?"

Stone sounded exasperated. "It's not a bar. I told you that in the car. Many times."

Sally whined, "You said you were taking me to *a* bar."

He shook his head. "I said I was taking you *out* of *my* bar."

"That's too bad." Sally released her grip from Stone's bicep and stepped shakily into the foyer. Glancing around, she almost lost her balance. "This is a fancy bar. It makes The Rail look like crap." She turned to Rae and asked, "Would you be so kind as to show me the ladies room?"

After closing the front door and locking it, Rae obliged, leading Sally to the nearby powder room. Then Rae looked at Stone with a grin.

Reading her expression, Stone explained, "Sally has a really good mind for business."

"It's true," Sally called from inside the bathroom. "I used to run my own cleaning business. Started out with just me and my sister, cleaning houses. Four years later, we made our first million, cleaning companies. I retired eleven years ago when I turned forty-five." She belched. "Hey, if you're waiting in line for this bathroom, it's going to be awhile." She then started singing "Let It Go".

Rae laughed and offered Stone a glass of water. He graciously accepted and followed her to the kitchen. As they sat across from each other at the table, drinking ice water, she noticed the dark shadows underneath his eyes. "You look exhausted. What made you stop by *now*?"

Stone looked deeply into her eyes. "Bash told me about the dead body. I was worried."

Her body tingled from his warm gaze and she forgot about all things nerve-racking. "Strange stuff happens to me all the time. Remember chemistry class our senior year?"

Stone chuckled. "You blew up the teacher."

"That sounds horrible. Can't we just say that I started his face on fire a little bit?"

"You burned off his eyebrows, his mustache and his full, woodsman beard."

Chuckling, Rae argued, "But I didn't blow him up entirely."

"No," Stone agreed as he laughed. "He did quit after that though."

Rae changed the subject. "Hey, remember my boss's dog that I told you about? Well, he isn't my boss's dog after all. He lives with an elderly couple and is named Toto."

"A Great Shepherd named Toto?" Stone looked puzzled. "Why was it around here?"

Rae shrugged, not wanting to tell the whole sad story. "Anything new with you?"

Stone bit his bottom lip. "Nope. Did you recover from last night's party?"

Rae eyed him suspiciously again. "You *are* checking on me."

He held her gaze with his. "You were so out of it. How much did you drink?"

Rae widened her eyes at the new memory of wine. "I had one glass of fuzzy wine."

"*Fuzzy* wine? Wine shouldn't be fuzzy, Rachel. Did she drug you?"

"Why would she do that?"

"So that you wouldn't remember anything," Stone said, "and it worked."

"But why wouldn't Maeve want me to remember anything?"

"Because she doesn't want you to really know about her."

"That's silly." So was Sally's new song choice, Rae thought as Sally now crooned "Release Me" by good ol' Bobby Darin.

Stone asked, "What do you know about Maeve?"

"Well," Rae began, "she lives in the woods."

"What's her last name? Is she married? Does she have kids?"

"I only know that she's not married."

"Ever?"

Rae snapped her fingers when old memories formed. "She's a retired art teacher and likes to do arts and crafts with the other members. That's what we were doing last night."

"Arts and crafts?" Stone raised his eyebrows. "What did you all make?"

Rae slouched in defeat. "Well, she made this necklace for me, but I don't remember making anything." Sally switched songs again and swooned to "Coming Down Again" by the Rolling Stones. "Sally sure likes a wide range of music."

Stone nodded and then asked, "Do you remember the other members?"

She shook her head. "All I remember are shoes."

Stone inhaled deeply and then exhaled. "Bash thinks that Maeve is The Birch Grove Banshee and she's out to get you."

Rae snorted. "You don't believe in that stuff, do you?"

He shrugged. "I don't know, Rachel. Who am I to say whether or not Maeve is The Birch Grove Banshee? There are some things that I didn't believe in before, but I do now."

Rae's curiosity rose. "What things?"

Stone shifted in his seat and glanced at the ceiling. Finally, he answered, "Fate."

His answer surprised Rae. She leaned toward him. "For a minute, I thought you were losing your mind and going to say *ghosts*."

He stared at his hands. "So, you think people are crazy for believing in ghosts? Doesn't Bash believe in that stuff?"

"Yeah, but he's just a twelve-year old kid. Adults who believe in ghosts are all kinda nutty. Those shows with the paranormal investigators are even fake."

Stone kept his eyes lowered. "What about the people who not only believe in ghosts, but can also see and communicate with them? Do you think they're nutty too?"

Rae shrugged. "No, I think they're liars."

Stone looked up, squinting. "Really? Why would they lie?"

"For attention." She yawned. "So, what time do you work tomorrow?"

"I usually get into work by one in the afternoon and work till closing time."

"Two in the morning? That's thirteen hours. And you're open seven days a week? No days off?"

He slowly smiled at her. "Have you been *checking* on me?"

Rae felt her cheeks warm. "I'm just curious about the life of a bar owner." She waited for his teasing remark, but it never came. Instead, Stone just stared past her in a trance-like state. Leaning forward in her chair, she rested her hand on top of his and asked, "Are you okay?"

■ ■ ■

Unbeknownst to Rachel, a white mist swelled behind her, eventually forming into the shape of a person. Stone couldn't take his eyes off it.

"Stone," he heard Rachel say faintly, "you're scaring me. Can I get you anything?"

He couldn't answer. The ghost girl with the blonde ponytail and sad brown eyes now stood directly behind Rachel. She pointed toward the backyard, but Stone remained seated and silent. The girl stared into his eyes as the cuts on her face bled. Falling deeper into a trance, a name suddenly popped into his head and he heard himself say aloud, "Honey."

Rachel blinked. "What? You want some *honey*? Like, on toast or something?"

Her questions broke his hypnotic state and the ghost quickly vanished. He cleared his throat. "Never mind. I'm good." His lips trembled, but he tried to hide his uneasiness. The last thing he wanted was for Rachel to think he was nutty or lying for attention.

Rachel grabbed both of his hands and squeezed. "You need rest. Why don't you and Sally crash here tonight? There's a guest room with a daybed for Sally and since Bash is already sleeping on the couch, you can stay in his guest room."

Stone liked the feel of her hands in his. "What if he wakes up and finds me in his bed? Should I move into yours?"

Rae smirked. "Bash is a very sound sleeper. You don't have to worry about that."

After waiting for Sally to finish in the bathroom, the three of them walked to the staircase. Stone stopped the procession and inquired about locking the front door. Rachel smacked herself for forgetting and once the door was locked, she moved a chair in front of it. Stone gave her a quizzical look, but said nothing. They all marched upstairs and Rachel led Sally to her guest room first. Now Stone stood opposite of Rachel in front of their respective rooms.

With her arms crossed, Rachel said, "I'm right across the hallway, if you need anything."

Stone raised his eyebrows. "Anything?"

She stuck her tongue out at him and he stuck his out farther. Smiling, she turned and entered her room, closing the door behind her.

Now, with the lights off, he lay on his back and emptied his mind by naming the states in alphabetical order. He fell asleep just after Wisconsin. When he awoke, he knew two things. First, it was still early as the soft morning light cast a gray hue over the bedroom. Second, he wasn't alone. At the foot of the bed stood the ghost girl. As her full name popped into his head, her brown eyes begged him to follow. Slowly turning, she glided to the door and passed through it. Stone held his breath and thought of Rachel. After quickly dressing, he slipped on his shoes, leaving the bedroom to follow Honey Ward into the woods.

CHAPTER THIRTY THREE

Rae awakened to the sound of her phone buzzing. It was a text from ChAdonis, teasing her: *Six more days until I see your naked ass.* She gagged. Needing a run, she jumped out of bed and changed into her running gear while thinking of Stone. Maybe he would run with her?

Now standing in the hallway, Rae puzzled over the open bedroom door and the empty bed that should have been occupied by Stone. Hoping to find him in the kitchen, she instead met Sally. Her long purple wig had been replaced with a short white one, choppy-layered with pink highlights. She looked comfortable while cooking at the stove as a cigar hung out of her mouth.

"Hi, doll," she said to Rae. "I found your cigar stash in the cupboard." She puffed a perfect smoke ring. "I keep my Cubans in the cupboard too. How about some eggs?"

Rae declined the breakfast and clarified, "I don't live here. My boss does and you're smoking his cigar. Please don't smoke any of the others. He'll kill you and then me." She then crossed over to the kitchen window and opened it.

Sally took the cigar out of her mouth. "Should I put this back?"

Rae shook her head. "I don't think that'll help. Looking around the room, she asked, "Have you seen either Stone or a twelve-year-old boy named Bash?"

Sally's face lit up. "Dimples is in the other room, but I haven't seen Stone at all."

Rae strolled over to Bash who sat cross-legged on the couch, eating eggs. She said to him, "Hey, dimples, wanna come with me on a run?"

"Um, yesterday, you found a dead person on a run."

"Finding another dead person today would be like a tornado striking the same house twice. It can't happen."

Bash's mouth dropped open. "Aunt Rae, haven't you ever heard of Codell, Kansas? A tornado hit that place in the consecutive years 1916, 1917, 1918. All on May 20."

"Alright, but I'm talking about one house, not one city."

Bash shook his head. "A church in Guy, Arkansas was hit three times by a tornado."

"Seriously?"

Bash nodded. "It's documented."

"My point is finding dead bodies is a lot different than natural disasters. I'm sure that my run today will be uneventful. Sure you don't want to come?"

"Sure you still want to go?"

Rae bent down to him and whispered, "Do you mind staying here with Sally?"

Bash widened his eyes at her question. "No. She's super cool."

"Okay," said Rae. "I'll be back around eight thirty. Call me if you need anything."

Soon, she was running on the path. She purposely chose to run the same route as yesterday strictly because of morbid curiosity. As she approached the crime scene, she became startled at the surprising development. Three men stood inside the caution tape and she recognized them as being Bronco, Orangutan Man and Howie. Howie deceived her!

Bronco's wheelchair was pushed to the side as they talked comfortably with each other. Rae crept into the woods and crouched behind a birch tree, listening intently to the men's dialogue. Absorbed in their conversation, they never noticed her prowling.

Next to her, a voice then whispered, "Hey, lady, you're standing on my foot."

Rae's head snapped to her left and there was Gio, crouching next to her and pointing at the ground. Removing her foot from the top of his, she asked, "What are you doing here?"

Gio answered casually, "It's none of your business. What are you doing here?"

Rae replied just as casually, "It's none of *your* business." She turned, watching the three men disperse. Orangutan Man lumbered to his Ford and drove away. Howie shook Bronco's hand before strolling down the path toward the park. Bronco sat in his wheelchair and waited a few minutes. He checked the time on his phone and Rae did the same. It was a quarter past eight. Then using his hands, he pushed the wheels in the same direction as Howie.

Rae looked at Gio as he stood and wordlessly left, walking deeper into the forest. Then against all the voices inside her head, she quietly followed, wondering about his attraction to these woods. Keeping a distance, she trailed after him and watched as he crawled through a small opening in a mound of earth covered with moss.

Remaining on the outside, she debated her next move, when she heard Gio ask, "Aren't you going to come in?" Damn, she thought. He knew that she followed him all along. Dropping to the ground, she crawled inside the small enclosure and settled herself near the entrance.

Using her phone's flashlight, she inspected the area. There were books, notebooks, a calculator, pouch of pencils and a pile of branches and twigs. She shone the light on Gio's face. "What is this place?"

Gio answered smugly, "I study here for college entrance exams."

She lifted her eyebrows. "Seriously? *Here*?"

Gio crossed his arms defensively. "My friends would give me hell, if they knew. I want to go to college and don't have a lot of money, so I need a scholarship in order to afford it, which means I need a good score on my ACTs. I study out here and hide my stuff in this place."

"If you need money, why don't you get a job?"

Gio sounded irritated. "I can only find small odd jobs that don't pay a lot."

"Is scamming twelve-year olds out of fifty bucks one of those odd jobs?"

Gio's eyes widened. "I gave Bash's money back, lady."

Rae scolded, "You should never have taken his money to begin with or taken him on a wild banshee chase at three in the morning."

Gio sheepishly studied his hands, explaining that he felt desperate. No one in his family was a college graduate and he wanted to be the first. Most of his friends dropped out of high school already and were pressuring him to do the same. He, however, had a goal.

"I want to be a civil engineer and build bridges."

Rae commented in a mocking tone, "Build bridges out of lies?"

Gio narrowed his eyes. "What have I lied about?"

"The woods and Honey Ward. You told Bash that you don't like being in the woods, yet here you are. And you told Bash that you didn't know Honey, yet you dated her."

"I told you I come here to study. As for Honey, that's nobody's business."

Rae gave her best bored expression. "Really? I'm pretty sure it's police business, especially since you were the last person to see Honey alive."

Gio glared at Rae. "That's not true. We were supposed to see each other that night, but she never came. Why would I hurt her? I loved her."

Rae scoffed at the idea of thirteen-year olds being in love and watched Gio lean over the pile of branches, brushing them away to reveal a small gift box wrapped in pink paper.

He carefully untaped the sides and opened the box. Inside were two penny keychains, each with a heart shape cut out of its center. "I was going to give this to her that night. We both wanted to see the Grand Canyon. So, the keychains meant that when we got our driver's licenses, we would go there together." He gave her a sober look. "Like I said, I loved her."

Rae was dumbfounded. "Love at thirteen. That's nuts."

"You don't understand first love, man." He returned the penny keychains to the box and buried it under the branches again. Looking at her, he asked, "Anything else?"

Rae studied him briefly before saying, "Were you crying in the woods that one day when Bash and I were talking to Bronco?" When Gio nodded, Rae asked, "Why? And why didn't you just show yourself to me?"

"I *cried* because I miss Honey. I *hid* because you scared me. At first, I thought you were my friends sneaking up on me and then I thought you were the banshee. But then I saw your face and knew you were a stranger. That scared me even more." He smirked.

Rae noticed that he seemed unusually calm and ready with answers, like he was used to being questioned. She continued, "Who's Bronco?"

Gio paused. "Just an old dude."

Rae pressed him. "Why were you watching those guys? Do you know them?"

"Look, lady, I know nothing." Gio grabbed the ACT book and set it on his lap. "I need to study." He turned on his pocket flashlight and opened the thick book, no longer interested in her.

With the conversation being decidedly over, Rae left and tried to retrace her footsteps out of the woods as her mind reeled. He knew so much more than he was letting on. And his love story regarding Honey was *unbelievably* touching. Way too shmaltzy. One thing was very clear to her though. Gio was definitely a liar.

. . .

"Gio is not a liar," Bash said to Sally as he floated on a raft in the pool. "My aunt thinks he's responsible for Honey's disappearance and Purple Stiletto's death, but she's wrong."

Sally warmed herself on the chaise lounge under the morning sun, still smoking the cigar. She looked at Bash and said, "What about Honey's parents?"

"They divorced and her dad died a month ago. That's all I know." Bash was now halfway off the raft with both of his legs in the water. "Purple Stiletto was doing something in the woods with Bronco a few hours before my aunt found her body."

Sally licked the side of the Cuban. "Is that her real name?"

Bash chuckled. "No, that was a nickname that my aunt gave her. My aunt always comes up with nicknames for people. I think it's a fun game she likes to play with herself. She used to call me Bashquatch because my name is Bash and I like Sasquatch." He slid entirely off the raft. "I don't know what Purple Stiletto's real name was."

Sitting upright, Sally said, "We gotta find that out. Now, tell me about Bronco."

Bash felt elated. He finally had a sidekick. "Bronco is this guy who hangs out at the park in a wheelchair, but he can really walk. He threatened my aunt, sort of. He told her that he was watching her and she should leave this area." Bash snapped his fingers at a recollection. "Bronco was the first person to tell my aunt and me about Honey Ward."

"Really?" Sally moved to the edge of the chaise lounge. "And you said he hangs out at the park?" Bash nodded and Sally added,

"I'm pretty good at striking up conversations with men. Why don't you show me the way?"

Bash leapt out of the pool, excited to start the investigation. Maybe with Sally's help, they could figure out the connection between Honey and Purple Stiletto? His thoughts were suddenly disturbed by the many sounds of sirens invading the area. He quickly snatched his phone laying on the patio and his stomach dropped. It was just before nine. Aunt Rae said she would be back within thirty minutes. That was a half-hour ago.

CHAPTER THIRTY FOUR

Using her good sense of direction, Rae tried to exit the forest, but the trees confused her and she found herself standing on the path by the park. With her hands on her hips, she wondered how she ended up way over here? She sighed and glanced at her phone. Since she left the house thirty five minutes ago, she only ran for fifteen of them. The rest of her time involved following Gio *into* the woods and then eventually finding her way *out of* the woods. Shaking her head, she began her jog back to Bash, hoping that she didn't stick him with the task of babysitting Sally.

A few minutes later, nothing could stop her stride, except for an empty wheelchair around the corner. She collided into it and then rolled with it for a few feet. It took her many moments to stop her world from spinning. When she finally could stand, she set the wheelchair upright and searched the area for its occupant. Rae knew the man who owned this assistive device and she knew what she was going to say to Bronco when she found him. *Fortunately*, it didn't take her long at all to spot the man in his jean shorts. *Unfortunately*, he was dead.

Bronco was sprawled on his back along the edge of the path in the same manner as Purple Stiletto. This time, however, there was no poor attempt at covering Bronco's body with leaves. Feeling more curious than frightened, Rae bent over and examined his face. She had seen those same slashes across Purple Stiletto's face yesterday. What could make those marks? Her eyes scanned the area for anything resembling a whip or belt. Maybe even a rope or leash? She squatted, being careful not to touch anything. Around his body were only small rocks, leaves and branches. Wait a minute, Rae thought. The branches were long like switches. Gio collected a pile of switch-like branches in his study cave. Taking out her cellphone, she snapped a picture of the long sticks on the ground. Then moving carefully, she leaned over to look at the back of Bronco's head. His white hair turned red and looked wet, like new, fresh paint. Purple Stiletto had the same head wound. Quickly standing, she noted the time. It was eight forty-six. Her fingers then flew across the screen on her cellphone and she rapidly dialed 9-1-1.

Rae timed the first responders behind a tree thirty feet from Bronco's body. They arrived exactly twelve minutes after she called them. After thanking the dispatcher for her calm words during the wait, she watched the frenzied crew work when a heavy hand from behind landed on her shoulder. Turning around, she squeaked at the hunched-over presence of Howie who held a white bakery bag and a large styrofoam cup of coffee.

He peered at the new crime scene. "What happened?"

Rae was cross. "You lied to me. You knew Bronco all along."

Howie interrupted her. "Is that Bronco?" Rae nodded and he exclaimed, "I just talked to him. What happened, Rae?"

"I don't know," she said. "I was running and found him like that. How did you know him? And how do you know Orangutan Man?"

"Orangutan Man?" He shook his head, visibly upset. A voice suddenly sounded from his transceiver and he quickly spoke into it. "I got her right here. 11-10." Howie handed the coffee cup and bag to her. "Do you mind holding these?" She complied and he took out the small notepad and pen from his shirt pocket. "Look, Bronco's real name was Cook. He was the private investigator I told you about. He was investigating the disappearance of Honey Ward and was close to solving it." His whole face instantly perspired. "Rae, this is bad. This is really bad."

Rae asked, "What does 11-10 mean?"

"It means that I'm conducting an interview. With you, since you found him."

"Well, I have a few questions for you too." said Rae.

"Well, if you don't mind, I'll start." Howie grabbed his coffee from Rae, took four gulps and gave the cup back to her. His voice cracked. "Where were you about forty minutes ago?"

Rae replied, "I was crouched in the woods, watching you have a chummy conversation with Cook and *Orangutan Man*. Who is he?"

He paused and then said, "First, tell me everything."

"I went for a jog. *Then* I saw you three talking and hid in the woods right off the path. *Then* I stepped on this kid named Gio and followed him into the woods. I had an interesting chat with him about Honey Ward by the way. *Then* I came out of the woods, started jogging again and ran into Cook's wheelchair. *Then* I discovered his body right there on the path." Rae almost drank his coffee, but stopped herself. "Your turn. Who's Orangutan Man? And what was Cook's connection with Purple Stiletto? There's evidence that they were killed in the same manner."

Howie only wiped more sweat from his entire face, which seemed to pale. Looking at her, he asked angrily, "Why did you go for a run *today* on the same path where you found a dead body *yesterday*? I told you to stay away from trouble."

Rae turned her head, rolling her eyes, and noticed that the onlookers from yesterday formed again. At the head of the crowd was Bash with Sally surprisingly at his side. No Stone though. Bash raised his cellphone to his face as Sally puffed two perfect smoke rings. Rae sighed and then spotted Bryson on the other side of her nephew, looking all sunny as he tapped a long stick on the ground. A mental picture of Gio's pile of sticky weapons flashed through her mind. She searched for Gio, but found Boozy Candice *with* a glass of brandy and *without* her husband, Movie Star Bob. Interesting, Rae thought. She then noticed Gio emerge from the woods and he hung near the back of the crowd. His shifty eyes locked with Rae's. Quickly glancing away, Rae scanned the crowd for Stone, but he was nowhere to be seen.

Calmer, Howie resumed questioning Rae. "Did you see any suspicious activity?"

The unexpected sound of the barking distracted her. Was it Toto? She appeared distrait as she quietly answered, "Pile of sticks."

"What?" Howie gave Rae a quizzical look.

The barking became demanding. It sounded like a Great Shepherd in trouble. Rae began nibbling her thumbnail when a voice from the group suddenly rose.

"I saw something suspicious." Gio stepped forward. "A crazed guy was in the woods early this morning."

"Crazed?" Howie wrote quickly. "What do you mean?"

"His eyes were wide open. Real wide. Like he was in a trance." Gio held out his palm. "Can I get paid now? A detective told me yesterday that if I see anything suspicious and reported it, I would be rewarded for my civic duty."

Looking at Howie, Rae raised her voice in order to be heard over the dog's wild barking. "That's Gio. You can't trust him. He's a liar."

Howie spoke to Gio, "Did you get a good description of the guy?"

Before Gio could answer, Toto sprang out of the woods, followed by Stone. Rae blew out a sigh of relief, seeing Stone lessened her anxiety. Then she noticed his clothes, scuffed with patches of dirt, and his hands held a stiletto heel in one and a tan cowboy hat in the other.

Gio pointed his finger at Stone. "Yeah, it was that guy."

▪   ▪   ▪

Around six o'clock in the morning, Stone quietly unlocked the back door as he stepped onto the patio. He saw Honey standing by the trail, waiting for him, and as he walked toward her, she disappeared. He never stopped walking though and soon hiked the path, heading toward Maeve's house. Briefly, he paused when he heard something softly moving among the trees. Then Honey appeared to him, beckoning him to continue, and he obeyed.

Stone wasn't aware of time passing. Maybe it had only been ten minutes? Maybe a half hour? It didn't phase him. And it didn't phase him when he saw the Great Shepherd waiting for him at the edge of the cliff. He instinctively knew that the dog had been following him all along.

Stone smiled. "Hey, Toto, I knew I'd find you here." Approaching the dog, Stone gave him a good ear-scratching. "You belonged to Honey, didn't you?" Toto whined and motioned his black snout toward the cliff. Stone stepped to the edge, scanning the rocky ground below him. It looked to be about a twenty foot drop. The side of the cliff was roughly carved into the earth with jutting tree roots and jagged footholds. Nodding to Toto, he knew what he had to do.

Toto guarded as Stone carefully descended the rugged cliff. Even with years of experience free soloing, he was still extremely careful on the descent. At the six foot mark, he jumped, landing on the large boulders all around him. About forty yards away, he saw sand meeting the lazy waves of the great lake as the stench of fish overwhelmed him. Then he felt the lightest touch on his hand as though someone held it. He turned and saw Honey standing next to him. With her messy blonde hair now stained red, her torn clothes dirtied and her face wet from tears and blood, Stone understood what happened. She fell to her death by someone else's hand.

Kneeling, he knew exactly where to find her remains. First, he saw the yellow fabric and then her bones, nestled between a wider space of two boulders. They were hidden well inside the crevice. Laying on his stomach, he reached for Honey with one arm, but could barely touch her with his fingertips. "I'm sorry. I can't free you." His soul instantly emptied and all he could do was cover his face with his cold, dirty hands and weep.

A warm sensation cascaded through his entire body and he raised his head as Honey appeared to him again. No longer feeling sorrow, he watched her appearance change. Her blonde hair was pulled neatly into a high ponytail, her yellow romper was clean and new and the deep facial cuts vanished, leaving a bright and unmarked complexion. The biggest transformation was her expression. The sadness dissolved as Honey beamed at Stone.

They stared at one another for several seconds. Then a bright ball of light slowly materialized behind her. As it grew, it became blinding. Stone raised his hand to shield his eyes. He saw a male figure approaching Honey and knew it was her father. When she turned and saw her dad, they hugged and walked into the light together.

Stone was now alone. He sat in peace for a long time. Hours seemed to pass and he enjoyed the solitude. No more head pain. No more tingling forearms. Taking a deep breath, he held it and listened to the soft sound of distant waves slapping at the shore. Slowly, he exhaled, smiling as the tension drifted from him.

Toto woofed above him. When Stone looked up, the dog had a stiletto heel and a cowboy hat in his mouth. He set the two items on the ground and barked at Stone once more.

Stone said, "You're right." Not knowing what the shoe or hat meant, he knew that he needed to inform the authorities about Honey.

Climbing the ascent was longer and harder, but Toto's encouraging yelps helped. When he reached the top, Toto pushed the shoe and hat over to Stone with his paw. He followed Toto's instructions, picked up the items and headed with Toto out of the woods. However, Toto didn't stay on the trail. He instead weaved through the trees, barking loudly. Suddenly, the dog shot out of the forest and Stone quickened his pace. He suddenly found himself on the path, surrounded by people wearing white coats and blue vinyl gloves. Three policemen quickly encircled him while another larger cop waddled toward him.

Stone spoke first. "I found these in the woods. The hat belongs to a guy named Bronco." A woman in a white coat approached with two plastic bags. Carefully taking the items, she placed each in their own bag and hustled toward a van. Stone then saw a body on the ground, covered completely by a white sheet. Perplexed, he asked, "Who's that?"

The first officer said, "The guy you call Bronco. Was he a friend of yours?"

Stone felt uneasy for some reason. "No, I never met him."

The second policeman asked, "But you knew his name and that this was his hat?" Stone slowly nodded and the policeman gave him a skeptical look. "Why were you in the woods?"

Perspiring, Stone explained, "I found the remains of Honey Ward. They're between two boulders at the bottom of a twenty-foot cliff. They're hard to find, but I can show you the spot."

The three policemen glanced at each other while the heavier-set cop rubbed his forehead. Stone noticed Bash and Sally as they now stood behind the policemen, shaking their heads. The third policeman asked, "But you found them? How do you know that the remains belong to Honey Ward?"

Whoops, Stone froze as he thought. He probably shouldn't have said that. Panic set in. Clasping his hands together, he pleaded. "Listen, I can't tell you. I just need you to believe me that I had nothing to do with her murder." Whoops, he thought again. He probably shouldn't have used the word *murder*. He even heard Bash gulp and Sally choke on smoke.

The second policeman spoke, "Interesting choice of words. Why don't you show us this cliff and then we can all drive down to the station and you can tell us everything. Starting with your name."

Stone felt drained. "Sure, it's Stone Winters and can I take my own car?"

The first policeman replied, "I'll ride with you. First, though, let's see the remains."

As Stone led the police through the trees, he kicked himself for throwing away the name of Zalen's lawyer.

CHAPTER THIRTY FIVE

Rae watched as the police talked to Stone, but she couldn't hear what he said to them. At one point, Stone looked like he swallowed glass and paled. When the three policemen and Stone headed for the woods, she reached for Toto and nervously petted his head.

Howie, Bash and Sally returned and Rae asked Howie, "What's happening?"

Holding out his palms in a peaceful gesture, Howie explained, "Stone found remains and is showing the officers where they are. That's all."

Rae snapped, "Whose remains?"

Bash answered, "Honey Ward's. That's not good. Stone shouldn't know that. Only the killer would know the name of his victim before a forensic scientist could figure it out."

Howie addressed Bash. "You stay out of this." He then spoke to Rae, "The police are then going to take him to the station for questioning and he'll *probably* be released after that."

Puzzled, Rae asked, "Probably?"

Howie scrunched his face. "Eh, most likely."

Sally sounded frustrated. "Let's cut to the chase. Is Stone a suspect? Yes or no."

"As of right now, maybe." Howie looked at Rae. "He looks the most suspicious."

Bash said, "In *all the* investigative shows I watch, that's never good."

Rae felt hot. Tired of holding Howie's bag and coffee, she thrusted the items at him, saying, "Look, I've been in this crazy neighborhood for the past six days and have never been surrounded by so many suspicious-acting freaks in my whole life. Starting with Gio. Any of *them* could've killed Bronco and Purple Stiletto and Honey Ward easily. Who's in charge of this clown show? I want to speak to *that* person."

At first, Howie just stared at her. Then he took his bakery bag and coffee cup from her hands, nodding his head in a manner to make her turn around. "That's him over there. His name is Detective Nelson and he's a homicide detective."

Rae spun around and flinched. Ahead of her, wearing a maroon coat and inhaling a cigarette, stood Orangutan Man. He took one look at Rae, rolled his eyes and strolled away from her. She slapped Howie's shoulder. "Orangutan Man is a homicide detective?"

Howie chuckled. "Fair warning, Rae, you don't want to get in his way."

She was already gone.

Moving through the crowd, Rae hustled toward Detective Orangutan with Bash, Sally and now Toto all trailing after her. "Detective," Rae called, "wait. You got the wrong guy."

As she approached Detective Orangutan, parts of him looked young while other parts looked old. His forehead and cheeks had no wrinkles of any kind, making him seem like he was in his thirties. Yet his balding head and general physique put him around fifty. His scowl, however, reminded her of a cranky eighty-year old grandpa.

"Calm down," he immediately told her. "Stone is fine. What's his last name again?"

"Winters. And he had nothing to do with this. He's just a bar owner."

Detective Orangutan rubbed his chin. "That's right. It's called The Empty Keg, right?"

"No, it's actually called The Rail."

The detective smiled. "Oh, yeah, that's right. The Rail. That's on Jefferson Street."

Rae shook her head. "It's on the corner of Pleasant and Hawthorne."

Detective Orangutan waved over a policeman. He said to the officer, "See if you can get a search warrant for Stone Winter's bar called The Rail on the corner of Pleasant and Hawthorne." He smiled smugly at Rae. "Is there anything else you want to tell me?"

Rae bit her tongue.

"Good." Detective Orangutan took a long drag from his cigarette and blew a puff a smoke, which swirled lazily around their heads. Then looking at her squarely in the eyes, he said, "I think it would be best if you just let me do my job." He turned toward Bash. "Stay out of those woods. Especially at three in the morning."

Bash looked surprised. "So, it was you who I was saw smoking in the woods."

The detective grinned and then noticed Sally or, at least, her cigar. "Cuba is a nice place."

Sally shrugged. "I wouldn't know. I've never been to Cuba."

"Really? Then how did you manage to acquire a Cuban cigar?" He seemed amused at Sally's silence. "Do you have a proof of purchase for that, ma'am?"

Sally looked all around her. Shocked, she asked, "Who's the ma'am?"

He held out his hand. "May I?" Sally reluctantly gave the cigar to him and as he strode away, he said to Rae, "Don't go anywhere too far, Rae. I may need to ask you some more questions." He then chuckled while enjoying his Cuban smoke.

Bash said, "Oh. My. God. He knows your name. Aunt Rae, you're a suspect."

"No, I'm not," Rae argued. "Howie probably told him about me, that's all."

Bash started to pant. "What if you get arrested? What am I supposed to do?" Toto joined Bash in the panting.

"Stop the drama. Detective Orangutan didn't say anything about me being a suspect."

"I can't believe he took my cigar," Sally said in astonishment. "And he smoked it right in front of me. What a bastard." She looked at Rae. "I wonder if he's married."

A belch interrupted them and Rae turned to see Boozy Candice standing near them. She belched again, saying to Rae, "You come to town and suddenly dead bodies pop up everywhere." Rae didn't respond. She instead watched as Candice steadied herself and eventually walked down the path toward her home, almost in a straight line.

Bash suddenly spoke, "We need a murder book."

Sally looked at Toto who looked at Rae. She asked her nephew, "What?"

Bash continued, "I know what to do. According to the TV show, *Murder Manhunt*, the first forty-eight hours of *one* homicide investigation are the most important. We have *two*. Plus a cold case. The way I figure it, if we work now and order Chinese takeout for dinner, we should have two strong leads by seven this evening." His voice rose with excitement. "All good detectives have a murder book for their notes and I have a notebook back at the manor that we can use for our murder book. Now, any thoughts on where we should start?"

Sally answered, "The neighbor with the loosest lips."

Rae asked, "Who around here has lips loose enough to give us all the gossip?"

Sally reasoned, "Someone who's drunk enough. I'm speaking from experience."

Rae and Bash said in unison, "Boozy Candice."

Sighing, Rae continued, "I guess there's no harm in asking questions. For Stone's sake."

While heading to Travis's, Rae filled them in on Bronco's real name and occupation. Bash added the new facts to his notes and the four of them now stood at the foreboding front doors of the Harrison residence, waiting for someone to answer the doorbell. Bash studied Toto. "Instead of Toto, can I call you Typhoon, after the world's biggest submarine?"

Toto groaned and shook his head.

"How about Big Chip?" Sally patted the top of Toto's head. "I once dated an amateur wrestler whose stage name was Big Chip because of his big--"

"No, no, no," Rae quickly interrupted Sally's story. "My nephew is only twelve, Sally."

Sally looked surprised. "I was going to say because of his big *chip* on his shoulder."

Rae rang the doorbell one more time and Boozy Candice finally answered, clutching a brandy glass that was half full. She gulped the rest of her drink. "What on earth?"

Rae spoke first, "Sorry to bother you. We just need some neighborhood information."

Swaying, Candice asked, "What kind of neighborhood information?"

Bash replied, "Did you know the victims?"

Sally quickly added, "Especially the first victim. She wore purple high heels."

When Candice shook her head, Bash asked, "How about Cook? He was a private eye who also was known as Bronco. Or Honey Ward? You must've known her since you were next-door neighbors." Bash had his pen upright, ready for writing, and Toto's ears pointed straight up to the sky. He also waited expectantly for Candice's answer.

Candice looked at Toto and then at everyone else. "What kind of fucked up Scooby Doo gang is this?" She hiccupped. "You're all coming on way too strong. Get off my porch already. You're all scum." Candice stepped back, grabbed the edge of the door and tried to slam it in Rae's face. However, the door stopped within inches of her nose because of Sally's body.

Using her own foot as a door jamb to keep it from closing entirely, Sally sneered at Candice. "You're going to help us, or we'll call the National Helpline and report you. So, I suggest you pour yourself another brandy and the sooner you do, the sooner we'll leave. And I'll have a gin and tonic, thanks for asking. Easy on the tonic."

Candice winced as she opened the door and gestured for them to enter, except for Toto. "The dog will have to stay outside. I'm allergic to dog hair."

Bash quickly asked, "You don't have a dog?"

Shaking her head, Candice said, "Absolutely not. Never have. Never will."

Rae turned to Toto and said, "You'll have to stay here on the porch." Suddenly, she felt Toto's paw on her foot. His brown eyes filled with concern. Patting his head, she winked at him. "Don't worry. We'll be alright." Seeming to be satisfied, he removed his paw from the top of her foot and winked back.

• • •

Stone sat on a cold metal folding chair in a small room with a tiny square table. Feeling relieved that the mystery of Honey Ward's remains was now solved, he wondered how much trouble he brought onto himself by trying to help the police. He could tell that they didn't believe his story about innocently stumbling upon the bones, but he couldn't tell them about her ghost.

The door opened and a stocky man wearing a maroon trench coat entered. His orange hair receded, leaving only a fringe around the sides and back. His face glistened and he reeked of smoky earth. After sitting in the other chair across from Stone, the man said,

"Hello, Stone Winters. My name is Detective Nelson. Can I get you anything? Coffee? Soda? Water?"

Stone narrowed his eyes. "Are you trying to get my DNA or fingerprints?"

"We already have your fingerprints on the shoe." Detective Nelson drummed his fingers on the table while staring at Stone. "According to what you told the officers, you were alone in the woods from six o'clock this morning to nine o'clock this morning. Is that correct?"

Stone nodded. "I left around six and met the police at nine."

The detective shook his head. "Why were you in the woods for three hours? You don't live in the area."

Stone felt his upper lip spasm. "I stayed with a friend who's house-sitting in that neighborhood and I went for a walk this morning."

The detective then asked, "And you just happened to find the remains of Honey Ward? Buried between two boulders? Unable to see from the cliff? How do you know it's her? Why do you think she was murdered?" When Stone said nothing, Detective Nelson continued, "Do you know Bill Cook?"

Keeping his lips steady, Stone asked, "Who is he?"

"He's a retired cop turned private investigator. He worked on the Honey Ward case."

Stone nodded. "Shouldn't you be talking to him?"

Detective Nelson watched Stone very closely as he said, "He's dead. Murdered. This morning on the path right where you came bursting out of the woods."

Stone blinked in surprise. "I thought his name was Bronco."

The following seconds felt heavy for Stone. Eventually, the detective cracked a small grin. "Look, I've been a homicide detective for eighteen years and can easily smell the guilt on a person the same way a hammerhead shark can smell the blood in the ocean. You're not a murderer. You have that dumb deer in the headlights look. But I know that you're keeping something from me about your walk. Am I right?"

The detective was definitely right, Stone thought. His upper lip spasmed again.

Detective Nelson squinted at Stone's mouth and then nodded. "I'm going to ask you again, Stone. What were you doing in the woods for three hours this morning?"

Highly doubting that the detective would accept Stone's explanation of Honey Ward's ghost leading him to her remains, he repeated, "I was just walking."

Leaning closer, the detective focused on Stone's lips. They stared at one another when a name suddenly popped out of the detective's mouth. "AJ Williards."

Stone's face relaxed. "Who's AJ Williards?"

Unexpectedly, the door opened. A young woman approached, dressed in a well-cut black suit. Carrying a briefcase, she first asked Stone, "Have you been read your Miranda rights?"

The detective answered, "He's not arrested."

The lawyer grabbed Stone underneath his bicep and pulled him to his feet. "Then we're finished here." As they left the little room and hurried down the hallway, she said, "Hello, Stone. I'm Taylor D. Drake, your lawyer. Please call me TD." She smiled. "Zalen called me. He's waiting for you outside the station. It looks like I came in nick of time."

CHAPTER THIRTY SIX

Candice waved at them to follow her down the hallway and into her husband's office. After she fell onto the leather chair behind the enormous walnut desk, she grabbed a crystal brandy decanter and knocked over the framed photograph next to it. As Rae steadied the picture, Candice fumbled with two glasses and poured brandy into both, spilling on the desk. She pushed the drink toward Sally and said, "I hate gin, but brandy and I have been best friends for the past month. Let's get on with the interrogation."

Bash spoke first, "What can you tell us about Honey Ward?"

Candice burped. "She was a typical rich kid. Only wore designer clothes. Had a taboo boyfriend. Enjoyed pissing off her parents, but they still paved her way in school with their many monetary contributions."

Rae reached for the photograph. "Who was the taboo boyfriend?"

"Gio. Nice kid, just too poor. He mowed my lawn a few times. Funny thing is Honey only dated him to make her parents angry."

Sally leaned forward in her chair. "Did Gio know that she didn't like him?"

Candice laughed before replying, "Yes. Everyone did. Even her parents. I think that's why they were so mad at her. They knew that she was just trying to get back at them."

The keychain that Gio bought for Honey entered Rae's mind. If he knew that Honey was using him, why would he give her that touching gift? She prodded Candice. "Get back at what?"

Candice closed her eyes. "I don't know."

Rae examined the photograph. The picture showed four people, or two couples, gathered closely together for a selfie. Candice and Movie Star Bob acted as bookends while cuddling with the other couple in the middle. The familiar exterior of the manor with the looming tower gave Rae a powerful clue as to whom the other couple was. Rae asked, "Are those Honey's parents?"

Candice peeked at the picture with one eye and then closed it again. "Yes. That's Laura and Ryan. There was a time when we were all *very* close. Closer than any friendship I ever had. But that friendship ended even before Honey's disappearance. And then Ryan died a month ago." She raised her glass to the ceiling. "To Ryan." After two gulps, the glass emptied.

Sally leaned over the desk, speaking loudly, "Was Honey fighting with anyone?"

Candice yawned. "Everyone. She liked drama. She fought with her parents, me, my husband. Whoever crossed her path."

Bash asked, "Why was she fighting with all of you?"

Candice struggled to open her eyes and sat motionless, squinting at Bash. A wistful and forlorn smile hinted at the corners of her mouth as she murmured, "So young, so innocent."

Rae returned the picture to the desk and glanced around the room. Her eyes settled on a display case against the wall, free-standing and tall, with five glass shelves displaying many different kinds of whips. When Rae turned toward Candice, her eyes were fixated on Rae.

Candice said, "Those belong to my husband. It's just a stupid collection of whips."

Bash nudged his aunt and mouthed to her, "Facial lacerations."

Rae thought the same thing and remembered how Bronco was alive around eight o'clock, but was dead by eight forty-five. "Where was your husband this morning between eight and eight forty?"

Candice snorted. "At work. He left at seven."

Sally asked, "He works on Sunday?"

Candice looked calm. "He works every day. He always leaves at seven."

Rae interrupted. "That's not true. He was here yesterday around eight in the morning. You both watched the crime scene."

Candice tipped her head back. "He had nothing to do with Honey's death."

Rae narrowed her eyes. "I didn't ask that."

Candice covered her face with her hands and Rae noticed her very long acrylic fingernails. Through her fingers, Candice mumbled, "The room is spinning."

Sally pressed Candice, "Are you sure you don't know the woman in the purple heels?"

Candice still hid her face. "I already said that I didn't know." Burying her head in her folded arms, Candice said, "My husband gets bored. That's all. It was all supposed to be harmless fun, but she found out."

Bash jumped on that. "Who found out what?"

Candice moaned. "That it was his idea. Honey threatened to ruin him without realizing that it would ruin all of us." Sliding off the chair, Candice crawled to the nearby waste basket. "You should go now. I'm not feeling very well." Then she threw up.

Glancing at Bash and Sally, Rae nodded and said to Candice, "We'll see ourselves out."

. . .

TD said to Stone, "Let's go over your defense one more time." Stone, Zalen and TD sat inside his car still parked at the police station. He and TD rehearsed in the front while Zalen relaxed in the back.

Staring out the windshield, Stone took a deep breath and exhaled. "I assumed that the remains were Honey's because--"

"Stop," TD interrupted, "you need to look people in the eyes when you talk. Eye contact exudes confidence. Also, always say Honey Ward, never just Honey. That sounds too familiar, like you knew her. Start over."

Stone looked the lawyer straight in her eyes. "I assumed that the remains were Honey Ward's because of all the media coverage that I've seen on television lately. Because of the news, I knew that she lived in The Birch Grove area and that she had been missing for the past two years. Because of the news, I knew the anniversary of her disappearance was yesterday. So, when I found the bones, I instantly thought of Honey Ward."

Zalen spoke from the backseat, "Because of the news."

"Remember," TD spoke to Stone, "We're establishing that the media has the power to suggest. Every day, we are exposed to advertising on TV, radio, the internet. We are constantly told to buy, eat or do something and many of us eventually act on that suggestion. That's what happened here. It was suggested that Honey Ward was missing for two years. A missing person for that long always suggests that they're dead. It was also suggested that Honey Ward went missing from The Birch Grove area, specifically from the woods. Therefore, when you found the remains in the woods, you acted on that power of suggestion and told the police that you found Honey Ward's remains without really knowing."

Zalen said, "That happened to me the other day when I saw a commercial on sauna pants for weight loss. I bought two pair and I don't even have a sauna."

Stone asked TD, "How do I explain me walking in the woods early this morning and finding the bones between the rocks? That wasn't the media's power of suggestion." TD didn't respond, but read texts while he talked. "You believe me about following Honey's ghost, right?"

Without looking at him, she replied, "Lucky for you, I've been friends with Zalen for a long time. So, yes, I do." TD then placed her hand on his forearm. "Don't worry. This is just a start. I'll come up with a much stronger defense by the end of the day. Any questions so far?"

"Detective Nelson knows that I had nothing to do with Cook's murder. Am I off the hook with that?"

"No." TD sighed. "I know Detective Nelson and everything with him is a tactic. He probably told you that you're not a suspect to make you feel comfortable so you'll slip up."

Stone clarified, "I'm still a suspect in his death then." TD nodded and Stone continued, "And why did he ask about AJ Williards? I don't know who that is."

TD thought for a moment before saying, "I don't know either. I'll dig into that. In the meantime, I have your number and you have mine. Don't talk to anyone about any of this and I'll be in touch with you later tonight. Okay?"

Nodding, Stone thanked her and asked, "We never talked about payment."

TD opened the door and stepped out of his car. "I'm doing this as a favor for Zalen. I owed him one. Possibly two." She bobbed her eyebrows and closed the door.

"It was actually three," Zalen said from the backseat. "Do you want to hear the story?"

"Not on an empty stomach." Stone turned the car key, bringing the engine to life.

CHAPTER THIRTY SEVEN

Rae, Bash, Sally and Toto left the Harrison residence in silence. Once they stood at the end of the driveway, Bash commented, "You guys are good at interrogating people."

Sally explained, "I've had a lot of experience being interrogated." Crossing her arms, she said, "There's something that *really* bothers me about Candice."

Bash asked, "What?"

"She hates gin. What self-respecting drunk *hates* gin?" Sally tsked in disgust.

They stepped onto the sidewalk and Bash immediately picked up the pace. "Let's go back to the house, have lunch and turn a room into headquarters. All we need is a glass board, glass board dry erase markers, a printer and a scanner."

Feeling like a top with everything spinning out of control, Rae's anxiety rose. To make matters worse, she recognized the black Ford pulling up to the curb. It took Detective Orangutan a few minutes to free himself from the driver's seat and to lumber over to the pack. Toto stood on all fours and Detective Orangutan approached him, offering bacon treats. Toto, however, kept his mouth closed, refusing the snack.

"I see where your loyalties lie," said the detective to Toto. Then looking at Rae, he said, "Can we talk?"

"Here?"

"Would you rather sit in my car or go down to the station?"

"Nope."

Detective Orangutan shrugged. "Then this sidewalk will do." He kept his hands in the pockets of his maroon trench coat. "You have bad luck."

Bash said, "Ah, so you've been asking around about her?"

Rae looked at her nephew. "Why don't you take Sally back to the house? Toto and I will meet you there shortly."

Bash patted Toto before leaving with Sally and Toto moved to sit next to Rae.

Detective Orangutan nodded toward Toto. "What kind of dog is it?"

"Great Shepherd."

"How old is it?"

"Two years."

"His name is Toto?" When both Rae and Toto nodded, the detective said, "He doesn't look like a Toto at all. You should call him Gladiator."

Rae asked dryly, "Are you here to talk to me about dog names?"

He grinned. "No, I'm *here* to find out why you're *here*."

Rae narrowed her eyes at him. "I'm house-sitting for my boss, Travis. He and his husband are adopting a boy from China. They'll be back by Tonyay."

He narrowed his eyes right back at her. "Right and how do you know Stone?"

Rae replied flatly. "We grew up next door to each other. We've known each other since we were three. He's a good person and would never hurt anyone. Ever."

"So, you know him well?"

Rae sighed. "That's a silly question. I know him *very* well."

"Alright. Can you tell me what his favorite movie is then?"

Toto rolled his eyes right after Rae rolled hers. "I don't know."

"How about his favorite meal? Drink? Color? What's his favorite pastime?" Rae shrugged and Detective Orangutan continued to speak calmly. "Did you know that Stone doesn't have an alibi? He was alone in the woods for three hours. No alibi."

Toto burst out barking and Rae placed her hand on top of his head, quieting him. She then asked, "Why would he hurt Cook or Honey or that other woman? He didn't know any of them."

"Do you know that for a fact? You just told me that you knew him for a very long time, yet you don't know the simple stuff about him." Detective Orangutan grinned tightly.

"We kinda lost touch." Wanting to cast suspicion from Stone, Rae blurted, "Did you know that Bob Harrison has a collection of whips and that Honey threatened to ruin him about something? And Gio knew Honey didn't *like* him. He was supposed to meet her at midnight in the woods on the very night she disappeared. Have you looked into them as suspects?"

"Yes," Detective Orangutan answered. "I was the homicide detective first assigned to this case and know all their stories. After the case went cold, I vowed to keep investigating. And now with the recent events, I'm determined more than ever to solve it, especially with the new lead."

"You mean Stone?"

"He found the remains."

"So? I found two dead bodies these past two days. Why aren't I a suspect?"

"You were. Then Officer Howard Scott intervened on your behalf."

"Howie's a good guy. You should take notes."

The detective smiled at her crack. "He says you are a good egg who just has bad luck."

Rae looked at Toto and then at the detective. "I wouldn't say *bad* luck."

"Howie told me some outrageous stories about you double-crossing some gypsies, ninja-fighting four guard dogs and almost falling off the Eiffel Tower."

"It was unusually windy that day. Nobody seems to understand that."

Detective Orangutan stiffly chuckled as he glanced at his buzzing cellphone. Walking toward the driver's side of his car, he said, "I know why you're *here*. You're snooping around this neighborhood on Stone's behalf, but it won't help him." He opened the door. "So, stop. Got it?" Then he slid behind the wheel and was gone in a matter of seconds.

"Got it." Rae slowly smiled as an idea struck. "I won't snoop around this neighborhood anymore." Then she slyly winked at Toto and he slyly winked back.

• • •

Stone stopped his red Dodge in front of the drive-thru speaker at Espresso Lane and ordered his lunch. "I'll have a ham and egg sandwich with ranch dressing. And I'd like my egg cooked over medium, please. And a bottle of water."

In a monotone voice, the male cashier asked, "How do you want your egg?"

Speaking clearly into the microphone, Stone answered, "Over medium."

"And did you say mayo dressing?"

"No, I said ranch."

"So, one ham and blue cheese sandwich with one raw egg and french dressing?"

Stone sighed. "No, I want the egg fully cooked with ranch dressing and no blue cheese."

The young man said, "I'm sorry. Could you repeat that?"

Stone leaned his head out the window and yelled, "One egg *cooked*, no *blue*, just *ranch* dressing!"

"Just to be clear, you said cooked blue ranch?"

Leaning over, Zalen positioned his head by Stone's right ear and spoke around him. "Hey, Erik, how are you doing today?"

The cashier heard Zalen's voice and said, "Is that you, Zalen?"

"Yeah, my man. It's been awhile."

"Hey!" Erik said with his voice full of inflection. "I thought you were supposed to be in South Africa, helping children with special needs?"

"I ended up in a small snafu at the airport and the security took my passport. I'm hoping I can go next year once my name is off the no fly list."

"I got in a small snafu at the airport about two years ago. I was carrying drugs. What was your crime?"

"Wearing spandex shorts."

"Oh, man, that's harsh." The drug mule turned drive-thru cashier sounded genuinely deflated. "Would you like your usual?"

Zalen replied, "Yes, please. And Erik, let's get our Barbershop Quartet back together."

Erik said, "Definitely. Your total is fifteen eighty-seven. Pull up to the first window and I'll have everything ready."

Erik was true to his word. He smiled at Stone while handing him the bagged order and drinks. "Here's your ham and egg over medium sandwich with ranch dressing. And Zalen, I put some extra special sauce on your spinach and mushroom sandwich. Just the way you like it." After saluting Zalen, Erik began taking another order and closed the window.

Stone parked his car in a nearby spot, took out his sandwich and handed the rest of the order to Zalen. With his mouth full of spinach and mushrooms, Zalen asked, "You don't like *blue* cheese? Only *ranch* dressing on your *cooked* egg sandwich?"

Maybe it was the way Zalen said it, or maybe it was the number times Stone heard the words cooked, blue and ranch? Whatever the reason, Stone suddenly had a vision of a blue ranch house with two arbor vitaes and a mailbox with the name of Cook on it. He looked at Zalen. "Are you trying to lead me to Cook's house? Why, in God's name?"

Zalen replied, "I can't really feel the answer to that, but I feel it's important."

"Did you know him? Do you know where he lives?"

"Nope, but I feel that you do." Zalen slurped his iced tea and said, "I also feel that we need to go there."

Stone turned his head toward Zalen. "Why?"

"Because I feel that she's there right now."

Stone's heart flipped. "Who are you talking about?"

"Rae. Or Rachel, as you like to say."

Stone tore out the parking lot, clipping part of a hedge with the bumper as his sandwich hung out of his mouth.

CHAPTER THIRTY EIGHT

Rae turned into an old subdivision on the outskirts of the big city. The small houses lining the street screamed from the 1960s era. Pulling over, Rae parked in front of a ranch with faded blue siding and a beaten up driveway. Two arbor vitaes stood on either side of the large bay window. Untrimmed and overgrown, their branches crept over the glass, hiding both the contents and actions from inside the home. Weeds dripped down from the gutters. The once solid blacktop for the driveway now moaned in pain from all the cracks, leaving the pavement broken and aching. Gaping at Sally in the passenger seat, Rae said, "I can't believe we actually found Cook's house."

Sally placed her cellphone in her gold sequins purse. "It pays to know the right people."

Bash sat in the back with Toto whose large body took up all the space, burying Bash. Even though Rae couldn't see her nephew, she heard him. "Who's the right person?"

"His name is Johnathan W. Thomas. He's a retired judge who worked with a bailiff who had a brother who worked in the same force as Cook." She smiled at Rae. "Good ol' Johnny. He loved my flexibility, especially when we--"

"Nope," interrupted Rae. "Remember, Bash is only twelve."

"I was going to say when we *danced*."

Bash asked his aunt, "So, we're going to break and enter Cook's house?"

"No," Rae answered, "just enter. I'm hoping to find a key, so we don't have to break in."

Toto, who hung his head out the open window, glanced disapprovingly at Rae and made an inquisitive sound in his throat. She looked at him and shrugged. "Hey, this is Bash's idea. So, look at Bash like that, not at me."

"How did I give you the idea of breaking into Cook's home?"

"*Entering*, not *breaking*. And you were the one who said that every detective has a murder book. Well, we need to find Cook's."

Sally commented, "I'm always up for a thrilling time, but I gotta ask. How do you know he actually has a murder book and how do you know it's in his house? Somebody else could already have it. Or maybe he had it with him when he was killed and now the cops have it."

Toto's back pressed into Bash's face, making Bash sound muffled. "Cook may not have worked from home either. He may actually have an office somewhere."

Rae nodded. "Those are all good insights. But this is the only place I know to start and since I told Detective Orangutan that I wouldn't snoop in Travis's neighborhood anymore, this is where we are. So, here's plan A. Let's go in and search for any clues that may help us in figuring out who Cook suspected in the murder of Honey Ward. Maybe there's a murder book or maybe there's something else?" Rae turned around in her seat to face the team. "We should come up with a code word, just in case we need to alert everyone that there's trouble and we need to run for our lives. How about *pineapple*?"

"Pineapple?" Sally frowned. "Why can't we just say *let's get out of here*? Or *run*?"

Bash quickly said, "Run. Let's get out of here."

"Already?" Rae asked, "Why?"

"I see a car parked in the backyard."

Astonished, Rae looked at Bash and saw only Toto's stomach. "How can you see anything?"

"Well, I can see the back end of it." Bash craned his head way back to look out the window. "It looks new and doesn't seem to fit with the house."

"So," Sally said, "someone's home. Now what?"

Rae asked Sally, "Did good ol' Johnny say if Cook had a wife? Or kids?"

Sally shook her head. "I didn't ask. Could it be Cook's car?"

Rae replied, "Cook drove a convertible."

Bash struggled to be heard. "You're not listening to me. I said the car doesn't seem to go with the house. It looks too good to belong here."

Rae asked her nephew, "What kind of car is it?"

"I can't tell. But it reminds me of every other kind of trendy mom car I see on the road."

"Okay," said Rae, "plan B. I'm going around the back to knock on the door. Maybe the car owner is a relative? Maybe they can help? I'll try to nonchalantly find out."

Bash's bangs peeked over Toto. "Why the back door?"

"I don't want to be seen by any neighbors. The last thing I need is for a neighbor to describe me to Detective Orangutan. The rest of you stay here." Toto grumbled as Rae removed the key from the ignition and gave it to Sally. "If things go awry, save my nephew and leave." Rae emerged from her car and Sally, Bash and Toto emerged as well. Rae looked at them. "What are you all doing?"

Bash replied, "We're coming with you."

Toto nodded and Sally flipped the car key back to Rae. Then she dug into her purse, pulling out vinyl gloves and passing a pair to each of them. "I always carry these with me. It's out of habit."

"Oh," said Rae, "because you used to have that cleaning business?"

Sally looked surprised. "I forgot about that."

Rae shook her head. Her last words to the group were, "Try to look inconspicuous."

The four of them strolled up the driveway, all giving their best impressions of looking normal in this neighborhood. Rae knew though that they stuck out like four sore thumbs. For starters, Sally sported a white wig with hot pink highlights. Meanwhile, Toto's large size blended easier with planets rather than ranch houses. As for herself and Bash, they almost impersonated regular people, but the blue gloves gave them the appearance of being either nurses or serial killers. Rae speculated that those were two unnerving professions for the other older homeowners. When the next-door neighbor stepped onto her front porch to retrieve a newspaper, she jumped at the sight of them and knocked the glasses off her face with her flailing arms. Rae waved at her with her blue hand, but the neighbor didn't return the friendly gesture. She instead ducked inside her home, quickly closing the front door and leaving the eyeglasses on the stoop.

Rae alerted the others. "We've been spotted. Let's go around quickly and not attract more attention." After hustling everyone to the back door, she knocked on it three times. Glancing at her phone, the time was near noon. She rapped on the door again, but no one answered.

Bash reached over her shoulder and rang the doorbell. They all leaned in, placing their ears against the door.

Sally said, "I don't hear anything."

Rae nodded and tried to open the door, but it was locked. "Back to plan A. Let's search for a spare key and enter the house to find Cook's murder book or other clues."

Sally began looking underneath various objects, like rocks, a grill and a garden hose. She called over her shoulder, "Why aren't the police here? I mean, shouldn't they be here since Cook was murdered this morning?"

Rae shushed her, replying quietly, "Maybe they came already?" When Bash shook his head at her in dismay, she huffed. "Well, I don't know. Do you?"

Bash nodded. "If the police came already, they would've left caution tape everywhere. I think they're on their way."

"Well, then." Rae was impatient. "We better hurry."

Bash pointed to the car. "That car bothers me. Who does it belong to?"

Sally now was head over heels in a bush. "I can't find a spare key anywhere."

Rae pointed to a hanging birdhouse and said to Bash, "Look in there for a key."

Toto arfed and Bash said, "I agree with Toto. There's something fishy about that car."

Rae widened her eyes and sucked in air out of frustration. "Fine," she said and blew out her breath. She saw Sally drop to all fours near a basement window. Turning her full attention to the car, Rae said to Bash, "It's a rental."

Bash stared at the car. "How do you know that?"

"It has brand new license plates and no dealer markings." Rae pointed to a sticker on the driver's window. "See that? It's a barcode for the car rental company to keep track of it." She saw the astonished look in her nephew's eyes and said, "You know about banshees and I know about cars. Now let's get going."

Bash stalled. "But who's renting it, why are they here, and *are they dangerous*?"

Rae bit a fingernail. "Okay, new plan." She looked at Bash. "You wait in the car." Toto whined and Rae added, "With Toto."

"No way, Aunt Rae. You can't physically make us."

"Yes, I can." She looked up and into Bash's face. He seemed taller than yesterday. Then she studied Toto. He also seemed taller and heavier. Both of them smiled at her triumphantly. "Fine," she said. "Why waste time debating this when there's a good chance that we won't be able to get into Cook's house anyway?"

Just then, the back door opened and Sally stepped out of the house. Smiling, she explained, "I opened the basement window and crawled through." She sighed longingly. "Boy, I miss those cat burglar days."

Before Rae opened her mouth to speak, Bash and Toto pushed past Sally into Cook's home and Rae quickly followed. All four now stood in the middle of the kitchen, listening to the eerie silence. Rae called out, "Is anyone here? We're just harmless neighbors doing a welfare check." Bash gave her a quizzical look and she shrugged at her fib.

After a few quiet moments, Sally said, "I think we're alone. So, what exactly are we looking for?"

"A murder book." Bash's apprehension had been replaced with newfound excitement. "It's a file full of notes, photographs, witness interviews, stuff like that."

Rae added, "Or look for anything with Honey Ward's name on it. We need to find out who hired Cook too. Or any information to get Stone off the hook. Whatever that may be."

The four of them shifted into high gear, swiftly moving through the house. Rae tackled the catch-all dining room table, Bash foraged a kitchen desk littered with everything from old newspapers to empty coffee mugs, Toto tipped over the kitchen trashcan with his nose, digging through the refuse, and Sally studied the mini bar in the living room.

"Does it have to be a book or file?" Sally asked, "Can it be something else?"

"Why?" Bash asked excitedly, "What did you find?"

"Post-its." Sally paused. "Weird. They're just old lists that he used for bottle coasters."

"Never heard of such a thing." Rae sounded stressed. "All I found are unpaid bills. Look, it's been five minutes. We gotta hustle. I'll quickly search his bedroom."

As Rae strode out the dining room and into the foyer, she heard a key being inserted into the front door. Fear took over her mind and body, rendering her speechless and immovable as she watched the doorknob turn.

The door flung open and two men entered. One held a half-eaten ham sandwich and the other one held a key while happily exclaiming, "Rae!"

 .   .   .

Rae recognized the exaggerated smile. "Zalen? Where did you find that key?"

"It was under the welcome mat." He then returned it.

Her eyes shifted over to Stone. "You're not in jail?"

"Technically, I was never arrested." Shoving the rest of his sandwich inside his mouth, he spoke with his mouth full. "We should go."

Zalen disagreed, closing the door behind him. "Don't worry. We have some time."

Rae asked Stone, "What are you even doing here?"

Stone squinted. "We saw you on the road and followed you. What are you doing here?"

Bash interjected, "We're here on important business. The man who lived here was a private investigator."

Stone nodded. "I know. Detective Nelson told me all about it. Let's go."

Chuckling, Zalen said, "Relax, Stone."

Rae winced. "You mean Detective Orangutan? He's a piece of work."

Sally looked at Stone. "Do you have a good lawyer?"

Zalen said reassuringly, "He has a great lawyer. She's actually my personal lawyer and very good friend. She's very smart and won't let anything happen to Stone. Plus, I think she likes him." He winked at Stone. "I get a feeling."

Rae's eye twitched once.

"She *likes* likes him?" Sally asked, "What's her name? Does she have a lot of experience in the law field?"

Zalen replied, "Her name is Taylor D. Drake and she's *very* experienced in all fields."

Rae's eye twitched twice.

Stone added, "TD already has a great start for my defense."

Sally crossed her arms. "TD? Is that your pet name for her?"

"She told me to call her TD. They are her initials." Stone grinned.

Sally sneered. "Gag me. Before you two elope, I want to meet her first."

Rae's eye twitched three times.

Toto cocked his head to the left when Bash asked, "Is she pretty?"

Stone nodded and Zalen said, "Definitely. She looks like that one alien movie actress with the full lips and naturally glowing skin. I can't remember her name."

Rae suggested, "Tom Skerritt?"

Zalen said, "No, not that one. The other beautiful actress."

Stone said to Zalen, "I think you're thinking of the actress in those action movies where she searches vaults for her missing father. She has long brown hair and a killer body."

Zalen smiled in adoration. "Yes. Fit, but still feminine."

Rae's eye was having a full-blown spasm. While covering it with her hand, she said sharply, "We're here to look for Cook's murder book. It may have imperative information about Honey's case in it. So, let's stop wasting time." Glaring at Stone, she said, "You should go."

He smiled smugly. "Not without you."

Bash asked Rae, "What's wrong with your eye?"

"Nothing." Rae marched down the hallway. "I'm searching the bedroom. If anyone has questions, ask Bash. Now hurry!"

Zalen said easily, "Don't worry, guys. We don't have to hurry yet. We have some time."

Rae now stood in Cook's bedroom, which looked like a storage facility for boxes. He was apparently a hoarder. Stone sauntered into the room, squeezing his hands into blue vinyl gloves, and exclaimed, "Whoa. This is nuts." He looked at Rae. "So, what's a murder book?"

She did not look at him. "Why don't you ask your girlfriend?"

Stone spoke calmly, "I don't want to ask TD. I want to ask *you*."

She felt the heat of his general presence all around her. Moving away from him, she lifted a lid off one of the boxes. "It's a file that detectives use to keep all of their notes."

"So, it's not an actual book?"

Rae shrugged. "I really don't know. I'm just looking for anything about Honey Ward." She looked him straight in the eye. "I'm doing this to save your ass."

Reaching around her waist, he pulled her toward him and hugged her tightly. "Thanks."

Rae melted into his chest for a hot minute before freeing herself from his arms. "Let's just find the book."

She opened a box, discovering a stack of spiral notebooks with months and years written on the covers. After quickly rifling through them, Rae learned that each was dedicated to one of Cook's cases. These were his murder books. Now, she just had to find the right box with the current year. She closed the lid, noticing that Stone watched her.

Leaning against a tower of boxes, he asked, "Ever hear the name AJ Williards?"

Opening a new box, she shook her head. "No, why?"

Stone shrugged. "Detective Nelson mentioned his name to me, but I never heard of it either." He blew out a sigh. "So, how did you find this place?"

"Sally. She knows a lot of people." Returning the notebook to the pile, Rae closed the lid and opened the third box. "Did Detective Orangutan wonder about your morning walk?"

Stone smirked. "Yes and I bet that you're wondering too."

Rae closed the lid to the third box and opened the fourth. "Yep."

Stone crossed his arms. "Do you think I had something to do with Cook's death?"

Rae looked at him. "Maybe?" His mouth dropped open and she smiled. "It occurred to me that I don't really know the present-day Stone. I don't even know your favorite movie."

Rubbing his forearms, he gave her a complacent look. "It's Step Brothers. And you do know me, Rachel. Present-day Stone hasn't changed that much from the past."

"Yeah, I guess." Rae turned her back to him. He clearly wasn't going to answer her question about his walk. "Maybe you can help me look instead of just watching?"

Suddenly, she felt something slap the side of her thigh. She looked at Stone and he pointed to a spiral notebook on the bed. She picked it up and opened to the first page, gasping at the name entered on the first line. It was Honey Ward. Crossing her eyebrows at him, she asked, "Where did you find this?"

Stone gestured to the nightstand. "I had a feeling that it would be in there."

"Damn, that makes sense." She smacked herself in the head with the notebook. "Why would he store this in a box when he was still using it? Duh."

"Don't be so hard on yourself. This is your first ransacking." Stone grinned.

Rae quickly flipped through the notebook, disappointed at all the blank pages. However, she noticed that chunks had been torn out of the book, including most of the first page.

Stone shook his head. "The old tear-the-important-pages-out-of-the-book trick."

Rae bit her fingernail. "What if Cook tore the pages out and hid them in a safe place?" Suddenly, Rae snapped her fingers as a thought popped into her head. Crossing the room to the closet door, she placed her hand on the doorknob, glancing at Stone. "My parents keep a safe in their closet for important papers. What if Cook did too?" Swiftly swinging the door open, her body crumbled under the weight of the falling boxes, spiral notebooks and another dead body.

CHAPTER THIRTY NINE

Still unsuccessfully searching the kitchen drawers, Bash froze when he heard what sounded like an avalanche of his falling sleuth aspirations. He looked at Toto who stood at attention. Then he heard Stone curse loudly and he raced past Zalen in the foyer, around Sally in the hallway and toward the bedroom. Toto followed closely behind and they both skidded to a stop before tripping over Aunt Rae and a dead woman. Looking down at the floor, Bash said, "Oh, Aunt Rae, this makes three dead bodies in two days."

Stone pushed the woman's body off Aunt Rae and helped her to stand while the whole group gathered. Bash noticed that the deceased hadn't stiffened yet. Bending down, he inspected the mark around her neck, which was about one centimeter in width and dark brown in color. "She was obviously strangled, which is different than Cook and Purple Stiletto." He looked up at his aunt. "And not too long ago."

Stone asked Aunt Rae, "Purple Stiletto was the first victim, right?"

Aunt Rae looked at Bash. "How does he know that?" Bash smiled innocently and his aunt sighed, pointing at the new corpse. "She looks familiar to me."

Studying her thick brown hair pulled back in a ponytail, she seemed familiar to Bash as well. He glanced over the rest of her, noting her expensive sporty outfit. "I've seen her before too, but can't place it." He spoke to Zalen, "Are you feeling anything?"

Zalen patted his stomach. "Just a little gut rot."

Aunt Rae snapped her fingers. "That's Laura Ward, Honey's mom. She was in the photograph on Movie Star Bob's desk."

Sally agreed, "Yeah, it is." Bash turned to face her. In Sally's hand was a wallet. She looked at Bash's alarmed face and asked, "What? The dog found it."

Bash looked at Toto and he had a satchel bag in his mouth, which he dropped before wagging his tail. "Good boy," Bash commended.

Sally took three cards out of Laura's wallet and handed them to Aunt Rae. "Here's her driver's license and a car rental business card. But look at this one."

Bash's eyebrows rose as his aunt said to the group, "It's Cook's business card. Laura Ward must have hired Cook to find out what happened to her daughter."

"Wow," Bash said, "and now Laura and Cook are both dead. Along with Purple Stiletto and Honey Ward."

"Four murders," Sally clarified.

"In different ways," Aunt Rae pointed out. "Cook and Purple Stiletto both had head wounds and facial lacerations. Laura was strangled and we have no idea how Honey died. Are these murders even connected?"

Stone opened his mouth and then quickly shut it, pursing his lips.

Bash wrote in his notebook. "I personally think this could only mean one thing."

Zalen smiled. "Jack Daniels."

Sally raised her eyebrows. "Speaking of my good friend, Jack, I think I'll grab him." She left the group.

Bash shook his head. "It means that there are two killers."

Zalen stuffed his hands into his pockets. "We should go now. We ran out of time."

Suddenly, Toto whined at the sound of the distant police sirens and expletives exploded from everyone's mouths. Stone grabbed Aunt Rae by the shoulders and told her to drive straight back to the manor.

"Where are you going?" Aunt Rae looked concerned.

"Back to the bar. I'll call you later." They stared into each other's eyes briefly before bolting in opposite directions.

The next thing Bash knew, he sat in the passenger seat of his aunt's car with Toto stuffed in the back. He watched Stone hustle Zalen and Sally into his car before leaping into the driver's seat. Aunt Rae pressed the accelerator to the floor, squealing the tires and forcing Bash to clutch the grip handle.

Within minutes, a police car raced past them and Bash blew out a sigh of relief for not being pulled over. He then looked down at his gloved hands and wondered how the bottle of Jack Daniel's ended up in one. More interesting was the post-it stuck to the bottom of the bottle. He peeled it off and read the list of words scribbled on the piece of paper: Park, 10:00, AJ Williards. He showed it to his aunt. "What do you make of this?"

While glancing at the words on the post-it, Rae zigzagged through Cook's subdivision. There was that name again. AJ Williards. Looking at Bash, she said, "Search for that Williards guy on your phone."

Bash already found some information. "There are a lot of people with the name Willard, not Williards. The only AJ Williards I can find is a man named Andrew Jackson Williards. Wait a minute." Bash paused and then said, "He died in nineteen twenty." He slid his phone into his back pocket. "What we need to do is create a link chart back at headquarters. I need visuals."

As Rae approached a four-way stop, another car stopped across from her. Then they both accelerated through the intersection, passing each other. Rae recognized the handsome driver and she could tell by his surprised expression that he recognized her as well. "That's Movie Star Bob. What is he doing near Cook's house? I thought he was at work."

Bash opened his red notebook. "That's interesting." As he made note of that information, he asked, "Who do you think called the police on us?"

"My guess is the neighbor who saw us walk up to Cook's house. I'm still wondering about Movie Star Bob though. Why is he here?"

Just then, Rae's phone rang and Bash answered it, immediately putting it on speakerphone. On the other line was Sally. "Hey, I've been thinking. Candice said that her best friend this past month has been brandy. She also said that she and her husband were close friends of the Wards. I think the two couples were swingers."

Bash asked the group, "What are swingers?"

Rae didn't want to answer his question and ignored it. "Sally, why do you think that?"

"Because of something Candice said. She toasted Ryan's death, which happened a month ago. That's the same time that she started drinking. Could she be mourning her lover's death? And then she said that Honey was going to ruin Bob and inadvertently ruin all of them. The two couples were obviously doing something fascinating. I mean, wrong."

Bash held his phone as he read aloud. "According to dictionary dot com, swinger is a person or thing that swings, or someone who's fashionable. I don't get it."

Rae snapped her fingers at a memory. "I saw Movie Star Bob walking with Laura Ward last Wednesday. It was that day when Bash and I were looking for Toto. Remember, Bash?"

Gasping, Bash still read from his phone. "*Wife*-swapping? What's that?"

Rae continued, "Let's say you're right, Sally. On the night that Honey disappeared, Ryan wasn't home and felt guilty about it. Maybe he was with Candice?"

Sally agreed. "And I bet Bob was with Laura."

Bash gaped at his aunt. "Group *sex*? *That's* what you mean by *swingers*?" His phone fell from his grip. "I am young. I am innocent."

Sally quickly said, "I gotta go, sweetie. We're at the bar and the lawyer is here, waiting for us." Rae heard Stone groan before Sally disconnected.

Rae looked at Bash. "Let's say the four of them were sleeping with each other. What do these affairs have to do with these murders?"

Bash said, "I think Bob and Candice killed Honey. Bob lied in an interview I read. He stated that he was walking his dog at midnight on the night that Honey snuck into the woods, but his wife told us today that they never owned a dog. She's allergic to dogs. So, if he wasn't walking a dog, why was he there?"

Toto whined and Rae stared at him in the rearview mirror as a thought struck her. She said, "Unless he was talking about Toto, which proves that he was there with Laura, right?"

Bash shrugged. "I don't know. We have to stick to the facts. Laura Ward hired Cook to investigate Honey's disappearance. He was close to solving it and was murdered, probably by the same person who had something to do with Honey's murder. What else?"

Rae added, "Purple Stiletto knew Cook and I think they were working together."

Bash said, "Well, I think we should talk to Boozy Candice again. Maybe we should head over there now before Bob gets home?"

Rae pointed to the post-it. "Keep that in a safe place."

Bash opened his red notebook and stuck the post-it inside of it. Looking at her with an air of triumph, he said, "Done."

The rest of the drive was quiet and uneventful. As Rae pulled into the driveway, she felt relieved to see neither the police nor Movie Star Bob behind her. The three of them stepped from the car and, to Rae's surprise, Toto exploded toward the woods. He galloped across the backyard, stopping at the beginning of the hidden trail, and began that incessant barking.

"My trap!" Bash shrieked and bounded after Toto. Rae followed and caught up to him just as he squatted near a metal rectangular cage, which was the size of a large shoebox. Inside of it was a nonmoving white ball of soft fur and a dirty sock.

Rae peered over Bash's shoulder. "What on earth?"

"It's my banshee trap," he explained.

"That's a squirrel trap."

"Yeah. I tried to build my own, based off the book that Bryson gave me, but it didn't work out. So, I used this squirrel trap instead. My sock was supposed to be prey. The book said *not* to use real animals because they could attract owls." Bash leaned over the lifeless creature. "It didn't say anything about socks attracting guinea pigs."

Biting a fingernail, Rae asked, "Is it dead?"

Bash picked up a nearby stick and poked at it gently. The guinea pig never flinched. He poked at it again, harder, and Toto whined. Dropping the stick, he said to Rae, "It's dead."

Rae nodded. "I'm sure you know whose guinea pig that is, don't you?" Bash nodded and she continued, "How did Fluffy end up here? I can't imagine it escaped and then walked down the road, through Travis's back yard and into this trap."

"Well," Bash began, "you're not going to like my answer."

Rae bit another fingernail. "Does it involve Maeve?"

"Yes. Using her magical powers, she lured Bryson's guinea pig here to warn us. We're obviously getting too close to finding out what happened to Honey, Cook and Purple Stiletto."

"Are we?"

"I was right in suspecting her all along." He turned and started walking toward the house. "I'm getting a bag for Fluffy. We have to give it back to Bryson." Toto trotted after Bash.

Rae sighed as her head dropped to her chest and a warming sensation awakened at the center of her collarbone. At first, it calmed her. Soon, however, the heat began to heighten. She opened her eyes as her fingers felt the source of the heat. It was the charm again. Or the potion necklace or witch bottle. She remembered how Bash explained that a witch chooses her ingredients with that specific person in mind to help that intended person. Or was it to harm?

Just then, Rae jumped as the cage rattled all by itself. It was a quick shake, just enough to grab Rae's attention. She froze, still clutching the charm, when she heard something crack deep in the woods. Rae raised her head toward the intrusive noise, seeing nothing at first. As she searched the darkness, however, she recoiled after spotting a face among the trees, watching her. It was a pale face with dark eyes and white flowing hair. It was Maeve's face. Rae blinked and Maeve was instantly gone.

After Bash and Toto returned with a bag, Rae debated whether telling her nephew about seeing Maeve's creepy face. Deciding *not* to add more creepy ingredients to Bash's banshee stew, she held her tongue.

CHAPTER FORTY

TD stood in front of the entrance doors, gripping her briefcase and clenching her jaw. Stone unlocked the door to his bar and held it open, allowing his entourage to enter. Sally sprinted to the restroom, Zalen headed for a stool at the counter and TD walked to the nearest bar table. Shaking her finger at him and Zalen, she said, "I just got a call and heard the most ridiculous story. Tell me it's not true."

"What story?" Stone looked at Zalen.

"The story that a good-looking guy broke into Cook's house with a jolly round man, a woman with hot pink hair, a very large dog, a youngish boy and a little kid."

Zalen laughed. "Little kid? You must be talking about Rae. She is small."

TD looked at Stone in astonishment. "What were you thinking? Going to Cook's house was so stupid. How am I supposed to defend you when you do stupid things?"

Confused, Stone asked, "Who called you?"

"I have a friend who's a cop and he warned me about the report." She rolled up her sleeves. "A neighbor watched all of you go into Cook's house at different times. She said you looked suspicious and called the police. Why in the hell did you break into that house?"

Stone tried to reason with her. "We didn't break in. We had a key."

Zalen said, "We found it. It was under the welcome mat."

TD looked at Stone. "Why were you there, of all places?"

Stone explained, "Rachel thought Cook kept a murder book about Honey Ward's case and she hoped that he named the killer in his notes. She was trying to help me."

Zalen asked her, "Do you want to know about the dead body we found?"

TD raised both her hands in frustration. "I already heard." Slamming her briefcase on the table, the loud boom shook Stone's nerves.

Sally frantically appeared into the room. "Are we being shot at?"

Stone answered, "Might as well be. We were seen at Cook's house."

Sally pointed to herself. "Even me?"

TD spoke. "Your hair definitely was."

Sally whisked off her wig, exposing her gray short hair. She ran into the kitchen and Stone then heard running water followed the sound of the garbage disposal. He sighed.

TD continued, "Lucky for you, I've dealt with worse situations. So, when the police come to question you, tell them you won't say anything without me, your lawyer. Then we'll go from there." She shrugged. "They'll probably arrest you, but until then, keep doing your normal stuff. Run your bar, don't talk to anyone about what's going on and stay away from Rachel."

Stone squinted at TD. "Why?"

TD rolled her eyes. "My cop friend knows her and told me that she attracts trouble." TD touched his forearm, caressing it tenderly. "You don't need Rachel bringing anymore suspicion to you. Understand?"

Zalen chirped up again, "She prefers to be called Rae."

Stone sighed. "Go home, Zalen."

"Okay." He slid off the stool and pleasantly strolled out of the bar.

Stone turned to TD and spoke sternly, "I will not stay away from Rachel. Besides, I should warn her that we were all seen entering Cook's house."

TD never took her eyes off Stone. "Absolutely not. If she is questioned by the police, her reaction must be sincere and not rehearsed. Just stay away from her, for Christ's sake. I have a feeling that you two together is *dangerous*." Grabbing her briefcase, she said, "I have to go to court for the rest of the day. I wrote a killer closing argument for this elderly lady who tried poisoning her husband." She flew out the door with her head held high in the air.

After TD left, Sally approached Stone. "I have two things to say. First, you need Rachel as much as she needs you and second, your garbage disposal appears to be smoking."

Stone stood in front of Sally, crossing his arms. "What if TD is right, though? What if Rachel will be hurt if I'm near her?" Sally said nothing and Stone's mind replayed Rachel's body shattering again. His plan to act like an orange traffic barrel in guiding her to safety already landed him on the suspect's list and provoked Rachel into illegally searching a dead man's house. Maybe TD was right? The two of them together was dangerous.

As Rae, Bash and Toto followed the sidewalk to Bryson's home, Rae asked her two companions, "Do you think it's strange that Stone went for a walk early this morning and *happened* to find Honey Ward's bones?"

Bash adjusted his grip on the plastic bag, which held the deceased Fluffy. "Not really."

When Rae glanced at Toto, the dog looked upwards and shook his head. She narrowed her eyes at the both of them, not trusting their responses, and eventually said, "I do."

"I think that's more strange." By now, all three stood on the apron of Bryson's driveway, but Bash pointed at the Harrison's home across the street. "He's back."

Rae watched as Movie Star Bob pulled into his long driveway. He hustled out of his car and into his home. Biting a fingernail, Rae said, "And he's in a hurry."

Bash replied, "He's definitely on the run. I think he killed Laura Ward because she hired Cook to find out who killed her daughter. Cook put it together that Movie Star Bob is the killer and told Laura. So, he had to kill both of them."

Wiping the chewed nail pieces off her shoulder, she said, "What if Sally's right and they were having an affair? He wouldn't kill his lover. And why was he driving *toward* Cook's house and not away from it?" Toto nodded at Rae.

Bash guessed. "Maybe he forgot something and had to go back? And you have to remember, Aunt Rae, if the affairs happened, that was two years ago. Laura doesn't even live around here anymore. Judy said she moved to the west. Bob could hold some hard feelings against Laura, making it easy to kill her."

"Or maybe he had nothing to do with Laura's murder?"

"Then why was he in that area?"

Rae shrugged. "Maybe he was supposed to meet Laura at Cook's house to help her?"

"To help her with what?"

"Find Cook's notes on who killed her daughter."

Bash shook his head. "Why would he do that?"

"Because he still loved Laura the way Candice still loved Ryan." Rae held out her hand. "Can I see your notebook?" After he handed it to her, she leafed through the pages frantically as Toto peered over her forearm.

Bash asked, "What are you looking for?"

"I honestly have no idea. I'm hoping something jumps out at me."

Bash pulled his bottom lip. "I can't believe that married couples really swing."

"Well, it's true," said Bryson, standing behind them. When Rae and Bash spun around to face him, he continued, "Honey told me all about it. It made her furious. According to her, it was all Bob's idea and it was supposed to be just for fun. But then Honey's dad and Bob's wife fell in love and they both wanted to end their marriages in order to be together. When Honey overheard her dad telling her mom that he wanted a divorce, Honey flew into a rage and confronted Bob. Later that night, Honey left her house and was never seen again."

"Really?" Rae closed the notebook.

"She told me that she threatened to ruin him. But I *think* Honey was just angry, you know?" Bryson smiled. "This is some really twisted stuff, isn't it? My mom says this is what happens to people with way too much money. They get bored or greedy and act on their own selfish impulses without considering the consequences." He nodded to the plastic bag. "What do you have there?"

Rae heard Bash gulp. She then took a deep breath and explained how they found Fluffy. "I don't understand how it ended up over by us though. It doesn't make sense."

Bryson shrugged. "Don't worry about it. It's one less chore for me to do." He then strolled to the trashcan at the end of his driveway, lifted the lid and tossed the plastic bag into it. Turning to Rae and Bash, he quickly jerked his head, flipping his bangs out of his eyes. "I gotta go. My mom will be home soon and I still have to clean my room." He jogged toward his house when his high-top tennis shoe dropped off his foot, causing him to fall.

Rae reacted instantly and swooped up his sneaker on her way over to him. "Are you okay?" She offered her free hand to help him stand. After a quick pause, he grasped it with such a powerful pull that she unexpectedly bumped into him.

"Whoa," he said after they both caught their balance. "Careful."

Handing him his tennis shoe without any laces, she quickly apologized, feeling her cheeks warm.

Smiling, Bryson chuckled while squirming his foot into his shoe. "It's okay." He jogged off again, but this time he was careful to keep his high-top on his foot.

Bash stroked Toto's neck. "I guess he didn't really like Fluffy."

Distant shouting then caused Rae, Bash and Toto to look at the Harrison's house again. They saw Movie Star Bob carrying two large pieces of luggage to his car while he yelled at his wife to hurry. He heaved the luggage into the trunk and lunged at her, grabbing her by the shoulders. He said something in a gruff tone and pushed her into the passenger's seat. Then he rushed to the driver's side, jumped in the car and circled around. Careening down the driveway, Movie Star Bob turned sharply onto the road, squealing the tires. Rae glimpsed the shocked expression on Boozy Candice's face before her body rolled over from the force. They drove out of the area within seconds.

Rae said aloud, "Cuz that's not suspicious."

Bash asked Rae, "What do you think was in those suitcases?"

"Clothes? Passports?"

Bash shook his head. "Wrong. He packed all of his whips. Movie Star Bob is going to get rid of the weapon that he used to slash Cook's and Purple Stiletto's faces."

Toto whined and looked behind them. Rae followed Toto's gaze and only saw Bryson's front door in the distance.

Bash asked Toto, "What is it?"

Toto whined again and then licked his lips right before yawning. Nosing his head underneath Bash's hand, Bash smiled and began scratching behind Toto's ears.

"Bash, are you telling me that the weapon is *all* of Movie Star Bob's whips?"

"One of them could be, so he's being smart and getting rid of *all* the evidence."

Toto's ears sprang to attention. Turning toward a hedge, he suddenly barked twice at it. A chipmunk popped out of the bush, took one look at Toto and sprang back inside the evergreen shrub. Toto took a step toward the hedge, lowering his head and growling.

Rae scolded Toto. "Stop doing that." Turning to Bash, she said, "Maybe Bryson liked Honey? He said that he barely knew Honey, but, if they barely knew each other, then why did she confide in him about her parents' affair? Maybe he killed her in a jealous rage?"

Bash shrugged. "*And* Purple Stiletto? *And* Laura Ward?"

"But there might be two killers. Maybe Bryson and Gio are working together?"

Toto snarled at the hedge again. Hungry and tired, Rae snapped. "I told you to stop doing that." Her stomach then grumbled and she wrapped her arms around her torso. "I need cheese. Let's talk suspects after some sandwiches." As she and Bash began walking toward the manor, Toto stayed, staring into the thick shrubbery, until Rae called his name.

CHAPTER FORTY ONE

As Bash and Aunt Rae sat at the kitchen table, devouring their grilled cheese sandwiches, Toto sat on the floor next to them, licking his chops. At his feet awaited an empty plate. He placed his paw on it and slid it over to Bash.

Aunt Rae intervened, "No, Toto. You just ate two."

Bash asked his aunt, "How about one more?"

Aunt Rae shook her head while Toto nodded. The ringing of his aunt's cellphone then made Bash jump. He watched her face cringe in disgust. After a few *uh-huhs* and a couple of *take that backs,* she ended the call and said, "That was Travis. My co-worker named Tonya ratted me out. She told him that I haven't been working on these stupid logo designs." Her shoulders slumped. "I need to get a logo design approved by tomorrow or else."

"But," argued Bash, "you have been working."

"Unfortunately, my New York client is siding with Two-face Tonya and Travis is mad." Sighing, she added, "Suddenly, I'm not that hungry."

Toto lifted his head and salivated.

Aunt Rae quickly retracted her statement. "On second thought, I need food for creative power." The doorbell then sounded and Aunt Rae stood. She looked at Toto who was staring at the other half of her sandwich.

Bash said, "You better take that with you."

His aunt snatched it off her plate, hurrying to answer the front door, and Toto gave Bash a disappointed look.

"Sorry, dude," Bash said to Toto. "I don't want you to get a tummy ache."

Toto rolled his eyes, dropped to the ground and dabbed at the crumbs on the plate with his tongue.

Bash chuckled at Toto as his aunt returned with Howie. Surprised to see him, Bash said, "Oh, hi, Howie. Anything new?"

Howie took the bottle of water that Aunt Rae offered to him and pointed it at Bash. "Funny you should ask. Detective Nelson sent me here. It turns out that the body of Laura Ward was found at Cook's residence earlier today." He raised his eyebrows at Rae and Bash. "And guess what else?"

Rae shoved the whole half of her sandwich into her mouth and replied, "Mmbf."

"That's right. A neighbor reported that a boy, a short woman and a hooker with hot pink hair, all wearing surgical gloves, were seen entering the house."

Rae swallowed her lunch. "That could've been anyone."

Howie shook his head. "The neighbor also mentioned that there was a dog the size of a bulldozer with them." He looked at Toto, who looked at Bash.

Shrugging, Bash explained, "She was already dead when we got there."

Rae added, "She had been strangled."

"Really?" Howie asked, "Well, maybe the two men who were also seen there today strangled her? One was around six feet tall, strong build, brown wavy hair. The other one was plump and very smiley."

"Oh god." Aunt Rae looked alarmed. "The six-footer was Stone."

"I know." Howie nodded. "I remember him from this morning after he came out of the woods, carrying objects belonging to the victims and yapping about finding Honey Ward whom he didn't murder. Who's his accomplice?"

Bash chuckled at the word *accomplice*. "That's Zalen. He's just a nice intuitive empath."

For a long moment, Howie didn't speak. He just stood there with his mouth open and Bash could see the officer's tongue moving across his teeth in thought. Finally, he said, "Are those the shoes you wore over there today?" After Bash and his aunt both nodded, Howie asked, "May I see your hands?" Bash followed his aunt's move and showed the top side and the palm side of his hands. Howie then sighed. "This is a waste of my Sunday."

Bash became curious. "What's so important about our shoes and hands? What are you looking for?"

Howie ignored the question. "I have to go, but you two have to listen to me. Neither one of you is a detective. So stop sneaking into houses. Stop finding dead bodies and reporting them. Stop finding dead bodies and *not* reporting them. Just stop. You're not only making yourselves look guilty, but you're also charging the electricity for Stone's electric chair."

Aunt Rae squeaked. "Really? I'm trying to find the person responsible for these murders to get Detective Orangutan off Stone's back."

"Or people," Bash reminded Aunt Rae. Looking at Howie, he explained, "We think there might be two murderers."

Howie held up his hand. "Neither of you are allowed to think anymore." When Aunt Rae snickered, Howie suddenly sounded frustrated. "I'm serious, Rae. I *will* tell Danny and Clare about this and they won't like it." As fear rose in Bash after hearing those words, Howie continued, "So, no more thinking and no more aiding Stone."

"He really had nothing to do with any of this." Aunt Rae looked anxious.

Bash agreed. "Stone's not a killer. You should look into the Harrisons. They live next door and are on the run."

Howie looked exasperated. "I know. Bob Harrison called us already to tell us that he thinks he knows who's responsible for these murders and he's leaving town with his wife out of fear. Apparently, the killer is stalking them."

Surprised, Bash asked Howie, "Who does he think it is?"

"Your aunt. He saw her leaving Cook's subdivision today."

Aunt Rae jumped on that comment. "Did you ask him what he was doing there?"

"No," replied Howie. "He explained without us having to ask. He was meeting Laura Ward to search Cook's home for any information regarding her daughter. He was very forthright." Both Bash and Aunt Rae opened their mouths to speak, but Howie spoke over them, "I'm not getting into this with you. Look, obviously mental illness runs in your family and that is what's driving you two into making bad choices. I'm begging you. If you can't think of *yourselves* in these kinds of situations, then at least think of *Danny*."

Aunt Rae glanced at Bash before asking Howie, "Really? Danny?"

"Yeah, because I would hate to be the one to give him bad news about you or his son." He now implored her. "Please stay out of this, Rae. You're a graphic designer. You're an aunt. You're a good person, so I'm telling you as nicely as I can. Don't get involved with this."

In silence, Howie left the kitchen and Bash heard him leave through the front door. He studied his aunt who was nibbling on another fingernail. Clearing his throat, Bash said, "Don't mind him, Aunt Rae. He's a cop who has to say stuff like that. Let's take our minds off of that nonsense and set up our headquarters."

His aunt shook her head. "No, Bash. Howie's right. We're done playing detective." Without looking at him, she continued, "I need to get that stupid logo designed."

After she turned and dragged herself into Travis's office, Bash nodded at Toto. "It's time to end this. How about you and me go for a walk?"

Toto quietly woofed in agreement and they both tip-toed out the house, heading for the jogging path. Bash's plan involved Gio,

Honey and his paranormal equipment. At first, he thought of asking Stone for psychic help, but could he trust Stone to not tell his aunt? Nope.

After walking all the way to the park, they found Gio sitting on a swing, staring at Bash with no emotion whatsoever. "Hey, Gio," Bash said, "you okay?" Gio stiffly nodded and Bash continued, "I need a favor. I want to communicate with Honey in the woods, but need to know where your special meeting place was. Would you show me?"

Gio stood, raised his arms and pushed Bash, causing him to stumble backwards. Toto growled, but Gio paid no attention, yelling at Bash, "Get away from me! You don't belong here!" He then bolted down the path, completely out of sight within seconds.

Shaken, Bash's heart thumped loudly inside his chest. Stinging tears welled up in his eyes as he reached for Toto. Stroking Toto's head, Bash wiped his nose with the back of his hand and said, "It's okay, Toto. No big deal. Let's go back." As he and Toto turned around, they found Bryson standing behind them, wearing shorts, a bulky sweatshirt and flip-flops.

Bryson smiled. "Gio's bad news. He always fights with people. You okay?" Bash nodded and Bryson continued, "Listen, I can show you where their special meeting place was."

Bash's spirits rose. "Really? You know?"

"Everyone knew. They weren't quiet about it. When do you want to go?"

Toto woofed softly at Bash and began lightly prancing in agitation. As Bash looked at Toto, he said to the dog, "I need to try." Toto calmed down and Bash turned to Bryson. "How about three in the morning? That's when paranormal activity is at its peak. "

"Wow," said Bryson, "you sound like a pro. Do you have equipment and all that stuff?"

"I have some stuff." Bash smiled. "It's really cool."

Bryson agreed. "It sounds like it. So, what's your motivation?"

"I want to ask Honey to give me the name of her killer."

Toto whined as his ears pointed straight up to the sky. A blue sedan slowly pulled into the parking lot, causing Toto to prance again.

Bryson didn't seem to notice the car. Instead, he said to Bash, "I gotta go. Let's meet at the hidden trail along the cliff. Should we meet earlier than three to give us time to set up?"

Nodding, Bash said, "That's a good idea. How about quarter to three?"

"You got it. See you then." Bryson turned on his heel and jogged toward his home.

Bash heard a car door slam and noticed Judy waddling over to them. In her hand was a long, rope-like leash. Toto whined again as Judy approached.

"There you are," she said to the dog. "I've been looking everywhere for you. We have a grooming appointment, remember?" She clipped the leash onto Toto's collar. "We have to look nice for tomorrow."

"What's tomorrow?" Bash felt a weighted ball form in the pit of his stomach.

Judy lowered her voice. "With the news about Honey, I decided to find another home for you know who." She nodded toward Toto. "We're meeting a truck driver in the morning."

Bash's throat tightened. "Truck driver?"

"Yes," Judy said, "I know a truck driver who wants a big dog to take with him on his routes. He would like the extra protection when he has to sleep at those stops at night."

Toto exploded with many barks and Judy pointed her finger at him. "No," she said and the obedient Great Shepherd silenced himself at once. She then tugged on the leash, leading him to the backseat of her car. Toto filled the entire space and his head poked out the window. As Judy drove off, Toto gave a desperate look, causing those stinging tears to return for Bash.

. . .

Rae eventually fell into a creative groove and new designs poured out of her like water out of a fire hose. She completed her twentieth design and sent them to the client. Quiet minutes passed with no reply and Rae knew that she had to start again. While cursing at the computer screen, her phone rang and she froze with indecision. It was Stone. Reluctantly, she decided to follow Howie's advice and declined the call.

Rae needed a new life. Unfortunately, she was stuck with this one. Requiring a scene change, she left the office in search of a water bottle just as the doorbell rang. After swinging the door open, she groaned. No one was there. The doorbell ditcher was back. Rae stepped onto the porch and felt the soft fabric of a canvas tote under her foot. It had a hexagonal design on the front. Oh god, she thought as her stomach lurched at the sight of Purple Stiletto's missing bag.

Without thinking, she quickly picked it up. Once she realized her fingerprints could now be on the bag, she yelped, dropping it like a hot piece of coal. Looking around the street, she saw no one in either direction. She used her foot and looped the strap around her toes, lifting the evidence with her leg. Turning carefully, she kicked it into the foyer and checked her surroundings one more time. The street was still empty and quiet.

Closing the front door, she locked it and tried to set the alarm. After it sparked, she called for Bash. He never came and she called for him again. The back door opened and then she heard footsteps across the kitchen. Bash finally came into view and she asked him, "Where were you?"

"Outside."

"Did you see anyone around this house?"

"No. Why?"

"We're being watched. How do you work this alarm?"

He shrugged. "I don't know. What do you mean, we're being watched?"

Rae dramatically pointed to the bag on the floor. "That's Purple Stiletto's bag. The two times that I saw her, she had this bag. On the day I found her body, the bag was missing."

"Why do you have it?"

Rae dragged the chair over and placed it in front of the door. "Someone rang the doorbell and left it on the porch."

Bash's mouth dropped open. "Oh, Aunt Rae, this isn't good. On *Murder Manhunt,* innocent people are always framed by the killer planting evidence against them. We're doomed."

"Should I call the police?"

"You haven't already?"

Rae sounded defensive. "It just happened. Do I call 9-1-1?"

Bash shrugged. "I think that's for life and death emergencies only. Call Howie."

Rae nodded, removing her phone from her back pocket and dialing Howie's number. After many rings, she said to Bash, "It went to his voicemail." She then left a detailed message and begged him to call her.

Bash scrutinized the design on the bag. "I've seen this before. It's a molecule of something." Holding his cellphone with both hands, his thumbs flew over the keys. "See? It's the molecule of serotonin."

"Really?" Confused, Rae asked, "Isn't that the happy chemical in your body?"

Bash read from his phone. "It says here that serotonin is an important chemical and neurotransmitter in the human body. It regulates mood and social behavior. There could be a connection between serotonin and depression." He looked at her. "Since we can't reach Howie, maybe we should call Stone and tell him about this?"

Rae shook her head. "No, Howie's right. I am charging the electrical current for Stone's electric chair. I think he's in enough trouble and it's all because of me. The less he knows, the less he'll look like he's involved."

"How does Stone feel about this? Maybe you should call and ask him?"

"I'm trying to follow Howie's advice and think about you, Stone and Danny. The best thing to do is distance myself from Stone until this is all over." Feeling an absence, she asked, "Where's Toto?"

Bash looked glum. "Toto had to go to the groomer. He's being sold to a truck driver tomorrow morning."

Rae clutched her chest. "What are you talking about?"

"Don't get mad, but while you were working, Toto and I went for a walk. We ran into Judy who was looking for Toto. She told me that a truck driver wants to buy him and take him on his routes for more protection."

As Rae covered her face with her hands, a piercing pain struck her heart. "That's bad."

"Call my dad." Clasping his hands together, Bash begged, "Please talk him into taking Toto. My mom won't allow it, but my dad might, if you talk to him."

"No, Danny won't and you know it. He won't even let you get a fish, but I am calling your mom and having you picked up today."

Bash screeched, "What?"

"This bag left on the doorstop is too much. I need you to go home. Now."

"No way. If you call my mom, I'll tell her the truth about summer camp last year and how it was all your idea."

Rae opened her mouth in protest, but no words sounded.

"Yeah, that's right. You gave me the idea, I acted on it and then I almost *died*." He nodded with a hint of a smirk on his lips. "My mom will never let me see you again." When Rae clenched her teeth, Bash quickly stated, "I'll go home tomorrow. Just let me have one more night here with you. We can play games and eat garbage and come up with a plan to save Tiny."

"You mean Toto."

"No," Bash shook his head. "I mean Tiny."

Rae unclenched her jaw. "How are we going to save him?"

Bash smiled. "You'll come up with something."

"Fine, but you're going home right after breakfast." As she said that, her heart saddened, not only at the thought of Bash leaving tomorrow, but also at the thought of possibly never seeing Tiny again. Bash was right. She needed a plan and thought of Stone. Maybe he would like a dog? Nah, that didn't feel right. Oh well, she'd have to come back to that. Right now, a computer called her, begging her to end this logo suffrage movement.

CHAPTER FORTY TWO

Stone banged his forehead on the counter. His head swirled with confusing and contradicting Rachel thoughts. What was the right thing to do? The obvious answer hit him like a herd of wildebeests. The right thing to do was to ignore TD's order. Taking his phone from his back pocket, he dialed Rachel's number and listened to the other end ring many times. Finally, he heard her voice mail and he left a brief message for her. Ending the call, he frowned.

"Don't worry," said Sally as she filled up a beer glass. "Rae's probably swimming with Bash or tripping over more dead bodies." She laughed, but Stone groaned. "When you lose your sense of humor, it means you need a break. Go home and take a shower." She led him to the entrance door and pushed him out of it. "I'll handle this place until you get back."

A shower sounded reviving. He rushed home and was soon relishing the cold water trickling down his body. While vigorously scrubbing his hair, he pondered about Rachel. What if she did find another dead body? Worried, he covered his face with his hands and almost drowned himself in suds. Stepping out the tub, he wrapped a towel around himself and called her again, but she still did not answer.

Exasperated, he now sat on his leather couch, fully clothed, as thoughts of Rachel still engulfed him. What was she doing right now? Did Detective Nelson question her about Laura Ward? What if he arrested her and she needed him? He froze at that thought. Then he snatched his car keys and strode to the front door. He decided not to call Rachel anymore. He was going to see her instead. Only one thing could stop him. Opening the door, that one thing stood on his porch, wearing a maroon trench coat.

"Let me call my lawyer," Stone said.

"Not necessary. I just need to talk."

Stone debated and eventually stepped aside, allowing the detective to enter his dwelling.

Detective Nelson wandered to the dining room. "You got anything to drink around here?"

Stone replied, "Water?"

The detective nodded. "Sure, I'll take a scotch."

Stone raised his eyebrows. "Can you drink that stuff while on duty?"

"I can if nobody knows I'm drinking it."

One scotch later, they sat at the dining table at opposite ends, eyeing each other. Stone finally asked, "What are we talking about?"

Detective Nelson said, "You're no longer a suspect." When Stone opened his mouth, the detective cut him off. "And neither is Rae. Lucky for you two, I found stronger leads and I'm giving you the honors of telling her. And tell her to stop calling me Detective Orangutan. I find that insulting. Questions?"

Stone grinned. "None."

"Good." The detective stood, walking to the front door. "I'm glad you're back to being a bar owner instead of a thorn in my side."

"Me too." Suddenly, Stone's phone buzzed. It was a text from Sally in all caps: HUGE CROWD. NO GIN. NO TONIC. HELP ASAP.

▪ ▪ ▪

Toto returned home from the groomer, smelling like a bouquet of roses. He sneezed at his own floral stench and then shook his whole body, fanning the aroma from him. The old woman led him to a room at the end of the hallway. Inside was a white shiny chair. He knew that chair. It could make an interesting draining sound and the water inside of it would disappear. But then the water would return. And he couldn't drink that water even though the chair looked like a tall bowl of water. It would make the old woman angry.

Speaking of angry, he wondered if the angry lady would allow him to drink out of her white shiny chair. She seemed like someone who would only mind if she caught him.

"There." The old woman's voice made him look at her. "That should keep you from leaving." She patted his head. "I can't have you missing your chance at finding a new home." She smiled down at him and then left the room, closing the door.

Toto looked down at his leash and noticed that the old woman wrapped it around the base of the shiny white chair. He pulled on it trying to make the chair move, but the chair wouldn't budge. He was stuck.

Looking at the door, he cried out, hoping the old woman would come back and release him. He needed to be with the angry lady and the nice boy called Bash. He really needed another grilled cheese sandwich. The old woman never returned though and he fell to the ground in despair, wondering what to do.

CHAPTER FORTY THREE

Bash watched as his troubled aunt slumped into Travis's office and closed the door behind her. He then ran upstairs, flopped onto the bed and quickly made a note of Gio's baffling reaction. Afterward, Bash inspected his paranormal equipment, feeling satisfied that everything was in working order. The rest of the afternoon was spent in solitude. While watching a show about creepy things that lurked in the woods, his parents called, using the speakerphone so that they both could speak to him at the same time.

Bash's greeting sounded on the depressive side and his dad asked him, "Sick?"

"He's not sick, Danny." His mom sounded impatient. "You never listen. Rae said that Bash is bored and has nothing to do. He wants to come home tomorrow morning."

Bash pondered that somewhat inaccurate information. "What else did she say?"

His dad replied, "New York sucks."

Bash sat on the edge of the couch. "Did she mention a cool dog who needs a home?"

Sounding stern, his mom said, "My answer's no. We'll see you tomorrow at ten."

The conversation was cut short after that and Bash remained on the oversized sofa, completely deflated. Around dinner time, Aunt Rae finally made an appearance, looking downtrodden as well. The two of them cooked together, in silence, and sat across from the other at the table with a mound of spaghetti in front of each.

Twirling his fork in his pasta pile, Bash asked, "How's the logo coming?"

"I sent over twenty new designs, but my client rejected all of them."

"What are you going to do?"

Aunt Rae shrugged. "Play games, eat garbage."

Bash's excitement rose. "And come up with a plan to save Tiny?"

The remorseful look in his aunt's eyes gave him the dreaded answer. She had no plan. Tiny was to become a truck dog. At first, Bash felt disappointment in his aunt. Then he took a long look at her. Her hair resembled a nest suited for a hedgehog, stuck on the top of her head with a rubber band wound around it. If that wasn't bad enough, a paperclip held some loose strands of her hair to the side, like a barrette. She nervously played with another long piece, wounding it around her finger. At one point, her hair became interwoven with the pasta. Bash opened his mouth to stop her from eating it, but was too late. She choked. And then she gagged.

All of his harsh feelings toward her subsided after that. After dinner, they played card games and then switched to board games. However, neither of them was in a mood to think and they ended up watching reruns of *Murder Manhunt*. At one point, Bash heard his aunt's phone ring and she stared at the number.

Bash asked, "Is it Howie?"

"No, it's Potential Fraud." Aunt Rae declined the call.

Bash asked her, "Is Potential Fraud your nickname for Stone? You should call him back."

"Nope. I'm cutting off all communication." To make her point, she turned off her phone, giving Bash a smug look.

"What if Howie tries to call?"

"I don't think he's interested in us anymore."

Bash sighed at this loss and focused on the show. Around two, the sound of his aunt's soft snoring alerted Bash that he was now the only conscious person in the manor. Curled up into a tight ball, Aunt Rae snoozed in the corner of the oversized sectional and Bash covered her with a nearby afghan. He then snatched the remote control, turned off the television and stood in the darkness, waiting expectantly. As the top of the hour struck, he heard a melancholy wail, rising from the woods, and he smiled. "Thanks for the warning, Maeve, but I'm coming anyway."

• • •

Sally helped herself to new bottles of gin and tonic while Stone sat on the corner stool, his grandpa's stool, drinking sparkling water from the bottle. She toasted him again, making it her fifth time. "Here's to Detective Nelson finding stronger leads. What a great bastard." She drained all the liquid in her glass. "Have you reached Rae yet?"

Stone shook his head. "No, but I keep leaving messages."

"You should go over there." Sally bobbed her eyebrows.

"Now?" He glanced at the time on his phone. "It's after two."

"So? This early hour didn't stop you last night."

Stone crossed his arms. "I think she's avoiding me."

Sally poured herself another drink. "I don't think that's it. Obviously, there's a connection between the two of you that just scares her a little."

"But why does it scare her?"

"Because she doesn't understand it yet."

Stone asked, "Why does she have to understand it?"

"Because that's just how Rae works." Sally drained her glass again, turned from him and began telling the patrons that it was closing time.

The inner workings of Rachel Greyson were more hidden and unknown than the location of Cleopatra's tomb. Oh well, he thought. If she wanted to play cool, he would play cooler. Hopping off the stool, Stone ambled to the storage room where he needed to figure out a whole other problem: the bar's finances.

CHAPTER FORTY FOUR

It was now quarter to three. Armed with his equipment, phone and utility flashlight, Bash crept through the kitchen, carefully unlocked the back door and snuck into the night, heading for the hidden trail along the cliff. He found Bryson already waiting for him.

Bryson held his phone, shining the flashlight toward Bash. He smiled and asked, "Are you sure you *want* to do this?"

Bash eagerly nodded. "I *have* to know how Honey died and who's responsible."

"Okay. I guess there's no going back now." He stepped onto the trail, leading the way with Bash following close behind him.

Moisture filled the stagnant air, nearly suffocating Bash, but he never slowed his pace through the trees. They were eerily silent again, like they were trying to keep all the forest's secrets hidden. He wasn't interested in revealing *all the* secrets though. Bash only yearned to unearth the ones pertaining to Honey Ward.

As they hiked along the trail near the cliff, Bash glanced up toward the heavens. It was so dark that the canopies of the trees blended in with the black starless sky. Suddenly, his light flickered, forewarning Bash that something paranormal was near.

Bryson's voice broke the stillness. "We're here. This is the spot."

They were at the cliff, standing on a section of earth that jutted out and over the rocks below them. Bryson shone the light over the edge toward the ground. The twenty foot drop looked deadly. As Bash peered over the edge, he barely saw the yellow police tape arranged on the rocky bottom. He leaned for a better look, but the blackness of the cliff's depth hid the crime scene like an overprotective mother.

He asked Bryson, "This was the secret meeting place?"

"Yes."

Bash pointed to the rocks. "That's where Honey died? You know this for a fact?"

Bryson looked at Bash. "Yes." The flashlight flickered again. "Let's get started."

Bash checked the time on his cellphone. He had one minute to spare before the true witching hour. Opening his case, he made a quick decision and grabbed his favorite piece of equipment: the spirit box. He then closed the case lid and stood. After securing the memory card into the spirit box, he was ready to not only communicate live with Honey's ghost, but also to record their interaction.

Bryson shone his phone on the spirit box. "It's like a walkie-talkie with ghosts, right?"

Bash nodded. "That's a good way to put it."

Bryson asked, "You really think she'll say her killer's name? You *really* want to know?"

"I need to know. I need to end this." Bash turned on the spirit box and it instantly scanned channels, causing the static noise to pulsate. After pressing the record button, he raised the spirit box, speaking loudly, "Is Honey Ward here?" Sweeping his arm slowly across the area, he waited patiently for a response, but the choppy static only persisted. Bash tried a second time. "Honey, tell me who killed you." Again, he waited. Again, there was nothing. He turned up the volume. "Tell me the name of your murderer." Bash brought the spirit box closer to his ear. At first, he heard the same rhythmic static, but then a faint ghostly female voice spoke and she said a name.

Bryson seemed stunned as he walked backwards into a tree. "It can't be."

Bash stared at Bryson, not completely understanding what name he heard. Looking down at his hand, it began to shake uncontrollably and he dropped the spirit box on the ground. A rushing sound then erupted next to him as a dark form stepped from the blackness of the trees. It was Gio. In one hand, he gripped a long branch resembling a whip while in the other, he gripped a bat. It was his fierce brown eyes, though, that frightened Bash the most. They were full of fury.

Much time passed and the house grew quiet and dark. Toto remained in the small room, alone. He never changed his position and lay on his side with his head near the shiny white chair. The floor was hard and so were his feelings. He didn't want to be with a truck driver, whatever that was. He wanted to be with the angry lady and noticed that, lately, she smiled more. Or maybe he could live with Nice Bash who made him delicious grilled cheese sandwiches with four different cheeses? Toto licked his lips. Either owner would do.

His whole right side hurt. He needed to do something. He needed to move. Lifting his limp tail, he held it in the air for a moment before letting it slap to the ground. The repeating thump almost calmed his nerves, but his knotted stomach continued to tighten. What he really needed was some help.

A sudden warm sensation rushed along his back. He turned his head to find the sad girl sitting next to him, except she no longer seemed sad. Toto woofed once, explaining his predicament, but she held a finger to her lips. He watched as she unlooped the leash around the white chair and then raised it, showing him that he was free. Pointing to the door, she whispered breathily, "Hurry." Her transparent body began to fade as she waved a final farewell to him.

CHAPTER FORTY FIVE

A loud clap startled Rae awake. It reminded her of the flapping sound that she heard in the forest when Bash first arrived at Travis's. Frantically looking around the room, her breathing eventually slowed after realizing that she was alone on the sofa. There was no prehistoric bird near her and Bash must be in bed. Reaching for her cellphone on the coffee table, she turned it on and checked the time. It was two-fifty in the morning.

After she set her phone on the table, she wiggled her body into the thick cushions and switched her mental gears from spooky house noises to the beach. She closed her eyes as she imagined herself snorkeling with Stone in some exotic sea. The more she drifted in her daydream, the more she drifted from reality when a distant ringing of a doorbell brought her right back to it. With a thumping heart, she sat straight up. Did she imagine hearing the doorbell? Her body turned to immovable rock. All she could do was hope to not hear anything more.

While listening to the hum of the air conditioner, Rae felt the warmth of the pendant on her chest, calming her. She rested her head on the arm of the sofa, staring at the ceiling, when, ever so softly, she heard a footstep in the hall. Quickly lifting her head, she called out, "Bash?"

The house remained silent. Baffled, she kicked the afghan off her, reaching for her cellphone again. Standing, she felt an unusually tense buzz in the atmosphere. The floor creaked in the foyer and she spoke sharply, "Bash? Are you trying to scare me?" She heard no response. Convinced it was her nephew, Rae planned to turn this cat-and-mouse game around on him. On her tiptoes, she sneaked around the sofa, through the kitchen and into the foyer. She now stood by the chair at the front door, all alone.

The doorbell rang again and she jumped. After a few startled heartbeats, a gust of courage rushed over her. She moved the chair, unlocked the front door and swung it open. A cool breeze brushed past her, blowing Purple Stiletto's bag off the console table. Seeing no one, she firmly closed the door and locked it again. Leaning against the wall, her legs weakened from these unnerving events and she sat on the chair, staring at the serotonin molecule on the bag. What she would do for the happy drug right now. She picked up the bag, thinking of Howie and wondering why he hadn't returned her call. Didn't he care? A new determination overwhelmed her and she decided to investigate this bag on her own.

Using her cellphone to launch the internet, she researched serotonin and the top hits all related to mood and brain function. Then she switched directions and searched for bags with a design of the serotonin molecule. An image of a tote bag similar to Purple Stiletto's popped up on her phone. She scrolled down and saw a list of reviews about it. A chemist wrote the first review, followed by a STEM teacher, a genetics student and then a psychologist.

Rae nibbled a fingernail. Was Purple Stiletto a chemist? Nah. And she didn't look like a teacher either. Nor a genetics student. What about a psychologist? Rae pictured the purple heels and doubted it. But wait. Someone mentioned a psychiatrist. Bryson did. He said that Gio should see a psychiatrist. Why again? Oh yeah, Rae thought. Bryson believed that Gio was a sociopath.

Rae started a new search regarding child psychiatrists in Monroe. After scrolling past the ads, she clicked on the first website leading to a list of psychiatrists. There were tons. While thinking of the word *sociopath*, she used a filter and narrowed the search down to five psychiatrists with experience in the Psychotic Disorder area. The third name jumped at her: Amy Jullian Williards. With her mouth wide open, Rae knew that she found Purple Stiletto, aka Amy Jullian Williards, aka AJ Williards.

Rae bit another fingernail as she stood, picturing the post-it note. The words *park, 10:00, AJ Williards* replayed in her head like an old song. So, who was the connection between AJ Williards and Cook? The charm against her chest began to warm her skin, but Rae ignored it. Was AJ Williards Gio's child psychiatrist? If so and if AJ Williards knew that Gio killed people, wouldn't she have to notify the authorities? Maybe that was why she met Cook in the park that morning at ten, just like the post-it note stated? Maybe she was reporting Gio?

As heat from the charm started to sting, Rae bit a cuticle. Her mind was close to a breakthrough and she gasped. Gio was at the park that morning. He approached her to give the money back to Bash. He could have seen AJ Williards and Cook together. If Gio killed Honey and then told AJ Williards and then AJ Williards told Cook who told Laura Ward, Gio would kill all of them to save his own skin. Right?

The hot charm burned her. Rae looped it off her neck, throwing it to the floor. Rubbing the sore spot on her skin, she saddened at the thought of Maeve making her something that would harm her. Needing a cold cloth, she looked up and yelped, startled by her own horrified reflection in that evil-looking mirror. Cursing audibly, Rae turned toward the kitchen and almost collided into Jessica as she stood in the archway, slowly swaying from side to side.

Stymied, Rae asked, "What are you doing here? How did you get in?"

Jessica's voice wavered. "Bryson said the back door would be unlocked." Tears flooded her eyes as she raised her fists, pulling on a long shoelace and making it taut. Breathlessly, she continued, "I'm supposed to kill you." However, she lowered her hands and began to weep. "But I can't do this anymore. I just can't." She shrugged. "Bryson's such a good boy. He really is." Her voice sounded throaty. "I know deep down, he cares about people. I know he cared about his dad. His dad was just so controlling and manipulating. Even abusive. That's where Bryson gets it from." Jessica's seams of sanity were snapping. "And I know he even liked Honey. But she was wrong. Her parents paid the school administration for her election win. Honey didn't deserve it."

The thoughts in Rae's head swirled. She finally asked, "What?"

Jessica shook her head. "Don't you see? All Bryson wanted was to be the class president and Honey took that away from him. It broke him." Jessica sounded frantic. "That night on the trail, Bryson told me that she wouldn't relinquish her presidential duties for him. So, he had to push her off the cliff. She wouldn't back down. Just like he had to push my husband down the stairs. It was all in self-defense. You must understand that."

Rae nodded, feeling very warm, but wanting to hear more. "Sure. Did AJ Williards understand that?"

Jessica snapped. "No. She was another one who just pushed him too hard. You can't push kids like that."

Rae squeezed her phone, asking calmly, "What did she do?"

"She badgered him about taking anger and violence management classes. God, she wouldn't relax about it."

Stepping on psychotically thin ice, Rae asked, "Is that why Bryson killed her?"

"She *somehow* found out about Bryson's involvement with Honey's death and told Cook, which was illegal. Psychiatrists can't tell anyone about other people's past homicides, especially if it was in self-defense."

"Self-defense?"

Tears streamed down Jessica's face. "Bryson was bullied. First by his dad. Then by Honey. Then by his own psychiatrist. AJ Williards never should have told Cook! They obviously were out to get my son!" Her voice strengthened. "Bryson is the victim here.

He's a good boy. If you knew him, you'd see how special he really is."

Rae took a few steps backward. "Why does Bryson want you to kill me?"

Looking at her hands, Jessica whispered, "Bryson overheard you and Bash. He knew you were close to figuring this out. He tried to warn you to back off with the guinea pig and AJ's bag, but you both are so persistent." She raised her head. "More than Laura Ward."

Matching Jessica's quiet voice, Rae asked, "Bryson killed Laura Ward too?"

"No." Shaking, Jessica continued, "I did." Dropping to her knees, she sobbed. "I killed her because I'm a good mother to my son and he needed me. Laura told me that she hired Cook. I don't know why she told me other than to threaten us. She must've figured it out and was going to ruin Bryson unless I did something." Jessica suddenly looked remorseful. "Just like you and Bash aren't going to stop. Unless."

Wait a minute, Rae thought. Her throat tightened when the crippling realization set in and she could barely speak. "Where is Bryson right now?"

Falling over her knees, Jessica buried her face in her hands. Through whimpering, she finally managed to say, "He's in the woods. With Bash. At the cliff." She heaved forcefully. "I really liked Bash, but Bryson had to kill him. It was self-defense, I'm sure."

With bare feet, Rae leapt over Jessica and burst through the back door, shining her phone's flashlight toward the hidden trail and shouting her nephew's name.

.   .   .

At first, while sitting in the storage room, Stone had good work intentions. However, his eyes burned and he just needed to close them for a second, which he did. And then he just needed to rest his head on his crossed arms for a moment. And then he just needed to take a ten minute snooze, instantly dreaming of Grandpa Ed.

The setting was the storage room with Stone sitting at his folding-table desk as his grandpa stood over him. He seemed very agitated and mouthed some words to Stone. They were not audible and Stone remained stoic, not knowing how to answer. His grandpa began gesturing with his arms in agitation, but Stone did not move. Suddenly, his grandfather lifted his end of the table and slammed it to the ground.

Stone's eyes shot open. He felt Rae's terror, her adrenaline, her dread. The bottoms of his feet stung and his body ached as he tried to catch his breath. Suddenly, he saw the shocked look in Bash's gray eyes right as he fell into a pit of darkness.

Reaching into his back pocket for his cellphone, the time warned him that it was three in the morning. Quickly dialing the number, he hoped that he wasn't too late.

At the same time, Sally poked her head into the room. "Need anything before I leave?"

He tossed her the phone. "Yeah, I need you to talk to Detective Nelson while I drive." Then he grabbed her by the wrist and they both ran to Stone's car.

CHAPTER FORTY SIX

Rae raced to Bash. With every trip and tumble, she would rise. With every stone or stick piercing the bottoms of her bare feet, she ran faster. Now arriving at the scene, she stared in disbelief. Something was wrong. Bash was nowhere in sight.

Frozen with fear, Rae begged herself to move. On the other hand, to move would mean that time would continue and Rae wanted time to stop. If time stopped, Bash could still be somewhere. Standing near the edge of the cliff, her legs shook as her hands trembled, allowing her cellphone to fall to the ground. The flashlight's beam lit a small area, giving a glimpse of the dismal scene around her, and Rae couldn't believe it. Her mind wouldn't let her accept it.

Bash's paranormal equipment scattered on the ground and Gio lay face down, just a few feet from her. In the moonlight, his body looked still. Too still. Dead still. Crouching down, she raised her hand and reached for him.

"Don't touch him."

Rae snapped her head forward and was met with darkness at first, but then Bryson's faint silhouette began to form as he stepped into the beam's light. One of his hands held a bat; the other playfully swung a switch. On his face spread the biggest smile.

Bryson said to Rae, "I'm surprised to see you here. Where's my mom?"

Rae tried to speak, but the words stuck in her throat, sounding broken. "Where's Bash?"

He laughed. "Answer my question first."

A small flicker of anger ignited within her and Rae spoke a little louder. "She's at the house, calling the police."

Bryson said flippantly, "No, she's not. Don't lie to me." Raising the switch, he struck at the air with it, only inches from her face. "Well, Bash isn't fine. He is, in fact, dead. I pushed him over the cliff, just seconds before you arrived. You were so close to saving his life. But don't feel bad. It's his fault, really. He wanted to know how Honey died, so I showed him."

The small flicker of anger instantly transformed into an outbreak of untamed rage and a spine-chilling scream erupted from deep within Rae. Hurling her body at him like a linebacker, she felt him collapse upon impact. They both fell and with clenched fists, Rae blindly pummeled his body. Before she knew it, however, Bryson powerfully struck her across her left eye, sending her backwards and rolling into Gio.

She felt Gio stir and a new hope came to light. He still had a chance. Rae knelt next to him, pleading. "Gio, get up. Go get help." Without moving, he only moaned. Rae begged again, "Come on, Gio, I can't leave you here, he'll kill you." She knew that she had to stay and stall Bryson so that Gio could make a run for it. At least one life would be saved that night.

Bryson rose to his feet, scanning the ground. He then casually bent down and picked up the bat and switch. Resting the bat on his shoulder, he said matter-of-factly, "I could be a great baseball player. My mom says that I can be a great anything."

Scrambling to her feet, she stood to face the golden boy with the charred soul. He smiled at her and his game began. First, he would swing with the bat and then immediately whip at her with the switch, all the while steering her toward the cliff and laughing joyfully.

Her sore eye remained closed from the pain. Without being able to see well, she was no match for Bryson and he knew it. Boredom quickly rushed over his expression and he struck her with the switch. A hot stinging cut burned across her arm. Stunned, she looked at him, and using the end of the bat, he punched her in the sternum. An explosion of pain weakened her knees as she felt the ground rush to meet her. On all fours, she gasped for breath.

Confidently, he approached her, dropping the switch. His eyes were ablaze with excitement as he swung the bat around in a circle. Then, with both hands, he raised it high above his head. Rae didn't cower though. She rose to her feet as a strange calmness overcame her. Glancing quickly at Gio, she silently asked for his forgiveness. She couldn't save him after all. Then staring into Bryson's unreachable eyes, she lifted her chin and braced herself for the blow.

Suddenly, a low guttural growl sounded from the woods, stopping Bryson from advancing. In the darkness emerged the Great Shepherd as he slowly crept from the shadow of the trees with his long leash trailing from his collar. Curling his vibrating lips, he bared his sharp teeth as he crouched low to ground, placing himself between Rae and Bryson. With his body leaning forward, he snapped at the air as a warning.

Bryson hollered as he swung the bat at the dog, barely missing his head. The Great Shepherd then hopped onto his hind legs, but Bryson did not back down. The challenge seemed to make him stronger as he repeatedly lurched at the dog, almost striking him each time.

Shaking from fear, Rae watched helplessly as they fought when, suddenly, the trees swayed from side to side in a frighteningly brutal way. Mesmerized, Rae remained at the edge of the cliff and beheld the wonderment as the forceful wind bent the trees over and around Bryson, forcefully whipping their branches at his face.

He dropped the bat, striking at the trees with his hands while screaming, "Stop!" The trees only angered more and attacked him with greater force. As the howling wind grew louder, it began to change into the familiar, shrilling wail.

Standing immovable in the strong wind, Rae watched as a white mist crawled smoothly from the forest, deliberately encircling and rising above Bryson. It easily lifted the boy with the handsome face, now bloody and torn, off the ground and into the moonless night, throwing him over the cliff without any hesitation.

Then, in an instant, all was still; all was silent. The wind stopped roaring and the trees stopped attacking. Illuminating the night sky were trillions of twinkling stars as the content moon beamed down on her.

The Great Shepherd came to her unharmed, but whining. After a quick outward sniff, he licked her hand. Even though she felt the wetness, she couldn't react. She couldn't move.

Gio then slowly sat up, holding his head. After seeing Rae, he asked, "Where's Bash?"

Her lips trembled uncontrollably as tears stung her eyes. A lump in her throat prevented any words from forming. Burying her head in her hands, a surge of inconsolable emotion swelled in her gut and just as she was about to release, one meek voice sounded from the cliff.

"Aunt Rae, I need some help."

Overcome with elation, Rae dove to the cliff's edge and gasped as she saw Bash hanging onto an exposed tree root. On her stomach, Rae reached for him and with a strain in her voice, she said, "Take my hand."

Their fingertips were far from touching. "I can't reach it. My feet feel like they're about to slip off the ledge. I think I'm going to fall."

Gio now joined her, holding her cellphone with the flashlight shining on them. He asked her, "What should we do?"

The dog barked, prancing around Rae and bobbing his head in an exaggerated manner, which caused the leash to jiggle. Rae snapped her fingers as she remembered Zalen's words at the art museum. She quickly unhooked the leash from the collar while saying, "When you come to the end of your rope, tie a knot and hang on." After lowering the knotted end to Bash, he grabbed it, but she struggled to pull him up. Grunting, her sweaty hands lost their grip. The leash slipped through her fingers as Gio instinctively grabbed it. Even in the moonlight, his cheekbone, swollen and misshapen, seemed very painful, but he still managed to smile at Rae as they both pulled Bash to safety.

• • •

Bash wrapped his arms around Aunt Rae, feeling relieved that his aunt wasn't seriously hurt, that Gio was alive, that his large, furry friend was licking the top of his head and that his paranormal investigation was a success. Police descending upon them interrupted these good feelings and within seconds, they surrounded the area. Detective Nelson led the charge as Howie hustled behind him, looking pale and grim. Once Howie spotted Bash and his aunt, Bash saw Howie blow out a sigh of relief as he spoke into his walkie talkie.

Detective Nelson reached his aunt first. "Where's Bryson?"

Aunt Rae pointed toward the cliff. "He fell over it." Bash gave her a suspicious look as she continued, "On his own."

Detective Nelson nodded, hollering to his police crew, "We gotta get down there now!" As a team of paramedics raced by, he grabbed one. "I need an ice pack for her eye and for Gio's face." Then he looked at Gio. "What happened?"

Gio explained, "Bryson took my bat and hit me in the face. I was trying to stop him from hurting Bash. I don't remember anything after that."

Detective Nelson, looking redder and angrier than an infected toe, turned to Bash. "I told you to stay out of the woods."

Bash held up his hand. "Before you start, I have proof that Bryson killed Honey Ward." Looking over the detective's shoulder, he continued, "I just need to find my spirit box first. Honey's ghost actually said Bryson's name on it. That's what set him off."

Aunt Rae then spoke. "Detective, Bryson's mom, Jessica, was in on it too. She's at my boss's house right now, having a breakdown." She paused. "Well, I'm not exactly sure that she's still there, but when she was, she told me everything."

Detective Nelson interrupted them. "I know what happened." He looked at Aunt Rae. "I just got two phone calls, both around three this morning. The first was Stone."

Bash and Aunt Rae asked in unison, "Stone?"

Without answering, the detective continued, "Then Jessica Baraton called. She told me Bryson killed Honey and he thought Amy Jullian Williards told Cook about it and then Bryson killed them."

Aunt Rae asked, "Did she tell you about Laura Ward?"

The detective nodded. "Jessica strangled Laura Ward because she thought that Laura knew everything. I actually figured that one out on my own. Anyhow, she *calmly* told me that Bash was now dead and you were next. It was eerie. Scared the hell out of me. I called everyone I knew to get here as fast as they could." Glancing at his watch, he said, "Stone somehow got here a second before me and I was in the area."

Even in the moonlight, Bash saw the happiness grow on his aunt's face. He smiled too and said, "Two murderers." He looked at his aunt. "I knew it." Gio looked sad though, bringing the severity of the situation crashing back to Bash. "I'm sorry about Honey, Gio."

"I can't believe Bryson really killed Honey." Speaking to Detective Nelson, Gio asked, "Did Cook tell you that I was helping him?"

"Yes, I know all about you, Gio. You don't have to worry about your involvement."

Gio said to Bash, "After I saw you in the park and you asked for my help, I got to thinking that you'd be here tonight. I didn't want you to go into the woods. That's why I pushed you. I was trying to scare you into stopping."

Bash smiled. "Yeah, that didn't work."

A paramedic arrived and handed ice packs to both Gio and Aunt Rae. As they both brought the packs to their faces, Aunt Rae looked at Gio and said, "I was completely wrong about you. I'm so sorry."

Gio shrugged. "I was wrong about you too."

Aunt Rae chuckled. "If you need help studying for the ACT, let me know and I think I can help."

Gio gave her a skeptical look. "How did you do in geometry?"

Aunt Rae cleared her throat. "Well, I think I squeaked out a strong C."

First Gio laughed; then he winced from pain while managing to say, "Thanks, but no thanks."

Detective Nelson instructed an officer to take Gio to an ambulance. Before being led down the trail, Gio paused and gave Bash one last thumbs up.

Detective Nelson dug into the side pocket of his maroon trench coat, removing a nub of the Cuban cigar that barely hung to life, and lit it. "You know what's crazy about all of this?" He waved his hand around the area, seemingly talking to nobody. "Amy Jullian Williards didn't say anything to Cook about Bryson. She and Cook were actually just dating."

Bash raised his eyebrows at Aunt Rae who said, "Seriously?"

"Yep. They would meet out here at night, acting like horny teens. She called him Cowboy and he called her AJ." After two quick puffs, the detective continued, "And you know what else? I interviewed AJ once and she only knew Bryson pushed his dad down the steps, which she felt was in self defense. AJ truly believed that Bryson was a good kid. I thought Gio was the one responsible for Honey's death. Fortunately, I found Cook's murder book."

Bash asked incredulously, "What did you just say?"

Detective Nelson grinned. "Murder book. I don't expect you to know what that is, but every good detective has one. We found

Cook's in the dashboard of his convertible parked around the corner by the park." Bash groaned as the detective continued, "He took great notes."

Aunt Rae clarified, "Are you saying that Bryson and Jessica reacted in paranoia and killed Amy, Cook and Laura for really no reason?"

Nodding, the detective said, "It's actually called being a narcissistic sociopath. I think they both had that personality disorder." He shrugged. "Anyhow, we have Jessica in custody." One of the policeman then hollered for him and he quickly excused himself.

"Wait." Aunt Rae stopped him. "Does she know what happened to Bryson?"

Detective Nelson gave her a kind look. "You don't have to worry about that. It's all over. Go go Stone. He's waiting for you at the house." When Rae didn't move, the detective said, "Seriously, get out of here already and get someone to look at that black eye." He turned and walked toward the policeman, calling over his shoulder, "I never want to see you again. Or Stone. Or Bash. Or your dog."

Standing next to each other, Aunt Rae gave Bash a curious look with her one good eye. "How did Stone know that we were in trouble?"

Bash knew the answer. Stone was *obviously* a psychic and he *obviously* wanted to keep it a secret from his aunt. Bash suggested, "Maybe Zalen used his psychic power and told him?"

"Nah." Aunt Rae rolled her eye. "Zalen's a coo-coo."

"But he quoted FDR, warning us about tonight's events. How do you explain that?"

"He's a lucky coo-coo." Aunt Rae nudged him with her shoulder. "Seriously, I'm worried about you. Are you okay? Are tonight's events going to mess you up for years to come?"

Beaming at his aunt, his voice shook with excitement. "I'm not messed up! I'm fantastic! I can finally call myself an accomplished paranormal investigator!"

Aunt Rae choked. "You were thrown over the cliff."

Bash disagreed. "I wasn't thrown *over* the cliff. I was thrown *toward* the cliff and then rolled over it. Luckily, there was that ledge to stand on and a tree root to grip. So, no big deal."

Her mouth fell open. "You were slipping off the ledge."

Bash patted her back. "Let's not think about that. Or tell my mom. Or my dad, for that matter."

As the three of them limped down the trail, Bash whispered to her, "You know who really saved us, don't you?" His aunt pursed her lips together and Bash continued, "It was Maeve, the banshee. I heard everything. The flapping. The wind. The banshee wail. Bryson didn't fall off the cliff *on his own* the way you said he did. Maeve, the banshee, blew him off to save us."

Aunt Rae remained quiet and bent down to kiss the Great Shepherd's snout. He leaned into her, nuzzling his large head underneath her arm. Looking at him, she said, "Speaking of saving, if you're going to be my dog, I'm changing your name back to Tiny."

Tiny looked up at her, nodding, and Bash exhaled. "Oh thank god."

When they finally reached Travis's manor, there were many police cars, two ambulances, one fire truck and a red Dodge parked on the back lawn. Out of the darkness appeared Stone, running to Aunt Rae. He hoisted her into his arms and to Bash's surprise, she held Stone just as fiercely. As Stone set his aunt back on her feet, he lightly caressed her bruised eye, saying a curious thing. "You didn't shatter into millions of pieces." His aunt also seemed confused, but laughed and then slugged him in the shoulder.

Sally swung her arm around Bash, squeezing him. He looked at her short cropped hair peppered with gray and said, "You look great." She smiled, squeezing him harder.

A grunt sounded behind him and Bash turned to find Howie standing next to his dad, dressed in his paramedic uniform.

Then Bash heard his aunt say, "Hey, Danny. I can explain."

His dad just shook his head and, suddenly, took two long strides over to Bash, engulfing him with his strong arms.

Bash squeaked, "No need to tell Mom. I'm not hurt."

His dad sounded concerned. "Sure?"

"Yeah. I'm just sorta bummed." A lump formed in Bash's throat. "I just realized that I forgot all of my paranormal equipment in the woods. Can we go back and get it?"

Looking at Bash, his dad said, "No. Way."

ONE LAST THING

With each passing day at the manor, Rae's bruised eye changed from purple to yellow green and her mood also improved. Maybe it was because the New York client finally approved her logo design? Or maybe it had something to do with being alive? Quite possibly, it had a great deal to do with her new pet dog, Tiny.

As they both reclined on the oversized sofa, each at opposite ends, Rae stroked his back with her foot. Tiny panted happily in return. Fortunately for Rae, Judy readily agreed to have Rae become the proud owner of Tiny and he now was a permanent fixture at her side. Obviously, he felt eternally grateful for her. And possibly vice versa.

The buzzing of her cellphone caused her to sigh after recognizing that the text was from ChAdonis. While reading it, however, her heart soared. He was giving up the nude bike ride. It seems a new girlfriend of his forbade him from doing it and as an added bonus, this text would be his last to Rae. His new girlfriend said so.

Just as she was about to set her phone on the coffee table, it now rang and Rae smiled at the familiar number. "Hey, Bash," she answered. "Still grounded?"

He groaned. "Stop asking me that when you already know the answer. Is Tiny there? I want to talk to *him*."

Rae pressed the speaker button and set the phone by Tiny's face. After Tiny barked a greeting, Bash began telling him all about a little-known local werewolf.

"Ever hear of it?" Bash asked the Great Shepherd.

Tiny woofed.

"Exactly." Bash's voice started to rise in excitement. "It was first sighted near here in 1936. If banshees exist, werewolves must exist too."

Rae and Tiny exchanged looks and then they both shook their heads. Suddenly, the doorbell sounded and Rae immediately thought of the elusive doorbell ditcher. Racing to the door, she quickly opened it and once again, found no one. However, a possible tip as to the doorbell ditcher's true identity lay on the front porch, along with Bash's case of paranormal equipment. This clue came in a form of a note resting inside a green helmet. It read:

When I gathered Bash's equipment, I noticed his spirit box was irreparably damaged and tossed it. I then purchased a new one for him. Consider it a contribution toward his future science of the paranormal investigations. I'm sure he'll understand. By the way, have fun on the bike ride and remember, it's in two days. ∞ Maeve

. . .

It was now Saturday afternoon and Stone was not at the bar. He waited with Rae in the foyer as Travis crashed through the front door, carrying luggage and a two-year old boy strapped to his back in a baby carrier. Seth trailed exhaustedly behind his family with a smaller parcel strapped to his back. A fluffy white head belonging to a Bichon Frise peeked over Seth's shoulder and stuck its pink tongue at Rae. Stone chuckled when she stuck her tongue back at it.

Nudging Rae, he whispered to her, "I like your Tiny better."

With a sassy grin, she replied, "There's no contest."

A sense of heat began to singe Stone's face and he looked around for the source, finding Travis's glare upon him. At first, Travis said nothing. Then he scanned Stone from his head to his toe, dropped his suitcases and set his keys on the console table, asking Rae impatiently, "Who's this guy? I said *no guests*."

"Ignore him." Seth said to Rae as he lifted their son out of the baby carrier still attached to Travis's back. The little boy kicked until both feet touched the ground. Then he sped to the console table, picked up the keys and chucked them at that grotesque mirror. A horrific sound of smashing glass silenced everyone, except for Stone. Laughing softly, he saw Rae's reflection in the mirror shards, making her look like she shattered into millions of tiny pieces.

Rae pushed Stone out the manor before Travis's temper erupted with expletives. They sprinted to her car and Tiny greeted them from the back seat with a joyous howl. His melon head hung out one open window while his tail wagged out the other.

As they sat in her car, Stone watched Rae bite her fingernail. "What's wrong?"

Rae sighed. "I think I owe Maeve a favor." Facing Stone, she continued, "This afternoon, we have to ride a bike naked in protest of clearing these woods."

Stone smiled at her. "*We?*"

Returning his smile, Rae shrugged. "The only requirements are a bike and a helmet."

"I don't have a helmet." Stone smirked and then playfully added, "But I'll definitely wait for you at *the end*."

THE END

ABOUT THE AUTHOR

Like the protagonist in *The Shrill of it All*, BW Hoff has dealt with pushy employers in the graphic design field, has tangled with a band of French gypsies and has an aversion to beastly dogs. Unlike Rae, murder mysteries excite her, ever since she watched *Hart to Hart* with her mom while recuperating from pneumonia at the age of nine. High fevers aside, those were the good ol' days. BW Hoff currently spends her good new days with her husband, two children, mom and dad, cousins, friends, her older brother and sister-in-law, and Lambeau, her inspiration for Tiny.

NOTE FROM THE AUTHOR

Word-of-mouth is crucial for any author to succeed. If you enjoyed *The Shrill of it All*, please leave a review online—anywhere you are able. Even if it's just a sentence or two. It would make all the difference and would be very much appreciated.

Thanks!
BW Hoff

We hope you enjoyed reading this title from:

www.blackrosewriting.com

Subscribe to our mailing list – *The Rosevine* – and receive **FREE** books, daily deals, and stay current with news about upcoming releases and our hottest authors.
Scan the QR code below to sign up.

Already a subscriber? Please accept a sincere thank you for being a fan of Black Rose Writing authors.

View other Black Rose Writing titles at www.blackrosewriting.com/books and use promo code **PRINT** to receive a **20% discount** when purchasing.